C0060 00733
KT-158-230

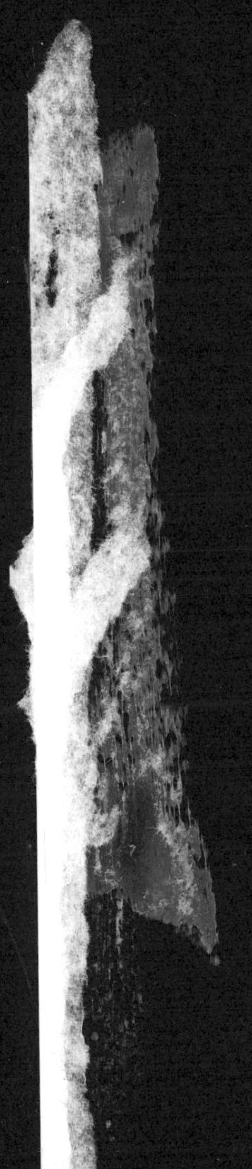

so many ways to begin

BY THE SAME AUTHOR

If Nobody Speaks
of Remarkable Things

so many ways to begin

jon mcgregor

BLOOMSBURY

First published in Great Britain in 2006

Bloomsbury Publishing Plc
36 Soho Square
London W1D 3QY

A CIP catalogue record for this book
is available from the British Library

Hardback edition
ISBN 0 7475 7946 6
ISBN-13 9780747579465

Paperback edition
ISBN 0 7475 8413 3
ISBN-13 9780747584131

10 9 8 7 6 5 4 3 2 1

Typeset by Hewer Text UK Ltd, Edinburgh
Printed in Great Britain by Clays Ltd, St Ives plc

The paper this book is printed on is certified by the © 1996 Forest
Stewardship Council A.C. (FSC). It is ancient-forest friendly.
The printer holds FSC chain of custody SGS-COC-2061

To Alice

They came in the morning, early, walking with the others along tracks and lanes and roads, across fields, down the long low hills which led to the slow pull of the river, down to the open gateways in the city walls, the hours and days of walking showing in the slow shift of their bodies, their breath steaming above them in the cold morning air as the night fell away at their backs. They came quietly, the swish of dew-wet grasses brushing against their ankles, the pat and splash of the muddy ground beneath their feet, the coughs and murmurs of rising conversation as the same few phrases were passed back along the lines. Here we are now. Nearly there. Just to the bottom of the hill and then we'll sit down. Cigarettes were lit, hundreds of cigarettes, thin leathery fingers expertly rolling a pinch of tobacco into a lick of paper without losing a step. Cigarettes were cadged, offered, shared, passed down to nervous young hands eager for that first acrid taste of adulthood, cupping a mouthful of it in the windshield of their open fists in imitation of fathers and uncles and older brothers, coughing as it burnt down into their untested young lungs, the spluttered-out smoke twisting upwards and mingling with their cold clouded breath as they made their way between flowering hawthorn hedges and cowslip-heavy banks, down towards the city walls. They wore suits, of a kind, all of them: woollen waistcoats and well knotted neckerchiefs, thick tweed jackets with worn elbows and cuffs, moleskin trousers with frayed seams tucked into the tops of their boots. The younger ones carried bundles of clothes, brown paper parcels fastened with string, slung across their shoulders or clasped to their chests, held tightly in their damp nervous hands as they started to gather pace, pulled down the hill by the sight of the city, by their eagerness to be first and by the impatience of the men and the boys pressing in from behind; still foggy from sleep, still aching from the long walk the day before, but forgetting all that as they came to their journey's end.

From the top of the hill, where others were only now beginning that last long downward traipse, the city looked quiet and still, wrapped in a pale May morning mist, weighted with the same brooding promise that cities have always held when glimpsed from a distance like this, the same magnetic pull of hopes and opportunities. But as those first men and boys came into the city, their boots beginning to stamp and echo across the cobbled ground, windows were opened and curtains pulled back, and the city began to wake. Sleepy children peered from low upstairs windows, the hushed chatter and the rumbling of feet signalling the start of the day they'd been looking forward to, calling to each other and pulling faces at the children in the houses across the street. Landlords opened the doors and shutters of their bars, sweeping the floors and standing in their doorways with brooms in their hands to watch their customers arrive. Stallholders finished preparing their pitches around the edges of the square, keeping an eye on the small group of guards by the steps of the new town hall. And from each end of the long square, from the road leading in from the bridge to the east, from the gateway under the lodge to the west, from the road winding out along the river to the south, the army of workers appeared, hurrying on with the growing excitement of arrival, calling greetings to friends not seen for the past six months, looking around for others yet to arrive, asking after health, and families, and wives. And the crowd of people in the square grew bigger, and noisier, and fathers began to lay hands on the shoulders of their youngest sons, keeping them close, wary of letting them drift away too soon, listening to the snatches of conversation echo back and forth, looking out for the farmers and foremen to start to appear, waiting for the business of the day to begin.

Mary Friel stood with her father and brothers, watching, her youngest brother Tommy clutching her hand. You okay there

Tommy? she whispered down to him. He looked up at her, nodding, a look of annoyance on his young face, and pulled his hand away.

Soon, as if at some unseen signal, deals began to be made all over the square. You looking for work son? the smartly dressed men would say, glancing down. How much you after? And the older boys, the ones who knew their price, or the ones who could say they were experienced, stronger, would get more work done, tried their luck with eight, nine, ten pounds, while the younger ones, who knew no better or could ask no more, said seven or six as they'd been told. Deals were made with a terse nod and a handing over of the brown paper packages, an instruction to meet back there in the afternoon, sometimes with a shilling or two to keep the boy busy for the day, sometimes not; sometimes the father taken for drinks to smooth over the awkwardness of the scene, sometimes not.

This was the first time Mary had been to town for the hiring fair. She'd only ever watched her father setting off with her brothers before; stood in the low doorway to wave them goodbye, her sister Cathy beside her, Tommy holding on to both their hands, their mother turning away before the boys got out of sight and saying no time to be standing around all day now. She'd had an idea of what it would be like from hearing her father those evenings he came back home alone; she and Cathy lying in bed listening while he talked in a low voice to their mother by the last few turfs of the fading fire. But she hadn't been expecting quite so many people, or so much noise, or the way her father would stare sternly straight ahead when a gentleman approached him and said your boy looking for a job?

They left the square as soon as the price had been agreed, telling Tommy to be good, to work hard and to do what the man said, and to meet them back here at the next fair day in six months' time. They walked through the town towards the river, Mary, her father, her two older brothers who were past the age of hiring now, out to the docks to catch the boat across to England. She listened to her brothers talking to her father as they sat waiting for the boat, talking and joking about their time as hired boys, the threshing and weeding and picking of stones, the early mornings and the endless thoughts of food. She sat slightly apart from them, looking up into the hills on the other side of the river, feeling the imprint of her young brother's hand across the palm of her own. Other men joined them, walking over from the square, lighting up cigarettes, sitting on sacks of grain and crates of wool, talking about where they'd heard the work was that year. Following the harvests from Lancashire up to Berwick and all the way on to Fife. Waterworks round Birmingham way. Munitions in Glasgow, Manchester, Coventry, Leeds. Talking of the best ways to get there, the cheapest places to stay, the names to mention to stand a better chance of work at the end of the trip. Some of the men looked across at Mary, curiously, wondering what she might have been doing there, wondering who she was with, until their gaze was interrupted by her father's hard glare.

They were going over the water early this year. The weather had changed sooner than usual, and the field was dug and planted, the turf cut, before fair day came. Work had been arranged for Mary, in London, and so their father had announced that they would all make the journey together. It's a long way for a girl to go on her own, is it not? he'd said, and her mother could only agree, making up slices of cake for their journey, taking out the brown paper from its place beneath the bed.

On the boat, the four of them found a place in a quiet corner and settled themselves in, the two brothers on either side, Mary resting her head on her father's shoulder, his heavy coat laid over them both. It smelt of damp soil and turf smoke and the cold clean air of their two days' walking. It smelt of him and she concentrated on the smell as she drifted into an uncomfortable sleep, broken by the tip and slide of the boat, by the shouts of other men, by the hard wooden deck beneath the both.

In the morning, in Liverpool, they put her on a train down to London. They stood on the platform for a few moments to be sure she'd got a seat, watching her put her bundle up on the luggage rack, watching her smooth out her skirt as she sat down by the window. Her brother William opened the door and jumped up on to the step, leaning in to wish her a good journey, telling her to say hello to Cousin Jenny and the rest of that shower, telling her to tear up London town, laughing as he ran his hand across the top of her hair and pulled it out of its carefully pinned place. She reached out to catch him a clip round the ear but he leant away, jumping down and slamming the door shut as she said goodbye and the guard blew the whistle with his flag raised high. Her father and her other brother had already turned away.

She spoke to no one on the journey, as she'd been told, and waited under the clock at Euston station for her cousin, who came running up to meet her a half hour after the train had arrived. Sorry I'm late, she said, out of breath and a little red in the face. The bus depot was bombed last night and I had to walk all the way. You had a good crossing?

The house was in Hampstead, close enough to the Heath to see the tops of the trees from an upstairs window, its large front door reached by a broad flight of stone steps she was never allowed to use. Her room was at the top of the house, squeezed in under the rafters at the back somewhere, overlooking wash-yards and alley-ways and gutters. The room was just big enough for a bed, and for a fireplace that was never lit, and for a small chest under the bed where she kept her clothes and a biscuit tin for her wages, ready to be taken home the next summer. But the size of the room was unimportant because all she ever did was sleep in there. If you were awake you were working, she said when she told someone much later what it was like. Cleaning out fireplaces, scrubbing pots and pans and boots and steps, washing and drying and ironing the clothes, lighting the fires in the family's rooms. On her first day off she stayed in her room, counting the bruises on her knees and shins and the angry red chilblains on her fingers, sleeping, looking out of the small window and wondering where she would go if she dared to leave the house.

She lived in the attic and she worked in the basement, and part of her job was to get from one to the other without being observed. You want to be neither seen nor heard, Cousin Jenny had told her, standing at the wide stone basin scrubbing potatoes and carrots that first evening. And you want to not see or hear anything neither. Mary nodded, pushing her paper-white cap back where it kept falling down over her eyes. She learnt how to time her trips through the finely panelled rooms and corridors of the main house, going downstairs before the family had risen, waiting for their mealtimes before going back up, or for the evenings when they sat together in the drawing room. She learnt how to tip her head a little if she ever did meet someone, to say Sir or Ma'am before quickly walking away.

The thing was to make yourself invisible, she said, many years later, so that everyone could pretend you weren't even there. You would do whatever piece of work you had to do and just slip away out of the room. Eyes down, ears closed, mouth shut. That was the thing to do, she said. So if you went in to light a fire one morning and your man was getting dressed, it wouldn't matter because you were invisible, and he wouldn't even know you were there. And if he asked you your name you'd tell him, and if he asked you to come closer you'd go, but you could pretend you hadn't because really you didn't hear or see him and he didn't hear or see you. It wouldn't matter at all. I was a pretty child though, she said. It wasn't always easy to be so invisible. I tended to catch people's eye, you know?

She would speak these words softly, eventually, but she would speak them.

Jenny took her out on their days off, showing her round London, walking through the parks if the weather was good, hiding in a picture house if the weather was bad, walking right up to the West End to look in through taped shop windows and watch out for boys. They talked about what they would do when they went back home, whether they would go back home at all, and they talked about marrying, about children, make-believing extravagant farmhouses to go with the size of the families they imagined into life. Sometimes they finished those days off in a pub in Kilburn or Camden or King's Cross, and there were so many cousins and young aunts crowded into their corner of the bar that Mary could half close her eyes and think they were all squeezed into the lounge bar at Joe's, with her parent's house only a few minutes' moonlit walk away. She saw people she hadn't seen since she was young, and others she'd seen only at Christmas for the last few years, and they all asked for news of Fanad. She told them about Cathy's wedding, and about the new priest, and about how her brother Tommy had gone off to work that year.

And how's that other brother of yours, young William? a friend of Jenny's asked once, a girl Mary remembered from church.

Oh he's fine, she said, and the girl lowered her voice and said aye he's more than fine, he's very good indeed, the whole crowd of them shrieking in shocked laughter and Mary not knowing quite what they meant but laughing along all the same.

On days when it wasn't as cold, another girl would have laid the fire the night before, sweeping out the ashes and piling up the kindling, and it didn't take a second to slip into the room with a box of matches and set it going. But on colder days, when the embers had been left to smoulder halfway through the night, it was a much longer job. The grate had to be swept out, the ashes scooped into a metal bucket, the hearth wiped over with a damp cloth when it was done. Paper had to be screwed up into little twists and laid over with twigs and splints and pieces of kindling, and the first flares of flame had to be watched over for a few moments to see that they caught, to see that it was okay to lay on the larger lumps of log and coal and close the door softly behind her. It was too much of a job to be done silently, or invisibly; the brush would bang against the side of the grate, or the bucket, the newspaper would crackle as she screwed it up, the match-head would spit as it burst into flame. She tried very hard, but it seemed impossible not to wake whoever was sleeping in the bed behind her, not to make some small disturbance that meant she would hear a voice saying her name. A man's voice, asking for her.

They sent her to light the fire in each of the rooms by turn, but mostly she was asked to go to the father's room, and it was here that she found it hardest to not make a sound. After a time, she went to the housekeeper and said that if it was at all possible she would very much prefer not to go into the rooms to light the fires any more, please.

She kept it hidden the whole nine months. She wore bigger clothes. She ate as little food as she could. She stopped going out with Jenny and the others, spending long evenings and days off in her room with the chest under the bed and the small window, saying she was tired, or poorly. She learnt, too late, how to make herself invisible.

Later, this would seem the strangest part of it all, that no one noticed, that no one asked, that she was able to keep it so well hidden while she carried on with her work, the cleaning and the sweeping and the scrubbing and the pressing. I suppose I was stronger then, she would say, one day, when she was finally able to talk. A girl that age, I suppose they're built for it, aren't they? Young and supple and all. You do what you have to do, I suppose, she would say.

She took a bus to the hospital when she could stand it no more, wrapping her saved wages in the middle of her brown paper bundle of clothes, leaving a note that said nothing on her bed and a month's money uncollected. Her waters had already broken by the time they took her on to the ward. When they asked, she told them her name was Bridget Kirwan and that she came from a village near Galway. It took her no more than a few hours to give birth. It was the easiest of the five, she would say, years later. I must have been tougher than I felt, though it still hurt more than enough. When the baby was born, an underweight boy, he was taken from her almost without discussion. They told her it would be the best thing, they told her it would be cruel to do anything else, and she was too shattered by pain and hunger and shock to raise a voice in disagreement.

They barely even let me say goodbye, you know? she would tell someone, eventually.

When she went home, after two weeks in a rest ward, she knew that she would never want to go away to work again. She didn't say, of course, why she had come back across the water before her time, and she did her best to make up for the shortfall of money in the bundle she'd brought back, walking three miles each day to milk and feed and mind the cows on the landowner's farm. And when the men came home towards the end of the year, older and fitter and better fed, swollen with talk and drink and money, she watched them carefully, waiting, choosing, and before the following year's hiring fair she was married to Michael Carr, waving him off the way she used to watch her mother do, turning away before he was out of sight to settle into a house of her own. She scrubbed and cleaned and polished her own pots, her own plates, her own clothes and boots and low front step. She lit a fire in her own grate. She opened the door to her friends, and she waited for her husband to come home.

He brought no money with him when he returned, and she could smell on his breath that she'd chosen wrong.

I can say this now, she admitted to someone, years later, when she lived on her own and waited for her grandchildren to call; it was a wonderful marriage for eight months of the year. And that's a lot more than some folk can say, don't you think? Laughing as she said it, glancing up at the photograph of him on the mantelpiece.

Her four children all had their birthdays in late September. And she wondered, each time she held a newborn child in her hands, where that lost one might have gone. She wondered it with each niece and nephew and grandchild she was given to hold, saying he's a fine one to the mother as she looked into the baby's clouded eyes. She wondered it as she changed and cleaned her own children's nappies, as she fed them, as she mended their clothes and sang them to sleep and sent them off to school. She wondered it as she watched them grow into young adults, going further away to find work, bringing back money when they ducked into the house, bringing back other young men and women with whom they shyly held hands at the supper table. She watched them marry, and she watched them make homes of their own, have children of their own, move away and move back and move away again, and she never stopped wondering, waiting, hoping for some young man to contact her from England, some long-lost solemn-eyed child to come calling across the water and tell her something, anything, of where he'd been gone all this time.

part one

Eleanor was in the kitchen when he got back from her mother's funeral, baking. The air was damp with the smell of spices and burnt sugar, the windows clouded with condensation against the dark evening outside. He stood in the doorway with his suitcase and waited for her to say hello. She had her back to him, her shoulders hunched in tense concentration, her faded brown hair tied up into a loose knot on the back of her head. She was icing a cake. There were oven trays and cooling racks spread across the worktop, grease-stained recipe books held open under mixing bowls and rolling pins, spilt flour dusted across the floor.

Hello, he said gently, not wanting to make her jump. She didn't say anything for a moment.

How'd it go then? she asked without lifting her head or turning around.

Okay, he said, it was okay, you know. The oven timer buzzed, and as she opened the door a blast of hot wet air rushed into the room. She took out a tray of fruit slices, turned off the oven, and went back to icing the cake. He put the suitcase down and stood behind her. The creamy-white icing looked smooth enough to him, but she kept dragging the rounded knife across it, chasing tiny imperfections back and forth. He put his hand on the hard knot of her shoulder and she flinched. He kissed the back of her head. Her hair smelt of flour, and of baking spices, and of her, and he kept his face pressed lightly against it for a moment, his eyes closed, breathing deeply.

It looks like you're done there El, he said quietly, reaching round to take the knife from her hand, putting it down on the side. It looks lovely, he said. He kept his hand on her hand, wrapping his fingers around hers as it clenched into an anxious fist.

It was okay then? she asked, her head lowered.

It was okay, he told her. She turned round, wiping her hands on her apron, and looked up at him, smiling weakly.

Good, she said, I'm glad. She picked up a palette knife, and eased the fruit slices from the baking tray on to another cooling rack. I got a bit carried away, she said, waving the knife around the room to indicate the cakes and buns and biscuit tins. I wanted to keep busy. She smiled again, shaking her head. She carried the baking tray past him and put it into the sink, the hot metal hissing into the water. Did you find the way okay? she asked.

Yes, he said, it was fine. He sat at the table, stretching out his legs, squeezing the muscles on the back of his neck, stiff from the long drive. She tried to undo her apron, her sticky fingers fumbling blindly behind her for a few moments, and gave up, turning her back to him and saying could you? over her shoulder. He picked at the tight double knot, awkwardly, his own fingers thick with tiredness, easing his thumbnail into the knot and unlooping the strings. She sat down, slipping the apron off over her head and folding it into her lap, wiping her fingers clean on one corner. She looked tired. He reached over and ran his hand up and down her thigh.

Hey, he said, you okay? She closed her eyes, resting her hand on top of his.

Yes, she said, I'll be fine. It's just been a long day. It's been a long few days.

They sat like that for a few minutes and he watched the lines around her eyes soften as she began to relax. Long strands of coarse hair had fallen free of the knot on the back of her head and were hanging around her face. He reached over and tucked them back, smoothing them into place. She smiled faintly, already half asleep.

Was it alright coming back? she murmured, just as he was about to slip his hand away and get something to eat.

It was fine, he told her, it took a long time but it was fine. Not too much traffic about. I stopped off at some services for a break.

You've eaten then? she asked, opening her eyes and rubbing at her face suddenly.

Well, a little something more wouldn't do any harm, he said, looking over at the racks of cooling cakes.

Oh, sure, she said, smiling, be my guest. He took a plate from the cupboard and fetched himself a large rock cake, blowing at the steam that poured out as he broke it open.

What about Kate? she asked, turning round in her chair.

She's fine, he said, I dropped her off at the station this morning. She sent me a text when she got home, she's fine.

She was okay with it all then, was she? she said, looking up at him.

Yes, he said, she was okay with it.

Oh, good, Eleanor said.

Later, as she got into bed, she said, so, will you tell me about it? She sat up, the duvet held up to her chest, the pillows wedged behind her back and her hair pulled round to one side of her head. She looked up at him as he took his shirt off and folded it over the back of the chair.

What do you want to know? he said.

Just what it was like, she replied. Who was there, what happened.

Well they were all there I think, he said, all the family, grandchildren, a few neighbours. A few dozen altogether I think, he said. He leant against the wardrobe to take off his shoes and socks, rubbing at the cracked skin across the back of his heels.

And was Tessa there? she said. He looked up. No love, he said, no. Tessa wasn't there. She pulled the duvet back from his side of the bed.

Come and tell me about it, she said, I want to hear. Was it a nice service?

He unbuckled his belt, slid off his trousers, and draped them over the back of the chair. He swapped his pants for a pair of pyjama trousers from underneath the pillow, and he told her about Ivy's funeral. He told her that a lot of them, the immediate family, had met at Donald's beforehand, and that Donald's wife had overloaded them with sandwiches and cake, and that this was where Kate had first met them all.

I picked her up from the station, he said. She seemed very quiet but I think she coped with it well enough. People were saying she looked like her grandmother, he said, and Eleanor looked across at him with a doubtful expression.

No, she said, I wouldn't say that. Does she? Do you think so? He smoothed his thumb across her creased eyebrows.

A little, he said, perhaps. It's only natural, isn't it? She thought about it, shaking her head. He told her about the service, that the minister hadn't seemed to know Ivy at all and had just talked in general terms about a long and full life but that people hadn't seemed to mind. He told her that it had felt very warm in the church, and she smiled and said well at least some things change then, and she started to close her eyes. He told her about the burial, about the corner of the cemetery which had trees along both sides and seemed to be well kept; that he'd spotted her Great-uncle James's grave nearby, and her father's of course, and that Donald had said her father's father's headstone was somewhere but they hadn't been able to find it. He told her about the wake in the Crown Hotel, how good the food was and how people had kept buying him drinks.

He didn't tell her about the question which had hung back on people's lips when they found out who he was, or that he'd felt like apologising and explaining for her every time, even though people were too polite to mention it. It's the travelling, he'd wanted to say; it's such a long way, it would be too much for her. But he didn't say anything, because people didn't ask. There was a gap in the conversation all day, no one saying well she could at least have, or after all this time, or I suppose she didn't feel she could; but it was a gap which was soon bridged by enquiries about work, or Kate, or how he was enjoying his stay.

She shuffled down into the bed, rearranging the pillows behind her, and turned her head on to his chest. He could feel the warmth of her breath. He leant down and kissed her hair. She spread her hand across his skin, tracing circles with each finger the way she'd always liked to do, pressing lightly against each of his ribs, his belly button, the short dotted scar above his waist.

He told her about walking around Aberdeen the evening before the funeral, and how different things were now; the massive oil tanks and pipeworks ranged along the harbour-front, the new shopping centre, the graceful blue-glass extension to the Maritime Museum, the rebuilt houses on Torry Hill where she'd grown up. You'd still recognise it though, he said gently. He told her about some of the people he'd met at the wake, what they were doing now, that they'd said to give her their love. He told her, as her eyes closed more firmly and her breathing settled into its familiar slowness, about the long drive home, past Dundee and Dunfermline and over the new Forth Bridge, past Hadrian's Wall, through the high bleak openness of the North York Moors. He told her how nice it had been, passing through all that scenery. He told her that there'd been no traffic problems, that it had been straightforward finding his way, that everyone had seemed to be driving carefully and sensibly.

He shifted down into the bed, kissing her on the cheek, and reached across to turn out the light.

You still want to go then? she said, opening her eyes suddenly. He looked at her.

Yes, he said, you know I do.

It's an awful long way again, she said, so soon.

I know, he said, but I want to go. It's important, you know it's important. I'll be okay. He kissed the side of her face again, stroking the top of her ear with his finger.

Have you packed? she asked. Have you written a list?

He thought of all the things he'd considered taking with him, stacked in the corner of Kate's old room: the photograph albums, the document folders, the bundles of letters and postcards and notes, the scrapbooks, the loose objects wrapped in sheets of old newspaper and filed carefully away. He went through them all in his mind, listing each item as though in a museum catalogue, picking out the few things he'd eventually decided to take.

Yes, he said, I've written a list. Don't worry about it now though. We'll talk about it in the morning. He turned the light off, and for a while he lay there listening to the quick shallow sighs of her breathing, the kick and twist of her legs as she tried to get comfortable.

Can't it wait David? she said. Why do you have to go now?

Please, he said. Don't. She turned away from him, pulling the cover around herself, shifting further down into the bed. It was a long time before she was still.

1 *b/w photograph, Albert Carter, defaced, c.1943*

He was going to start with a picture of his father. It seemed as good a way as any to begin. It was the first thing he'd thought of packing before he went off to the funeral, tucking it into a padded envelope to keep it safe. This is my father, he was going to say, holding up the small photograph for someone to see. When he was a young man, he was going to add, before I was born. Well now, someone might say, looking closely, and what are these marks here? And then he could explain, telling it the way his sister Susan always had, the words worn comfortably smooth with repeated use.

It was a story she liked to tell; it made her feel a part of something bigger than herself, tied to a time when there were bigger things to feel a part of. She'd told it again a few weeks earlier, looking at the same picture with a group of her friends after dinner one night. Someone had mentioned seeing it on the way in, and she'd led them all through to the hallway to stand around it, balancing their cups of coffee on thin white saucers while they listened and smiled and nodded, and remembered stories of their own, and went quiet at the appropriate time. Whenever he'd heard her tell the story, people had always gone quiet at the same appropriate time.

It was taken in 1943, she said, gesturing towards the photo, a small black-and-white studio portrait mounted on a greying cardboard surround, a name and number scribbled in soft illegible pencil along the bottom. Just before I was born, she said, placing herself firmly into that generation. He must have had it taken before going away on service for the second time, to the Med, I think, and sent it back from Portsmouth for my mother to put up on the mantelpiece while he was away. Pausing here, as she always did, picturing the man in the strange uniform above the hearth, watching over her and her mother while they crouched under the Morrison shelter in the back room, the ground shaking, firelight flashing past outside, or greeting them when they came home from the public shelter in the morning with the all-clear ringing out down the street, the house safe for another day and the garden strewn with rubble from next door but one. Remembering the morning her mother had tried to explain that a bomb had landed on her grandparents' house, and that her grandparents wouldn't be coming round for tea any more.

It was the Med, wasn't it? she asked, glancing across at him. I can never remember. Everyone turned to look, and he shrugged, smiling apologetically.

Don't look at me, he said, I'm not a historian, and they all laughed.

Albert Carter, their father, had been twenty-seven when the picture was taken, but he looked a lot younger; fresh-faced, smiling broadly, his skin so smooth that it was hard to believe he'd ever had to shave. His hair was slicked back, with the comb-lines as straight as a slide-rule, and his smile lifted the same creases around his eyes that David could remember seeing as a boy. The uniform looked a little too big for him, hanging loose around the shoulders, and there was none of the formal regalia which might have been expected in a portrait photograph, no spit-polished brass, or epaulettes, or braiding; it was a uniform which looked purely functional, ready for the serious business of crewing a ship into battle.

Of course, Susan said, I don't remember much about the war, I was too young. All I can remember, really, is this man arriving in the house, like the man in the picture but older and heavier, and not smiling. The others leant in towards the photograph as she spoke, looking at Albert Carter's fixed and frozen smile. He just appeared, she said, there was no discussion, he was just suddenly lurking about the place, making the house much smaller than it had been and taking up my mother's time. Smelling unfamiliar and damp, she said, laughing, as though she was unsure what she meant. But that's the thing I always remember, she said. His not being there and then being there, and nobody asking my opinion. The others smiled at this, as people usually did.

David was going to tell someone this story with the picture in his hand, holding on to it for a moment before passing it over, feeling the rough and crinkled texture of the greying card, turning it over to read the soft pencilled dates and numbers on the back, running his fingers again across the scratches scored into the photograph's dull surface. Dozens of scratches, mostly too faint to see unless the picture was turned into the light; mostly, except for three deep scars which had split and torn right through the skin of the paper, gouged across the young man's smiling face.

Susan explained that she'd made these marks, one afternoon when her father had been home for a few months. This was the part of the story where people always went quiet, and looked at the picture more closely, or turned to her and nodded, or smiled wryly because they could guess exactly what she was going to say. She'd been told to take a nap so that her mother and father could have a lie down while the new baby, David, was sleeping. Auntie Julia, whose house they were all staying in until they could find something of their own, was out doing some shopping. Restless and bored, Susan took a small metallic comb from her father's desk, grabbed the picture from the mantelpiece, and scoured frantically across its surface before making a tearful escape to the bedroom.

The most awful thing, she said, pointing out an ashtray on the hall table to a guest with a cigarette, is that nothing was ever said. The picture was replaced with another one, almost identical, and nobody ever mentioned it, she said.

Goodness, said a woman with a bright red scarf tied around her neck. Really? Susan nodded.

Not a word, she said. We found the damaged original in a box of his things after he died, and I insisted on keeping it. I've only recently put it up though, she added. The dinner guests peered closely at the picture for a few moments more, mentioning similar stories of their own before gradually moving back into the dining room.

My mother told me I used to try and drag my father out of their bed, the woman with the scarf said, laughing, and the man with the cigarette smiled at her, nodding.

Anyone want another coffee? Susan asked, as she followed them back to the table.

David stood in the hall for a moment longer, looking at the picture, tracing the scratches with his fingers, imagining the distress of the three-year-old girl which they recorded so well. He looked at the eyes, the smile, the face of the man who had brought him up so lovingly and was now gone, and he turned away.

You'll be careful with it though? Susan said, later, when he asked if he could borrow the picture for a while. She unclipped it from its frame and handed it over to him, and he told her that yes, of course, he'd be careful. And, I mean, are you sure this is a good idea? she asked, the whole thing? and he told her that yes, thank you, it was.

2 *Handwritten list of household items, c.1947*

When Dorothy Carter was twenty-seven she wrote a list, sitting at the kitchen table, tapping her pen against the side of her face while she thought of everything she wanted to include. When she'd finished she pinned it to the back of the utility-room door, where it stayed until the day she finally moved out, and as David was helping to pack away her things he took it down and slipped it quickly into his pocket, thinking that someone might be interested in having a look.

He imagined her sitting at the kitchen table that first day, with unopened suitcases and boxes all over the clean hard-wearing linoleum floor, a trunk, a bundle of bedding tied up with string. Susan stamping and clattering around the hard bare rooms, testing the echo of her voice against the walls, or playing in the sand and rubble at the back of the house. Albert would have been on his way back to London already, returning the borrowed bread van in time for that night's deliveries, having stopped on the way out to take a photo of Dorothy by the front door with the new handbag he'd bought her. He imagined her looking out through the window at the unfinished road piled high with timber and roof tiles, the other houses still skeletal, scaffolded, half-built; or standing to open and close the spotless cupboard doors.

It was so much more than we were expecting, she told David once. It was so much more than I felt we deserved.

The new house had its own front garden, and a path leading up to the door. It had an indoor toilet and a bath. There were fitted cabinets in the kitchen, and an airing cupboard, and electric lighting throughout. There was a cupboard under the stairs instead of a damp cellar. He found it difficult to imagine, when she told him all this, that these things had once been enough to seem like a miracle, to stun someone into speechless tears, but they had. Later, when he watched her saying the same things to Kate, he could see that Kate didn't believe her at all, saying, and did you make your own entertainment in them days Nana? Glancing at him and biting back a smile, not noticing how quietly her grandmother said yes love, we did, you're right.

She'd never been inside a new house before. She'd grown up in a tiny soft-walled cottage in the Suffolk countryside, where the only new buildings were the Nissen huts and hangars of the new airfields, where a bathroom was a kitchen for six and a half days of the week and the cooking was done on the fire, and she had no way of picturing what a new house might be like. Theirs was one of the first houses in the development to be finished, and they'd had to drive carefully through acres of Coventry's bomb-flattened streets to reach it, waiting for them, perfect and untouched. We could still smell the paint when we went inside, she told him. She'd never seen rooms without furniture before, and the emptiness made the house feel so large that she was convinced they'd made a mistake until his father went outside and checked the number on the door.

And after he'd left with the van she sat at the table, steadying herself, trying to write the list. She was frightened, she told David once. She didn't think they were entitled to it. All that work, for them, when there were so many people in worse off positions. She was worried for a long time that someone was going to come knocking on the front door with a clipboard, asking for forms they didn't have, saying there'd been some kind of mistake.

She sat there, thinking through all the things that needed to be done, while his sister played in what would one day be the garden and he slept in a pushchair in the room next door.

She made a list of jobs which needed doing straight away: putting sheets and blankets on the mattresses Julia had given them; laying out the clothes; cleaning the kitchen cabinets and scouring the surfaces; putting away their small stock of food; getting the rest of those boxes out of the way so some cooking could be done. And then she made a list of 'Things We Will Need', the list he still had now, a list which started with the immediate essentials and worked through to the fanciful and frivolous, a compendium of wishful thinking.

There was a space in the kitchen made especially for a refrigerator she told him, much later. Anything seemed possible.

By the time his father had got back from London the next evening, she'd measured the windows for curtains, and planned carpets for the floors and the stairs. She'd chosen colours and wallpapers for each of the rooms, and listed the ornaments and accessories which she'd seen in magazines and long wanted. She'd listed an electric iron, a top-loading washing machine, a vacuum cleaner, a new wireless set, an electric sewing machine. Albert laughed when he saw the list, the story went, telling her that she'd missed out the moon on a stick, but he kissed her all the same and said they'd see what they could do. They stood there for a long time, looking at it, their hands touching, until Susan came running in with a banged elbow, or David woke up crying in the next room, or the kettle came to the boil, and they both turned away.

And the list turned yellow with grease and flour and thumb-marks, and ticks appeared as each item was sweated and dreamed and saved into life. The lawn turned green with sprouting grass-seed, and rose bushes blushed into bloom all around it. A rug rolled out across their bedroom floor, and carpet stepped neatly down the stairs. Patterned nets were stretched across the front windows, and curtain material purchased, sewn, and hung. A carpet sweeper appeared for the new carpet, and settled in under the stairs with the brushes and buckets and mops, waiting to be put out of work by a new vacuum cleaner. And one bright day, six or seven years later, a gleaming white refrigerator, complete with icebox, was delivered by men in smart overalls from the newly rebuilt Owen's department store in town. It's not quite the moon on a stick, his father said, when he got home from work and saw the cold white cabinet humming quietly in the corner of the kitchen, but it's not far off.

This is the sort of person his mother was, he thought whenever he looked again at the list, when he imagined her reinventing her family's life in that way, with a new child, a new house, a new city outside waiting to be rebuilt. This was what he would tell anyone who asked, showing them the yellowed sheet of paper; my mother wanted all these things for us, and look how much of it she got. This was what he was going to say, if there was anyone who wanted to know.

3 *Local map, Whitechapel district, London, annotated, c.1950*

It was his father's idea to move to Coventry. He heard that from his mother, more than once, sitting around the kitchen table while his father read the evening paper and grumbled about some factory closure or rates increase. It was your father's idea to move here, she'd say, to David and Susan, pretending that she thought he couldn't hear. Or he heard it from their bedroom late at night, their tempered voices breaking through the thin walls and closed doors; this was your idea remember Albert, not mine. To which his father usually replied that they'd otherwise still be squatting in Julia's bloody spare room and how would she like that then, eh?

Julia had been Dorothy's closest friend at nursing college, despite being a few years older and more familiar with silver cutlery or linen tablecloths than anyone Dorothy knew. She'd been widowed early on in the war, and her young son Laurence was living with her brother in the country, so when she offered Dorothy lodgings in her house she claimed that it was as much to keep her from getting lonely as anything. You'll be doing me a favour dear, she said, and she refused to let Dorothy even think of finding somewhere else to live once Susan was born, or David, or even when Albert came back from the war for good, and Laurence returned from the country, and there were six of them squeezed into the house and making do. It hadn't always been easy, especially once Laurence came back and began to compete noisily for his mother's attention. But the house was big enough, just, and Julia generous enough, that they could easily still have been living there had Albert not heard about the houses being offered in Coventry for building workers, or had Dorothy not secretly done all that she could to encourage him.

They went back to Auntie Julia's house now and again, once a year if they could, using the postal orders she sent to pay the fares; David and Susan wearing their Sunday clothes and watching the train rattle past the newly built suburbs of Coventry, the long reaches of wasteground, the farms and woodlands and market towns which soon gave way to the smoke and noise of London. Look, that's where I went to school, his father would say, as they walked from the underground station to Julia's house, squeezing David's hand to get his attention, pointing to a tall high-windowed Victorian building; and this is where I took my first job, a few moments later, as they passed a builder's yard with a few small piles of bricks and sand and waste timber. This is where your grandparents lived, he'd add quickly, gesturing at an open scrap of wasteland between two houses; that's where I grew up. And this is where we all used to live, his mother would say, as they rounded the last corner into Julia's street, David and Susan both slipping out of their parents' hands in a race to reach the house first, stretching up to reach the doorbell before Julia, who would always be looking out for them, swung open the door.

Their visits usually followed the same pattern. Julia would have lunch waiting for them – cucumber sandwiches, sliced meats, fruit pies, all laid out on the big table by the window, with Laurence hovering sullenly while he waited for permission to begin – and once they'd eaten Albert would make some excuse and slip out to see old friends in the pub, leaving the women to talk and the children to get down and play. It was a tall and narrow terraced house, with three floors and a cellar, and although the rooms were small and crammed full of Julia's many possessions, there was plenty of space to explore. Sometimes Susan and David would play together, or with Laurence, while Julia and Dorothy did the washing up and chattered about grown-up things; playing hide and seek up and down the three flights of stairs, making handkerchief parachutes for Susan's dolls and dropping them with a quick thud from the top landing, daring each other to creep down into the dark cellar. Sometimes they'd play apart, allocating each other a floor of the house and muttering their imaginary narratives around cars and teacups and soldiers and dolls. And sometimes they'd make so much noise, encroaching on each other's games or flaring up over some half-imagined slight, that Auntie Julia or their mother would give them some money and some coupons to go to the sweet shop, telling them to run off some of their silliness in the park. Laurence never came to the park with them, and often ignored them altogether, barricading himself in his room to read comics or listen to the crystal radio set he'd built himself. He was five years older than David, so it almost didn't seem strange that he would keep himself apart like that, although sometimes he heard his mother complain about it on the way home, saying well Laurence was a bit rude, a bit sulky, nothing like his mother, and didn't Albert think Julia should be doing something about it?

Dorothy was up on her feet before he'd even opened the door, reaching for him, saying David David love, what happened? Lifting him into her arms, kissing the top of his head and wiping his eyes with a handkerchief, saying oh David, it's okay, it's alright, what's happened to you? And by the time she'd sat him down on a chair to have a good look at him, Julia had taken a wad of cotton wool from her useful drawer, and a bottle of antiseptic from the cupboard, and set them on the table.

She asked him again what had happened. There were some big boys, he said, in the park, and he didn't manage to say much more through his sniffs and juddering tears. He didn't say that they'd asked him what he was doing in their park, that they'd told him he wasn't from round there and to get lost, that one of them had pushed him off the swing and that another had thrown stones while he was running away, that he'd tripped and fallen and they'd all laughed. He was already learning that some things were easier not to say.

This is going to hurt a little now David, his mother said, as she dabbed antiseptic on to his broken skin. He nodded, wincing, sucking the breath in between his teeth, and when she was done he said are we going home soon? and his mother said yes love, we are, we'll go soon, but why don't you have a lie down first, have a little rest, okay?

And while David lay in the bed in one of Julia's spare rooms, a cool damp cloth folded across his forehead, and while Susan went up to see him, to offer him something from her thruppenny bag of sweets and say are you alright? I'm sorry I left you in the park, and while David thought about it for a moment and said that's okay, Dorothy was wiping at tears of her own with the same handkerchief she'd offered David a few moments before, sitting down on the chair and smiling up at Julia, saying well, you can't always be there with them, can you?

No dear, Julia said, sitting down next to her. You can't.

It's a good job I wasn't there, Dorothy said, smoothing her handkerchief. I probably would have belted them.

I daresay you would have done Dotty, Julia said, shaking her head, and where do you think that would have left us? A long line of upset mothers knocking on my door I'd imagine. Dorothy smiled, wiping her eyes again and folding the handkerchief away.

But where does it come from, this? she said, looking down at her clenching and unclenching fist. I mean, Julia, you know, from the first moment I set eyes on him, I— He was such a beautiful child, wasn't he?

They always are, said Julia, smiling.

No, but Julia, he was; I couldn't, I couldn't take my eyes off him; I couldn't put him down for more than a minute. I used to watch anyone who came near him like a hawk, you know I did. Julia nodded.

I know Dot, she said. Of course I do.

I would have stepped in front of a bus for him, Dorothy said. I still would. Where does that come from? she asked again. Julia shrugged.

It's only natural, she said.

Dorothy looked up, almost startled.

But this was different, she said, this is different. I'd never felt like that before, she said fearfully. Don't you remember me telling you that? Julia nodded, smiling, squeezing Dorothy's hand and then letting go as they both heard Susan stepping carefully down the stairs.

4 *Tobacco tin, cigarettes, Christmas card, 1914*

He pushed open the door of the room at the end of Auntie Julia's top landing, and stared. He'd never seen so many things in one room before. There were piles of books and magazines, dresses on hangers and dresses spread out across chairs, hats balanced on top of each other, photo albums still halfway through being filled from shoeboxes of loose snapshots, bunches of flowers hanging to dry, posters for West End productions, jewellery boxes spilling over with tangled necklaces and earrings. He edged into the room, his hands hovering over it all, not knowing where to begin. His parents kept a much tidier and more ordered house; clothes were kept in wardrobes, toys went straight back under the bed when they'd been played with, and the few photographs they had were neatly filed away into albums and rarely taken out. This was something very new. Later, once he'd been taken to the British Museum, and been patiently waited for while he tried to read every last caption, he would think of comparing this room to the collection halls of the Egyptian Pharaohs, where the many possessions they needed to accompany them to the next world were held for safekeeping, and he would shyly tell Julia this and be shocked by the volume of her laughter, by the ferocity with which she would gather him into her arms and kiss the top of his head.

Without thinking about it, he picked up a tobacco tin from the bookshelf, half hidden amongst the jewellery boxes and polished stones. It was lighter than he'd expected, and rough where the metal had rusted, and there were pictures of battleships around the edge of the lid. You can open it if you like, Julia said quietly, and although he hadn't realised she was standing behind him, he was too absorbed to be surprised. She came into the room, swept a pile of magazines from the bed to the floor and sat down. He looked at her and he looked at the tin in his hands.

Julia's mother had been an actress, and although Julia had never quite made it onto the stage herself, she had inherited something of that same gift for inhabiting a story; and that was what she did that day, as she told him about a long-gone Christmas. She told him about her father, a young schoolteacher with round glasses and a thin moustache, spending the Christmas of 1914 in a muddy hole somewhere in France. She said that even though it was a war they'd found the time for a celebration, and that by the light of a smoky paraffin lamp and a few stubby candles they'd drunk from small mugs filled with brandy, sung carols, and worn party hats made from sheets of old newspaper. It can't have been all that cheery, she said, what with men not there who should have been there, and all of them anyway wishing they were home with their families, but they did their best, and made jokes, and drank to the health of every last man they could think of. And then, she said, leaning in close as though it were a secret, their commanding officer gave them these: a Christmas present from the young Princess Mary herself. She reached across and helped him ease the lid off the tin. Inside, there was a Christmas card, a full pouch of tobacco, and twenty cigarettes. She smiled. He kept his, she said. He thought it would be worth hanging on to, he thought it might be worth something one day. She laughed. He could be very dull and sensible sometimes, she said. My mother was forever on at him to liven up a little. He looked at the unsmoked cigarettes and a strange excitement shook through him. It was a dangerous, thrilling feeling.

The thing in his hands felt at once indestructible and hopelessly fragile. He was terrified of dropping it, or of spoiling it in some way, of holding it out in the air for too long. It felt as though he had only to put one of the cigarettes to his lips and he would be suddenly transported to that foxhole in 1914, crowded around a mess table singing carols with his fellow soldiers. He wanted to put the lid back on, to have Julia take it out of his hands, but he couldn't move and he couldn't bring himself to look away.

Later, Julia took him to the Imperial War Museum and showed him soldiers' uniforms like the one her father had worn, and the type of rifle he would have used, and letters sent home from the front. She took him to the British Museum and showed him the treasures of Sutton Hoo, the Egyptian Mummies, the jewellery and weapons and costumes smuggled home from around the world. She took him to the Natural History Museum, the V&A, the Horniman, and each time he felt the same breathless excitement he'd felt when he'd first held her father's tobacco tin, the same thrill of old stories made new.

And it was this that he had spent most of his life looking for: these physical traces of history, these objects which could weigh his hands down with their density of memory and time. Something he could hold on to and say, look, this belonged to my fathers and forefathers, this is some small piece of who they were. This is some small piece of where I began.

5 *Shoebox of assorted domestic goods, bullets, shrapnel, 1953–1960*

Soon after those first museum visits with Julia, he started collecting things for himself: broken crockery, an alarm clock with the face smashed in, the trailing wires of an old radio set, an empty picture frame; the cracked and rusting remains of other lives which he found on the bombsites where he wasn't allowed to play. He brought them home, brushing the dried mud from them with an old toothbrush, looking for maker's marks or other inscriptions, looking for something which would give these objects a story, attaching small labels with the date and the place where they were found and lining them up along his windowsill and his desk.

What are you doing? Susan asked him one afternoon, not for the first time, standing in his open doorway with her arms folded across her chest.

Nothing, he replied, turning away from her, trying to shield his latest find with his body, waiting for her to go away.

Why don't you just collect cigarette cards like normal boys do? she said.

Why don't you mind your own business? he said.

It is my business, I'm older than you and I'm your sister, so there, she said, picking up a dented water flask from the floor and lifting it quickly out of his reach. Where did you get this from? she asked, looking at it, reading the label which hung from its neck by a piece of white thread. Have you been on the bombsites again?

David stood up, reaching for it.

Give us it back, he said. Colin's brother found it, he gave it to me.

Don't believe you, Susan said. You'll be in trouble if they find out.

Give us it back, David said again, jumping for it now, Susan lifting it higher and stepping back, turning towards the door.

Maybe I'll keep it, she said, smiling.

It's not yours, David said, his voice rising indignantly.

It's not yours either, she snapped back. You don't even know whose it is, it could be anyone's.

Finders keepers, said David, and Susan stepped out on to the landing, smiling again.

Well, I've just found this so I'm keeping it, she said. David grabbed at it, Susan shrieked, and their mother yelled up at them both to stop it whatever it was they were doing. She pulled a face and gave him back the water flask, whispering for good measure that he was a smelly stinker.

If she'd asked, if she'd sat down and said that she really honestly wanted to know, he would have told her that he collected these things because he was fascinated by them, because he couldn't take his eyes off them, because it was almost as good as having a real museum all to himself.

But she didn't ask, and he rarely talked about it to anyone. He found it hard to explain, when anyone did ask, why he liked museums so much, why he spent so many of his weekends catching buses to museums in other towns, or gazing frustratedly at the building site which would one day become the museum Coventry was so painfully lacking. I just like looking at all the things, he would say, and imagining how old they are and finding out about them and everything; muttering as he spoke, knowing that the person asking wouldn't understand.

He liked the smell of museums, the musty scent of things dug from the earth and buried in heavy wooden store cupboards. He liked the smell of the polish on the marbled floors, and the way his shoes squeaked as he walked across them. He liked the way that people's voices would drift up and be lost in the hush of the high-ceilinged rooms. He liked the coldness of the glass cases when he pressed his face against them. He liked looking at the dates of the objects, and trying not to get dizzy as he added up how long ago that was. He didn't understand why people had to ask, why they didn't enjoy museums as much as he did, and why some of the other boys at school started to call him a swot and a teacher's pet. It seemed perfectly natural to him, to be amazed by the physical presence of history, to be able to stand in front of an ancient object and be awed by its reach across time. A thumbprint in a piece of prehistoric pottery. The chipped edge of a Viking battle-axe, and the shattered remains of a human skull. The scribbled designs for the world's first steam engine, spotted with candlewax and stained with jam. It seemed like some kind of miracle to him that these traces of distant lives had survived, and that he was able to stand in front of them and stare for as long as he liked.

When he ran out of display space in his room he started keeping the collection in cardboard shoeboxes under his bed, and it was from underneath his bed that he retrieved one of those same boxes some fifty years later, lifting the crinkled lid and sifting through the contents a few days before his journey, trying to remember where all these things had come from. A brooch, a set of keys, a bullet, a handful of blank-faced coins, a lumpen twist of rusted shrapnel: they could have come from any number of the sites he'd explored as a boy – the cratered fields he took as a shortcut across to school; the motor-works which still hadn't been rebuilt; the numerous acres of cleared land which had been marked out with foundations for the housing his father would build to replace what had been there before the war. Coventry was a city of building sites when he was a child, great unmapped territories for him to explore, piecing together stories around the objects he found, guessing which buildings had once been where, or what might be coming, watching the way the city changed as all his favourite places were gradually rebuilt upon.

But the small leather shoe, in the bottom of the box, had come from his own back garden, not from a rubble-strewn bombsite. He'd dug it up with a handful of potatoes one evening after school and taken it to show his father, who was sitting on the back step with the paper. It fitted easily into his father's broad hand, and they'd both looked at it for a moment, cradled there, plastered with mud.

Well that's something, his father had said.

How old do you think it is Dad? David said, leaning over it with his hands on his knees. His father looked up.

I'd say it's probably been in the ground there since '44, he said, so it's older than you at least. He looked over towards the potato patch, David's spade still sticking out of the ground, the pale potatoes lying in a bunch beside the small hole he'd made. I wouldn't tell your mother about this one though, he added. She might be upset. She might not let you hang on to it, he said. He looked at David, solemnly, and winked, and David tried to wink back. Now, you going to finish digging up the spuds? he asked, passing him the shoe and turning back to his paper.

In the summer, if the weather was fine, his father liked to sit out on the back step when he got home from work. His mother would look out for him coming down the road and have the kettle and the pot ready so that by the time he got to the house there'd be a mug of tea there waiting. Sometimes she would meet him at the door, holding a damp handkerchief up to his face to wipe the dust and dirt from his mouth before kissing him hello. He would sit on the step and spread the evening paper out across his lap, steam rising from his mug, smoke curling from his cigarette, and he didn't like anyone speaking to him until he'd put the paper to one side and looked up again. He was always covered in dust when he got home, his face and hands coated with brick dust and powdered cement, his clothes scattered with woodshavings from the joiners working overhead, his hair threaded with thin white fibres from the panels they used in the roof and around the pipes. When he'd finished the paper, and got washed and changed before tea, he shifted back to being their at-home dad again, softer and more human seeming, but while he was sitting on that step, covered in the debris of work, waiting for his body to recover, he almost seemed to be someone else, some mythological character who built houses and schools and hospitals with his own bare and calloused hands.

At weekends, or on long evenings when the light held, he would work on the garden, swapping the dust of the building sites for the mud and soil of the ground. There were photographs, taken when they first moved into the house, in which the garden was nothing but piles of sand and builders' rubble, a few nettles and thistles springing up from the odd patch of soggy ground. By the time he died, he'd turned it into something out of a gardener's catalogue – a small lawn at the front, kept carefully trim and straight, bordered with rose bushes, hydrangeas, dahlias, and hollyhocks on either side of the front door. Long rows of vegetables in the back, carefully weeded, carrots and cauliflowers and brussel sprouts, potatoes and parsnips, wigwams of peas and fat runner beans.

Years later, when Dorothy first met Eleanor, she took great pleasure in showing her around the garden. This was all a wasteground when we moved in, David heard her say as she took Eleanor by the arm and led her around the borders. It took six years for the magnolia to flower but it was worth it, don't you think? And Eleanor smiled and said that she thought it was. And as David watched them, from his place beside the back step, looking at the pale pink flowers of the clematis, which had been trained to the top of the slatwood fence, looking at the heavy handfuls of lavender and thyme growing out of the half-brick rockery in the corner, looking at the gnarled and sagging branches of the two small apple trees, it seemed as if his father had hardly gone away at all.

6 *Postcard from Greenwich Maritime Museum, c.1953*

When David told Julia that he wanted to be a museum curator she didn't nod and say that's nice, or make a face, or ask him why; she clapped her hands and said it was a wonderful idea. You'll have to invite me to your first exhibition, she said enthusiastically and whenever he saw her after that she would ask how his collections were coming along, what lessons he'd learnt from the museums he'd been to since she saw him last, whether he'd have any jobs going for a work-shy duffer like her once he was open and ready for business. He started telling her about the sort of museum he would run, the exhibitions he would put on, the archives he would collect. I'll have some displays that people can pick up and hold, he said, and more people to explain what things are. And I won't have anything in storage, he said. It'll all be out on display and if there isn't enough room I'll buy a bigger museum because it's not fair to hold on to things and not let people look at them. And I won't have any replicas or artist's impressions, he said.

He reminded her about the boat he'd seen in the Maritime Museum; it was sitting in a small white-washed room of its own, beached on the bare floor and propped up by a pair of painted timbers. He'd walked around it, just able to see over the gunwales and into the plain interior, a couple of bench seats the only sign of comfort. The display panel on the wall had said that this boat, all twenty undecked feet of it, may well have been sailed across the Atlantic by the Vikings. He'd read those words over again and turned back to the boat, a storm of excitement breaking over him, pressing his hands against it breathlessly, wanting to climb in and run his hands all over it, to push his face into the rough-grained wood and smell the salt tang of sweat and sea and adventure, to sit on the bench and imagine the lurch of the open ocean, the endless tack and reach towards an unrelenting horizon. He'd looked at the wood, which must have been eight or nine hundred years old, and wondered why it wasn't roped off from the public, why it wasn't a little more crumbling and worn, why the varnish was gleaming under the spotlights. And he'd gone back to the display board, and read the last short paragraph explaining who'd built the replica and how, and he'd wanted to kick the whole thing to pieces.

It didn't mean anything, he told Julia later. It wasn't real, it was made up. You can't learn anything about history by looking at made-up things, he said, talking quickly and urgently. It's stupid, it's not fair. It's a lie, he said. They're lying. She held up a hand to steady him, smiling at his earnest scorn. It's better than nothing though, isn't it? she asked gently. It gives you an idea at least, wouldn't you say?

7 *Opening programme, Coventry Municipal Art Gallery and Museum, 1961*

It was still in good condition, kept clean and dry in a plastic wrapper, and when he slid it out to look through the pages the only marks of age were in the stilted language of the text and the starched formality of the photographs; the mayor, the director, the city treasurer, the benefactor's wife, sitting on the platform with their hands folded into their laps, their hair waxed neatly into place, listening attentively to one another's opening speeches, applauding.

He remembered their applause carrying out into the street, to the long crowd of people pressing and shifting back down the steps and away round the corner, five or six abreast, chatting and smoking and bending stiff legs, their hands stuffed into their pockets and their collars turned up against the last of the winter winds. One or two policemen were there, keeping order, walking up and down the line, asking people to keep out of the road and leave space for passers-by, keeping an eye out for light fingers and lost children. A pair of journalists were hanging around at the front of the queue, squiggling comments into a notebook, lifting a camera and encouraging people to smile, catching a shot where all the bleached white faces managed to look into the lens at once, a long stretch of them fading back into the dark evening; David near the front, waiting, unsmiling, half hidden by the heavy black coat of the man ahead of him.

The inky picture ended up on the front page of the *Evening Telegraph*, and the front page landed on the kitchen table for a while before being neatly clipped out and filed away into the box under his bed.

Didn't it occur to you to smile? his father asked, standing and leaning over the paper, still dressed in his dust-plastered work clothes. Didn't the photographer say cheese or something? David shrugged, embarrassed.

Wasn't bothered, he said. Susan, who'd come through from watching television when Albert called, pulled the paper across the table and said let me see, where is he? She searched through the faces and found her brother, smiling in spite of herself, reluctantly impressed.

Fame at last, she said. You'll have all the girls after you now. David ignored her, his face colouring, and leant over to try to read the article. Dorothy, standing at the oven to stir the gravy and check the chops and the potatoes, turned to Albert and said it's almost ready now if you want to get changed. Albert waved his hand at her in passing acknowledgement.

Listen, he said, taking the paper back from Susan. Crowds gathered last night to be among the first visitors to another of our city's proud buildings, the long-awaited Municipal Art Gallery and Museum. Guests were especially honoured to have in their midst the future director of the museum, one Mr David Carter Esquire, pictured here with a dirty great sulk on his face. David tried to pull the paper away, but his father whisked it up from the table and stood back, raising his voice above Susan's laughter. The city treasurer, he continued, a tight-fisted bugger if ever we saw one, said it's a shocking waste of money of course, but I was out-voted at the committee stage. It doesn't say that does it? Dorothy asked, lifting her hand to her mouth as she realised her mistake. They all laughed, and she joined in, embarrassed, and they kept on laughing until Albert began to cough and splutter and double over in an attempt to haul in some breath.

You really should go to the doctor's, Dorothy said when

he'd recovered, handing him a glass of water. Albert didn't reply.

And there was nothing now to show for this, in the archives he had kept. No medical records, no photographs of his father's face turning a violent red as he fought for breath, no prescriptions or bottles of pills. Just the memory of that cough, the angry defiant bark of it, dry and choked, as though his lungs were full of tangled steel wool. There should have been something, at least. Something to hold up to the light, or to pin to the wall.

If he was asked, he was going to say that he remembered his father as a strong man; as someone who could balance two dozen bricks on his broad shoulders while he climbed a ladder, who could swing both him and his sister up in the air at the same time, and dig the whole vegetable patch over in the hour or two of light that was left after supper. He was going to say that he remembered his father as a busy man; as someone who always seemed to be in a hurry to be somewhere else: home from work, out to the garden, away from the supper table and out to join his friends in the pub. And he was going to say that he remembered his father as a loving man; someone who could hold his wife in his arms without shame and kiss her as if nobody else was in the room, someone who could find the time now and again to tuck his son into bed, with broad strong hands that smelt of soil and dust and cigarette smoke.

No one was much surprised when he died, and Albert was probably the least surprised of all. It had been coming on quickly for months and he seemed to have given up and started waiting for it. It feels like I'm breathing in tiny splinters of metal every time I open my mouth, he told David once. It feels like there's a barrow-load of bricks weighing down on my chest. Dorothy found him when she got back from the shops one afternoon, his head tipped back over the arm of the sofa, a blanket wrapped around him like a shroud. She called out, and by the time David had run downstairs she was kneeling beside the sofa, holding Albert's hand and stroking the side of his face. The shopping bags were on the floor, split open, tins and packets and loose wrapped meats spilt halfway across the room, and it was only when the doctor arrived that she pushed herself back to her feet again.

My father wasn't one for talking much, he wanted to tell someone, and if he did it was never really about the past, about his family, or where he grew up, or what happened in the war. I know he was in the Navy and that's about all, I don't know where he went, or what he did when he got there, I don't know what my mother went through at home when the bombing was going on, if she saw anyone killed or injured at all. I only know that they were apart for a long time, and they couldn't even write, and that when they were together again there were things they didn't feel the need to talk about; not even, I suppose, to each other. I think that's how I got so interested in history, he would say, since there was so little of it at home. There weren't even any photos on the wall until after my father had died.

I suppose I didn't really know him all that well in the end, he thought he might say. Well, isn't that the oldest story, someone might murmur in response, he thought, or, who among us ever did?

They'd spent the afternoon at the Imperial War Museum. He was still uncertain about finding his way around London on his own, so Julia had gone with him, and had been very patient while he took notes and made sketches, and had gone quiet at one or two of the exhibits, stepping away a few paces and turning her back so that he knew it wasn't a good idea to ask her what was wrong. They'd found a Christmas tobacco tin from 1916, like the one she had at home from her father, but this one was empty and she'd laughed and whispered maybe it's worth something now, and he'd been shocked by the idea of her selling such a thing until she'd nudged him and he'd realised she was joking. It hadn't been until they were on the bus on the way home, the street lamps already spilling splashes of light on to the rain-polished streets, that he'd asked about her own experience of the war, and about her husband; and it was only after they'd run from the bus stop to the house, and wrapped their wet heads in warm towels from the airing cupboard, and sat down in the kitchen with a steaming pot of tea and thick slices of heavy cake, that she'd begun to tell him.

The war hadn't started when I met him, she began, but everyone knew it wouldn't be long in coming. She hadn't got very far with her story before she realised he didn't know what she meant by ballroom dancing, so she insisted that she teach him there and then. She put a record on, and had him push the table back, and talked him through the steps while a waltz crackled out of the small loudspeaker. He felt a tightening knot of embarrassment in his stomach as she took his hand and placed it on her waist, and laid her hand against his, but he knew there'd be no getting out of it until he'd got it right. So he listened, and he concentrated, and he started to relax a little, and the second time the record played he only stepped on her foot twice. Well! she said, clapping her hands as the record finished again, I think we'll make a ballroom maestro out of you yet, young man. We'll have the debs of London queuing up for you! He didn't know what she meant by debs, but he didn't get a chance to ask. Once more, she announced, as the needle jerked back to the start of the record. This is the way the story begins, she said, taking his hand.

A Friday evening in early June, 1939. A hotel ballroom just off The Strand, its high domed ceiling frescoed pale sky-blue with wisps of spindrift clouds, ringing with the fading echo of the orchestra's closing bars. A renewed rumble of chatter and a tinkle of glasses. A brief light-fingered applause for the musicians. The dancers returning to their seats, singly or in pairs, smiling and no-thank-you-ing, reaching for drinks with lowered eyes and private blushes or whispering reports to a neighbour's ear. A rustle of loose sheaf paper at the orchestra's music stands. The unaccompanied glide and twirl of the white-jacketed waiters refreshing tall glasses with a stoop and a bow, proffering hors d'oeuvres on broad silver trays, wordless, indifferent, impeccably polite. Seated guests rising for the next dance, taking the hand of those closest to them, or catching the eye of another nearby, or crossing the room with a smart-heeled step, a discreet straightening of the jacket, a two-fingered smoothing of the hair; determined, after much raw-humoured ribbing, to finally take the bull, as it were, by the horns.

We'd been watching each other all evening, she told him as the first few bars of the music swelled up against the sound of the rain outside and David led them correctly away to the right, towards the tall potted yucca. That's it! she said. You're getting it now, back two three. I'd noticed him almost as soon as he came into the room, she said. The smart cut of his uniform, you know, and an awfully manly jaw, and very clear pale eyes. I caught him looking a few times, she said, smiling. Or he caught me looking, she added; turn two three. I suppose it depends which way you look at it. She laughed.

Major William Pearson stood in front of Julia's table and introduced himself. Neither of them were surprised that he was there, after an evening spent watching each other's movements – checking who the other may or may not be dancing with, hazarding a smile from across the room, murmuring excuse me as they came close to colliding by the doors to the terrace – and neither of them expected her to decline his invitation to dance. But still, she went through the formalities of reluctance, and her friends carefully looked away and pretended not even to have noticed that the gentleman they'd discussed all evening had finally crossed the floor to their table, and was as smoothly good-looking close up as he was from afar. He insisted, politely, and she stood, churning with excitement, and accepted his outstretched hand. Thank you, she said. I'd be glad to.

They strode to the middle of the room, offering each other their hands and waists just as the conductor was tapping his podium. William smiled, and their dance began. Neither of them said very much at first, beyond an exchange of polite enquiries, a compliment on the other's dancing, a remark on the weather, concentrating instead on their crisp and flowing movement around the circular stage of the room. Moving away from her table, where her friends were speaking into their hands and offering gestures of encouragement as she looked over his shoulder towards them; turning across the floor to within earshot of her mother and father, her father looking rather glazed, her mother smoking a cigarette in an ivory holder and dropping her a wink in the middle of one of her actress friends' long anecdotes; past a table of boys she recognised from the school opposite hers, boys she'd once gossiped about and spied upon but who from the vantage point of Major William Pearson's arms now looked far more like boys than the men they were trying so hard to be with their fuzzy moustaches and their freshly signed papers; deftly sidestepping a waiter with a tray of drinks; twirling quickly away from a raucous gaggle of tail-coated medical students; changing direction, and pausing for a brief moment, in front of his table by the corner of the stage, the officers of his party in uniforms as smart as his, raising their glasses and making comments from the sides of their mouths before roaring with laughter and slapping each other's knees – ignore them, he said quietly, smiling a little nonetheless – and she blushed and dropped her eyes for a moment; sweeping past the orchestra which seemed to be playing for the two of them alone, as if nobody else was there, and although she'd partnered dozens of men in that same dome-ceilinged venue, and although the music was more than familiar, the dance still felt brand new for them both.

They found themselves talking a little more, confident in their dancing, asking about each other's lives, his short career in the army, her studies at drama school and her hopes of following her mother on to the stage. He talked about the prospects of war, the slim chance of it still being avoided. They both described their favourite walks, restaurants, pastimes, and they were both surprised by how soon they were sharing these small secrets and intimacies. And as they talked, almost forgetting that they were dancing at all, quite forgetting that others were dancing around them, or that they were not passing unobserved, they found that they were holding each other a little closer, a little firmer, his hand resting lower on her waist, his chest brushing lightly against hers, their hips even pulling tightly together once or twice; and they found that their voices were dropping lower, taking on a secretive inviting tone obliging the other to lean in a little closer to hear, tilting their heads to whisper in each other's ear, turning their faces to catch the murmuring lips against their cheeks.

I still don't really understand how it happened, she told David, dancing past the record player. I wonder if anyone really understands how it happens, when it's like that, so immediate. How could we possibly have known what we were doing? What did we think we knew about love, or any of that business? He didn't know how to answer her. He wasn't sure if she was still talking about one dance, one evening, or the first weeks and months of their being together. He didn't really understand her questions, and he was too busy concentrating on matching their steps to the music without colliding with the furniture. But she wasn't really asking him at all, he realised later; she was asking the photograph of Major Pearson on the wall, or the music which skipped and bumped beneath the worn-out stylus, or the rain which spattered against the windows outside.

Later, she told him how reckless she thought they'd been. He presented it as a matter of practicality, she said, almost the same day as war was declared. He said that he'd soon be leaving for France, that an opportunity had arisen for the purchase of a house, this house, which would be unsuitable for a bachelor. He said there was no benefit to our endlessly hanging around. But the truth really, David, is that we were stupidly and drunkenly in love. We didn't quite stop to think, she said. Not that I would have had it any differently of course, she added, but one does wonder.

One does wonder was a phrase she often repeated, always pausing before correcting herself in one way or another. But he was such a handsome man David! Such a handsome and exciting man! And when you're young nothing else very much matters, does it? Only that this handsome chap is offering you a ring and wants you to be his wife. Patience and caution weren't really in my vocabulary in those days, she told him, smiling, and he replied, teasingly, that he didn't think they would ever be.

And as the record started again – we danced for a very long time, she told David; it seemed to go on for ever but then it was over far too soon – Julia and William danced once more around the room, past her friends, past his colleagues, past the waiters and the medical students, and back to her parents, pausing and turning while William cocked an eyebrow at her father, inclining his head towards Julia, and her father nodded, lifting up the palm of his hand as if to say certainly, be my guest, and they turned, stepped, stepped, turned away, their waltz bringing them over to the centre of the room where William dropped quickly to one knee. The conductor raised his baton, the musicians paused and the whole room leant forward to listen. Yes of course, she said. I'd be glad to, she said. And the music resumed, and the whole room applauded, and the pace of their dancing quickened as they whirled back and forth across the floor, rushing to make the arrangements, a best man, a bridesmaid, a church and a vicar, choosing the hymns and booking the hotel room, and before she knew quite what was happening her father had taken her by the arm and danced her down the length of the room, up past a pressing throng of friends and well-wishers, up to where the vicar waited and nodded his head in time to the waltz. Will you? he intoned to Major Pearson, and Major Pearson replied I will. Will you? he asked of Julia, and Julia smiled. Of course, I will. The vicar joined them hand in hand, and they danced back down the hall, confetti showered at their feet, William's colleagues lining up to form an archway with their bayoneted rifles, a waiter leading the shout of hip-hip-hooray as Major and Mrs Pearson danced right out through the doors and into the hotel lobby, sweeping up the thickly carpeted stairs and straight into the first available room, William lifting Julia into his arms and slipping a coin into the bellboy's hand.

And when they emerged, sometime later, the music was still playing. So they waltzed back down the stairs into the ballroom, and it seemed as though no one had noticed their return, the whole room dancing together now, and when Julia looked around she saw faces fixed with concentration, eyes focused on distant points beyond the room, people moving with a stiff-limbed determination, lips pulled up into forced blank smiles.

David had long sat down by then, too embarrassed to dance any more, muttering that he thought he had the hang of it and he was out of breath. But Julia had barely seemed to notice him moving away, still stepping around the room with her hands held out in front of her. She was talking quickly, stumbling, not looking at David or following the music, saying and then, and then, no, that's not right, we, and then, as if everything had happened all at once, in that one room, on that one night, and not in the space of a few hurried months.

We only had a few days, she said, before he went away. It was difficult not to think about it, she said, raising her voice against the rain, turning to a slow halt, her hands falling to her sides, her face lined with shadows. The details of her story were becoming confused, and she seemed breathless, unsteady, nodding slightly in time with the music or in agreement with her own muddled recollections. He wanted the music to stop, or Julia to say something like, well really I think that's enough for now, let me just sit down, but she didn't. She leant back against the writing bureau, her eyes half-closed and her hands seeming to conduct the music, and she carried on talking.

He used to send me short little notes, she said. Writing wasn't his strong point but I loved to get them all the same. He couldn't tell me where they were, or what they were doing, but he'd mention little details about life with the men, and I'd feel almost as though I was there with him for a minute or two. I found out later that they hadn't got all that far at all, she said softly; they were heading back to Dunkirk when they got caught out. Shelling, she said. She stopped for a moment, tipping her head towards the record player, listening to the music and smiling slightly.

In the ballroom, the dance floor less crowded than it had been a few moments before, one of the tail-coated medical students and his partner danced alongside William and Julia, matching their movements step for step, the student looking at Julia with interest. She glanced across at him nervously, and he said excuse me, I'm sorry, may I? reaching his hand out to her stomach, slipping a stethoscope from his inside pocket and looping its end inside her dress. I thought as much, he said, nodding to his partner; three months on, and they smiled and turned and twirled away. Julia looked down at herself, startled, and up at William, his thoughts seemingly somewhere else entirely. She took a few moments to compose herself, her heels clicking time across the ballroom floor, and then she leant forward to whisper in his ear: My darling William stop Pregnant stop Surprised but happy be careful I love you stop. Quietly, almost inaudibly, he replied, with a hoarse whisper in her ear: Surprised but happy also stop Suggest Laurence if a boy stop Be careful yourself all well here stop.

And almost while he was still speaking the blue sky of the ballroom ceiling was covered over with smoke and oily clouds, and a kettle-drum roll from the orchestra sent the soldiers in the corner, the officers of William's party, clambering under a table which offered no protection when the mortar shells came raining down through the stained-glass skylight, tumbling and exploding directly amongst them, scattering shrapnel and mess tins and glassware and limbs.

There was a moment's startled pause in the room, a dramatic swish of cymbals, and then the waltz continued, the waiters moving in with stretchers to take the bodies away, the medical students standing around to see if there was anything much they could do, a pair of maids hanging back with sponges and buckets and mops.

And the music was slower then, quieter, and many of the guests were returning to their seats, some of them even fetching their coats and heading for home, and Julia and William were soon the only ones left dancing, with small tired steps, back two three and turn two three, and William was silent and pale-faced in her arms, not meeting her eye, barely keeping a hold of her hand or her waist, his shoes dragging rather than smartly clicking across the polished floor. William? she said, and waited in vain for a reply. The music came to an end, and there was a strange crackling hiss as the musicians put down their instruments and the conductor turned to face the two dancers with a bow. There was no applause, and William broke away from her, not hearing her thank you or acknowledging her smile, lowering his head as he shuffled towards the table by the corner of the stage where his men had once sat. Julia crossed the dance floor for the last time and rejoined her friends at their table. They silently poured her a drink, avoiding her querying gaze.

Oh, she said, as she sat down, as if something she'd not thought of before had only just crossed her mind. Oh. She wondered what the crackling hissing sound could be. A young waiter glided past with a silver tray, turning and holding it out to her, indicating with a nod that the slim white envelope was for her. Oh, she said, again.

She showed David the two telegrams later in the evening, while he sat at the kitchen table drinking hot chocolate, the rain still pounding against the window and traffic sliding wetly through the street. She had them in a brown envelope, at the back of the useful drawer where she kept string and sellotape and candles and cotton wool. The paper was blackened and cracked along the folds, and one of the corners was stained with damp. He read both of them, the one beginning Surprised but happy also, and the one beginning Regret to inform, and he slid them delicately back into the envelope.

People are very resilient you know, she said to him later, when he pressed her about it. People find all manner of ways of working things out. I wouldn't mind but it was just so quick, she said.

She stood up from the kitchen table, put the envelope with the telegrams back into the cluttered drawer, and headed out of the room.

I don't think I'll have any chocolate tonight, she said. Will you be okay to sort things out down here? All that dancing, she said, I've worn myself out, I'm not as young as I was. She stood in the doorway a moment and something blurred and drifted in her eyes, as though she was confused, trying to remember what she was doing. He turned in his chair, his bare feet cold on the stone floor, watching her.

Auntie Julia? he said, and she turned her focus back towards him.

Yes dear? she said.

What was he like though? he asked. When you knew him at least; what was he really like?

She looked at him, her hands weakly twisting and untwisting the hem of her long cardigan. She shook her head, as if she was still surprised.

I have absolutely no idea, she said.

9 *Contract, wage slip, duty sheet, from Coventry Museum, 1964*

They gave him a small rectangular name badge when he started work at the museum, three years after that opening night; its white plastic soon yellowed from sunlight and the nicotine stain of the staffroom. *David Carter*, it said, *Junior Curatorial Assistant*. His mother insisted on him wearing it when she took his first-day-at-work photo, and said it was a pity they didn't give him a uniform as well but she supposed it was all modern these days. He told her that it was only the attendants who wore uniforms, but she said she couldn't see the difference. She said oh if your father could see you now he'd be so proud, and he said do you think so? Julia, when she saw the photograph, sent him a postcard of the British Museum, with *Onwards and upwards!* written on the back.

His first day was a disappointment. He spent the morning being shown around the galleries by the Senior Keeper, despite knowing every last inch of the place, and the afternoon sitting in the staffroom while someone tried to work out what jobs they could give him to do. He'd half expected to launch his career with a dramatic discovery in some lost corner of the basement stores, or at the very least to be given immediate responsibility for the design and layout of a groundbreaking new exhibition. But instead he spent the first few weeks doing odd jobs for the rest of the curatorial staff; looking for records in the enormous card-index boxes, taking draft documents to the secretaries' office to be typed up, checking the mousetraps and the thermohydrographs, keeping the stores spotlessly clean, making the teas and taking away the post. By the end of his first week he had an encyclopedic knowledge not of the archival filing system but of the milk and sugar preferences of each member of staff. It's not what I thought it would be like, he told his sister, and she told him he'd better get used to it, he was the new boy, and what did he expect without any proper qualifications?

But after a few weeks things started to improve. He was assigned to the Keeper of Social History and cast more into the apprentice role that he'd been expecting. And once the Director had convinced himself that this was a career David was serious about, there was mention of training courses, placements, personal responsibilities. He began to be allowed away on research visits, to Leeds, Liverpool, Newcastle, as far north as Edinburgh and Glasgow, even Aberdeen. But he still spent most of his time flipping through card indexes, cross-checking records, inspecting stored objects, looking for mouse droppings in the basement, and it was a few years more before the job started to involve any of the work he'd imagined doing when he'd been a twelve-year-old boy poring over hand-drawn gallery designs and displays.

Julia came to see him after a few months, once he'd settled in. He was talking to an attendant in the foyer when she came through the main door; she stopped and looked for a long moment, surprised, she admitted later, by the pounding sensation of pride she'd felt.

Excuse me young man, she said, approaching him finally, Dorothy waiting by the door, I wonder if you might be able to show me around the museum? He turned to her, looking taller than she remembered, looking suddenly much older than the boy who'd visited her so often, and said I'm sure I can manage that Auntie Julia. She took his arm and let him lead her slowly around the first gallery, stopping to look at each of the display cases, asking questions, asking some of the questions more than once. He wondered if there was something wrong with her hearing. Dorothy had been before and hung back a little, noticing at the same time how grown-up David seemed and how much Julia had suddenly aged. She watched him showing Julia the case of medieval artefacts, lumps of pottery and ironware and stonework, most of it found during the recent rebuilding of bomb-damaged sites, scraped out of the mud as new foundations were dug into the ground. She watched him showing her the prehistoric case, a few bones and brooches and artist's impressions, telling her that he didn't think they were very reliably dated or sourced. Julia winked, lifting a finger to her lips. I won't tell if you don't, she whispered. He moved on to the natural history displays, a whole rack of beetles balanced on nail-heads, a cotton-wool drawer of speckled birds' eggs, a tray of pinned butterflies, a panoramic landscape crowded with stuffed birds. His enthusiasm dropped when he showed her these; he half turned away even as he dutifully described each panel.

I don't even know why they call it natural history, he said. It's not the same at all.

Well, Julia said, starting to smile, gesturing towards the birds' glassy-eyed gazes and tensed jaws, I'd say they were history now Daniel, wouldn't you? She turned towards the other side of the room, but he didn't move, looking at her curiously. Dorothy started to say something, but stopped herself, meeting David's eye, shaking her head, glancing away. He hesitated, stepping towards Julia.

Auntie Julia? he said. She stopped a few feet away.

What's that dear? she asked.

Auntie Julia, he said, you called me Daniel. She looked at him blankly.

No I didn't, she said. Why on earth would I do a thing like that?

You did, he said, quietly insistent. You said Daniel. She turned to Dorothy, half-smiling, as if asking her what he was talking about. Dorothy shrugged, tutted, and peered closely at a case of flint axe heads. Julia looked back at David.

Don't be silly, she said tiredly, indignantly. I think you need to get your ears checked, don't you? And your manners. He watched her walking back down the gallery, sitting in a chair by the door to the foyer and looking pointedly away from them both. His mother nudged him. Well done, she murmured. Good work.

But by the time they rejoined her she seemed to have forgiven him, smiling pleasantly and waving her hand at the room. Are you going to show me around? she asked. He looked at her. Are you going to show me around? she asked again.

10 *Letters, handwritten, 1966–68; Paper napkin, 1966*

Their first letters were short, tentative, neither of them wanting to put into words what they had both felt the first time they met, neither of them wanting to allude to what could so easily seem absurd. I'm sorry but it's so far away, they each imagined the other replying. It would be different if we both lived in the same town. Really, I'm sorry, but I barely know you at all. Instead, they asked each other polite questions, and wrote safe remarks about their own lives, as if they were pen pals enquiring about life in another country – *What's your house like? Do you have brothers and sisters? What's your favourite film? Today I spent the whole afternoon up on Tullos Hill just looking at the sea.* But gradually the questions, and the answers, developed into something more, something which began to imply a deepening interest in each other – *What do you want to do when you're older? Will you always stay in your town? Are you going out with anyone at the moment?* And, gradually, they stopped worrying about how long the letters were becoming, and how frequent, and they started signing off *with love,* without quite thinking what it would mean, and they started writing things like: *It would be good to see you soon. I can't wait to see you. When will you be coming up again?*

He had all her letters still, of course, filed neatly away in a shoebox with everything else in Kate's old room, the tops of the envelopes smudged with fingermarks where he had taken them out and put them away over the years. And there were phrases he could quote from memory: *It's deadly boring working in the tea room but sometimes it's worth it for the folk you meet. There are seals on the beach near here you know, I can show you if you're ever up again. I heard there was a job going in the museum today. Isn't it funny to think we almost never met?*

He didn't tell his mother, or Susan, but they both noticed the letters he'd started getting, and it wasn't long before his sister asked him who they were from. It's no one, he told her as they were walking to the bus stop one morning, David heading for the museum, Susan for her job in a solicitor's office. Susan was still holding the latest letter just out of his reach, studying the envelope's girlish scrawl, and David tried to look unconcerned. It's just someone helping me with my research, he said. She looked at him over her shoulder, grinning, making a questioning face. What? he said. I met them when I went up there to study the museum. He grabbed at the letter but she pulled away from him, laughing.

Them? she said. Them? She stopped and turned around. What's her name? she said. David looked at her, and realised that no matter how old they both got she would always be his older sister and would always eventually get her way. He was twenty-one but he might have been twelve for the way she was holding the letter away from him, taunting him with it. He gave her a shove, snatching the letter, and he couldn't keep himself from smiling when he said Eleanor, her name's Eleanor alright? She's just a friend, alright? Susan gave him a shove back.

Alright, she said, she's just a friend. David put the letter in his pocket, keeping his hand on it, running his fingers across the ink-smudged paper. Aren't you going to read it? she asked, as they walked on.

No, he said. Not now.

Why? she said. It's not private, is it? I thought she was just a friend? She nudged him again and this time when he looked at her it was with a smile which admitted something he wasn't yet willing to say.

You won't say anything to Mum though? he said quietly, just as they got to the bus stop. She looked at him, made a zipping her lips shut gesture, and winked.

But she did tell their mother; or if she didn't tell her then she at least said enough for her to guess. Or perhaps Dorothy simply worked it out for herself, because when he came back from his second trip to Aberdeen she said, so, tell me, you're serious about this girl then?

What girl? he said. She smiled, shaking her head at him. She was ironing his shirt for work the next day, knowing that he wouldn't have thought about it before he went away.

Well, she said, what's her name? How old is she? What does she do?

He laughed, dropping his bag and holding up his hands in defeat, pulling a chair out from under the table. Her name's Eleanor, he said, sitting down. She's eighteen. She's still at school but she works in the tea rooms at the museum sometimes. Dorothy rearranged his shirt on the board, turning it over so the buttons ran down one edge, pulling the seam straight as she slid the iron across the creases.

And have you met her parents yet? she asked, trying and failing to say the words as if the question didn't mean anything much. David pulled a face.

It's not like that Mum, he said. Not— and he caught himself, bending down to look for something suddenly important in his bag. His mother looked up, standing the iron on its rest.

Not yet? she suggested, smiling. David screwed up his eyes and shook his head.

No Mum, he said, his voice muffled by embarrassment and exasperation. It's not— I don't know. I like her, but, I don't know. It seems a bit soon to be meeting her parents, he said. Dorothy picked up the iron again, pressing it down on to the shirt's folded cuffs, resting her weight on them a moment.

I met your father's parents almost before we started courting, she said. He took me to his house after picking me up from Auntie Julia's and introduced me to them. It was very formal. I think he just wanted to show me off. They were very nice you know; it was so sad what happened. She put the iron back on the rest and started to fold the shirt, smoothing it out with the back of her hand. Of course, my parents didn't get to meet him until the wedding, she said. London was a long way from Suffolk in those days. David looked up at her and stopped himself from saying I know this Mum, you've told me all this before. I'd only met him a week earlier, she said, at a church-hall dance. Julia made sure I went and she made sure I talked to him as well, not that I needed much encouragement. She stopped, looking down at her hands where they rested on the folded shirt, looking at the ring still on her finger there.

I miss him David, she said. I really do. Her voice faltered. He stood up and moved awkwardly towards her. They both waited.

I know, he said. She took a sharp breath, blinking quickly, and held the shirt out towards him.

Anyway, she said briskly. So. Did you meet this Eleanor at the museum, was she working there when you went up? Or did you, I mean, was it something else? He took the shirt and shook his head, smiling, as if to say that she knew too much already, that he wasn't going to tell her anything more.

I don't know really, he said, I just did. It just happened, he said.

He went upstairs, and as he carried the folded shirt out of the room she mouthed thank you? behind him, shaking her head and unplugging the iron from the wall.

It just happened.

He could have walked straight past. The door might not have been ajar. She might not have been struggling to work the new coffee machine, and so the sudden shriek it made might not have caught his attention the way it did. He might not have had the money to spare, or the confidence to push the door a little wider and ask if she was still serving. He might not have misunderstood the museum layout and missed an entire room of exhibits, and so he might have been rushing to catch his train and not turned and seen her there.

These things, the way they fall into place. The people we would be if these things were otherwise.

The coffee machine shrieked, he turned his head, the door was ajar. Behind the gleaming mahogany counter, partly shrouded by a jet of steam, he saw her, frowning, pulling levers, banging her hand against the side of the machine. There didn't seem to be any customers. Sunlight was pouring into the room through tall sash windows, every surface shining, every spoon and coffee pot glinting, and as the steam cleared he caught his first sight of her face.

Or it was raining, and the room was dull and grey, and he couldn't see her properly from the other side of the room – the details slip away, arranged and rearranged over the years.

She might have turned away at that point. He might have heard footsteps along the corridor behind him, the jangle of a janitor's keys. The woman who usually worked in the tea room with her might have come bustling out of the kitchen instead of having left half an hour early to get to the post office on time. But none of that happened. He stayed looking at her, and caught the expression on her face: a purse of the lips, a shake of the head, a brief and secret smile. He noticed the way she tucked her hair behind her ear, the small coloured bead necklace she wore, the freckles on her nose, the high arch of her eyebrows. He noticed the open neck and the close fit of her tight white blouse. He caught his breath for a moment, and he didn't turn away.

And there were so many ways it could have been different.

She might not have had the job in the first place. The friend of her mother's might have mentioned it to someone else first, or her mother might not have thought it suitable. He might not have been able to get the time off work to make the long journey north. Trains could have been missed, or delayed, timetables misread. She might not have changed her scowl to a smile the way she did when she looked up and heard him ask if she was still serving.

He walked up to the counter and she said what can I get you? Looks like the coffee's a problem, he said, so I'll have a tea if that's alright. And she smiled again, blushing a little, and said aye they got the stupid thing on the cheap, it never works properly, and she went out to the kitchen to use the urn instead. She came back with a pot of tea, and poured out a cup, and glanced quickly up at him before pouring out another cup for herself. He stood across from her, his satchelful of guidebooks and leaflets propped against his feet, sipping from the thin china cup with the saucer in the palm of his hand. She leant across the counter and they talked. And there it was, already, in the way her long thin fingers fiddled with a sugar cube, in the way she held his eye when she spoke, in the way he wanted to reach across and tuck a stray wisp of hair back behind her ear.

She asked how he liked Aberdeen, and he said he hadn't had much chance to look around, he'd been in the museum all day. He asked if it was worth a return visit, and she said it was nice enough but she wasn't planning on hanging around, she was going to get out as soon as she could. I'm going to university, she said, looking him in the eye as she said it, as though challenging him to say she wasn't. This job's only while I finish my Highers. Her eyes were wide and pale brown and her eyelashes were so much the same colour that they were almost invisible; he must have stared at them a little too long because she turned away and said would you like a piece of cake? They'll only throw it out otherwise.

She asked him what he was doing there and he told her, and she was only the second person who'd ever been interested or taken him seriously when he'd said he wanted to one day open a museum of his own. Will you need a tea room? she asked, her smile softening the edges of her narrow angular face, and her boldness surprised them both into silence for a moment.

I'm going to be a geologist, she said, restarting the conversation, and he told her he'd never met a geologist before and asked her what they did. We study rocks, she said, laughing, and told him about fissures and seams and glacial deposits. It sounds like it's boring but it's not, she said, and he assured her that it didn't sound boring at all. He noticed the colour of her eyes again, and then he noticed the time.

He said he had a train to catch. She asked him when he might be there again and neither of them seemed surprised by the question. He said soon, probably, as if it were the most natural thing in the world to make such a long journey for the sake of an afternoon in a museum. She said my name's Eleanor by the way, Eleanor Campbell, and he told her his. She wrote her address on a paper napkin and he put it in his pocket, and he wrote his telephone number on another napkin and she put it in hers. He told her he'd write, and she said she'd like that, and he picked up his bag and walked away, replaying the conversation over and over again in his head.

These things, the way they happen. These things, the way they begin.

Will you write again soon? Isn't it funny to think we almost never met?

11 *Cigarette holder, tortoiseshell, believed 1940s*

It was only when Julia started smoking again that they realised something was really wrong. Before that, her slips and slides of memory had seemed like absent-mindedness, eccentricity, nothing more. I've been a dizzy old bat ever since the war, she said once, looking for her keys, it's nothing new, and his mother said which war's that then, the Boer? and they both yelped with laughter while he and Susan rolled their eyes.

But when she started smoking, it seemed different somehow.

They were having dinner at her house – David, his mother, a woman called Alice, Alice's husband – sitting around a large table in the bay window of the back room, listening to Julia and Dorothy talk mostly about their time working together during the war. Dorothy told the story, not for the first time, of how they'd once had to use sterilised strips of torn bedsheet when they ran out of bandages, and Julia did what Dorothy assured everyone was a note-perfect impression of the merciless ward sister inspecting the resultant dressings. Alice's husband asked Julia why, when she was clearly in no need of the income, and could have gone to live with her brother in the country to be with her son, she'd gone into nursing at all, and Julia said that she'd just felt the need to be useful for once. One got the impression from the newspapers, she said, that there was an awful lot of nursing to be done. David sat and listened, and asked questions occasionally, and tried not to look as though he'd let the heavy red wine go to his head. Towards the end of the meal, when the puddings had been eaten and the talk had turned to coffee, just as a warm sighing quiet had settled on to the room, Julia took out a packet of cigarettes and lit one up, offering them round to the rest of the table. It surprised him, because he'd never seen her smoking before, or smelt smoke around her, or seen ashtrays in the house.

Alice and her husband both took one, leaning in towards the candles to light them. David shook his head quickly as Julia held the packet out to him, and his mother just looked at her. Julia put the packet away, inhaled deeply, coughed and tapped a few flakes of ash into her pudding bowl. Dorothy watched her. When did you start smoking again Julia? she asked, sounding surprised.

Cigarettes weren't a problem at the time. Most people seemed to smoke to some extent; pubs were always clouded with it, cinemas provided ashtrays, and people often offered a packet around at the end of a meal. He didn't know why his mother was so worried about it. Later, she told him that they'd both given up after the war, when a surgeon had shown them some photographs of tar-blackened lungs and told them what medical opinion was only just beginning to suspect. It was something we decided together, she said. It was like a pact between us, something to do after it was all over. I don't mind, she told him later, I'm just surprised, that's all.

Julia looked at Dorothy blankly, as if she hadn't heard her. Dorothy repeated herself. My dear girl, what are you talking about? Julia said. I've been smoking since I left school, since before I met you, you know that. The room shifted to a very different sort of quiet, a catch of breath and a stilling of hands.

Dorothy tried to laugh and said but Julia I thought we both gave it up, didn't we? Julia frowned, took a long draw on her cigarette, and coughed again.

I think you've had too much to drink Dotty, she said, smiling. Should I make those coffees now? They were all looking at her, wondering what to say. David didn't quite know what was going on, but his mother, and Alice and her husband, obviously did.

They looked at each other, and then Alice said, quite calmly, do you have an ashtray Julia? I hate to make a mess of your dishes here.

Of course, of course, said Julia, getting up from the table with a jolt, how silly of me. Now then.

And she swept around the room, her hands reaching for the ghosts of ashtrays which had long since been got rid of, on the sideboard, on the coffee table, on top of the piano, beside the record player. She went twice around the room, and then spun to a standstill by her chair, looking at them with a sudden flicker of fear in her face. She looked at the cigarette in her hand. She said, oh bugger, oh bloody bugger, and for a moment she looked like a child, shrinking in front of them. She looked at the cigarette and stubbed it out on her pudding dish. She laughed, and said well that's me showing my age already then, eh? twirling her finger around the side of her head, her bracelets spinning and rattling against each other. No one else laughed. She sat down slowly, covering her face for a moment with her hand. She looked up at Dorothy. Oh Dotty, she said quietly, her voice cut with disappointment as well as fear, her eyes flitting to each of them, looking for some kind of reassurance.

It wasn't long before her fears began to be realised, piece by disjointed piece. Conversations started to peter out in the middle, names were repeatedly forgotten, doctor's appointments missed. She got lost in a department store in town, bursting into confused tears at the top of an escalator, and when the staff took her into a back room and tried to calm her down she was unable to remember her address. Dorothy began to realise that she wasn't eating properly, or changing her clothes, or keeping the house as clean as she had once made a point of doing. They started to visit her more often, doing her shopping for her while they were there, trying to prompt her into using the bathroom and changing her clothes. They took her to the doctor's, looking for a name for what was happening to her, looking for things they could do to make it better. I'm too young to be doolally, she said, and the doctor said he couldn't approve of the term but unfortunately there were cases where loss of faculty could have an early onset. It seems, bluntly, that yours might be one of those cases, he said. Laurence was an officer in the army by then, and when they tried to encourage him to take leave so he could look after his mother he told them he didn't think that would be possible. You carry on there, he wrote, in a short letter to Dorothy, I'm sure you're doing a fine job. Julia asked about him, often, and continued writing to him for some years, and when even people's names began to slip out of reach his was the last name she forgot.

12 *Picture postcard, Union Street, Aberdeen, c.1966*

When he made his first journey back to Aberdeen, five or six months after they'd met, they still hadn't used the words boyfriend, or girlfriend, or going out, and there were a few awkward first hours where they realised how little they still knew of one another – taking a moment to recognise each other at the train station, standing a little way apart, avoiding eye contact and having no idea what to say. But eventually, helped along by a couple of beers and a gin, they stood at the end of the harbour, next to the coastguard's tower, and dared to put their hands together, and to kiss, and it was a fierce, breathless, impatient kiss which lasted so long that the coastguards banged on the window and shouted at them, laughing and cheering. They walked quickly away to the end of the harbour wall, embarrassed, laughing, looking out at the calm bright sea, looking across the harbour mouth to the lighthouse and the half-ruined gun battery on the rocky knuckle of Girdleness, and the black cormorants standing along the jetty like a funeral party, waiting for whatever the next tide might bring. She pointed out her house, anonymous amongst the rows of stone-built terraces that climbed the low hill away from the shipyards, cut off from the rest of Aberdeen by the River Dee, and she pointed out the rooftops and towers of Union Street's grand procession, and he smudged his thumb along her narrow eyebrows and kissed her again.

They walked back along the harbour wall, through the huddled rows of fishermen's cottages and out on to the long unexpected sweep of beach which stretched for two miles or more up to the River Don. Everyone had their deckchairs turned away from the sea to face the sun, and as they held hands along the prom they felt as though they were on a stage. They walked past the ice-cream huts and candyfloss sellers and postcard stalls, and she told him how in winter the waves would race each other up the steps and over the refreshment huts, lunging landwards with the full weight of the North Sea rushing in behind. You should come back and see it then, she added.

They didn't go to her house that first time. They walked back into town along the harbour road, through streets piled high with fish crates and ropes and chainlinks as fat and heavy as Brunel's, wandering through the richer part of town to Duthie Park and the old Winter Gardens, scrambling down from a small station platform on to a recently abandoned railway line, hopping along the sleepers and make-believing they could follow the tracks all the way to America. My brother Hamish has been to America lots of times, she told him, once they'd given up and turned back towards the park. He's in the merchant navy, she said proudly. Donald's over to see him there next year; him and Ros are thinking about emigrating.

Have you ever thought about emigrating? he asked her lightly. Or going south at least? Slipping his arms around her waist and pulling her towards him, kissing her cheeks and her eyelids and her lips.

Aye, of course I have, she said indignantly, as if the very question was an insult.

Where would you go? he asked.

I don't know, she said, kissing him back. Anywhere, she said. Away from here.

School's the same as ever, it's difficult and it's not much fun but I'm going to stick it out, I'm going to get my Highers. Sometimes I think it's my only chance. I do spend an awful lot of time in class just thinking about you though, and I'm looking forward to seeing you again soon. I suppose really it's my turn to come see you, but I doubt my folks would let me do that. My da's already asking after you, he says he wants to know when he's going to get a chance to meet you! I told him it was nothing like that, but now I'm not so sure – what do you think?

Eleanor's house was small, as all the houses were on that side of the harbour; gloomy inside, draughty and probably difficult to heat, but well built, with granite blocks from the local quarries, and solid enough to last a couple of centuries or more. There were two bedrooms upstairs, divided by a steep and narrow stairway, a small front room, a kitchen at the back of the house, a scullery and an outside toilet. Her parents didn't own the house, but her grandfather had lived there as well, and his father before that, so the family history felt as though it was etched into the hard grey stone.

From just outside the house it was possible to look right down the street to the harbour, to the tall crooked cranes of the shipyards, the freighters unloading at the docks, the seagulls clouding and clamouring around the fishmarket on the end of the central pier. From just outside the house it was possible to hear what people were saying in the front room, or in the hallway, or, if they were talking loudly enough, in the kitchen. If there were more than a few people in the kitchen, as there were the first time David went there with Eleanor, it was possible to stand at the front door and hear them all raising their voices to make themselves heard over each other, laughing, banging on the table to get themselves some attention.

It was dark by the time they got there, that first time, finally braving an introduction on his third visit to Aberdeen. The light from the kitchen was shining out through the pane of glass over the front door and Eleanor hesitated before going in, listening. I don't believe it, she whispered, it sounds like they're all here. I'm sorry, she said. Her father, Stewart, came out into the hallway and greeted them loudly, shaking David's hand and inviting him in to meet the rest of the family. It just so happens they were all passing, he said, and from the corner of his eye David could see Eleanor shaking her head as he came into the kitchen and was introduced to her mother, Ivy, her brothers, Donald, William and John, Donald's wife, Ros, a couple of young children, and a great-uncle James sitting in the corner by the stove. There were bottles of beer out on the table, and the remains of a meal stacked up by the sink, and he was peppered with hellos and how-are-yous before he'd managed to get his bearings. He found himself answering questions about how far he'd come and what he was doing in these parts and what it was he did for a living back home, struggling to understand their flinted accents, and struggling to be understood in return – Eh? What's that son? Say again? – one of them still asking him to repeat himself while another was asking him something new, all turning to each other and discussing what it was he might have said once they'd given up on asking him again.

It was a small room, mostly taken up with the big wooden table they were sitting around, the wood worn to a shine by the years of scouring and cleaning, the crumbs from the meal already wiped away. There weren't enough chairs for all of them, so the younger men, Eleanor's brothers, were standing along the back wall, in front of the window and the kitchen sink, blocking the door to the scullery and the backyard, looking him up and down and muttering remarks to each other.

Coventry? asked one of them suddenly, while David was trying to explain to Stewart about being from London originally but having left there as a small child. Is it Coventry where they make all the cars? David nodded.

You make cars then? he was asked.

No, he told them, no, I work in a museum.

There was an awkward pause, and then another brother said museum, eh? You're no a geologist like our Eleanor reckons she's going to be? David shook his head, smiling, and tried to make a joke about being involved with more recent history than the formation of the earth's surface. There was another awkward pause and then the same brother said aye right, so what do you reckon then, is it true what Ellie says about there being oil under the sea? Great-uncle James, sitting in the corner, burst into a laugh that sounded more like a cough, and even Stewart smiled and shook his head. David didn't know what to say.

It's not just me, Eleanor protested, everyone's saying it. Mr Read showed me the maps and everything.

Aye, said Donald, the oldest of the brothers there, and there's a herd of camels going by outside just now. Eleanor tutted, and pretended to smile, and nudged David towards the door.

Well, we've got to get to the pictures, she said. We're meeting Ruth and folk, we'd better get going.

What's on? John asked. *Lawrence of Arabia*? Everyone in the room laughed, Great-uncle James slapping his hand against his knee, and Eleanor turning and pushing David ahead of her, and as they opened the front door he heard one of the men saying make sure he gets you home in plenty of time now, and another man saying oil be waiting up, and the hard-edged laughter followed them both as they hurried away down the hill.

13 *Pocket appointment diaries (incomplete set), dated 1935–1959*

The first time they persuaded Laurence to visit Julia in the nursing home, she was smoking again, sitting by the window with her back partly turned to the door. They stood behind him in the doorway, and he looked back into the corridor as if he thought they might have the wrong room. They nodded, and he stepped forward. Hello, Mother? he said tentatively. She didn't seem to hear him. He took a half-step closer. Mother? he said again, and she still didn't move, the cigarette held out on the arm of her chair, a steady plume of smoke trailing towards the ceiling. Dorothy interrupted impatiently, pushing past Laurence and putting a hand across Julia's shoulder as she spoke, leaning over to look her in the eye.

Hello there Julia love, she said, it's Dorothy. We've brought Laurence to come and see you at last, and she said the at last so quietly that only Laurence could hear. Julia turned round, looking at David first, curiously, and then at Laurence, some level of understanding that wasn't quite recognition passing across her face.

Hello darling, she said, smiling abruptly. Hello, how good of you to come and see me. Have you got a kiss for poor Julia? Laurence stood in front of her for a moment, looming over her, gripping the fingers of one hand with the other, running his thumb back and forth across his palm. Julia looked up and turned her cheek towards him. He bent down to her so slowly and hesitantly that he almost lost his balance and had to grab on to the back of her chair, and as his lips touched her face he held them there, closing his eyes and seeming to hold his breath before lifting away and stepping back slightly. David looked at his mother, and past her to the window, and at Laurence. The room felt suddenly very full.

Laurence sat down on the edge of Julia's bed, his hands in his lap, looking at her. He reached up and smoothed his hair back across his head with the heel of his hand. He said, look, I'm sorry it's taken me so long to come and see you, I've been posted abroad an awful lot, you know. She ignored him, as she'd learnt to do when there was something she didn't understand, gazing steadily at the room as if he hadn't spoken at all. He tried again. So, how are they looking after you in here? Is the food good? Have you met many people? His voice was loud and slow and he leant towards her slightly as he spoke. She looked at him, and at Dorothy.

I don't think you need to shout dear, she said dryly, we can all hear you. She squashed her cigarette into the ashtray.

Laurence had signed up for officer training when he did his National Service and had been in the army ever since. He'd never married, and there were no children that anyone knew about, and from the few letters he wrote to his mother it seemed as though the army had become his entire life, talking about *my boys*, and *the old man*, as if they were his family now. David only once heard Julia say she minded these long and repeated absences, or how seldom he ever wrote to say how he was, and even then it was with an insistence that she was just being silly, that he was a grown man and what did she have to complain about? I mean, she said, he's only following in his father's footsteps, isn't he?

He was stationed in Germany when they moved her into the home. He'd had to be sent the admissions papers to sign, and the financial documents, but he'd refused to discuss the situation with them. Dorothy had written, and even spoken to him by telephone on one occasion, but he'd only ever said that he trusted her judgement. I'm out of the picture here, he'd said, you're the one on the ground. I don't think she's looking after herself properly any more, Dorothy had told him, I don't think she's able to. Right, absolutely, he said, if you think so. We're trying our best, she told him, but we can't be down there every weekend. No, of course, he said, whatever you think's best Dorothy. You're the expert, he said, leaving her to talk to Julia about what was going to happen, to arrange a place for her, to make sure that the house was cleaned occasionally. And when they'd met him outside the home that morning, running a few minutes late, he'd seemed reluctant to go inside at all, standing away from the door and tracing lines in the gravel with the toe of his shoe. Ah, hello there, he said, seeming surprised to see them. This is it then, I've got the right place? I wasn't sure what to expect, he said.

They sat quietly for a while, the four of them, drinking the tea Dorothy had sent David to fetch, looking out into the garden. Julia asked for her cigarettes, and Laurence sprang up to find them for her, holding one out of the pack and lighting it when she put it to her lips. He looked pleased with himself, relieved to be able to do something for her at last. She smoked, and they waited for her to say something. She said, I hear they're building a new school at the end of the road there, where the theatre used to be, that'll be nice. Laurence looked at Dorothy, questioningly, and she discreetly shook her head. She said, I had a letter from Kathleen. Kathleen wrote and said she was coming to stay. I hope she does. I'm sure she will. She will, wouldn't you say? she said, turning to Dorothy, lifting her head to blow a stream of smoke towards the ceiling. She said, David, how's that girlfriend of yours, what's her name, the Scottish one, how's she? He looked at her, and at his mother, and his mother smiled and turned her face away.

She's not my girlfriend Auntie Julia, he said, embarrassed, trying to remember when he'd said anything to his mother. Not really, he said.

Oh, Julia said, smiling, my mistake, sorry, and she winked at Laurence, making him roar with sudden delighted laughter.

They left him alone with her for a couple of hours, walking out around the streets, down through the park to Julia's old house and back along the canal.

You know she's not going to get any better, his mother said, and David nodded, and they didn't say anything more about it.

14 *Pair of letters, handwritten, February 1967*

That's so sad what you told me about your Auntie Julia. I told my friend Ruth about it and she said her Gran went like that too, but she was much older which makes it almost not so bad. I hope it's not upsetting your mam too badly. It's funny saying that when I've never met her, but you've told me so much about her that I feel like I know her somehow. Sometimes I feel like I know her better than my own mam.

There's something strange about my mam at the moment though (more strange then normal I mean!). I think she's upset about something, or worried, but Da won't tell me what's wrong. She's barely speaking to either of us, or going out the house, and I think I maybe heard her crying last night. She was like this sometimes when I was a wee girl, she used to blame me for it then. She said I'd tired her out completely and she needed a rest. I'm sure she'll be better soon but it's funny seeing her like it again – it seems like such a long time since it happened before. I wonder if she thinks it's my fault again, I don't see how she can when I'm hardly ever in the house. Me and Ruth stayed out until almost eleven o'clock last night! We weren't doing anything, just sitting in town and talking and walking about, but it was great to be out like that. I almost caught it when I got home, and Da said I was lucky Mam was away in bed already and not to do it again. Ruth was looking at boys all evening but I told her I had no need.

She's like a wind-up toy that's all wound down, my mam, I mean. She moves all slow and shuffly, like she's no sure what she's doing. I hope she's not like it long this time – it gives me the creeps. I'd rather she was shouting at me, you know? I think my da is maybe taking her to the doctor's tomorrow.

Anyway I'm sorry, you didn't need to know all this. I'm just blabbering what's on my mind. How about you? What have you been doing this week? How's the museum? Have you been on any more research trips? Is Mr Newbold still giving you grief about taking time off? Write to me soon, won't you. Tell me some more things about – oh I don't know, anything. I want to know everything, David!

Everything's a bit of a tall order, Ellie-Na. Do you want to know what I had for breakfast this morning? (Fried egg and toast.) Or how many cups of tea I made at work? (Not sure, something like twenty-eight, but I usually lose count after lunch.) Or how many files I had to look through before I found the lost index card for a thirteenth-century dish that's been on display since the museum opened? (No idea, but it felt like half the files in the whole office.) If I told you everything, Ella-Nor, I'd spend my whole life writing letters, and there'd be nothing left to tell!

Sorry, that's a bit pedantic of me, I know. What should I tell you? My Auntie Julia's not getting any better but she seems to have stopped getting worse for the time being. Mum went down to see her again this weekend and left me and Susan on our own in the house. If you think eleven o'clock's late you should see what time Susan got home! I think she might be seeing someone she met at work but she's being very mysterious about it. I promised not to tell Mum if she paid my bus fare for a week, and she said that was bribery but she still agreed. On Sunday me and Danny took the train up to Birmingham – I wanted to go to an exhibition at the Gas Hall and he wanted to see a jazz group in a pub, so we did half of each. He was asking me about you again . . .

15 *Picture postcard, John Lewis shipyard, Aberdeen c.1967*

Eleanor's parents didn't approve. Or perhaps it wasn't as dramatic as not approving, nor as genuine; perhaps they simply didn't consider David a serious proposition. She wrote about it in her letters: he's from so far away, she told him they said, it's just not practical. He's older than you. He's not got a proper trade. He's English. She spiked these quotations with exclamation marks, as if to deflate their power, and underlined the words she most objected to: practical, proper, serious. She joked about it, sometimes, but he knew that she resented the way they felt able to interfere in her life, to set such narrow limits for her. Is that English boy still writing to you? her mother would ask, when his letters dropped on to their hallway floor and Eleanor hurried from the breakfast table to retrieve them. You should tell him to find himself a local girl, she would add scornfully.

But beneath their disapproval and scorn lay a simple fear that Eleanor's father eventually voiced one afternoon while he and David were sitting together in the kitchen. He looked at David across the table, two mugs of tea between them, and he said so when you taking her away then son? He was sitting back in his chair, but his gaze was fixed and intent, his thick eyebrows hunched darkly over his eyes. David stalled.

I beg your pardon Mr Campbell? he said, leaning forward as if he hadn't quite caught the question. Stewart Campbell didn't even blink.

You heard, he said.

Eleanor and her mother Ivy were out on the front step, talking to one of the neighbours, the neighbour doing most of the talking, Eleanor laughing occasionally, her mother keeping up a steady supply of ayes and reallys and oh-no-I-knows.

Stewart's hands were resting on the table, his fists clenched, the knuckles white. I asked when you're planning on taking Eleanor away from here, he said, laying a slow emphasis on each word. His self-contained ferocity took David by surprise. There was no shouting, no banging on the table, but for a few moments it felt as though one wrong word would bring Stewart vaulting across the table towards him. And even though he was in his late sixties by then, and often short of breath, it was obvious what a lifetime of working in the shipyards had done for the steel-rope hardness of his body. Shaking his hand had been evidence enough.

Mr Campbell, David said, trying to look him in the eye, I haven't, we haven't, really thought about that.

Stewart looked back at him, saying nothing, waiting for him to continue.

I mean, Eleanor's got her life here, David said. Her friends, her job, it wouldn't make any sense to, you know.

Aye and you'd know about that, would you? Stewart asked quickly, his voice picking up volume. You'd know all about her life here then? You want to tell me about it, do you? He leant forwards as he said it, gripping the edge of the table now, peering in at David's face as if looking for something. David could still hear Eleanor laughing outside, the sound coming through the open door. He wondered if the back door was open behind him.

But almost as quickly as Stewart's temper had flared, it softened again. He sat back, held out his palms, laid them in his lap. His face lost its pointed glare. Let me tell you something, he said, his voice calm again, distant. Let me tell you. It's not long ago, not long ago at all, that Eleanor was sitting here with her legs halfway to the floor and her chin resting on the edge of the table. David nodded and rubbed the sweat from his palms under the table. They were all that small once, Stewart said, and then before you know it they're banging their heads on the ceiling and popping out the door and that's them gone. Doesn't take long, he said. Hamish was gone before Eleanor was even born, and Eleanor will be gone soon enough.

He looked at David again, his eyes clear. But it's fine, he said. Your children grow into adults, and they leave, and they make a life of their own. It's the way the world turns, he said. He closed his eyes for a moment and eased out a loud slow breath. He lowered his head, rolled it from side to side, and looked up. But there's leaving and there's leaving, he said. You understand me? David nodded, and he knew from the look in Stewart's eyes that he hadn't meant to say all these things, and that when Eleanor asked him later what they'd been talking about he should say oh nothing much, he was just telling me about when you were small.

Ivy came back into the room, asking David if he wanted another mug of tea before he was on his way, and stopped for a moment, looking at him, looking at Stewart. Years later, David thought about the two of them in that kitchen and imagined them there when they were much younger, the children asleep in bed, both of them exhausted from a long day's work, sitting and talking while all around them wet sheets, hung from lines strung across the ceiling, steamed and dripped and swayed like storm-sodden sails; other people's laundry putting food on the table. And he imagined them sitting at that same table much later, the house empty around them, unspoken regrets and recriminations swept out of sight like crumbs from the table, silence blanketing the room, the two of them avoiding each other's eyes.

No, thank you very much, he said, standing up. That's enough tea for me, thank you Mrs Campbell. He smiled. I'll be on my way now, thank you. He glanced at Stewart briefly.

Ivy stepped aside to let him pass, and he walked down the hallway and out into the sunshine, where Eleanor was waiting for him.

And as his visits became more frequent, their letters to each other became less guarded, their thoughts less veiled. They began to make half-serious suggestions about one day living not so far apart. They said that they missed each other, and thought about each other as they were going to sleep. They told each other more, much more, about their lives and their families and their secrets. And after he'd been there half a dozen times, and after they'd written maybe a hundred letters and postcards between them, she wrote this at the end of a short note she sent, almost as an afterthought, almost as if she thought he might not notice: *You could come up again the weekend after next. My parents are away to Glasgow and Donald and Ros will be gone as well. You could come and stay at the house. If you'd like that.*

He remembered thinking, on balance, that he probably would.

16 *Birth Certificate, 17 March 1945*

And this was the part of the story they would most want to hear, he thought. This was where they would quieten, and lean forward, and when he'd finished they'd say so that's how it was. You know, I always wondered.

I was sitting in Auntie Julia's room at the nursing home when it happened, he was going to start by saying. My mother had gone down the corridor to get cups of tea for the three of us, and even though she was gone for a long time she still managed to be back at just the right moment, nudging the door open with her foot as she carried the tray into the room. He imagined someone leaning towards him as he said it, as they realised what he was talking his way towards.

He could pinpoint the moment precisely. Julia with her cigarette held up beside her face, his mother nudging into the room. The window open and a woman zimmer-framing her slow way across the garden. The sound of television laughter coming from the main room, and an unanswered telephone ringing somewhere. The cymbelline shaking of the teacups as his mother gasped and put down the tray. And David not knowing where to look or what to say or whether to just stand and leave the room as quickly as he could.

It was a small room with a single bed, a pair of easy chairs, a side table, a wardrobe, and a large window that opened out on to the enclosed garden. His mother had helped Julia try to make it her own – there were photographs on the wall, and one of her jewellery boxes on the side table, and flowers – but it still had the feel of a hospital room. The bed was metal-framed, with rails that could be cranked up to keep her from falling to the floor. There was a button on the wall which would bring a member of staff running if it was pressed. There were charts – medication, temperature, blood pressure, behaviour – and although they were kept on a shelf in the wardrobe rather than clipped to the end of the bed, they were still there. And there was a distinct hospital odour lingering about the place, that clinging smell of endless cleaning. But it was still Julia's room, and she seemed comfortable enough to feel somehow at home there. Perhaps she thought it was a hotel, or a room in an absent-minded friend's house, a friend who seemed to have forgotten she was coming, or had even forgotten that she was there at all.

They sat in silence for a while, Julia smoking one of her long menthol cigarettes and staring out of the window. He didn't know what to say. She'd always done the talking when he was growing up and it had been enough for him to listen, to say, really? or, what happened next? or occasionally, can you tell me about . . .? but since moving into the home she had mostly just sat and waited to be spoken to. His mother was much better at doing what was needed, skating briskly over the cracks in the conversation, the inconsistencies and the repetition and the hard-to-understand, seeming to always find a way of stopping the whole thing sinking into the icy chill of who are you, and where's Laurence, and why haven't we had breakfast yet?

How are you feeling Julia? he asked eventually, not knowing what else to say.

Bored, she said sharply, turning to look at him. Bored, and tired. She stubbed her cigarette out in a glass ashtray and gestured at him to empty it. He leant across, and as he picked it up she whispered, loudly, the trouble is the other people staying here are a little sub-normal. He emptied the lipstick-tinged cigarette ends into the bin.

Really? he said.

Oh, yes, she said. Some of the things I hear about, you wouldn't believe your young ears, really. There's an old man out there, she said, haven't a clue who he is but they have to put plastic sheets on the furniture when he sits down, due to his tendency. She said tendency with pursed lips and a note of disgust, as though the word itself was somehow unhygienic, and she nodded delicately, to confirm what she was saying.

His tendency? David asked.

She leant towards him, mouthing the words: he wets himself if he laughs too much. She took another cigarette and lit it with a quick flourish. Not really my kind of people, David, she said.

He smiled and said no, I'm sure, and for a moment the Julia he'd grown up with was back there in the room. She turned to look out of the window and they both watched a young boy kicking a football up and down the garden path until a woman opened a window and told him to stop it. The boy sulked slowly back into the building, and when Julia turned to speak he could see that she'd already slipped back into vacancy and confusion.

She said, I wanted to go home but they wouldn't let me, can you believe that?

He tried to explain, gently, that there were reasons she couldn't go home just then but she didn't seem to hear. And that bloody lot in there are no good either, she said, pointing through the door to the main room where most of the other residents sat and watched television. Half of them are stone deaf, she said. He nodded. Mind you, that's often a result of the explosive impacts, she said, and the shock, you know, and suddenly she was talking about the war, talking as though the mist had cleared and she'd found herself twenty years younger, working in the hospital through years of air-raid sirens, walking home in the morning to find whole streets flattened, seeing doodlebugs droning their way through a bare blue sky.

They were all given cigarettes for Christmas and he kept on to his you see, she said. Sometimes even the bandages were in very short supply but we did what we could. Your mother used to get back from a shift exhausted and we'd just have time to eat together before it was my turn to go out, she said.

He wondered whether to interrupt her, to bring her carefully back out of her confusion or to let her just chatter on. He heard footsteps in the corridor and his mother nudged the door open with her foot.

Julia said and of course we never saw the poor girl again. He moved to clear a space on the table for the tea tray, stacking the magazines to one side, taking his mother's cardigan and laying it on the bed, putting the radio back on the shelf. Julia said Mary, wasn't it? His mother looked up at her. She was all for insisting that it only be for a few days, Julia said, but of course we never saw her again, she disappeared off the face of the earth. Very sad for the poor girl, she said, and she turned and looked him clearly in the eye. She said so when your mother asked me what to do, I said well Dorothy my dear, you'll have to keep the little darling now, won't you? She said you were such a lovely baby, and anyway we couldn't very well give you back, could we?

He sat back down, looking at Julia, looking at his mother, looking back at Julia, gripping the arms of his chair as if he was afraid he might fall to the floor. He heard his mother putting down the tray, the cups and saucers shaking against each other.

Oh Julia, she said.

The poor girl hadn't even left you with a name, so we chose David, after that actor, you know the one, what was his name? said Julia, and she looked up at his mother on this last question, smiling fondly, trying to remember, looking for help. His mother was holding both her hands up to her face, covering her mouth.

Oh Julia, she said.

They left soon afterwards, catching an earlier train than

they'd planned, leaving Julia in her room, asking did I say something wrong? Dorothy did I say something wrong? They didn't even drink the teas, leaving them on the side table for a member of staff to clear away while they walked quickly and silently down the corridor. He heard his mother crying as they walked from the home to the tube station and he reached back to hand her a clean handkerchief from his pocket. She tried talking to him a few times, asking him to slow down as he paced through the tunnels at Whitechapel and Euston, and later, on the train, asking if they could talk, if she could explain, if he would at least say something. But he kept his face to the window and he didn't say a word, seeing nothing, hearing only the sound of Julia's voice, fragments of it repeating over and over again.

Of course we never saw the poor girl again.

You'll have to keep the little darling.

She disappeared off the face of the earth.

Did I say something wrong?

When they got back to the house, they sat in the lounge and looked out into the garden. The rose bushes had been in full bloom for a few weeks and were in need of dead-heading. The lawn was starting to yellow. The spade had been left out, sunk into the earth. They drank cups of scalding tea, and finally looked at each other.

David, his mother said.

She looked smaller than he'd always thought of her as being, and suddenly much older. As she spoke, her words came out on the back of long sighs, as if she'd been holding her breath all those years and was finally able to let it go. David, she said, you mustn't be angry with us.

Later, he realised that by us she'd meant only her and Julia. But at the time, it sounded as though she was saying us to include Susan, his grandparents, Laurence, his aunts and uncles, his teachers, the neighbours, anyone and everyone he had ever known or met. He had a sudden feeling of the walls of the house being pulled down, and of everyone he knew standing there behind the settling clouds of masonry dust, sniggering and smirking behind their hands.

Please, David, let me explain, she said. The room, the whole house, felt very quiet. He looked at the photos of his father on the mantelpiece, the one taken during the war, the one taken shortly after they moved to their new home, the one taken a few years before he died. He looked at her. Later, he would go for weeks without speaking to her, without looking her in the eye or even acknowledging that they were living in the same house. But for the moment, before Julia's words had properly begun to settle into his ruptured thoughts, he wanted to talk.

Is it true? he asked her first. She looked surprised that he was asking. If she'd been quicker, then, or on the journey home, or in Julia's room, she could have laughed the whole thing off, putting it down to the confusion and muddle of Julia's illness. Perhaps if she'd been ready, she could easily have convinced him that the whole idea was ridiculous, and perhaps he would have thought little more about it. But her immediate reactions, and her reactions in the days and weeks that followed, were a helpless confirmation of what Julia had so casually and forgetfully blurted out. Is it true? he asked her, and what he actually meant was: tell me yourself, say the words, I want to hear it from you.

The story was simple enough, and, when it came down to it, not so unusual. There was a girl; she had a baby she wasn't supposed to have; she gave the care of the baby to someone else and she disappeared. It happens. It has always happened. In those days, his mother said, it was considered neither unusual or fit for discussion. It was kept a secret, or else it was ignored, unstated, denied. Children grew up to realise their sister or their aunt was actually their mother, or they grew up with the names of orphanage directors who had taken them in, or the name of the street where they'd been abandoned. The tale of Moses, floating downstream in his woven rush basket, would not once have seemed so strange, in the days when baskets and blankets placed on doorsteps could turn out to contain wrinkled babies still dazed from the shock of birth. David's story, or the fraction of it which Julia and his mother had known between them, and kept to themselves all those years, did at least have a little more detail than those tales of early morning finds.

Her name was Mary, his mother said. She was young, fifteen or sixteen or seventeen, it was never quite clear. Julia was working in the ward when she gave birth. There was no father pacing expectantly in the waiting room, and she refused to give the name of one. There was no one in fact, no relatives, not even a friend, and afterwards, when she'd come round from the sedatives they'd given her, Julia had sat and talked with her for a few minutes, held her hand, comforted her.

Sometimes he thought he could picture her there. Young, too young, her limbs a little too long and slim for her body, the way that teenage girls' limbs sometimes are, her face small and neat and framed by a damp slick of dark brown hair. Or perhaps broad-shouldered, with taut muscles running down her arms and a slightly squared jut to her jaw. Blonde hair, or auburn, pale brown, coal black. Long hair, tied up, curled, straight, cut sensibly short around her face. Brown eyes, flecked with grey. Green eyes. Blue eyes, a pale watery blue. Sitting quietly in the bed, her chest heaving, trying to catch her breath, the curtains drawn around her and the rest of the ward quiet for a moment. She was Irish, his mother said. She told Julia she was from Donegal, and had been in London for two years, working in a big house, saving money to take back to her family. She told Julia her family wouldn't have her back if they knew, that she couldn't go back but she couldn't stay in London, she had no work, there were too many people she knew, the shame was too much. Afterwards he was surprised by how easily his mother had spoken the words. Her voice quivered a little, but she spoke clearly, and laid out the few facts for him as though she had long been practising them in her head. The poor girl asked Julia what happened to babies whose mothers left them, his mother said, and Julia told her what there was – Barnardo's, St Catherine's, social services – and the girl, Mary, said she didn't want that for a child. Julia asked her what she was going to do. Mary said that if she could go home she could find someone who would take you, without her parents knowing, and then at least she would see you growing up. Julia asked who that would be, and Mary said she didn't know, she would find someone. She said she would find someone and come back for you, but Julia told her it might be difficult to place you in a home and take you out again. His mother faltered here, bringing a hand to her face and squeezing her cheeks, and from behind her hand he could hear her whispering sorry. She breathed in sharply, put her hand down, and continued. Julia always said she didn't know why she'd done it, she said. There were plenty of hard things happened in that hospital, especially then; we couldn't let it get to us. Julia always said the words came out before she knew what she was doing, she said. He watched his mother going over the well-rehearsed words, the sunlight fading through the back garden and the photos of his father looking down on them both. Julia told the girl, Mary, she said to her, you can leave him with me, I'll look after him until you get back, and before she'd even finished speaking Mary had turned to her and said can I? Will you?

These things, the way they happen. The way they begin.

Sometimes he felt as though he could hear the words being spoken. Sometimes he felt as though he had been there, sitting up in his cot, studying the two women's faces, wondering which way the conversation would go. But he hadn't been there at all. He'd been off in some other ward, a numbered baby in a row of numbered babies, sleeping or stretching or wailing, waiting to be taken back to his mother.

And these words became something like a treasured fragment of parchment script, studied over and over again, handled in a humidity-controlled room, learnt by heart. It didn't matter that they were second-hand, third-hand, blurred by time and mistranslated, rubbed smoother and cleaner by his own re-telling. These broken pieces were all he had; like keepsakes pulled from the ruins. Fragile traces, dug from the cold wet earth.

A young woman, too young, fifteen or sixteen, crying it's no use, I can't do it; one of the nurses turning to her, brushing her hot damp hair away from her eyes and saying yes you can, come on my darling, you're nearly there. Slumping back on to the bed, giving up, and the nurses saying her name, saying, come on now, come on, Mary, raising their voices as if calling her back from another room. Covering her face with her hands and crying louder to block them out. Or not even thinking of giving up, even when the pain and the fear were enough to make her pass out – breathe, they tell her, keep breathing, as if her body had become so alien that she couldn't remember how to work it properly – sitting up, and grinding her teeth, and doing what young women have always had to do, her body and her choices no longer her own. Calling out for her mother, or her eldest sister, or her father. Calling out a man's name, and two of the nurses catching each other's eye. Or perhaps even in the middle of it all managing to keep such a thing to herself, not out of loyalty but out of fear and an instinct for self-preservation. Slamming her hands down on to the mattress, clutching at the cold metal rails of the bed; soiling herself, more than once, a nurse reaching quickly beneath her to clear it away, her humiliation complete, the nurses looking at her that way, knowing the sort of girl she was, thinking only that she was paying the price and it was too late to go crying now, but not saying this, maybe not thinking it at all. Praying aloud, oh dear lord Jesus have mercy on me now, her voice quiet and song-like between screaming contractions. Or not daring to pray, thinking who was she to turn to God at a time like this?

The nurses saying come on, just a little bit more, we're nearly there now, howling out a cry which seems to burst from somewhere in her spine, and the baby is born and it's over. Looking on in dazed confusion as the baby is lifted, cleaned, examined, and the cord cut. Someone telling her to push just a little bit more, and the afterbirth being scooped up and removed. A nurse wiping her down and giving her an injection. The baby being carried away, and her eyes following it out of sight before she falls into a long, dark, drugged sleep.

Julia didn't tell him any of this. Julia didn't tell him anything. Soon after the day she first let the secret slip, forgetting for a moment that it was supposed to be a secret at all, she went into a sudden decline. She forgot his name. She forgot Dorothy's name. Eventually she seemed uncertain of who they were at all, although they always told her when they arrived, and she always smiled in pretend recognition, gamely entering into conversation with them for a moment or two before losing her thread and gazing vaguely out of the window. Her body began to age rapidly. She lost weight. Her skin scrunched up into an old woman's wrinkles, her hair thinning out until there were only a few loose wisps floating around her scalp like a halo. Her eyes began to sink back into their sockets, and her shoulders started to round and hunch forward until she looked twenty years older than she was. She rarely looked at them when they spoke, and if she did she showed few signs of understanding what they said. But even when it came to feel useless, he kept asking her about what she'd said.

Auntie Julia, he'd say, can you remember Mary? Do you remember the young girl with the baby? What was her second name again? I can't remember. Where was she from? She'd look at him, her eyes empty of expression, the make-up she insisted on applying each morning beginning to look out of place, frowning or nodding or looking right past him. Whatever happened to that girl – Mary? he'd say, hoping to catch her in one of her lucid moments. But he never did. She'd only ever gaze back at him, or out of the window, or turn and look for her cigarettes.

I'm awfully sorry my dear, she said once, tapping ash into a saucer, but sometimes you do seem to talk such absolute bloody sodding nonsense, really you do.

He got desperate. He asked her over and over again. He took photographs in to try and prompt her, photographs of her and his mother during the war, of his mother and Susan, of her house. Her puzzlement seemed to turn into amusement, as if the whole thing was a game. Is it time to go home yet? she'd sometimes say, getting to her feet and looking around for her coat. No Julia, he'd have to tell her, it's not time to go home, not just yet.

There was one thing, his mother admitted to him once. There was one thing Julia told me, a few years after, she said. She told me the girl had a bad time of it, told me they thought they were going to lose her, she said. And it was obvious, after so many years of silence, how difficult it was for her to have told him even this much. But it wasn't enough. It was nowhere near enough. Nothing she could ever have told him would ever be as much as he wanted to know, and so he started to fill the vast gaps for himself, to read books about London and Ireland, to buy maps and brochures and magazines, to lie awake at night until he could make a story, any story, to fit.

Perhaps it was raining when she got off the bus, but she was already feeling better, just standing by the side of the road and breathing in the wet air. Everything feeling familiar, at last. The loose chippings on the tarmac beneath her feet. The walled-in tree where the bus was turning around. The frosted glass window of the shop on the other side of the road. The boxes of vegetables on a trestle table outside the grocers. The noticeboard by the bus stop behind her.

The bus turned its circle and drove back up the hill, and the place was quiet except for the water running along the gutter into the drain, a steady slurping gurgle, the same song of streams and ponds and falling water that she'd always known and grown up with. She looked at the wet grey veils of the sky, smiling for the first time in weeks, months, wiping the dampness from her face. I don't mind a bit of rain, she said, beneath her breath, and picked up her suitcase.

It was nearly three miles from the bus stop to her family's house, but the rain-sodden walk seemed to take no time at all, and the suitcase which carried the last two years of her life was as light as a handful of feathers in the clutch of her fist. Every step of the road was just as she'd dreamt it all the time she'd been away. Every step took her further away from the smoke and the noise and the loneliness and fear of the city she'd left behind. Every step drew her deeper into the hollows of the landscape, the green hills and shining rivers and mist-tangled treetops, as though she was clambering into the postcard she used to keep propped up on the mantelpiece of her small room at the top of the big house. The rain didn't let up, and the damp seeped through her thin clothes, clinging to her skin, the whole place wrapping itself around her, but she couldn't stop smiling and she felt like yelling her hello again into the hills. She was soaked by the time she was halfway home, but she knew that when she opened the door there would be a smouldering fire, a kettle on the stove, a slab of cake in the larder. She knew that the neighbours would be sent for, her brothers called in from the fields, the bottle of whiskey brought down from the sideboard.

Perhaps she remembered with a sudden cold shiver why she was there now, how different this walk might have been, how much colder her reception would be then, and she knew that she'd done the right thing. She told herself again that she'd done the right thing.

She passed the house at the top of the rise, and saw old John there in his open barn, still fiddling with that useless lump of a tractor that no one had ever seen run. His wife was coming out with a cup of tea for him, a ragged cardigan wrapped around her shoulders; she called out a little hello to the two of them as she walked past. They raised their hands and gave her a how're you doing there, and then they looked at her twice and their faces lit up in recognition. She smiled, but she kept on walking. They'd be along down the road soon enough, too wise to say they were the ones who saw her first, and she could say a proper hello then.

And then she could see her house at the bottom of the hill, caught between the road and the strip of woodland which ran along by the stream. There was a curl of faint yellow smoke lifting into the mist, and somebody moving around down in the yard. There was a good tall stack of turf by the side of the house. One of the dogs was ambling around in the yard, getting under the feet of whoever that was down there, getting in the way of whatever it was they were doing.

She'd done the right thing, she told herself. He'd be alright where he was, he'd be safe and well, it was the right thing to do; she said it to herself like a prayer.

Halfway down the road, while she was still far off, the man in the yard, her father, happened to turn round and catch sight of her. He looked up, lifting a hand to his forehead, as if shielding his eyes from the absent sun. He took a few steps in her direction, stretching his head forward. She kept walking. She didn't wave. Or perhaps she stood still and she waited. Perhaps then there was a moment's doubt in her mind as to how she might be received, how fast news and gossip and broken secrets might travel. She gripped her suitcase tighter and the thought that she could always turn and flee entered her head, the knowledge that with the case in her hand she could carry on her exiled life; but it was a small thought, and she did her best to blink it loose, to let the rain wash it away. She kept walking. Her father dropped the tools he was holding, lifted his head to call someone from the house, and ran towards her, his steps clumsy and lumbering, the dog barking suddenly now, confused, running a tight circle around the yard and then outpacing her father towards her. She kept walking. Or she stopped and she waited. She tried to keep the smile from breaking out all over her face, or she didn't, and when her father had nearly reached her she saw the door of the house open and her mother appear, wiping her hands on her apron, looking first to the yard and then to the commotion on the road, lifting her hands to her mouth, stepping towards them, breaking into a scurrying run. And already, while her father was still rushing to meet her, breathing hard, his muddy boots clumping on the tarmac, she could feel the all-encircling bulk of his embrace, the tickle of his woollens on her face, the rub of his chin on the top of her head, the pad and scratch of the dog jumping up to claim his place in the moment, the rush of her father's breath in her ears, the rich mumble of his voice saying ah now, Mary, it's been a while has it not? And she knew that she'd done the right thing. She told herself again that she'd done the right thing.

Perhaps it was like that, he would think, sometimes, or perhaps it wasn't like that at all. Perhaps she went to Ireland, but never made it as far as home, kept away by fear, or by warnings of how she would be received. Perhaps she went to Dublin, an exile in her own country, finding a place to stay through someone who knew someone, finding work, making friends, pushing what went before to the back of her mind. Perhaps she married, had children, gave them names and raised them. Three children, four children, five children. Brothers and sisters born and bred in Dublin, and her north-western inheritance didn't pass on to them but faded from view. Or perhaps she had no children, no more children, perhaps she didn't marry and she lived out her life further south, Waterford, Cork, nestling into some small village community and busying herself with work and the intricate weave of a new social life, and she grew old and built herself a new history to talk of in the village shop or at the club, fond talk of do you remember when with no need to think of what went before. Or she became a nun, clothed herself in righteousness and hid herself away in the cloisters and the rituals of religious life, praying and meditating and good-deeding her way out of the skin of the young girl she was when she first joined. Or she didn't go back to Ireland at all. She went as far as Liverpool, and put her savings together with a few weeks' work in a hotel kitchen, and bought herself a ticket to the New World, following in the wake of so many who had gone before, walking the gangplank aboard the White Star liner without a backward glance, keeping away from the deck until the ship was well clear of land so as not to have no one to wave to. Or she went back to London, losing herself in the crowds, walking out every day in the hope that she would bump into Julia, or Dorothy, or David; lingering by the hospital gates, waiting, hiding without hiding, never able to actually step inside. Or she went to Leeds, or to Birmingham, or to Coventry and she got a job in the Hotel Leofric and served David his very first under-aged pint. Or she died young, killed in various road accidents, explosions, struck down by illness and disease, drowned on her way to America, sodden with cheap drink in a one-room flat on the Kilburn High Road. Or she did go home, eventually, a few long years smoothing over the rough calluses of shame and gossip, a family's love and longing for a lost daughter overcoming any talk of sin and curse and letting down, a father brimming with tears as he brings himself to look her in the eyes and say, well, come inside, welcome home, it's been too long.

It was the not knowing, he would say to someone, much much later. The not knowing was the hardest thing.

part two

He woke early, stiff and tired from the previous day's long drive but restless with preparations for the journey to come. He left Eleanor sleeping, her fists clenched against her face, and slipped into Kate's old room, looking out the two albums and the scrapbook he planned to take, glancing at all the other scrapbooks and albums and shoeboxes and wondering if he should maybe take a few things more. He went over the route in his mind, uncertain even now that he was doing the right thing, sitting down on Kate's old bed, smoothing the pillow and the duvet, looking at her old postcards still Blu-tacked to the back of the door.

He heard Eleanor getting up and moving around downstairs, and then she appeared in the doorway with two coffees, squinting slightly, her face puffed with sleep. She put one down on the windowsill, glancing at the pile of boxes and folders he'd been going through. She looked at him, the faint lines on her face softening as she smiled, and said you're a case though, aren't you David? He looked at her, sharply, and stood up.

What? he said.

Well, she said, waving her hand vaguely, all this stuff. I mean, it's a bit much, isn't it? He looked down at the floor, and then at the window, holding his hands tensely by his sides. He didn't say anything.

He said, Eleanor, couldn't you just for once take something I'm doing a bit seriously? I mean, couldn't you do me that favour, just once? He said, it's not as if I'm taking it all with me. I was just looking; what's wrong with that? He gripped the edge of the windowsill, and realised he was shouting. He said, I'm sorry but— She moved towards him and put a hand on his shoulder, and she felt him tense against her touch.

She said, I'm sorry I didn't mean anything. Her voice was flatter, the teasing note of a moment before drawn out of it by his reaction. She said, I am taking it seriously, it's just— It seems like you're rushing into this a bit.

He looked at her, disbelievingly, shaking his head.

She said again, I am taking it seriously.

He lowered his head and said well it doesn't feel like it. She sighed, loudly, and pulled away from him, moving towards the door.

I'm sorry love, he said, rubbing his forehead with the knuckles of his fist, I'm just tired. It was a long drive. She held on to the door frame, and closed her eyes.

It was the first argument they'd had for months. The last time had been when her brother Donald contacted them to say that her mother was very ill and would Eleanor consider going up there at all, and David had tried to insist that she should. She'd shouted at him then, and told him that he must be stupid if he still didn't get it after all these years, and he'd shouted back that maybe he was stupid, for marrying her in the first place. There was nothing like that being said this time at least. But there was something of that same bristling tension; in their voices, in the tight grip of their hands on the windowsill and the door frame, in the way their eyes dared one another to go further. Later, over breakfast, they would agree that they were getting too old for that kind of thing, that it wasn't worth getting so wound up about it all, and the sharpness of their words would be forgotten. But for a moment, as they stood there facing each other, trying to think what to say, it felt as though they were newly married all over again.

Perhaps you shouldn't go today then, she said quickly, if you're really so tired, if it was such a long drive. Perhaps you should leave it. He raised his hands, shaking them in the air.

But I've bought the ticket now, he said, almost shouting again. It's all been arranged. They'll be expecting me, he said, his voice suddenly trailing away and his hands falling to his sides. And something like resignation or defeat must have shown on his face, because when he looked at her he could see that she regretted what she'd said. Maybe I shouldn't go at all, he said. She let go of the door frame and stepped back towards him, touching a hand to his arm.

Oh no, she said. I didn't mean that, I didn't mean that. I'm just saying, she said, you said you were tired. He turned away from her, looking out at the small back garden. She said, I'll put some toast on. She left the room and went downstairs to the kitchen. The steam rose from his coffee mug, settling to a steady twisted stream as the stillness seeped back into the room. He glanced at the clock.

They were in the middle of breakfast, still catching breath from their brief argument, when the phone rang. It was his sister Susan, wanting to know how things had gone at the funeral. I'm not interrupting anything, am I? she asked.

No, David said, reaching across to the table for his toast, you're fine.

Only it seemed like a good time to call, she added. How had it been at the service, she asked, and afterwards – were people friendly enough, how did Kate take it all, had Eleanor changed her mind at the last minute? No, he said, she hadn't. She asked him how Kate was in general, if she was still living in London, if she'd had any luck finding a proper job yet.

She's still in London, he told her, and she's working. She seems happy enough for the time being, he said, and Susan must have heard the slight edge in his voice because she said oh no, no I'm sure she is, I was just wondering. He heard the splash of something being poured into a glass, juice perhaps, and pictured her sitting at her breakfast table in the bay window, with toast and yoghurt and folded white napkins, looking out at the long stretch of garden between her house and the road. She asked him what he had planned for the day, and he said well I'm just getting things ready and then I'm heading off, on my trip.

Oh? Susan said, sounding surprised. You're still doing that? So soon?

Yes Susan, he said tautly. So soon. How much longer did you want me to leave it?

I didn't mean that, she said. You know I didn't mean that. I was just thinking about Eleanor, if she'll be okay while you're gone. He held his breath for a moment.

Yes, he said, well, I don't know about that. You'll have to ask her that yourself. He held the phone out towards Eleanor, saying it's my sister, she wants to talk to you, ignoring the faint sound of Susan telling him not to be silly. Eleanor looked at him suspiciously and took the phone.

Hello? she said.

David looked at the clock, put his breakfast dishes in the sink, and gestured to Eleanor that he was going upstairs. She watched him go, and he heard her say well it's difficult to explain Susan, it's mixed, you know? He washed, and dressed, and folded some clean clothes into his suitcase, standing by the window for a moment to look down at his car parked outside. When he went back downstairs, putting the kettle on to boil, Eleanor was saying oh is he, is that right now? I thought he wasn't going to. He spooned coffee and sugar into a flask. Eleanor said yes, he's still here, you want to speak to him again? He looked up, shaking his head, and saw Eleanor holding the phone out towards him. He reached out for it, and she put her hand across the mouthpiece.

Maybe I should come with you after all, she said.

He stared at her, trying to catch her eye, mouthing a confused what? while Susan asked him how their mother was coping with the new bungalow. Eleanor shrugged, smiling a little, as if it had just been a passing thought. David? said Susan. Are you there? He turned away and said sorry, yes, she's fine. I saw her last week and she seems to be settling in fine.

He looked at Eleanor, standing on the other side of the table, her hands resting on the back of the chair, waiting. He remembered the first night they spent together, and not being quite able to believe the sheer unadorned fact of her skin against his, and he thought how strange it was that after all that time she still slept beside him in their bed, with her hand spread out across his chest and her face turned in to his shoulder. They were both so much older now. Their bodies had crumpled and softened and worn, and no matter how many creams she kept by the bed the skin on her face had become as creased and lined as his. Her hair was shot through with threads of silver and grey. But her eyebrow still arched exquisitely when she didn't believe what someone was saying, and her lips still folded together when she was concentrating or frowning or confused. She still tucked loose wisps of hair behind her ear with a single long delicate finger. Sometimes, it was an effort to keep from kissing her while she slept.

Susan was saying of course I'll never be able to keep up with this garden, and he said no, well, oh. He said, Susan, look, sorry, I'm going to have to go now, I need to get on with things, it's been good talking to you, and as he put the phone down Eleanor jolted slightly and turned back into the room, wrapping the rest of the cakes she'd baked the day before in tin foil and stacking them into a bag.

He said what do you mean maybe you should come with me? She filled the flask, put it into the bag beside the cakes, and looked around the room to see what was missing.

Well, I just thought, she said. It's a long way, you might need someone to keep you company.

But I don't mind the journey, he said, I'm fine with that. I've done it before, he reminded her.

She took some fruit from a bowl on the side and tucked it into the bag, saying but that was a long time ago; things will have changed since then. He sat down, he looked at the ceiling, and he laughed.

I didn't realise it was me we had to worry about with long journeys, he said. I thought that was your department.

But I'm getting better David, she said. I am. Maybe it would do the both of us some good, she added quietly. He looked down at his hands on the table, turning them over, peering at his fingerprints and tracing the lines worn into his palms. He didn't know what to say.

He said, you really want to come then? and when he looked up at her she nodded. He sat back in his chair suddenly, the chair creaking with his weight. He said, bloody hell Eleanor, I really wasn't expecting this. He said, have you got any travel tablets? She smiled.

Are you still going over to your Mum's first? she asked. He nodded.

There's a few more photos I wanted to pick up, he said. And I should see how she's doing.

So have a think about it while you're there, she said. I'll get dressed and packed and we'll talk about it when you come back, she said. He looked at his watch, and he rubbed his face.

He said, but, I don't know El, this was something, I was planning— He stopped, and tried again. He said, I imagined doing this on my own. She moved towards him and put an arm across his shoulder. She leant forwards and kissed the top of his head, his hair thin enough now that he could feel her lips against his scalp.

She said, with her face still so close to his skull that he could feel the breath in her words, you've been doing this on your own for too long now, don't you think?

17 *Pair of cinema tickets, annotated '19th May 1967'*

Tell me something.

I don't know, anything.

Tell me something about when you were a boy.

Anything. The first thing that comes into your head.

But he said nothing, and there was only the quietness of two people breathing, the scratch and shift of a skirt being straightened, a trouser leg awkwardly tugged.

Are you not going to say something?

I'm thinking, he said.

Her eyes, when she looked at him, kept flicking from one small point of focus to another, the way they would if they were looking at a waterfall, or a fire, or the view from a moving train. It felt as though she was looking for something, something new, or something familiar but forgotten. The skin around her eyes stretched and folded into tiny creases with the movement. As she blinked, an eyelash caught and fell on to her cheek. He looked at it. He wanted to reach out and dab it away.

What do you want to know? he asked.

Anything, she answered quickly. Just, I just want to hear your voice a while. He looked at the eyelash on her cheek and she reached a finger up to rub it away. Gone? she said.

Gone, he told her, smiling. There were footsteps somewhere, someone coughing, men's voices, and they both turned their faces towards the noise until it had passed.

How about, she said, were you ever in the hospital? Her voice was quiet and tense, as if she was afraid of being overheard. He thought about it for a moment, trying to think of something to say. She closed her eyes, and he noticed for the first time that she had faint bobbles of skin on her eyelids, like tiny colourless freckles, and he wondered why he'd never noticed them before. She opened her eyes and looked back at him, and almost without meaning to they leant slightly closer together.

He told her about when he was eight years old and Susan had left him in the park near Julia's house, and the boys had thrown stones and chased him until he fell.

Did it hurt awful bad? she said.

I've still got a very small scar, he said. It bled all the way back to Julia's house and they had to put a bandage on it. As he said this, they were both looking down at his knee, as if they could see through his trousers to the tiny pink stitch of a scar which was hidden there. He rubbed at it with the palm of his hand.

The room was very quiet again. She looked down at the floor, put her hands on the edge of the chair, crossed and uncrossed her feet. His shoes squeaked as he rubbed them together. He looked around the room, at their jackets folded together on the back of the chair by the door, at the clock ticking loudly on the mantelpiece, her parents' wedding photo on one side, photos of her and her four brothers on the other. She looked up at him and smiled. This feels a little strange, don't you think? she said.

She told him that her earliest memory was of being lifted on to her father's shoulders, having to hold on tightly as his long steps bounced her up the hill leading out of their side of town and on until they could turn round and look out over the city and the sea. She turned and pointed as she said this, as if the high open moorland was just in the next room. He told her that he was ten years old before he saw the sea.

I couldn't believe how cold and grey it was when I finally got there, he said, or how huge.

Aye, she said, but I'll bet you it's even colder up here, and she laughed.

Their voices were soft and low, pressed close together, and when one of them spoke, murmuring, their words seemed to curl towards each other like a twist of smoke from a candle flame. Tell me something else, she said.

He told her about how when it was very hot in the summer his father liked to spray them with the hosepipe while he was watering the rose bushes, and how his sister and her friends would creep up behind his father until he span suddenly round and sent them all scattering into the road to escape the icy shock. He told her about the summer holidays they spent at his grandparents' house in Suffolk, about vague memories of pink cottages and fields full of poppies, of being taken by his grandfather to watch the blacksmith at work, of his uncle driving them all down to the sea. She told him about racing a cart down the steep streets, and how much trouble she'd got into when she fell out one time and hurt herself.

When neither of them had spoken for a few moments, he leant forward, resting his hand on the arm of her chair, and kissed her.

What was that for? she said.

He shrugged. Just because, he said. She lifted her face towards him, and he kissed her again, slowly this time, and she raised her hand to touch the side of his neck, his jaw, the faint rub of stubble around his chin. He moved his hand from the arm of the chair and up on to her shoulder. He lifted a finger to her cheek, trailing his hand down the neckline of her shirt. Their movements were slow and tentative, as if this was still the first time they had kissed. She leant away from him, opening her eyes, and he pulled his hand back. She looked at him for a moment, touching his lips with the knuckle of her thumb, then looked away.

Just, she said, just, I want to keep talking for a while, okay?

He said, but I thought—

I want to hear you talking, she said. I like the sound of your voice. There's things I want to know still.

He told her about the museum he and a friend had made in his bedroom, and about the exhibition he curated at school, and about how he tried to get his first Saturday job at the archives, and about how he would one day have a museum of his own. He'd told her these things before, but she listened again. He didn't tell her what had happened with Julia, what Julia had said, the unbelievable truth she'd revealed. It seemed an impossible thing to say out loud. She asked about his first kiss, and he told her about a girl called Rebecca. She laughed and told him about a boy called Jack.

There was a muffled sound from somewhere, from next door, footsteps going up and down the stairs, low voices clouded by the thin walls. She looked round, bringing the tips of her fingers to her mouth, staring at the wall, her breath held tight in her chest. She looked back at him and smiled, faintly, her bottom lip dented by her two front teeth. The voices faded.

They looked at each other, waiting uncertainly. He shivered, suddenly very cold, a draught coming in through the kitchen and the open door and skidding across the bare wooden floorboards. He rubbed his hands on his trousers to warm them up.

You want to hear more? she asked him, turning in her seat and pulling her legs up beneath her, straightening her skirt around her knees.

Yes, he said.

Well then, she said. When I was seven I fell in the water by the harbour and a man had to jump in and rescue me.

Really? he said. What happened? How long were you in the water for?

Oh, not very long, she said, smiling, looking pleased with herself. I don't think I was in any danger; they didn't have to give me the kiss of life or any of that. But it was a big upset all the same; I near choked myself with crying until my mam told me to stop making a scene. He leant forward, fascinated.

But how did you fall in? he asked her. Was it cold?

I don't know really, she said. I was just standing there waiting for Ma and Da to come back from doing something and next I knew I was in the water. Aye, course it was cold, she added, rolling her eyes and crooking the arch of her eyebrow at him.

Was it cold, she repeated, laughing. I remember hearing a ship's hooter out at the harbour mouth, she said, so I must have turned to look and just slipped in. This man was in something fast though – felt like he was there by the time I came back up above the water almost. And he just grabbed me by the neck and pulled me over to the side, and he said don't worry love you'll be fine, or something the likes of, and I couldn't see him, I could only feel his great big hands on my neck, and I could see all the lights from the harbour front shining off the black water, and the cranes along the jetties further off, and the ship that had blown its hooter still out by the mouth, and when he got me over to the wall there were all these faces looking down at me – my ma and da, some other people I didn't know – and they were all talking at once and reaching down towards me and it felt like they were miles away. It was only once they'd hauled me out and I was stood there with them all looking at me and someone asked if I was alright that I started crying my eyes out. She spoke quickly and breathlessly, her hands fluttering around her mouth, or sweeping her hair back behind her ears, or smoothing down the hem of her skirt.

He watched her talking, the room suddenly bright and loud with it, and when she'd finished he said but Eleanor, what if that man hadn't been there? What if he hadn't seen you?

Aye, she said, I know. She reached out and ran her finger along the back of his hand, a little out of breath. But he was, she said. And he did. So it's okay.

He leant forward again and kissed her cheek, touching the corner of her jaw with two fingers as he did so, running his fingers across her face as he pulled away, nudging the tip of one finger between her lips. She kissed his finger, and he drew it back, and they both dropped their eyes, looking across the floor, looking around the darkened room, waiting.

She looked up at him again. Do you want to go upstairs? she said.

It was a small room. There were two beds, one along the end wall and one under the window, opposite the door. There was a chest of drawers and a wardrobe next to the door, and a small wooden chair in the corner. Opposite the bed, there was a small table with an oval mirror hanging above it, cluttered with make-up and hairbands and books, folders and files and notes for her Highers revision, an underlined timetable of exam dates pinned to the wall, a stack of seven-inch records against a record player.

Shall I put some music on? he asked her, standing at the table and flicking through the records.

No, she said, whispering, lifting a finger to her lips. It's late, the folk next door don't like the music this late. He looked up at the wall, startled, wondering how much they could hear. She waved her hand at the bed. Come sit down, she whispered, and as he moved back towards her he was suddenly conscious of the sound of his footsteps on the bare floorboards, the sound of his breathing. She laughed at his tiptoe steps, covering her mouth with her hand. You don't need to be that quiet, she said. It's not as if they're listening up against the wall or anything. He sat down carefully, looking at the wall again, unconvinced.

She said, have you done this before?

She was looking down, at her hands in her lap, twisting one of her fingers from side to side. No, he told her. He was too embarrassed to ask in return. He assumed by the way she asked that she hadn't. She looked up at him, shifting her weight towards him on the small narrow bed. They kissed, and her hand resting on his thigh felt suddenly charged with anticipation. He lifted his hand to her hip, fitting his fingers to the curve of it, easing his fingertips beneath her shirt and on to her bare warm skin. She lifted her mouth away from his, pulling back a few inches and opening her eyes. They stayed like that for another long moment, uncertain, nervous. He dipped his head and kissed the soft part of her throat where her collarbones met, the way he liked to do. He liked the way it made her tremble very slightly, the faint sighs brushing against the top of his head. He did it again, but the second time she lifted her head and moved away a little, resting her fingers on his chest. Wait, she said.

It had been a long day. They hadn't met until late in the evening, by the clocktower, barely catching each other's eyes before turning and walking quickly to the cinema, heads down, not touching. Neither of them, when they talked about it later, could remember a single scene of the film. They'd held hands, briefly, but she'd pulled away. She'd kept looking over her shoulder, as though the usher might have seen them sitting too close together, as though somebody might be standing waiting to catch them as they left. Her parents had gone away to Glasgow for two days, but it felt as if they were still lurking behind every corner.

It wasn't until they'd got back to her house that she'd kissed him; and even while she was kissing him she'd been looking carefully over his shoulder until she was sure that no one was watching from behind any curtains. When she was sure, she'd opened the door and quickly pulled him inside, leaving him standing in the hallway until she'd rushed around the house and tugged all the curtains tightly closed. And finally, then, she'd come to him, and slipped her hands inside his jacket, around his waist, and kissed him slowly, and said hello.

Hey, she said. It's getting late.

She leant towards him, kneeling up on the bed, putting her hands on the blanket either side of him and dropping her head to kiss his upturned face.

Her weight, resting on his, her hand sliding inside his shirt and across his chest, his hands tugging at the buttons of her shirt.

She sat up, kneeling astride him, and undid the rest of her

buttons, letting her shirt hang loose and watching his gaze fall to her chest. She slipped the shirt from her shoulders with a wriggle, pulled her arms loose, and dropped it on to the floor. Now you, she said, smiling, and he took his shirt off, undoing the top few buttons and dragging it over his head. He felt cold for a moment, awkward.

Her flat hand on his chest, polishing his skin. His fingers compassing around the curve of her breasts, his thumb pressed flat against each of her nipples. The way she closed her eyes, the sounds she made.

She lowered herself again, kissing his throat, his breastbone, his nipples, his shoulders, and as she did so he felt the weight of her breasts pressing against his skin. He had to bite both his lips to keep from calling out. And as she rolled away from him, on to her back, and drew him towards her to kiss and stroke her bare chest in turn, they were both thinking of the same thing, of the only other time they'd been exposed to each other in this way, that long hot afternoon at the start of the summer when they'd walked up past the brow of the hill, and looked down at the flat grey sea, and somehow dared each other into unbuttoning and removing their tops. Then, they hadn't kissed each other the way they were now, too embarrassed perhaps, too afraid of some stray walker or farmer appearing suddenly, and so they'd only looked, and laughed, and blushed slightly, and turned away from each other to get quickly dressed again.

Take your trousers off, she said.

And the rest, she said.

She looked for a moment, tilting her head to the side, curious. She stood up and pulled her skirt and her tights and her knickers to the floor, stepping gracefully from the gathered heap like a magician's assistant. The sight of her made him want to applaud. His whole body was straining and taut, arching towards her.

There was so much skin to touch, and so much skin to touch it with. They stood there, shivering a little, pressing their hands together, their chests, their legs. He held on to her hips for balance and brushed his mouth across her breasts, her stomach, her thighs. She did the same, and then, delicately, cautiously, knelt down to kiss the very tip of his erection. She looked up at him and laughed quickly, and he turned his face away, smiling, embarrassed.

She lay on the bed, waiting, looking up at the ceiling. He couldn't get into the packet. He was worried about ripping the thing itself as he tore it open. When he'd eventually got it on, and knelt between her legs, she looked down and smiled briefly behind her hand. Sorry, she said. It looks funny though, in its wee mackintosh like that. Sorry.

He couldn't get it to go in. He wasn't sure about the angle, or the position. She waited for a moment, not looking at him, and then reached down to try and help. It didn't seem right at all. It was uncomfortable, for both of them. She said, you should probably – I think you need to – you know. He didn't know what she meant, but when he looked down he saw that she was pushing him away a little and rubbing at herself, and then he thought he understood.

She made little gasps and sucking sounds, winces, like the noises he'd once heard her make when she got her hair caught up in the zip of her coat and was trying to untangle it. Are you okay? he asked. Is it; does it? She nodded, quickly, it's okay, she whispered, it's okay. She laid her arms across his back and clung tightly to him. His face was pressed against the pillow beside her head, his arms squashed either side of her. He felt fragile, overbalanced. He held his breath.

She shifted uncomfortably beneath him, and the movement made him spill over into sudden regretful delight.

Don't stop, she whispered, it's okay. He mumbled something, his face still pressed into the pillow. No, he said, I've finished.

Oh, she said. He lifted his weight away from her. Oh, she said again.

They lay on their sides, looking at each other for a long time, wondering about what they'd just done. The room seemed suddenly very quiet and still. She smiled, and he brushed his finger against her lips, resting a knuckle in the squeeze of her teeth. She moved her leg very slightly, bringing her knee up towards his hip. He let his arm slip from her shoulder to the small of her waist.

He said – he whispered – bloody hell, Eleanor.

She smiled, pulling the covers up across them both, her eyes dimming and closing. He looked at their clothes, spread out across the room like stepping stones. He asked her if she was okay, if she was glad they'd done that, and she kissed him and stroked the side of his face, her eyes closed, her breathing slowing and deepening.

He said – he whispered – bloody hell. I feel like I hardly know you. She opened her eyes.

You do too, she murmured, you know me well enough.

No, but really I mean, he said, bringing his leg up towards hers, running his hand down her thigh, there must be plenty that I don't know at all. She pressed a finger to his lips, smiled, and closed her eyes. She opened them again after five minutes or ten minutes or an hour, and looked at him.

Are you awake? she whispered. He looked back at her.

Just about, he said. She shifted a little closer to him.

Would you tell me something? she said. Would you tell me something nice so I can get to sleep?

18 *Disciplinary letter, typewritten on headed paper, January 1968*

Your failure to fulfil the obligations of your position, or to meet the reasonable requests of your superiors, has been noted.

There were weeks when the only time he spoke to his mother was to ask her again what she knew. There must be something else, he would say. A second name, a date of birth. Tell me something, please. Why didn't you tell me before? he would ask again. And his mother would insist that there was nothing else, that there was no more she was hiding from him, that she knew she'd done wrong but could he please stop all of this, it was breaking her heart. He would always leave the room when she said that, slamming the door behind him.

It was like a hunger, an insatiable hunger, this need to know. There were weeks, months, when he could think of nothing else, could hear nothing else besides the slow refined sigh of Julia's voice, saying the words over and over again. Of course we never saw the poor girl again. You'll have to keep the little darling. Did I say something wrong? Of course we never saw the poor girl. The words repeating like a stuck record in a locked room, haunting him, so that he could get to sleep only by drinking too much and leaving the radio on, loud. You'll have to keep the little darling. We never saw the little darling. You'll have to keep the poor girl. And of course she disappeared off the face of the earth. Did I say something wrong?

He thought about leaving home, about cutting himself off and starting again, about never speaking to his mother again, but he was too numb to do anything about moving out, and his mother was the only person he could ask for answers, and so he stayed, seething with hurt and anger and betrayal and loss, wishing he'd never found out.

And even when he was at work he struggled to concentrate, his thoughts blurred by the many questions he wanted answering: why he'd never been told; why he'd never suspected; whether Susan was lying when she said she'd never known; what he could do now to find the answers he was looking for, to find the people he'd never known he'd lost. One of the curators would ask him to repair a broken display cabinet, to rewrite an outdated label, to take a parcel to the post office, and within moments of being asked he would forget, sitting down on a gallery chair, or in the staffroom, or in the pub, knocked off his feet again by the memory of Julia's words. His colleagues started to comment, joking about his forgetfulness, his empty stare, his vacant tone of voice. The Director called him into the office to discuss his attitude towards work.

The poor girl hadn't even left you with a name, so we chose David, after that actor, what was his name? And of course, she disappeared off the face of the earth. What was his name?

Your difficulties with punctuality, and with timekeeping in general, have become of increasing concern.

He was surprised, when he asked, that it had taken him so long to think of it. What did Dad say when he found out? he said, and as soon as he'd said it he knew what the answer would be. His mother was in the back garden when he asked her, kneeling over the border, pulling out weed seedlings and heaping them into a small basket. How did you tell him? he asked, something cold and fearful turning over in his stomach. She straightened up, pulling her gloves off before answering him. She seemed uncertain what to say.

David, she said, and she looked up at him.

Did you even? he asked quietly. She put the gloves back on and pulled more weeds out of the dry soil, working her way around the thickly spiked stem of a rose bush.

I thought it was best, she said. He'd been home at the right time, she said. She pulled a bulb out by mistake and pushed it quickly back in, packing the soil in around it. Her voice was stretched and thin. The dates fitted, she said. I didn't think he needed to know. David turned away before she'd finished speaking. I thought he'd find it easier, not knowing, he heard her say, her voice falling away into the earth.

Sometimes, it was light outside before he was able to sleep. He would sit on the edge of the bed, reading, listening to the radio, his hands shaking. Or he would stand by the window, looking out at the lamplit blur of the night sky, hearing the occasional shouts and sirens drift faintly across the city. Or he would slip out of the house and walk through the shadowed streets, thinking, unable to think, trying to pound some sleep into his tired body. His colleagues got used to him rushing through the front door half an hour or an hour late, toast crumbs around his mouth, his shirt tucked in and his tie knotted as he ran from home. I'm sorry, I slept through the alarm, he would say, and Maureen on the front desk would usually reply that he didn't look as if he'd slept at all, beckoning him over to straighten his collar and tell him to wipe his mouth before the seniors saw him. They started to joke about it in the staffroom, marking up a graph of his arrival times on the noticeboard, and he had no answer when Malcolm asked him what was on his mind so much these days, and he could only smile and pretend to look embarrassed when Anna said odds on it's a woman and they all laughed. It was easier to let them think like that. He wouldn't have known where to begin if he'd wanted to tell them what it really was.

Your misuse of museum time and resources has also been noted, with particular regret.

He went to the archive office at the Royal London Hospital in Whitechapel, where Julia and his mother had worked, and under the pretence of a research project he searched through the lists of patients in the maternity wing at the relevant time. But he found nothing. He contacted trades unions, and Irish emigrant workers' associations, and even tracked down a domestic service museum in Bath, looking for more archives he could search through, looking for a box of files which would reveal a line of detail on a Mary who had stopped work suddenly in 1945. But he found nothing. Domestic employment tended to be rather informal, he was told. The names weren't always recorded, or even known. He went to Somerset House and found that the entry for his own birth matched the birth certificate he had, listing his mother and father as *Dorothy Carter and Albert Carter*, and when he got home he asked furiously how such a lie had been incorporated into official history. But his mother could tell him nothing. He wrote letters, on headed museum paper, to museums and social centres across Donegal and the north of Ireland, asking for artefacts and recollections connected with domestic service in England during the war, and although he accumulated a large boxful of photographs and transcribed interviews he found no answers there. He discovered that history's secrets are not always easily found, that all the archives in the world weren't enough when he didn't even know who or what he was looking for, or where he should be looking.

These matters have all been discussed with you, formally and informally, on previous occasions. This letter therefore serves as a written warning that if an immediate improvement in your standard of work is not forthcoming, disciplinary proceedings will commence with a view to terminating your employment. As a valued member of staff we would very much hope that this does not become necessary.

He sometimes wondered what would have happened if he had lost his job then. He tried to construct an alternative story from the scraps of what would have remained, wondering if he would have gone to see Eleanor again, wondering if he would have found another job in a museum or whether that would have been the end of it, wondering whether he would have read and re-read Eleanor's letters with bitter regret instead of excitement and then fond recollection. He wondered what other story he would have ended up with, carried on the backseat of his car to show someone who at long last wanted to know.

But it was impossible to say, he knew. There was no clear parallel life into which he would have fallen had his job been taken away from him, just as there hadn't been a celibate loneliness waiting for him in the event of his failing to notice Eleanor in the tea room that day. Just as he hadn't been irrevocably formed, or broken, the moment Julia had said you can leave him with me, I'll look after him until you get back. It was more complicated than that. Lives were changed and moved by much smaller cues, chance meetings, overheard conversations, the trips and stumbles which constantly alter and readjust the course of things, history made by a million fractional moments too numerous to calibrate or observe or record. The real story, he knew, was more complicated than anything he could gather together in a pair of photo albums and a scrapbook and drive across the country to lay out on a table somewhere. The whole story would take a lifetime to tell. But what he had would be a start, he thought, a way to begin. What he had would be enough to at least say, here, these are a few of the things which have happened to me, while you weren't there. This is a small part of how it's been. You don't need to guess any longer, you don't need to imagine or wonder or dream. This is a small part of the truth.

19 *Identity badge, Junior Curatorial Assistant, Coventry Museum, w/photo, 1967*

He came out of work one evening, almost a year after Julia had first let everything slip, and saw his mother, waiting for him. He stopped, hesitating, looking back through the foyer towards the stairs to his office, wondering if there was some work he could catch up on. He carried on down the steps, saying goodbye to two of his colleagues and catching Dorothy's eye as she turned round. She smiled at him, and he nodded, glancing away up the street.

Hello love, she said. I just got off the train and I thought I'd see if you were around, you don't mind, do you? Who are those two? I don't think I've met them before. She was talking quickly, her hands fidgeting at her waist, and she leant in towards him as he told her that that was Paul from Conservation and a girl called Anna who was doing her second work placement from university. He didn't look at her as he spoke. Well, they both seem nice, she said, her hands still pulling at each other. Is work going okay then? He shrugged and started walking, and she walked with him, saying oh, well, as long as work's going okay, her voice trailing out as she waited for him to pick up the thread and tell her something more, some new project he'd been working on, a disagreement he'd had with another curator, something funny a visitor had said, any small part of his day he might want to share with her. But he said nothing.

They turned the corner towards the two cathedrals, Dorothy having to break into a half-run occasionally to keep up with his long strides. She said, I just got back from seeing

Julia. She said, she's not doing too badly, all things considered. He didn't reply. She said, the nurses there are doing a very good job with her; it can't be easy.

They walked past the old cathedral, and David glanced up at the ruined north wall, the unroofed sky a burnished August blue through the arched hole where the windows had once been. He'd seen archive photos of the fire, the great billowing folds of flame reaching up through the sky to light the bombers' path, and he'd read the accounts of the churchwardens who'd put themselves on fire duty, chasing across the lead roof with buckets of sand, booting fizzing incendiaries into the road until they'd had to retreat down long ladders and watch the whole city burn. She said, I went over and cleaned her house afterwards. It doesn't look like Laurence has been there for a long time. We'll have to think about doing something with all her things sooner or later, I mean, there's a whole lot of it in there. We'll have to talk to someone about it, she said. She touched his arm, and he jerked it away. Oh, she said. Sorry love. He didn't say anything.

They walked past the looming walls of the new cathedral, with its tall narrow windows letting the light squeeze in, with the skeletal steel spire that crowds had gathered to watch being lowered into place by helicopter, and she said, well anyway, we'll have to talk to Laurence about it, when the time comes. She said, I don't suppose he'll be much use though. David didn't say anything. They stood across the road from the bus station, waiting for the traffic to clear so they could cross. She said, when are you going down there next? She said, I'm sure she'll be very pleased to see you again you know. A heavy lorry clattered past, loaded with rubble and soil from a building site, and they both stepped back.

She said, David, don't be like this, please. She was out of breath from trying to keep up with him. She said, David, please, I can't.

They crossed the road, and as they walked round past the bus station she said, I thought I might have a go at getting the garden tidied up this weekend. It's been getting a bit out of hand again. She said, of course it was your father who was the expert, and they both flinched a little at her use of the no longer comfortable word. She glanced at him, and continued, saying, but I imagine he'd have a thing or two to say if he saw the garden now, don't you think? He looked at her, not quite meeting her eye, and made a gesture with his head which was almost a nod. She sighed impatiently, and said, yes, well, it's up to you whether you want to give us a hand or not. Give me a hand I mean, she said, correcting herself.

She said, David, are you even listening to me? They crossed the route of the new ring road, following the fenced footpath between a maze of trenches and banks and towering concrete stilts. She said, this isn't going to make things any easier you know. She said, I mean, I know you're upset, but I don't see how this is going to help David. He didn't say anything. She held his arm, and said, David, and again he pulled it away.

They walked through the streets beyond the city centre, past flat-fronted terraces which opened straight out on to the street, past bay-windowed semis by the park, past a row of houses which had once been watchmakers' workshops, the attic windows built tall and broad to let the light flood in on their intricate work. They crossed the road by a parade of shops and started walking up the long hill which led towards their house.

She stopped for a moment to get her breath back, and when he didn't wait for her she scurried after him, turning to try and meet his eye, saying, David, how long are you going to keep this up? He didn't say anything. She said, what do you want me to do? She said, David, I've said I'm sorry; I've said it over and over again; what else do you expect me to do? It's not fair David, she said, it's just not fair. And if it hadn't been for people walking nearby she would have been shouting, the force of it already trembling in her voice.

Do you think I never worried about this? she said, a moment later. He was silent, and she said again what she'd already said so many times: I was going to tell you; I wanted to tell you. I was waiting for the right moment and I never found it and then it only got harder. I couldn't think of a way to begin. I'd have had to tell your father as well, and I thought you'd both be better off not knowing. She reached into the sleeve of her jacket for a tissue, and David still didn't speak.

They walked past the school Albert had been working on before he died, built to take the pressure off the over-crowded grammar Susan and David had both attended, where temporary classrooms had hidden the bomb-craters in the playground and lunch breaks had had to be taken in shifts. They turned the corner into their estate, past a small strip of woodland, and left again into their street.

She said, in desperation, David, I never lied to you. If you'd ever asked me I would have told you the truth, but you always seemed happy with the way you thought things were; it didn't seem fair to upset things for you. I wouldn't have lied to you, ever, she said. You believe that at least, don't you?

He stopped abruptly and looked at her, meeting her eyes for the first time since he'd seen her at the bottom of the museum steps. He peered at her for a moment, closely, as if watching to see what else she had to say, and when he saw that she was starting to cry he allowed a smile to open out across his otherwise impassive face before turning away. She watched him go. She called his name, quietly in case the neighbours heard. She followed him to the door. She said, oh if your father was here you wouldn't, and he turned, waiting for her to finish her sentence, but she said nothing more. He stood in the opened doorway, blocking her path, and saw Susan walking up the street towards them.

He said, almost in a whisper, you've got no idea, have you? He stood aside to let her into the house, and as she squeezed past him the phone started to ring. He left it a moment, watching her disappear upstairs, and when he picked it up he was almost breathless with the adrenalin pulsing through him. He said hello and Eleanor said guess what? Guess what? Oh David, you'll never guess what.

20 *Examination results, Scottish Highers, July 1967*

A single sheet of paper, slightly larger than letter-size, an expensive-looking rough-grained texture with a circular watermark just visible about halfway down the page. The name of the examinations board at the top, an address, a reference number. An official seal at the bottom, lipstick red and frilled at the edges. A ruled table with columns for subject, paper, date, and grade. The thick black type that can change a life. The paper held delicately, at arm's length, as though creasing it or tearing it would invalidate what it said. As though the ink were still wet and could be smudged or removed.

She hadn't got any sleep the night before it came, she told him. He imagined her sitting up all night, drinking cocoa and trying not to think about it. Sitting in the kitchen, sitting in the front room, in her father's chair, standing out in the backyard, looking down at the lights in the harbour, softened and wavering in the warm night air.

She didn't want to open it when it came, she said. She heard the letter box go and she sat in the kitchen and she didn't move. The envelope landed with a tap and a skid across the smooth stone floor, and it was a minute before she stalked out of the kitchen with a butter-knife at the ready to slit open the envelope. The brown paper broke into two rows of jagged teeth. She slid out the letter and unfolded the clean white sheet.

She didn't know what she was expecting. For months she'd been going over it in her head, going backwards and forwards, convincing herself she'd passed, convincing herself she'd failed. She didn't know what was going to happen. She didn't know what she wanted to happen. It was new territory; her staying on at school at all had been new territory for the whole family. Her mother had left school at fourteen to work at Williamson's, learning to gut and split and fillet the heavy flat fish with vicious speed, salting and carrying them into the field and spreading them out like great white sheets in the sun to dry. Her father had left school at eleven to help his father's friend in the shipyard at the bottom of the hill; there was a photo of him from soon after he'd started there, half-hidden in a group of hard-looking men all bristling with moustaches and hammers and tongs, his small eyes shut tight against the blaze of the flashgun, his cap a few sizes too big for him still. So they didn't understand, either of them, what Eleanor had been doing at school those last few years, why she'd carried on fussing with books and things when she could have been bringing money into the house.

She unfolded the sheet of clean white paper, and read the words in thick black type. *Chemistry, B. English, C. Geography, B. Mathematics, C. Physics, B.* She read the words over and over, holding the paper up to the light, a pale gasp of excitement breaking out from her pursed lips. The first in the family to stop on at school, and now the first in the family, the first in the street, to go on to university. She refolded the paper and put it back into the jagged-toothed envelope. She propped it up on the kitchen table, leaning it against the empty cocoa mug, staring at it, checking her name and address on the front. She didn't know what to do straight away, who to tell, whether to have a drink and celebrate, whether to start packing her bags there and then.

All the different ways there were of leaving home, and the one she'd chosen had finally settled within reach. Her first brother, away with the merchant navy before she was even born. Her second and third brothers married. Her sister, gone with a story that no one ever spoke of. And now her, with a place waiting at Edinburgh University, ready to slip out of the house for good.

She heard footsteps on the wooden stairs and her mother came into the room, standing just inside the doorway, looking at her. What's that you've got there? she asked, her voice a little slow with sleep.

Eh? It's just a letter from the school, Eleanor said, leaning over it slightly. Is Da awake? she asked. Is he up yet?

No, he's still sleeping for now, her mother said, walking across to the kettle and filling it with water. What's the letter for? she asked. Eleanor turned round in her chair.

It's the results, she told her. Ivy put the kettle on top of the stove.

Oh aye? she said. I didn't know you were expecting those. There was a creaking from upstairs, the sound of someone getting out of bed, footsteps across the floor. So what does it say? Ivy asked. Eleanor listened for the steps to come downstairs. She glanced up at the ceiling, and at her mother, and at the empty doorway. Well? her mother said. Eleanor handed over the piece of paper in its thin brown envelope.

It's good, she said quietly, pre-emptively, watching her mother's eyes scan over the words. Or she didn't say anything, and looked the other way.

Ivy read the sheet of paper, nodded, and made an mmhmm sound in the back of her throat. Oh aye, she said. Stewart came into the room and looked at them both expectantly. Ivy handed him the sheet of paper and went back upstairs. Will you make that pot of tea? she said, as she left the room. Eleanor watched her go, unsure whether to be shocked or not, waiting to see if she would come back and say anything more. Her father looked at the results and let out a long low whistle, breaking into a shuffling jig around the kitchen table, pulling Eleanor into a tight and startling embrace, rushing to get dressed and knock on the neighbours' doors, launching a day of toasts and hugs and hearty thumps on the back – and never you mind what your mother thinks, he whispered to her at one point, wonderfully – a day in which the letter would take pride of place on the front-room mantelpiece, repeatedly taken down and unfolded and passed around from hand to careful hand.

And by six o'clock, when the front room was crowded full, the men still in their workclothes and the women quickly changed out of their aprons and headscarves into something a little smarter, their glasses full to the brim, and the conversations falling round to work and weather and sport, she managed to slip out of the house to the telephone box, dialling the number she still had scribbled on a paper napkin from work.

It was the first time she'd actually phoned him. After all their letters, and after all the times they'd spent together, it was still somehow unexpected. Her voice sounded strange and thin, coming all that way down the line while he stood in the entrance hall of the house, twisting the cable in his hand and glaring at his sister who had come down from upstairs to look at him accusingly.

That's bloody brilliant Eleanor, he said when she told him the news, and his excitement was as much from her phoning at all as from what she had to say. Her voice, breaking into his neat house like that, made him feel as though he were passing some kind of test. I knew you'd do it, he said.

Oh, she said, and then she was quiet for a moment. I've been waiting for someone to say that all day, she said.

She told him everything that had happened, how she'd waited a few moments to open the letter, how she'd hoped her father would see it first, how she hadn't really been surprised by her mother's reaction, and as her money started to run out, she said quickly, so you'll be coming up to see me again soon, aye? I'll see if I can't arrange for my folks to go away again, she said slyly. And he grinned and said you do that as the line went dead.

He sat on the bottom of the stairs for a minute, holding the warm receiver in his hand, looking out through the still open front door. His mother had gone outside with a pair of shears and her gardening gloves, and was busily cutting the hedge. She hacked at it with loose, stabbing gestures, letting the cut branches fall around her, stopping now and again to wipe the backs of her wrists across her eyes, glancing at him through the doorway once or twice. He put the phone down and went upstairs.

21 *Train ticket, Aberdeen–Coventry (single), 15 September 1968*

Eleanor took a model wooden boat from her bottom drawer, wrapped it in an old piece of newspaper, folded it into a navy-blue sweater, and tucked it down into a corner of the suitcase. She pressed folded skirts and blouses around it, a pair of shoes stuffed with balled-up socks and stockings, a handful of knickers, a pair of blue jeans, a dress still wrapped in the dry-cleaner's bag. She packed her field notes and sketches, her textbooks, her washbag, a packet of tissues, a hairbrush which had once belonged to her sister. She packed a magazine, a pillowcase, an envelope full of photographs and a thick bundle of letters, and when she pressed the lid down and forced the catch closed there was still plenty left that she wanted to squeeze in. Her father appeared in the doorway.

You all done there then petal? he asked, his head angling towards her and his thick eyebrows crinkling upwards. She looked at him a moment and tried a smile.

Aye, I think so, she said, as much as this case can manage anyhow, and she pushed on the lid to make sure the catches weren't going to burst open and spring her possessions back out into the room. She stood by the window, looking out down the street, towards the harbour. Stewart sat down on the chair in the corner of the room.

What time's he here? he asked.

About five, she said, looking at her watch.

Not be long now then, he said, folding his arms.

No, she said, not long.

Stewart must have sat in that room before, watching a son or a daughter pack up and leave, and now he was having to watch the last of his children go through the same routine; looking around for something forgotten, stroking the hair on the back of the head, not being able to look him in the eye. It was no easier now, surely, than the first time must have been.

You're not going for long then? he said. Just for a week or so?

No, she said, not long.

And you're sure you don't want to wait for your mother to come home first? She'll be awful surprised. Eleanor shook her head.

The train will go before she comes back, she said. She won't be back from work until six.

No, he said, I know. He narrowed his eyes, briefly, and she turned away, embarrassed, looking out of the window again.

It's not five yet, is it? he asked.

No, she said; I just wanted to be sure. He stood, slowly, lifting himself to his unsteady feet by pushing on the wooden arms of the chair, and picked up the suitcase.

Well, he said, puffing a little, let's at least get you all downstairs and ready for the young man. You sure you've got everything in here? he asked again, moving awkwardly towards the door and the top of the stairs. Eleanor tried to take the case from him.

I'll be alright with that Da, she said, let me take it. He put it down and turned to her, breathing heavily, and said now Eleanor, you're not out that front door yet. She didn't say anything. She looked at the floor and nodded, or she looked straight at him and tried to say all the things she was feeling, or she turned to the window again. He picked up the case and went downstairs, one heavy step at a time, clutching on to the handrail, stopping twice to get his wind, and by the time he got to the bottom his breath was pinched and loud. Eleanor stood in her room, trying not to listen, looking at the two neatly made beds, the chest of drawers, the wardrobe, the chair in the corner, the window.

He was sitting in his armchair in the corner when she got downstairs, wiping his forehead with a white handkerchief, the suitcase squatting in the middle of the room. She stood in the doorway. The street outside was quiet, the children and their families away to the beach, and the only sounds in the room were the ticking of the clock on the mantelpiece, the softening wheeze of her father's breath. They heard hurried footsteps outside, and a knock at the door, and they looked at each other.

That'll be David then, she said, and he nodded.

He was standing in the entranceway at home when she told him what had happened, just as he'd been standing there when she'd told him about her exam results a year earlier, fiddling with the address book and pens on the phone shelf, the last of the evening's light falling through the glass panels of the front door. It took him a while to understand what she was saying, her words not making sense even once he'd told her to slow down and start again.

But she can't do that, he said. It's not up to her; she can't just not let you go. Eleanor sighed impatiently, and it was years before he realised just how wrong he'd been. He heard her dropping more coins into the slot, and she said so what am I going to do?

She'd come in from supper, she told him, a bit later than usual because she'd been round the shops with Heather after work. There's something we need to discuss, her mother had said, as she sat down at the table, and straight away she'd heard something in that voice, in those words, something she was more than used to. She'd turned to her father, but he'd looked down at his empty plate and said only, are you not going to wash your hands before you come to the table now? She got up from her chair, washed and dried her hands at the sink, and sat down again, and as she did so her mother took a large white envelope from her lap and slid a stapled bundle of papers from it. A letter came for you from Edinburgh, from the university, she said.

It's not the first time she's done that David, Eleanor told him. I wasn't surprised about that part of it at all.

It's a list of all the things you'll be wanting when you start down there, her mother said. It's an awful long list. There's a couple dozen books and some of them are costing near ten bob each. Eleanor caught her father glancing up at her, and she could see already what was happening. You'll need a set of bedlinen for your room, her mother said, and a whole lot of stationery. And you know what else? It says here you'll be needing formal wear on occasion. On occasion!

She said all this, she told him, with a voice put on, a voice Eleanor described as her airs and graces voice.

So tell me, her mother went on, since you're the bright spark of the family now, where were you planning on finding formal evening wear, and bedlinen, and all those books? How were you thinking we were going to pay for it all? Because I don't think a year's worth of serving teas has quite covered it, has it now? She leant towards Eleanor, lowering her voice. Or had you not given it any thought, eh? she said.

The food was ready on the table. A large brown casserole dish on a mat in front of Stewart, steam piping out of the small hole in the lid. Butter melting over the hot salted potatoes in their bowl. Half a loaf of bread ready to be cut on the board, and no one touching a thing. Eleanor looked back at her mother, and perhaps allowed herself a smile as she saw a way around all these objections. Or perhaps she didn't dare smile. Perhaps she sat lower in her chair, dropping her gaze from the cold stillness of her mother's eyes.

There's a grant will pay for that, she said, quietly, or

proudly, or defiantly. They give you a grant for all your expenses.

I thought that would be enough David, she said, her voice stumbling and rushing down the phone line towards him. I thought she'd maybe smile or say that's okay then at least, she said.

But instead there was her mother's hand cracking down on to the table, a flinch from both Eleanor and her father, her mother's voice cutting sharply into the room, saying this family has never taken charity and it's not about to start off now.

It's not charity, replied Eleanor, and David imagined that there were already tears in her eyes as she realised how soon the conversation would be over. It's a grant, she said. Everyone gets one, she said.

She'd worked a year for this, saving her wages from the tea room and working spare shifts at the social club so that her mother wouldn't have this excuse, couldn't say these things, and it seemed impossible that it would all come to nothing now, that the plans she'd made so carefully were not going to work out. She'd studied the prospectus so many times it was falling apart; she had a room booked in the halls of residence, and a suitcase ready to pack, and textbooks already bought. She'd been waiting a year for this, she'd been waiting her whole life for this.

It's a grant, she said again, hopelessly. Everyone gets one.

A couple of times before, waiting together at the station for his train, he'd said why don't you come with me, only half as a joke, and both times she'd been cross and said he wasn't to say that, it wasn't funny, it wasn't fair. But that August evening, with Eleanor waiting on the end of a 400-mile phone line, with the sunlight pouring through the frosted glass, with all the bearings he'd always taken for granted so recently pulled away, he saw with absolute clarity that it could be as easy as saying the words. That things can sometimes happen just because you ask them to.

What am I going to do? she asked him again.

He walked from the train station to her house in a slight daze, uncertain of what was going to happen, or whether he was even doing the right thing. The harbour quays seemed quieter than usual, the road less busy. A trawler headed towards the mouth, the low sputter of its engine floating back across the water. From somewhere on the north side came the sound of hammer on sheet steel, ringing through the afternoon. The still dry air was salted with the smell of fish and diesel and rusting iron. He got to the bridge, and crossed over the Dee into Torry, stopping a moment to wipe the sweat from his face, his hands, the back of his neck.

He walked up the hill, quickening his pace as he got closer, anxious to get it over with. There were very few people around, and his footsteps sounded out loudly along the narrow street. The front-room window of her house was open when he got there, and as he knocked on the door he heard her voice through the net curtain saying that'll be David then, and her father muttering something in brief reply.

He didn't go inside. He waited by the door, listening to their low voices, listening to her footsteps clattering quickly up and down the stairs, and then she was there, ready, with him. Stewart met his eyes just once, as the three of them stood there shuffling their feet.

David, he said, nodding.

Afternoon Mr Campbell, he replied, as though they were bumping into one another in the street, as though it wouldn't be long before they saw each other again. He picked up Eleanor's suitcase. He said, well. He turned away, while Eleanor said goodbye to her father, and then he walked with her back down the hill.

22 *Book of Co-op dividend stamps, 1968*

Stewart took a white handkerchief from his pocket and wiped at the sweat on his forehead, to keep it from trickling into his eyes. He stood, with one hand on the door frame, one foot on the front step, watching the pair of them until they'd rounded the corner at the bottom of the hill, waiting to see if one or other of them might turn around, just once. Or he went back inside as soon as they'd said their goodbyes, closing the door sharply behind him, breathless with rage and regret. Or he waited a moment, went inside to put the kettle on, and came back out to see whether they might not, after all, still be there.

Later, with a cup of tea poured out but not yet drunk, sitting in his armchair by the window, he heard the front door open and Ivy come in, talking to Donald. They stood in the doorway, Donald holding two baskets of shopping from the Co-operative, Ivy out of breath from the long walk up the hill. She smiled. Enough in the pot for us, is there? she asked.

Aye, but it'll be stewed by now, he replied quietly. He nodded hello to Donald. Ivy looked at him and stepped into the room.

What's got you? she asked.

You're home early, Stewart said.

The job was done, so they let us go before time, she said. She studied his face. What are you not telling me? What's got you? she asked again. Stewart said nothing, looking away into the empty fireplace. Has something happened? she said. There been an accident?

No, he said. No accident.

What then? she insisted. Eh?

Stewart took a deep breath, and waited. Donald turned away, saying something about putting the shopping down in the kitchen and making a fresh pot.

Our Eleanor's away to the train station, Stewart said, pinching at the loose skin on the back of his knuckles.

Where's she going? asked Ivy sharply. Was she with that English boy?

Aye, he said. The two of them are away to the train station with a suitcase of Eleanor's things. She'll not be back for a time, he added.

Aye right, you're no mistaken there, are you? Ivy snapped sarcastically. She's no just away to the beach?

Stewart didn't reply.

Did you not try and stop them Stewart? Did you not try and keep them at least while I got back? Or did you just wave them off goodbye, eh? She came towards him as she said all this, her voice rising and breaking, and he looked away from her and he didn't say a word.

Aye and what happens now Stewart? Where are they going to? How are they going to get by? What did she *say* Stewart, what did she say? And by now she was shouting, until her voice collapsed and she sat suddenly down on the small sofa across from the fire.

In the kitchen, Donald was standing by the window, his hands gripping the edge of the stone sink, his head bowed, listening.

Ivy looked at her husband. She said, is she in trouble?

Stewart pulled at the skin on the back of his hand again. He twisted his finger until it clicked, painfully, in its joint. I don't know, he said.

Oh, aye, she said, her voice hardening again, I'll warrant she is. I never trusted that pair. She stood up again, peering out of the window, checking that no neighbours had seen or heard what she'd said. Stewart looked up at her, running his hands along the seams of his trousers, not knowing what more to say. In the kitchen, Donald poured out the tea and wiped his face with the sleeve of his shirt.

Ivy took out a handkerchief and rubbed a smear of finger-grease from the window. She said, well, she's an adult now; she can do as she pleases. She turned away from the window, and as she left the room she said aye and she always was a handful anyway.

Stewart watched her go. He remembered when Hamish had left home, and the room had been full of people wishing him well on his way, chairs squeezed in around the walls and barely any space to move. He looked at it now, and the small house felt suddenly huge. He had the feeling that if he called out to Ivy she would be too far away to hear him. He imagined he could hear floorboards creaking, and joists settling against brickwork, as though the house were subsiding after a storm. He imagined he could hear the echo of footsteps, fading away. Children's voices whispering into the distance.

He stood, and walked slowly through to the kitchen.

He said, Ivy, don't be too hard on the girl now, eh? He said, you've been doing that for too long.

23 *Handwritten list of Coventry addresses, August 1968*

No one ever said it out loud, but he knew that people thought he was rushing into things, acting carelessly, stupidly even. His friends, when he told them, all paused for a moment too long before offering their congratulations, as if they were checking that they'd heard him right, wondering who this girl Eleanor was even. His colleagues at work, when he gave out the invitations, read them and said oh, you're really going ahead with this then? And his mother, trying so hard not to say the wrong thing, not to make things between them any worse than they already were, still managed to say too much when she said but David, I'm just worried. I just want what's best for you.

And the front door slammed, again, and she noticed that the paint was starting to flake away around the edges of the frame.

Susan, being Susan and having a better idea than Dorothy of what not to say, asked him about it more disinterestedly: meeting him for a drink after work and saying so anyway, when did you ask her to marry you? How long did it take her to say yes? When is she coming down? Nodding and smiling when he said not long; saying oh I'm only joking when he refused to tell her whether he'd gone down on one knee. She waited a moment, reaching into her pocket for a packet of cigarettes muttering don't tell Mum as she lit one, and then she said so tell me about her anyway David. I mean you haven't said much. What's she like?

There were so many things he could have said.

He could have described the way she looked; she's shorter than me but not by much, she's got quite long hair, it's a kind of faded brown but it goes blonde in the sun and it falls across her face when she's daydreaming, she doesn't smile all that often but when she does the whole shape of her face changes, it gets rounder and softer, and her eyes are the colour of honey and her skin, her skin's so smooth it's like it's been polished by the cold north wind, and her body, I mean, her skinny hips her slip of a waist her pebble-round shoulders her smooth small breasts I mean I can't keep my hands to myself when I'm with her she's so warm and alive and she's just so I mean when she undresses I just want to applaud and do you know what I mean?

But he didn't say this. He took out a photo and showed it to Susan, and she smiled and said oh, well, she's pretty isn't she? and he took it back and said I know.

He could have described the way he felt when he was with her; she's the only girl I know who laughs at my jokes, and the sound of her laughing is my favourite sound in the world, we do so much talking when we're together, we talk about so many things and it's exciting to find out about her and have her find out about me, it's great to have someone so interested in who I am, and she loves making plans, she makes plans for us, we make plans, what we'll do in the future, where we'll go, she makes anything and everything seem possible and she wants to do it all with me, she wants me to be a part of her life and that's all I've ever wanted, does that make sense to you at all?

But instead he shrugged and said, I don't know, we just get on well together. And Susan said well, that's good. That's the main thing.

He could have said I've never felt like this about anyone before.

He could have said and you know what? She doesn't keep any secrets from me.

To which Susan could have replied how do you know that? You can't know that.

But he didn't say these things, and she didn't reply.

Instead, he talked briefly about Eleanor leaving school with good exam results, about her saving up for a year to go to university and her family now not allowing her to. He said that she was going to study geology at the new university, once they were settled in. He mentioned the flat he'd found, and the social club he'd booked for the reception, and Susan said it sounded like he'd got it all worked out, she was impressed.

And you're sure you're doing the right thing? she asked. He laughed.

No, I'm not sure, he said. But I can't imagine doing anything else.

24 *Doorkey on a knotted loop of string; Wedding certificate, October 1968*

It rained the day they moved into their first home together, a second-floor flat on a main road about half an hour's walk from the museum. It was early evening by the time she unlocked the door and they burst in, rainwater streaming from their hair and down the collars of their damp clothes.

You said the weather was finer in England, she said, laughing accusingly, wiping her face with her hands.

I lied, he said, holding up his hands in surrender, letting her come for him.

It had rained all day. It was raining when he left home in the morning, a thin drizzle which seeped through his new suit and clung to his skin, and it was raining when he stood on the steps of the registry office to wait for her, the rain thickening and the woman behind the front desk coming outside to hand him an umbrella, saying he wanted to be careful he didn't catch a cold. It was raining when Eleanor arrived, ten minutes late, in a car his friend Danny had borrowed from his uncle and strung with white ribbon, and she had to lift the skirts of her dress a little as she came up the steps towards him, smiling and avoiding his eyes, sheltered from the rain by a folded newspaper Danny held over her head. It was raining when they repeated their vows, raising their voices over the noise of the rain rattling impatiently against the wired-glass skylights, the dozen of them in that small office-like room glancing up at the heavy sky, and it was raining as they drove to the reception.

Everyone was waiting for them when they arrived, David's family and his colleagues from the museum and his friends from school, and some of them rushed out with umbrellas to gather the two of them safely in, and some of them stood in the doorway and laughed, and everyone raised the first glass of many as David stood on a chair to welcome them all, and thank them for coming, and ask them to tuck into the food which had been provided. And the afternoon went by as fast as the rain flashing past the window – people shaking his hand and offering advice, or tipping a cheek towards him for a kiss and beaming congratulations, and his mother crying, of course, partly from happiness and partly from his father not being there to see it, and his grandparents, all the way up from Suffolk for the first time, saying they couldn't believe how much he'd grown and they couldn't believe he was marrying already and how happy they were for him, and Eleanor sitting quietly for a while when Susan said something about welcome to the family, but she couldn't sit for long because someone drifted by to talk to her and squeeze her hand and fill her glass. And the speeches came and went, and the music got louder, and the tables, littered with half-eaten sausage rolls and cucumber sandwiches and emptied-out bowls of cheese and onion crisps, were pulled to one side so the two of them could be pushed across the carpet to dance.

I kept wanting to stop and take pictures, they told each other later. I wanted to write things down so I wouldn't forget them. I just wanted to stand still and watch and not have anyone say anything to me for a moment because I was worried it was all passing me by.

The photos they ended up with, mostly taken outside the registry office and stuck into a slim red album, didn't seem quite enough. He wanted more. He kept the cards people gave them, with their messages of love and good luck and best wishes, but they had nothing in them about the day itself, and he wanted more. I'll just have to keep telling you about it, she said, smiling, when he said these things to her, so you don't forget.

There was more dancing, and more speech-making. There was a table loaded with gifts, a cake, balloons being burst by excited children, singing. There was his mother crying again, there were people catching him for a quick hello and well done before someone else interrupted, there were people saying they knew it was early but they were sorry they had to be off, and then it seemed like no time at all before they were calling out their sudden goodbyes and running back through the rain to the car. And his family and his friends all crowded together in the entrance to wave and cheer them both on their way, and the children threw rice and confetti over the car, and the rice falling against the window sounded like yet more rain. Danny drove them the short distance to the flat, and as they got out of the car the rain seemed to fling itself down with one final flurry of temper, soaking them through in the brief time it took to run from the car, up the steps, and in through their new front door.

The flat seemed lighter and larger than he'd remembered. She whirled around in excitement, the lace-edged skirts of her white dress lifting and billowing out around her pale legs for a moment before she stopped and looked at him, proudly, and said what do you think?

He hardly recognised it. She'd obviously been busy during the few rushed weeks between coming down from Aberdeen and their wedding day. When the landlady had shown him around the flat he'd worried that it might be too cramped, or too gloomy, and he'd worried about what Eleanor might think. But she'd said it was fine when she'd first seen it, and then she'd banished him, insisting that she stayed there and he lived at his mother's until they were married, not letting him see what she was doing to the place.

She'd cleaned the windows and thrown away the filthy net curtains; she'd scrubbed and polished every possible inch of floor and wall and surface; she'd arranged the furniture so that there was room to move around. There were new sheets on the bed, and clean covers on the settee. There was a vase of flowers in the bedroom, and the lounge, and even the kitchen. There were large framed pictures of butterflies on the wall. It felt like a different flat entirely, and for the first time he understood what it was going to mean to share his life with somebody.

It's not bad, is it? he said. You've done a smashing job, he said, and there was something almost child-like about the look of proud pleasure which swept across her face. She turned and rushed suddenly around the room, closing the curtains, locking the door, taking out her earrings and putting them in a small bowl on the mantelpiece over the gas fire, turning back to him with a smile.

Hey, she said, hooking a finger into the waist of his trousers and pulling him towards her. Can you help me out of this dress now?

Their nakedness felt strange all over again. He felt inadequate, set against her. His body seemed shapeless, awkward, where hers was poised and flowing, delicate, ready to knock him into silence at the first sight of her. It didn't take long for them to grow more comfortable with each other – to insist on the abandonment of towels, sheets, needless underwear; to allow each other the long slow looks they needed to grow used to the bareness of their skin – but that first morning they dressed quickly, turning away from each other, barely speaking. They walked out into the cold-edged sunshine, their steps a little clumsy together, dazed by the rush of the day before, dazed by the rush of the weeks and months since they'd first made their plans. They went to a café for breakfast, walked through the Memorial Park, and, because they couldn't really think what else to do, went back to the flat again. She quickened her pace as they got closer, and broke into a run, taking the steps two at a time and racing him to the front door.

They only lived in the flat for six months; it was a time which would later come to seem unreal, a time which was almost entirely spent preparing for the future. They talked a lot, sitting in the darkened lounge with bottles of wine, or lying together in bed, or walking round and round the park; asking each other questions about their lives before they met, getting to know each other, telling secrets and sharing ambitions and making plans. They asked each other, more than once, if they thought they had done the right thing, and each time they said yes, of course, what else could they have done? It was a cold winter, and they spent a lot of time apart, working or looking for work, or visiting Julia, or looking for a new place to live. The one gas fire didn't work very well, and there was a crack halfway up the bath which meant it could only be filled about six inches deep. They were short of money. They had their first arguments. But it was their home, their first home together, and Eleanor wore the front-door key on a long loop of string around her neck as though it were a talisman, and always raced him home so she could be the one to unlock the door.

Once, he was reading a magazine in the lounge when he heard the bathroom door open. He looked up and saw her walk silently into the kitchen, pour herself a glass of water, drink it, and walk back past him to the bedroom. She didn't look at him. She seemed not to notice he was there. Her skin was flushed red from the hot bathwater, her hair brushed back away from her face and hanging in straight stretched lines to her shoulders, water beading down her back. She was naked, except for the long loop of string with the key dangling from it hanging between her breasts and swinging against her stomach as her wet feet padded across the bare linoleum floor.

25 *Lacework placemats (wedding gift), 1968*

It took him much longer than he'd expected to tell her what Julia had said, and the longer he didn't tell her, the more difficult it became. He didn't tell her when they spent that first night together in Aberdeen, or when he wrote, or when he went to see her again. He didn't tell her while they were talking and deciding if what they were planning to do was the right thing, while he was trying to persuade her that it was. He didn't take the opportunity when they made the long journey south together, her small suitcase on the seat beside them, her home country sliding away past the window. He kept it to himself until they were married, and he kept it to himself the six months they lived in the flat, and finally he spat it out in the middle of an argument they had soon after moving into their new house, when she said he knew nothing about her parents, that he didn't understand what she'd been through as a child, her voice loud and trembling, and he banged his hand against the table and said that at least she knew who her parents were.

She flinched violently at the sound of his hand on the table. She stared at him. What are you talking about? she said. His eyes were shut tightly, and his hand pressed flat against the table, the skin whitening under his fingernails. He didn't say anything.

David, what are you talking about? she said again, putting down her knife and fork, reaching her hand out across the table, leaning towards him.

I don't know El, he said, opening his eyes. It's a bit complicated. She waited. They sat like that for a minute or two, their dinners going cold on their plates, while outside it got dark and the lights started to come on in the houses behind.

David? she said eventually.

He told her what he knew, what Julia had said so casually and mistakenly, how his mother had tried to explain, how he couldn't get it to make sense in his head. His hands were shaking when he'd finished talking, and he looked down at them in his lap, intrigued, as though he wasn't quite sure that they belonged to him. He looked up at her, smiling, embarrassed. Jesus, El, I'm in a bit of a state. I'm sorry, he said.

He wanted her to stand up, to rush round the table and hold on to him. But she didn't. She just sat and looked at him, and when she spoke she sounded confused, frightened. She asked him all the questions he'd been asking; about whether his father and his sister had known, who else knew, how it had managed to be kept secret for so long, what it said on his birth certificate, what he knew about this girl Mary from Ireland, what he was going to do now, how long he'd known about it, how long had he known?

She tilted her head sharply towards him when he told her how long it had been, disbelievingly, as if she hadn't quite heard him right. Why didn't you tell me? she asked, and he looked down into his lap, shaking his head. How did you manage not to tell me? she said.

It's complicated, was all he could say. I don't know. I didn't know where to begin. The words sounded familiar even as he said them; they were the answers his mother had given him to the questions which had haunted their conversations since he'd first found out. How did you manage not to tell me. What were you thinking. How could you bear not to tell me.

They did the washing up together, scraping the uneaten food into the bin, standing in close silence while he stacked the pans and filled the bowl with hot water and she waited with a clean tea towel. She touched his arm. You okay? she said. He nodded, not looking at her. She slid her arms around his waist, pressing her face against his chest for a moment. I don't know what to say, she told him. I don't know how to make it better for you. He put the plates in the bowl.

There's nothing to say really, he said. It can't be changed. I'm just sorry I didn't say anything before.

No, no, it's okay, she said, don't worry, it's okay. She took her arms back from around his waist. I just wish there was something I could do, she said awkwardly. To make it easier, she said.

You could start by drying these, he told her, rinsing the plates and balancing them in the drying rack. She smiled, and didn't say anything else, and they did the rest of the dishes in silence.

Later, years later, she told him she'd been frightened. She told him that she had the sensation of his not being who she thought he was, of his slipping uncertainly away from her. It made me really panic though, she said; it felt like anything might happen. It made me feel a bit lost. It made me wonder if I'd even made a mistake, if I'd have to go back home after all or where I could go. But she didn't say these things at the time. She kept them to herself. She finished the drying up, and put everything away, and sat with him for the rest of the evening watching television, resting her head against his shoulder, slipping her hand inside his shirt and running her fingers backwards and forwards across his skin. You okay? she murmured, after a while, and he nodded.

I just can't stop thinking about it, he said. I don't know what to do about it. She kissed his cheek, and stroked his head, and kissed his cheek again.

It's okay, she said. It'll be okay. He nodded. He didn't seem convinced.

26 *Geologist's rock-hammer, in original case (wedding gift, unused), c.1969*

They had plans when they first got married, when he asked her to come to Coventry, to leave her home and be with him, so many plans. She was going to apply for a place at the new university in Warwick, and study for her geology degree there while he worked at the museum; she could go on and do further study, or get a job with an engineering firm, or a surveying company, or she could find a job abroad somewhere, in mining or drilling or research; there were museums all over the world where he could find work. You'll be able to do anything, he told her, and this was all she'd ever wanted to hear, and she fell in love with him saying those words. He would get a promotion by the time she finished her degree, they decided, maybe two, and he could begin to plan the new museum of his own that he'd always had in mind, and each evening they'd come back and sit together in their own home, telling each other about their days.

She would start by studying at the new university – and maybe once she'd got the degree she would take it home to show her family, to say look this is why I came away, it was worth it, was it not? Don't you think so? – and after that she'd be able to do anything. I'll be the first ever Campbell with a degree, she told him excitedly, more than once; won't that be something? She could even find a job, later maybe, with one of the oil companies that had begun to move into Aberdeen, they could live up there for a time, and things would be okay with her family again, once she'd proved herself like that, proved that all that schooling was worth it after all, and even her mother would have to say well now, Eleanor, perhaps I was wrong. Won't that be something? Eleanor said, laughing at the thought of it, standing in their kitchen with a tea towel clenched in her fist as she did an impression of her mother trying to say sorry – her face pinched and sour, her eyes lowered, the laughter cracking out of her again as she mimicked her mother's muttering voice. Won't that be something David? she said again, clapping her hands.

But it was too late to apply when she first got to Coventry. She went to talk to someone about it, about applying for the following year, and they said there was an issue with the funding, that she'd have to contact her local authority, that special rules applied for Scottish students. David didn't understand her explanation when she got back, and when he phoned them about it they weren't at all helpful. She tried to apply, but she did something wrong and the funding was refused. She went to the admissions office again, insisting that there must be a way for her to do the course, and they said there was, but unfortunately she'd have to wait until the following year.

His mother arranged a job for her, assembling component boards at the GEC factory, and after her upset about university she was glad to have something to get her teeth into. It'll be interesting to do something different for a while, she said. It'll make a change from studying books or breaking rocks or pouring teas. The new plan then was that she would work there until she could start the degree course the following year and they could save some money from her wages for books and materials. And for formal evening wear and bedlinen, he said, smiling, and she smiled back, shaking her head, tutting fondly. It'll be a good way of meeting people, his mother said; you'll want to make plenty of new friends if you're planning on settling here. But she didn't make any friends. She said it was too noisy to talk to people, or it was too busy, or that people just weren't all that friendly. She said she couldn't get the hang of the work, it was too fiddly, they wanted her to work too fast, the woman in charge of the line kept shouting at her when she got things wrong. He came home in the evenings sometimes to find her face red with furious tears, telling him she couldn't do it, she wasn't cut out for it, she didn't want to do it any more. She started not getting up in the mornings, saying she was ill, and when they sent a letter saying her services would no longer be required she said she was glad. She said she just wanted to stay at home for the time being. She could get back to doing some studying, she said; she didn't want to lose touch. Maybe she could make herself useful doing some decorating, she said, because that flowered wallpaper in the back room was really getting too much and wouldn't it be nice to have their home just as they wanted it? Just the way they'd planned it, wouldn't that be nice?

Susan found her a job, not long afterwards, working in the canteen at the council offices, and although she said it was strange to be pouring teas again she seemed to get on well with the other people working there. It'll do for now, she said, when he asked how her first week had gone; at least until I get things sorted out with the university. They went out a few evenings each week – to the cinema, to a restaurant, for a drink after work – and they started to tackle the decorating in the rooms upstairs. They went to his mother's for Sunday lunch now and again, or had her round to theirs. He took her to visit Julia, and even though Julia was too ill to say very much, Eleanor said how glad she was to have gone. They spent long evenings talking, watching television, pulling off each other's clothes as they scrambled up the stairs. They had people round for dinner, and talked about work, politics, sport, the weather, the news. Things weren't quite as they'd expected, not yet, but they had all the time in the world for things to fall into place.

27 *Model fishing boat, handmade c.1905*

Her father gave her the boat when she was no more than four or five years old. She could remember running from the kitchen to the front room one cold autumn evening, she said, the backs of her legs bright red and stinging, bruises rising blotchily beneath the skin on her arms, and her da looking down at her from his chair.

I can't remember what I'd done wrong, she said. Probably I didn't even know at the time; probably it was nothing more than my ma being in a short temper.

She stood and looked at her father, her small grubby fingers wiping her cheeks, wanting to turn around but not wanting to go back. She could hear her sister listening to music upstairs, and she could hear her mother turning the squeaking handle on the mangle in the kitchen, muttering and sighing as she crammed the wet clothes into it and choked out the water. She locked her arms around his leg and pressed her face against his hand.

That's my girl, he said, picking her up and setting her on his lap. You okay now? he asked. She thought for a moment, and nodded fiercely. Good girl, he said, smoothing down her short fair hair with his hand. Her mother had cut it again, roughly, and the sides were uneven and coarse, her fringe a slanted line across her forehead. The sun's got your hair again, hasn't it girl? he said, tracing the lines of blonde brought out of the mousey-brown by the sun. That'll be the Viking coming out of you, he said, smiling.

She'd liked the feel of his touch, she told David, the rough loose skin on his hand, the warmth of it. She'd liked it when he pinched her cheek and when he wiped her tears away with a stroke of his broad flat thumb.

Now then, he said. There's no need for all that crying, is there? Eleanor shook her head, shamefully. Would you like to see something special then, something your da's been saving for you? he said. She looked at him, not daring to nod, and he pulled a shabby cardboard box from the cupboard beside him, opening it up and peeling back the layers of crinkled yellow newspaper inside, lifting out the small model fishing boat and cradling it in his hands, feeling the scrapes and scratches which still pockmarked the hull, feeling like it could have been yesterday he was sailing this boat across the soap-sudded scullery floor while his mother scrubbed pans and sang high above him, remembering launching it off the edge of the worn back step, flipping it upside down and sending men and fish and ropes and sandwiches down into the endless ocean. He held the boat out towards her, straightening the unsteady mast and wiping it down with his handkerchief. It's an old fishing boat petal, he said. Your Granda used to go to sea on one like this. Look, see, there's the net for all the fishes, eh? He unfurled a knotted string net from the stern and draped it out across his thigh, sailing the boat across imaginary waves to his daughter, the net trailing across his oil-stained trousers, the blunt-pointed bow bucking and yawing into her outstretched hands. Do you think you can look after that for me then Eleanor? he asked. Will you keep it safe now? She looked up at him, holding the old wooden boat protectively against her chest, her eyes wide and clear, nodding solemnly. They heard the back door open, and her mother letting out a loud and weary sigh. Go on and play with that now, he whispered, gently pushing her forwards, and she slipped away to her room to sail the boat across the grey waters of a fraying rug, to cast weatherbeaten men into the hold and tip them back out into the sea.

Later, she heard her mother come up the stairs and, with a quick-thinking wisdom beyond her years, she sheltered the boat beneath the harbour of her over-hanging bedsheets before the door had even swung open. And there'll be no supper for you either my girl, so get yourself away into bed now, her mother said calmly. Eleanor undressed and got into bed without saying a word, and her mother closed the bedroom door. It was five o'clock, and she was already hungry. She closed her eyes against the daylight still flooding into the room. She listened to her father's voice, rumbling below the floorboards, and to her mother's brief muttering response. She stretched a hand out under the bed, finding and running her fingers over the gnarled and knotted wood of the model boat as she waited for sleep to come.

Sometimes, if he woke in the middle of the night and found himself alone in their bed, he would go downstairs and find Eleanor sitting on the sofa there, wide-eyed and unable to sleep, holding the model boat in her lap once more and stroking the grain of the wood. Go back to bed, she'd say, not looking at him, I'm fine. I can't sleep, that's all; it's nothing, I just can't sleep. He'd sit next to her, fetch her a glass of water, ask her if she wanted to talk, smooth her hair away from her face. You've got to work in the morning, she'd say. I'm fine, go back to bed. He'd ask her to come back to bed with him, to talk if she needed to talk, to lie down and close her eyes and come back to bed with him.

I'm fine, she'd say, leave me be. Go back to bed yourself.

28 *Page torn from* Aberdeen Press & Journal, *crumpled, August 1968*

Sometimes, if she was prompted, Eleanor would tell other people besides David about her life before she came to Coventry; Susan perhaps, or Susan's husband John, or one of David's colleagues from work, if the wine had been around the table a few times and she felt for once that no harm could come from it. You never tell us about Aberdeen, Susan would say, somewhere in the lull between main course and pudding; what's it like?

Aberdeen? she'd say. There's not all that much to tell. It was a bit colder than it is down here, there were fewer jobs about – what did you want to know?

Well, Susan would persist, I don't know. I mean, what did your parents do, and your brothers and sisters, what was your house like, that kind of thing.

And Eleanor would tell them about the small house in which all eight of them had lived, making a joke out of the bed-sharing and the outside toilet, the tin bath hanging on the wall, the belting for getting soot on the laundry that hung around the fireplace, making it all sound distant and unreal. She told them about her father's job in the shipyard, and her brothers leaving the house one by one to work in the merchant navy, the shipyard, the railways, the joiner's shop at the far end of town; and she told them about her own first job at the museum tea rooms. We didn't have much for entertainment, she told them once, mainly I had my head stuck in a book and just about the only place I could find quiet enough for reading was in the lav so long as it was warm enough. That got me in trouble as well, she said, laughing, filling her glass again, bawling out an imitation of one of her brothers – Mam! Ellie's been in there for hours, will ye tell her? – and lowering her head for a moment as she ran out of steam.

People laughed when Eleanor told these stories. Not at the stories themselves, but at the delight she took in turning these things into bleak caricatures, at the unexpected contrast with her usually quiet and self-contained self. Sometimes, David thought, people laughed more from an awkward embarrassment – especially when she joked about being sent to bed without supper for cursing, or being smacked in the teeth for losing a schoolbook – than because they were amused. She'd usually had too much to drink when she said these things, and by the time everyone had gone home she would tip over into regret. Did I say too much David? she would ask, as he helped her up the stairs. Did I embarrass myself any? Did I say too much?

Was that true? he asked her, once. What you said last night? He was standing halfway up a stepladder as he said this, a paintbrush balanced wetly on the lip of a tin. They were decorating their back room, finally, the furniture stacked under a sheet in the middle of the room, wallpaper shreds scattered across the floor. Eleanor was rubbing down the wall on the other side of the room, her hair tied back from her face with an elastic band and the sleeves of an old work-shirt rolled up to the elbow.

Hmm? she said, above the rough shush of the sandpaper. Was what true?

You know, he said, about being smacked, in the teeth you said. The words felt odd even as he said them.

Oh, that, she said, aye, of course. She seemed distracted, surprised that he'd even had to ask.

I mean, literally in the mouth? he said. She laughed a little, picking at a stray scrap of wallpaper still stuck to the bare grey plaster.

Yes David, she said. Right in the mouth. Why?

Well, he said. It just seems a bit much, that's all. She didn't say anything, and he lifted the brush to press another wet slick of pale yellow paint against the wall. They both worked in silence for a few minutes, Eleanor taking a damp cloth to wipe the dust from the wall, David dipping the brush in and out of the pot.

It didn't just happen once then? he said. She looked at him blankly.

What? she asked.

Being hit like that, he said, and again she seemed surprised that he was asking.

Well no, she said, I suppose not. It didn't happen all the time, and I suppose getting hit in the mouth was unusual. But I can't really remember. Why?

David climbed down, moved the ladder further along the wall, and climbed up again. Because it bothers me Eleanor, he said. It's not normal, it's not right. Why didn't you ever tell someone about it? She laughed tightly, as if she thought he was being naive, and she took the cloth into the kitchen to rinse it out.

Oh, come on, she said. Tell who? She came back into the room and began wiping along the top of the skirting board. Anyway, she said, changing the subject, what did you think about John last night?

John? he said. Oh, right. He seemed okay I thought. I mean, Susan seems very happy with him, doesn't she?

Aye but he doesn't say much, does he? she said. He barely said a word all evening.

David laughed.

That's because he couldn't get a word in edgeways, he said, the way you were going all night. He laughed again, and Eleanor was silent. He finished painting what he could reach from the ladder, and climbed down, and it was only when he turned round and saw how flushed her face was that he realised how much he'd upset her.

Oh El, he said. I didn't mean it. He moved towards her and she pulled away very slightly. I was only joking, he said.

I ruined the evening, didn't I? she said, whispering, staring straight ahead.

Of course not, he said. Don't be silly.

I did, she said. I ruined the evening. She put her hands over her face, as if she was ashamed even to be looked at. He sighed and put the pot and the brush down on to a sheet of newspaper.

Eleanor, he said, I was only joking. Everyone had a lovely evening. He took hold of her wrists and gently lifted her hands away from her face.

Really? she said.

Really, he said, licking his thumb and wiping a smear of plaster dust from her forehead; I promise. She wrinkled her nose and looked up at him, and the flush of embarrassment ebbed out of her face. She smiled.

I'm sorry, she said. It just worries me, what people think, especially your family and everyone. He kissed her forehead, then her nose.

They all think the world of you, he said. And so do I. He let go of her wrists, kissed her lips, and started to unbutton the worn-out shirt she was wearing, uncovering her small neat breasts. So do I, he murmured again, stooping to kiss each dark nipple, unbuttoning the rest of her shirt, slipping his hands behind her back. Eleanor stepped away, covering herself and fiddling with the buttons.

David, she said, quietly. Not now. I'm not— she said, and stopped. We've hardly started in here, she said. Give me a brush. David passed her another brush, wiping his mouth with the back of his hand, surprised and a little embarrassed at himself. He moved the ladder, and went back to the painting without saying anything more.

Later, sharing a bag of chips while they waited for the first coat to dry, she said, I'm sorry about before. I just wasn't feeling like it; I was a bit preoccupied.

It's fine, he said, pretending to have forgotten. Don't worry about it.

And the next day, when all the painting was done, the brushes washed and the spattered newspaper thrown away, the furniture shifted back into place and the pictures rehung on the wall, when they were looking around the room and each wondering if they'd ever really like the colour, she turned to him and said well, I think we're all done here now, aren't we? She swept the loose strands of hair away from her face and unbuttoned her shirt. He noticed that she still had yellow paint under her fingernails, and across one of her knuckles, and he noticed that she was shrugging her shirt to the floor.

Afterwards, lying across their bed together, he said now tell me something. She turned her face towards him, questioningly. Tell me what it was like, at home, when you were growing up. I want to know more, he said.

So she told him about watching her mother clean the kitchen floor when she was a child barely old enough to speak; hiding under the table, watching soap bubbles balloon and burst into the cold sunlight as her mother's wooden-soled shoes slid like skates across the wet flagstoned floor. The hot soapy water slopping towards her, and her mother hoisting the chairs from the floor and slamming them up on to the table as she caught glaring sight of her daughter.

She told him about her mother not talking to her for days at a time, not talking to anyone, stopping in bed with a mystery illness that nobody ever discussed.

She told him about having to make her brothers' beds each

morning, slipping out of her own to straighten the mess left from the morning's rush into work, gathering the tight-rolled balls of yesterday's socks and heaping them into the wash-bag, untangling the sheets and blankets from their heap at the bottom of the bed.

She told him about her mother cutting her hair, insisting on keeping it short so that it wouldn't be any trouble, never taking any time over it so that she always came out looking hacked and shorn and the other children would tease her. I didn't dare say anything though, or ask to get it done in a shop, she said, Mam would have walloped me. It was only when she was older, fourteen, fifteen, that she resisted and persuaded her mother to let her be, and her hair began to grow long and straight and fine. I couldn't keep my hands off it for a long time, she said, smiling, playing with it even as she spoke; it seemed like such a new part of me.

She told him that once, when it had reached down to her shoulders, her brother's wife Rosalind had brushed it for her, telling her how she could keep it nice, showing her different ways of wearing it, running the brush and her fingers through it over and over again. It was the first time anyone had touched me like that, she said.

29 *Set of clothes pegs, traditional style, w/hand-drawn faces, c.1920s–1950s*

When Eleanor was seven years old her sister Tessa told her something awful, whispering it in her ear while they sat in their bedroom one long Sunday afternoon. Tessa was already laughing to herself when I ran downstairs to find Mam, Eleanor told David, but I didn't know if that meant it was true or it wasn't true. She found her mother in the kitchen, sitting on a chair with her hands pressed against her lower back, arching her spine, a pile of freshly wrung sheets leaking murky water into a tub in front of her. Outside, more sheets were hanging on the line, swinging and snapping in the hard wind blowing up from the sea.

Oh you've come to help, have you? Ivy said, and Eleanor looked at her blankly. Because there'll be no food on the table while these sheets are waiting to be hung. Eleanor nodded and followed her mother as she hauled the washtub out into the backyard. She fetched the basket from the scullery and took the end of the first unpegged sheet from her mother, bringing the corners together and pulling them tight, bringing the corners together again, passing the ends back to her mother and fetching the hanging end up to meet the top until there was a neatly folded square in the basket. She knew exactly what to do. She'd had plenty of practice. They folded two more in this way, and then Eleanor said Mam is it true that when you have a baby all your stomach comes out and they have to stick it back in again? Ivy looked up.

Eh, no, she said, not quite. Feels like it mind, she said, unpegging another sheet. Eleanor looked at her, eyes wide.

Does it? she said. She was quiet for a moment while they folded the next sheet, thinking. But is there any actual blood? she said, and her voice was quiet and disbelieving.

Oh aye, said Ivy, there's blood all right. She passed Eleanor the end of another sheet. When I had you, she said, looking at her daughter carefully, the whole bed was covered in blood, and every towel in the house wasn't enough to mop it up off me. Her daughter stared back at her, bringing corner to corner and fetching up the hanging end, the colour fading from her face.

Did it hurt? she whispered, and her mother laughed, a single hard snort of unamused laughter. Or she laughed long and hard, sarcastic but also genuinely entertained by her daughter's innocence. Or she didn't laugh at all, but stared and thought there's a lot I've got to teach you yet my girl.

Did it hurt? she replied. Oh, aye. Felt like my whole body was ripping in two. Felt like my bones were cracking every time I pushed. Wasn't as young as I used to be, my body was too old to be coping with that kind of nonsense. I shouldn't really have been having a baby at all at that age. Midwife said I was lucky, said she thought she was going to lose us both with all the blood that was pouring out of me.

Ivy watched the effect her words were having on her daughter. She wanted her to know how it was, to understand and be grateful. Or she deliberately wanted to frighten her, to find revenge for what had happened. Eleanor stared at her.

But your stomach didn't come out at all? she asked eventually, confused. Her mother shook her head.

No girl, she said, smiling thinly. May have felt like it, but no, my stomach didn't come out at all. Who's been telling you that? she asked, and Eleanor's eyes immediately dropped away.

No one, she muttered.

Aye, well, of course, no one, said Ivy, hoisting the first wet sheet into the blustery air and pegging it to the line, glancing up at the house. Drops of water fell from the sheet on to the cobbled ground, spattering up around Eleanor's ankles, winding their way between the stones to the gutter running along the backs of the yards. The wind began to blow stronger as they hung out the rest, Eleanor passing the ends up to her mother and holding out the pegs, and as they went back into the house one of the sheets was lifted and flapped suddenly into shape by a sharp gust, the sound like a whipcrack echoing off the dark stone walls.

A letter came from the university in the summer, and where Eleanor thought that it would confirm her successful deferred application and forthcoming start date, it said instead that the course had been withdrawn due to lack of interest. She opened it while they were having breakfast, and slammed it down on to the table so hard that her wedding ring left a dented crack in the formica. David watched her, a slice of toast halfway to his mouth, reaching across the table to read the letter for himself. No, no, no, she said, her voice brisk and determined, no. That's not fair, it's not good enough. She stood up, and her voice rose with her, building to a rarely heard shout. They already accepted my application David. They said it would be okay! They can't do this! He stood, and held her, and her voice fell away again. Can they? she said.

She telephoned the admissions office, and they said they were very sorry but they'd had no alternative. They hoped to be able to run the course the following year, they said, and she slammed down the phone with a yell of frustration. He tried to persuade her to try another university – Birmingham, or Leicester, or one of the new polytechnics – but somewhere among all that shouting she seemed to have lost her nerve. Maybe it's not a good idea, she said. Maybe it's not what I'm cut out for. He sent off for the prospectuses, but she just smiled and said thank you and put them away. Maybe next year, she said softly. I'll try again next year, eh?

30 *Girl's hairbrush, wooden-handled, c.1940s*

And then she told him about Tessa leaving home. It happened quickly, she said. One day she was there and the next she was gone. I woke up in the middle of the night and I heard people talking downstairs, shouting, Tessa and my ma and da, in the front room and the hall and the kitchen, doors slamming and all sorts. I heard Tessa coming up the stairs, stamping, and then it sounded like she fell.

She was eight years old when it happened, ten years younger than her sister, lying in bed with the covers pulled up over her face, trying not to listen to what was going on. But she could hear her mother asking where were you? Where've you been? over and over again, and Tessa yelling nowhere, nowhere, what do you mind? in return. She could hear her father, his voice low and insistent, and she could picture him standing between the two of them, holding them apart, trying to lower Ivy's raised hands.

She knew that there'd been talk. Talk of a man Tessa had been seen with, and how much she'd been seen with him. She didn't know what it meant to be seen with someone, but she knew that her parents didn't like it. Folk have been talking, her mother had said a few weeks earlier; I'll not have folk talking about any family of mine, you hear me?

Eleanor lay in bed, wondering what people had been saying, wondering when the shouting was going to stop. She heard her mother say aye, well I know very well where you've been young miss, do you think I'm soft in the head or something? She heard her sister's voice saying something she couldn't quite catch, a slap, and a sudden clatter of footsteps up the stairs. She lifted the covers, peering out from beneath them, holding her breath, and dropped them again as soon as the door swung open and the light burst on. And in that short bright instant before she dropped the covers she saw her sister for the last time, looking straight at her. Something had happened to her face. The skin around her eyes was coloured a pale powdery blue, her lips a swollen cherry red. Eleanor listened to her sister's heavy breathing as she stood in the doorway, and the slow pound of her mother's footsteps following up the stairs.

A few nights earlier, she'd heard another argument, in the hallway and on the street, waking up just in time to hear her father use a voice she'd never heard before nor would ever hear again, a voice which had seemed to come blazing from somewhere deep in the hold of his belly. Aye, you go on, he'd yelled. Away you go now son, away you go! And see if I ever catch sight of your face again I will batter it for you, you hear me?

She heard her mother get to the top of the stairs, and her father coming up behind, and she heard everything happening at once, everyone talking over each other and stumbling into the furniture, the sound of smacks and slaps and yelps and whispers. She closed her eyes tightly and lay perfectly still, hoping that if they thought she was asleep they would none of them talk to her, or say it was her fault, or ask her questions about it in the morning.

She heard her father saying now Ivy, let's just calm down a little.

She heard her mother saying no Stewart, no. She's gone too far now.

She heard her father saying Ivy, Ivy.

She heard her mother saying quietly and calmly, that Tessa was to pack her things and leave, that she was no longer a daughter of the family and would never again be welcome in the house. She heard a soft sniffling, and the sound of drawers being opened and closed, and footsteps up and down the stairs, and people moving around and talking in the kitchen.

And when she next opened her eyes it was morning, and the room was still and quiet and bare. The sheets had been stripped from her sister's bed, and the suitcase from the top of the wardrobe was gone. Her mother came in while she was getting dressed, and without saying anything or even looking at her, she cleared the rest of Tessa's things into a black bag and put it outside by the bins.

I barely heard her name mentioned again, she told David. And if I did it was my ma saying something like, aye she'll not be coming back here again, or, she'll see what she gets if she shows her face around here. Things like that, she said, you know.

David looked at her, astonished. No, he said, I don't know. I don't know at all.

31 *Nurse's fob watch, engraved RCN, 1941*

When he went to visit, Auntie Julia would usually be sitting by the window, turned towards the garden, her face as blank and unconcerned as if she were gazing out to sea. Sometimes he would stand in the doorway and wait for her to notice him, wondering how long she could stay so still. Sometimes the cold afternoon light would make her skin look waxed and unreal, and he would wonder if she was there at all until he saw some slight movement in her face, the rise and fall of her breathing, a flicker in her eyes.

Julia, he would say eventually.

Julia. Softly, not wanting to frighten her.

Well, come in if you're coming in, she would reply, sharply, instinctively learning to cover up for herself. No use standing there all day, my dear.

Now she didn't even say this; he had to come into the room and lay his hands on her shoulders, crouching beside her and saying her name over and over again as if calling her back from a deep sleep.

Hello Julia, he said, when she finally turned her face and met his eye. It's good to see you again, he said. How are you doing? She didn't say anything. Are you warm enough? he asked. It's cold out, are you warm enough in here? She looked at him. She seemed to be thinking about it.

What's that dear? she said.

Are you warm enough? he said again, raising his voice a little.

You're not Laurence, are you? she said. They said Laurence was coming. Is he coming?

I don't know, he told her; he should be, he will be soon I'm sure.

When? she said, leaning her ear towards him, as if he'd told her and she hadn't quite heard.

Soon, he said. Soon, I'm sure.

But when? she insisted. They said he was coming. They said he'd be here soon, she said.

Tomorrow, he told her, regretting it as soon as he'd spoken. Laurence is coming tomorrow.

Oh good, she said, I am glad. Tomorrow, she repeated, reminding herself.

But you're not Laurence, are you? she said, a few moments later.

No, he said. No, I'm not Laurence. I'm David, he said, raising his voice, slowing his words, David. I used to call you Auntie Julia, remember, Auntie Julia? She looked at him indignantly.

But I'm not your aunt, she said.

No, he said, no, you're not. It was just something we used to call you. Me and Susan.

Yes, she said, relaxing, that's right, Susan. She smiled suddenly.

She asked him for a cigarette. He found the packet in her bedside drawer and helped her to light one. She turned her face to the window, closing her eyes with each long and slow inhalation. He waited. She seemed to have fallen asleep. Her cigarette was smouldering in the ashtray, half-smoked, the filter smeared with lipstick, smoke spiralling into the air. He reached across to stub it out, and emptied the ashtray into the bin.

Julia, he said. She turned towards him. Julia, I'm thinking of going to Ireland, he said.

She looked at him.

What's that? she said. Ireland, he repeated. I want to see if there's anything I can find out, he said. She smiled.

That sounds nice, she said. What time will you be back?

He closed his eyes, drawing his finger and thumb along his eyebrows, pinching the tip of his nose. He couldn't help smiling a little.

I don't know what time I'll be back Julia, he said; it's a long way to go, I might stay the night. I might stay a few nights, he added.

He looked out of the window. A gardener was raking up fallen leaves, working his way around the five trees in the enclosed garden, leaving a trail of molehill heaps behind him. It had been a dry autumn, and the leaves were small, curled up at the edges. The man looked old, and was working very slowly, his breath condensing around his face as the last warmth ebbed out of the day.

Angela wanted me to come over to dinner, she said. I told her it would have to wait until next week because you were coming to stay. She smiled broadly, a brief laugh breaking out of her as she turned towards him. Her smile slipped as she caught his eye. She squinted at him, and smiled again. Hello dear, she said.

I thought I might go to Donegal, he said, leaning towards her. She was watching the gardener retrace his steps, stooping down to gather up the armfuls of leaves and put them in a wheelbarrow. I thought I might go to Donegal, he said again, when I go to Ireland, I've heard it's nice there. Do you know Donegal at all? He shuffled his seat a little closer towards hers. Do you know of any good places to visit? he said. She kept her face turned to the window. The tone of her skin was softening as the light faded, and her eyes were half closed. She didn't say anything. She seemed to be just listening to the sound of his voice.

Eleanor doesn't think I should go, he said, persisting. She says I haven't got any idea where to start, she says I'll just upset myself. She says it's too late now, after all this time, he said. Julia smiled, and nodded, and opened her mouth to say something, and closed it again.

The gardener scooped up the last little pile of leaves and

pushed the wheelbarrow towards the archway at the far end of the garden. It was almost dark, and lights were beginning to come on in some of the other rooms. He could see the other residents sitting by their windows, gazing out at the bare-boned trees, their faces as blank as Julia's.

I'd like to be able to tell her I'm okay, he said, that's all.

Julia held her hands together in her lap, perfectly still. He noticed that the gardener had forgotten to take his rake, leaving it leaning against the branches of one of the trees.

Did she never try and get back in touch? he said. Didn't she write, just to ask? He spoke softly, as if being careful not to wake her. It's difficult, he said, not even a surname. To know where to start, he said.

She reached out towards the ashtray, looking for the cigarette, and caught his eye. For a moment he thought she looked frightened. She seemed to flinch away from him.

Have you seen my cigarettes? she said irritably. What have you done with my cigarettes? He took the packet from her bedside drawer and helped her to light another one. She smoked it quickly and unsteadily, spilling flakes of ash on to her cardigan.

They're digging up the road again, she said. I told them. Josephine wanted to come and stay and I said you'd be more than welcome but it's not the best time. I was terribly surprised but there wasn't all that much I could do. That man, what was his name, he told me, what did he say, that man?

He listened to her talking, watching the small movements of her hands, shrunken versions of the expansive gestures she used to make when she spoke, her fingers twirling tiny circles in the air as she tried and failed to pull her thoughts together. She faltered back into silence, her cigarette burning down to the filter in her hand. He reached out and took it from her, squashing it into the ashtray, and sat looking at her in the near darkness. He noticed, in the garden, the man coming back for his rake.

32 *University prospectuses; 1969, 1970, 1971, 1972, 1973, 1974*

Someone came to the door this afternoon but I don't know who it was, Eleanor said. They rang and rang and I didn't want to answer it. I didn't know who it might have been or why they wouldn't go away.

Her eyes faint and distant, refusing to meet his.

I meant to go to the shops, she said; there's some things we need; I'm sorry but I couldn't face going outside just now.

Her once-clear voice cracked and whispering.

I don't feel too good, that's the thing, she said. I don't feel too good at all.

It wasn't what they'd imagined, this life. It wasn't what they'd planned. She'd been going to study geology, get her degree, get a job, maybe go back to Aberdeen and show them all what she'd achieved, show them why she'd come away and hear them say, well, it was worth it after all. The stalled applications, the funding problems, the withdrawing of the course – these weren't part of the plan. The unhappy and unfulfilling jobs which she couldn't stick at weren't part of the plan. Her increasing reluctance to leave the house unless she was with David wasn't part of the plan. She was going to get her degree, the money from his job would help her through university, she could get any job she wanted when she left, they could go anywhere, she could do anything. Sleepless nights and uneaten dinners weren't part of the plan.

People started to tell him she wasn't well. I'm sorry David, but I'm worried about her, they would say. I don't mean to intrude but. They would say these things quickly, quietly, on the telephone, or while Eleanor was waiting outside in the car and he was struggling into his coat, or once she'd made her excuses and wandered upstairs to bed.

I don't want to interfere but I'm worried you can't quite see it, they would say; she's not well. Putting the emphasis on the word *well*, as though it was some kind of euphemism.

She needs help, they would say, with the word *help* said in the same way.

But it came and went, whatever it was, and each time it went he convinced himself that this time it had gone for good, that it had just been a difficult time of adjustment she'd been going through; that being in a new town would of course be bewildering as well as exciting; that of course she couldn't make new friends straight away. It's okay, he told people, when they said these things – Susan, or his mother, his friend Danny, Anna at work – she'll be okay. She's just feeling a bit down. She's tired. She'll be fine again in a while. It was only when she lost her job at the chemist's shop that he realised something was more seriously wrong; when they telephoned him at work and told him they were sorry but his wife didn't seem to be feeling well and would he be able to come and take her home?

She'd only started the job a week earlier. She'd mentioned it to him when he got home from work, casually, turning away to put the kettle on and saying so they gave me that job, as if she was embarrassed about it, as if it was nothing, really. But when he took hold of her waist and swung her round, when he said El that's fantastic, that's great, she couldn't help smiling and dipping her head in excitement, saying aye I know I know, taking his hands and jumping up and down. It wasn't the job itself she was excited about, she admitted to him later, but the fact that she'd found it and claimed it for herself. I feel like a real grown-up now she'd said, showing him the smart white coat they'd given her to wear, telling him how the interview had gone, telling him proudly what her duties would entail and saying that when she was on a morning shift they could walk into work together, couldn't they?

The chemist's was one of a row of temporary shops which had been hurriedly put up on Broadgate after the war. A large area of land behind the neat arched frontages was still derelict, weeds and shrubs growing up from the bomb-cratered ground. You must take your wife to see the doctor, the manager of the shop told him when he went to take her home. There are things they can do. She's waiting outside, he added, at the back. We didn't know what to do, he said.

Eleanor was crouching on the rough ground a few yards from the back door, smoking. She was staring at the back of the library buildings opposite, her face set into a hard blank mask. Her skin was pale, and each time she lifted the cigarette to her mouth her arm shook weakly. Eleanor, he said. She didn't react. Eleanor, he said again.

Do you want to go home now Eleanor? he said. He put his hand on her knee, gently, and she started but she didn't pull away. She let the cigarette fall to the ground from her fingers, the smoke scattering across the dirt in the light afternoon breeze. They heard a bus revving up on the corner, someone shouting. Her eyes were red and sore, as if she'd been rubbing them.

Come on then, he said, let's go home now.

I can't go home, she said urgently, her voice no more than a whisper. He crouched beside her, lifting his hand to her shoulder, moving her hair away from her face with one finger. She stiffened beneath his touch, but she didn't move away.

Come on, he said. We'll go back now, okay? I'll run you a hot bath and make you some dinner. We'll see if we can work this out, eh? And I won't burn the dinner this time, he said, smiling, I promise. She tried to smile in reply but managed only a sort of pale grimace, wiping quickly at the tears spilling from her eyes.

I can't go yet, she said. I'm not off until six. I have to go back into the shop. Her voice was strained and taut.

No you don't, he told her, it's okay, you can come home early today. Mr Jenkins said it would be alright. He stood up and held out his hand to help her. She looked straight past him, out across the craters and ditches and weeds, looking past the ruins of the old cathedral to the sheer glass soar of the new, its scaffold spire breaking into the sky. He leant down, putting his hands under her arms, and lifted her gently to her feet. Her body was soft and limp, unresisting, like a sleepy child's. Come on then, he said, let's go home now.

I can't go home, she said again, almost too quietly for him to hear. He walked with her through the shop, nodding to Mr Jenkins as they passed. When they got back to the house he helped her to undress and get into bed, and sat there for a time while he waited for her to fall asleep. She stared at the wall, wide-eyed, flinching when he tried to stroke her hair or her shoulders, eventually asking him in a small quiet voice to please just leave her on her own now thank you.

Maybe he wouldn't tell them this part of the story, when it came to it. It wasn't what they'd planned. It wasn't supposed to be a part of the way things were. He could say we had our ups and downs, you know. He could say, it was difficult for a while but then it was fine.

33 *Pill bottles, prescriptions; dated variously 1973–1987*

There were some things which should have been kept hidden from view. Pill bottles. Prescriptions. Days spent in downcast silence, days spent refusing to leave the house. These were things which shouldn't have been discussed. But it was difficult to lie, always, when someone said and how's your wife, what's her name again, Eleanor? Haven't seen her for a while, is she okay? It was difficult to always shrug and say oh, she's fine, you know, not working at the moment but she's fine.

He was having lunch with a colleague at work when he found himself saying she's not so good actually Anna, she's not very well at all. He hadn't expected to say it, and he regretted it almost as soon as he had. Anna put the remains of her sandwich down and looked up at him, leaning a little closer.

Oh, she said, lowering her voice, what's wrong? He was embarrassed, immediately, and he wished he hadn't said anything.

No, he said, no, it's nothing really, I mean, it's nothing serious. She's just been feeling a bit under the weather lately, you know. She pushed her plate to one side and wiped her mouth with a paper napkin.

David, she said, reaching across the table and touching his arm, it's more than that, isn't it?

No, he said, really, thanks. I shouldn't have said anything, sorry. He moved his arm away. She stood up.

Oh, she said, okay. Well, if there is anything. I mean, if you need to talk about something. He nodded, looking down at the table, looking at her crumpled napkin smeared with lipstick and food.

Thanks, he said. I will.

It's hard to explain, Eleanor insisted, when he asked. She said, you know if you're on the phone and something distracts you, like someone outside the phone box or something on the TV and suddenly you can't concentrate? I mean you're listening but you just you can't quite hear what they're saying on the other end of the line. I mean, you can hear the words but you can't put them in order, you can't make them make sense, you know? It's like that. It's like there's always something distracting me but I don't know what it is, she said. It's like I just feel distant from everything and I don't know how to get back.

He tried so many things to make her better. He tried taking her for walks, day trips, dinners out. He bought her flowers, presents, bottles of wine. None of it did any good, but he couldn't help trying.

She said it's not you, it's me. She said, I'm sorry there's nothing you can do. She pushed him away. She wrapped her arms around her legs and buried her face in her lap.

What do you want me to do? he asked.

Nothing, she said, her voice muffled against her skin and her hair. I want left alone, please; there's not anything you can do.

She said, I don't know what it is David. But don't worry, I'll be fine. Smiling as she said it, looking up at him, the ends of her cardigan sleeves unpicked and frayed, a wet tissue clenched in her fist.

These were things which shouldn't have been discussed, no matter how often someone said, are you sure? or, is everything really okay? or, you shouldn't keep these things bottled up you know. But he sat with Anna on the bus and he told her about it.

She seems to change so completely when she's like that, he said; I hardly recognise her. She's always been so fearless and now she's terrified of even leaving the house. Speaking quietly, so that no one else would hear. So that Anna had to lean closer to listen to what he was saying. I want to fix things for her but it just seems to upset her when I try, he said. It feels like it's my fault but I don't know what I've done.

Anna had a way of looking at him while he said these things, then, and later, her head tilting slightly to one side, her eyes widening, her front teeth biting sympathetically into her bottom lip. It was a way of looking which made him feel better about the things he was saying, even as it made him feel guilty for saying them to her.

I'm sure it's not you, she said.

The pill bottles were bigger than any he'd seen as a child; translucent brown, as big as a fist, three months' supply at once to save the trouble of too many trips to the surgery. The pills were small and colourless, stamped with illegible codes and offering no clue as to what was inside them or what function they might perform.

The prescriptions were always identical: a date, Eleanor's name and the name of the drug, the doctor's signature, all written in the same frenzied scrawl which suggested the sheet had been torn from the pad even as the prescription was being written. Which perhaps it had, the words inscribed as she went in through the consulting-room door, the doctor standing and saying hello Mrs Carter and what can we do for you today, nodding and mmm-hmming as he handed over the illegible paper, saying perhaps you should try and get more sleep, more exercise, find a new hobby, saying he'd see her again in three months' time.

Each day she came down for breakfast the first thing she would do was reach for the pills, shaking one out into the palm of her hand, a blank puzzled look in her eyes, while he stood at the sink and poured her a glass of water. She would swallow it with a hard gulp and a wince and only then think about starting the day, eating something perhaps, having a hot drink, even getting dressed, as the colourless pills sank down inside her, turning over, breaking open, spilling their powdery cargo into her stunned bloodstream. Each time he would want to stop her, his hands fat and useless by his sides; each pill felt like a failure on his part, like something he hadn't done for her, another mark of his inability to help. But he would watch, to be certain she'd taken them, and then he would pick up his briefcase and head out for work, kissing her lightly on the cheek or the top of the head, saying goodbye and take care and I'll be back soon while she gazed flatly at the window or the wall.

Sometimes she would still be in bed when he was ready to leave and he didn't have the time, or the energy, to persuade her out from under those heavy covers, into a dressing gown and down the steep stairs. He would bring the pills up to her instead, and ask her to please at least sit up. Sometimes she would only stare emptily back at him, and he would have to prod a tablet into her mouth with his thumb, holding the glass of water up to her lips. He would open the curtains, slam the door, and call out his pointless goodbyes from the bottom of the stairs.

Sometimes when he came home he would find that she hadn't eaten all day, and couldn't be persuaded to eat any tea, and he would look on helplessly as she poked at the food on the plate and said that she really couldn't eat a thing.

Sometimes she would stay up all night, unable to sleep, watching television or reading in the spare room or staring out of the window with tears pouring down her face in the dark.

This isn't me though David, she said to him once, despairingly. This isn't what I'm like. She waved a hand around the bedroom, at the heaped bedclothes, the empty mugs, the drawn curtains. I thought I was tougher than this, she said, I really did.

But mostly she denied there was even a problem. It's nothing, she'd say, when he asked. I'm okay, really, I'm fine. I just need some rest. Or she'd say it's not you, there's nothing you can do. I just want to be left alone a while.

But there were things he could do, and he did them. He took her to the doctor's. He made sure she swallowed the pills. He cooked her meals, usually badly, often burning the sausages or letting the vegetables boil dry, but he cooked them and served them and encouraged her to eat when all she seemed to want to put in her mouth were the bitten ends of her fingernails. He opened the curtains when she tried to leave them closed, walked with her to the end of the street, the park, the shops, trying to help her push back the boundaries of the world that had closed in around her like a clenched fist. He asked her what she was afraid of when she went outside. You never used to be worried, he said. You know this area now, what could happen to you out there?

Anything could happen, she said, her eyes wide and unblinking, looking up at him as if it was important that he understood. Anything could happen out there.

And he found himself talking to Anna about it more and more often, feeling even as he did so that there was something underhand or deceitful about telling her these things, but unable to keep himself from saying the words. She was alright for a while but she's back on the prescription now. I'm sure she'd feel better if she got out of the house more.

Standing in the doorway of her office, always on the way to somewhere else, just stopping for a quick hello. Or noticing that they both happened to be working later than everyone else, and popping his head round the door to see if she was okay, to see if she wanted a hand with anything, to see if she was alright for getting home. Walking around the building together, checking the lights and the windows and saying she's always got an excuse for not going out; that's the thing Anna, there's always some reason. I don't know if it's me, or something to do with her family. I don't know what she's scared of.

Maybe you just have to be patient, Anna said, looking out at the cars passing along the street outside. I mean, it's an illness, isn't it? Maybe you just have to wait for her to get better. And it can't be easy either, she added, turning to him, losing touch with your family and everything like that. Maybe it's just caught up with her and it's taking some getting used to. He smiled tiredly.

No, he said, I know, of course. It's just sometimes, I wish. He unlocked the main front door. Sorry, he said. I should get back. Are you catching the bus?

No, she said, I've got some work to finish off here.

Right then, he said. See you tomorrow.

Yes, she said. See you tomorrow. She locked the door behind him and they looked at each other through the glass for a short moment before he turned and walked away.

34 *Small vase, handmade by unknown Warwickshire potter, 1974*

The vase was still on their kitchen windowsill now, empty. And each time he looked at it he was reminded of the day he'd bought it, when they'd gone out walking and talked about things that were usually left unspoken, and had seemed to bridge the gap which had grown between them; when they'd walked from the clapboard bus shelter across fields waiting to be cut, the ripened stalks crackling against their legs, over stiles and gates and narrow streams, through a small patch of woodland which opened out into the next village, Eleanor picking flowers along the way; when he'd noticed the small narrow-necked vase with the cracked blue glaze in the window of a potter's gallery by the village green, and bought it for her while they waited for the next bus home; when, back at home, he'd watched her peel off its veils of white tissue paper and set it on the kitchen windowsill, the delicate and still warm flowers rising out from its mouth towards the light.

It was late August. He'd persuaded her out of the house, out of Coventry, out to the open country between Warwick and Stratford, to walk and sit and breathe fresh clean air together. The air was thick with drowsy warmth and distant traffic, the huzz and hover of blur-winged insects, the sentry song of a lofted lark. He looked at Eleanor walking beside him, and although he knew they'd only be here for a few hours, it felt like an achievement to have got out of town at all. They'd already seen dragonflies, and butterflies, and even the flash of a kingfisher hurtling along the stream, and he'd noticed Eleanor's hands unclenching, her shoulders losing some of their anxious hunch. An unfamiliar contentment washed through him as they walked together, quietly, slowly.

He said it reminds me of when we first met, don't you think? All those walks we used to go on, down along the coast and places. She smiled and nodded, and for a moment he had to stop walking, caught out by how long ago that suddenly seemed, how much older they both already were. He stopped her, put his hands against her hips, her shoulders, her cheeks, tilting her face towards him, looking at her. She laughed, embarrassedly, as if to say what, what are you doing? He studied her. There were no lines on her skin, no wisps of grey hair, but she was no longer the girl she'd been when they met. She'd put on weight over the last year or so, and her body felt different against his touch. There was a tiredness in her face, a weatheredness, as he realised there must now be in his own, and although he thought she was as beautiful as he had always done, it shocked him to realise how much time had passed since they'd first met, how the months had become years and the years had slid ungraspably away.

She looked at him, wondering what he was thinking. He kissed her face, and lowered his hands.

He said, I should tell you something; I've been meaning to tell you for a while. He said, I've been speaking to your brother a little, to Donald, on the phone. She jolted, as if she'd brushed her hand against a stinging nettle, and she said oh? Yes? What have you told him?

Just, how things are, he said. That we're well. That you were working but you're not at the moment, bits and pieces. He asked me to say hello, he added. He wanted you to know that everyone's okay, that any time you wanted to get in touch you'd be welcome. He told me your dad's been ill but he's okay now.

They walked on, reaching a stile between two fields, and she turned to him as she climbed over it.

You didn't tell him where we were at all? she asked.

Well, no, David said, only that we were living in Coventry.

You didn't give them our address though? Our phone number? David shook his head.

I didn't think you'd want me to, he said.

I don't, she said. Promise me you won't, will you? He nodded.

Of course, he said. She jumped down from the stile, stumbling as she landed, and stood looking out across the rise of the field, over towards a strip of woodland with a church tower rising behind it. She brushed dry mud and grass from her hands and made a noise that sounded like the beginning of a laugh.

You don't mind that I rang him then? he asked.

No, she said, I don't suppose so. But I don't want to speak to them myself. Not yet.

He climbed over the stile and jumped down beside her, and almost without meaning to he carried the conversation further.

He said, but when do you think you will? When do you think you'll want to see them again?

She said, don't ask me that. Come on David, don't say things like that.

He said, don't you think you should at least write and tell them you're okay?

And she said, utterly unexpectedly, I have done.

A letter when she first got to Coventry, a photograph of their wedding, a Christmas card once or twice. The envelopes addressed only to her father, the messages brief and uninformative: I am well; I hope you all are well; take care. She told him this, and he wondered if there would ever be a time when they knew everything there was to know about each other.

And it was after this, walking away from the stile and up over the hill to the woods, once the echo of her confession had faded, that something slipped inside him. Perhaps because they were suddenly talking about these things, perhaps because she was answering him so calmly and firmly, in a way that made it seem fine to be talking that way at all, perhaps because he felt some kind of safety in being out of sight in the field there, with a barely clouded sky overhead and the slow groan of a tractor three hedgerows away; something slipped and he felt a rush of tears rising to the surface like bubbles of air bursting through him as he turned to her and said:

Eleanor I can't stand it she's out there somewhere and I don't know where she is or who she is or why she did it and I need to know Eleanor I so so so want to know what am I going to do why can't I know I need—

And she turned to him, immediately, and he was still speaking as he bowed his head into her embrace, and her whole body shook with the force of his shuddering tears. She didn't need to ask him what he meant, and there was nothing more she could say than I know David, I know, I'm sorry, I know.

It was the first time he'd said these things so clearly, and it was years before he said them again.

After a few minutes he lifted his head, wiped his face and said nothing more. She slipped her arm around his and they walked on, leaning together into the rise of the hill, climbing up to the small patch of woodland and out into the village. They found a bus stop at the edge of the village green, and he noticed the shop window of the potter's gallery and wandered over to have a look, and bought the vase. They went home, and although it was years before they went out to the countryside again, she did at least seem to be better for a time; leaving the house, talking about university again, letting the pills gather dust in the bathroom cabinet. He dared to hope that that might be the end of it, that they could go back to the way things were always meant to have been; so when she went back on to the medication after Christmas, dulled and shaken by a higher dosage, he began to feel that things might never really change, that this was the life he'd stumbled into, that he was trapped by something he could neither understand nor control.

35 *Tobacco tin; used for storing buttons, beads, safety pins, c.1960s*

She was fourteen, she told him, sitting on the quayside with two of her friends, laughing and talking about boys, enjoying the long evening and glad to be out of the house. She heard her mother's voice behind her, and was pulled to her feet. Spun around to face those hard, narrowed eyes.

Let me smell your breath child.

The words spoken low and calm, the gaze intent and steady, the grip on the arm already bringing a soft smudge of bruising to the skin. Eleanor's friends looking carefully in the other direction, edging away, brushing down the backs of their skirts with their hands. The cigarette floating away between driftwood and dead fish and polystyrene scraps, rising and falling on the swell, the paper unfurling and spilling burnt tobacco down into the dark water. Ivy leant closer into her daughter's pale face.

Breathe, she said. Eleanor looked at her. She exhaled as weakly as she could but Ivy must still have smelt the damp sour stink of cigarette smoke. She stood back and slapped Eleanor hard around the side of the face. Her friends jerked their shoulders at the sound and moved a few steps further away. Eleanor's face coloured suddenly and her eyes started to shine.

I'm sorry Mam, she whispered. I'm sorry. Ivy pulled her closer.

Don't give me sorry, she said, it's too late for sorry child. You'll get what's due and keep quiet, aye? Standing close to each other, intimately close, blind to anyone else, their world reduced for the moment to this self-enclosed space of anger and resentment and shame.

Eleanor tried to say something, sorry perhaps, or I won't do it again, or they made me, or any of the other weak responses she knew wouldn't be enough. But her words crumpled under the weight of Ivy's glare, and all that came out was something like a whimper.

What's that? said Ivy. You say something? There was no reply, and perhaps it was only then that something snapped inside Ivy, the sight of her louring daughter, the embarrassment of people turning to watch, the knowledge that people would be talking later in the day. Or perhaps it didn't take anything to snap for Ivy to pull her daughter suddenly by the arm, to swing her round and point her in the direction of the steep road home. Get going girl, she spat into her ear, pushing the back of her head, get going quick or you'll see what I don't do. Eleanor walked quickly across the quayside, her head bowed and her shoulders turned protectively in, keeping her eyes to the ground. Or she walked tall, daring any of the onlookers to meet her eye, even turning to wave to her friends. Or she ran, her eyes a blur of tears. Before Ivy followed her, she turned to Eleanor's two friends and called out to them: I'll be talking to your mothers too, Ruth, Heather, don't think I won't. They watched her silently, and she turned and followed her daughter home.

The walk back to their house was a steep one. The pavement was stepped in places, and there were handrails bolted to some of the houses, to be caught hold of on icy days. The first time David went to see her parents he'd had to stop twice on the way to catch his breath, and Eleanor had laughed at him, saying he was nothing but a soft southern sass.

I never said a word more, she told him, safe in their bed with the lights out and the covers pulled up around them, I could just hear her steps and her breathing at the back of me. I thought she might have calmed down once we got to the top, or that she might be too worn out to do anything much. But she had this way of winding herself up, you know? David looked at her eyes in the half-dark under the covers; they were calm and clear, almost puzzled, as though she was considering something that had happened to someone else, as though she was still surprised by it all.

The door closed behind them, and Eleanor turned to face her mother's fury in the unlit hall. There were open-handed slaps at first, to the arms and legs, to the face, each slap held high in the air like a question – as if to say do you want this one too my girl? – and although Eleanor held out her hands to block them, Ivy was always quick enough to find a way through. There was nothing frantic about it. There was no loss of control. Each blow was considered, aimed, carefully delivered. And there was no sound from either of them; just Ivy's laboured breathing and the occasional wince or whimper escaping through Eleanor's tightly gritted teeth. The slaps closed up into tightly clenched fists, thudding into her ribs and the side of her head. Eleanor cowered under the punches, wrapping her arms around her head and crouching against the wall as Ivy whispered why don't you stand up, child, stand up now, eh? Or Eleanor refused to buckle, looking her mother in the eye, flinching with each thud of a fist but not falling down this time; Ivy realising with a sudden shock that her daughter was now an inch or two taller than her.

Didn't you ever try to push her away, or hit her back? David asked, stroking the side of her face.

It didn't occur to me, Eleanor said. I was used to it. I knew she'd stop eventually. I didn't want to make it worse, she said.

Ivy paused a moment, lifting her daughter's face to look her in the eye. Is that enough for you child? she asked. Will you be lying to me again? Eleanor didn't speak. Did you hear me there? said Ivy, raising her voice. I asked you a question. Eleanor looked at her, her mouth firmly shut, and Ivy, infuriated, lunged forward, shoving her fists against Eleanor's shoulders, knocking Eleanor off balance and against the front-room door, the door banging open and Eleanor stumbling backwards to the ground. Stewart was standing there, staring at Ivy, his fists trembling by his side.

God's sake Ivy, he said tensely. Do you not think that's enough now? The two of them looked at each other. Eleanor struggled to her feet, pushing past Ivy and up the stairs to her room.

You'll not be eating tonight, Ivy called out after her.

Later, she told him, after her parents had gone to bed, she stood in the washroom and eased out of her clothes, hanging them up on the back of the door and looking at her pale marked body in the mirror. She splashed herself with water, flinching against the cold, and worked a bar of soap into a lather across her skin. She ran her hands carefully across her body, working around the bruises and the swollen cuts, rinsing off the soap with cupped palmfuls of cold water which splashed down her chest and her belly and her legs and on to the dirty towel on the floor; taking her time, as though soap and water might wipe away the bruises and the hurt and the fear of it happening again one day soon.

And the next time she saw Ruth and Heather, nothing was said. They didn't ask if she was okay, or offer sympathy, or make any reference to what had happened at the harbour or to what they assumed had happened afterwards. There were things which didn't need to be said, or which had been said before. Instead, she told him, they took a packet of cigarettes each across to the golf course, and sat on a bench together, and smoked their way relentlessly through the evening until Eleanor was sick into the bushes, the girls laughing and applauding as she wiped her mouth and pretended to light up once more. It was funny, she said. We laughed about it for hours. It felt like some kind of triumph, you know?

36 *Catalogue from museum exhibition, 'Refugees, Migrants, New Arrivals', 1975*

The exhibition had been Anna's idea, but the senior staff gave it to David to take charge of, allocating him a budget and a month away from usual duties, telling him this was his opportunity to live up to what they had thought was his earlier promise. The Director made it clear that he wasn't entirely in favour of the form of social history the project would entail; but, as he conceded, it was becoming increasingly fashionable in certain circles and would do the image of the museum some good at a challenging financial time.

It wasn't difficult to find material. He did a series of presentations at social and religious centres – the Irish on Stoney Stanton Road, the Ukrainian on Broad Street, the Polish on Whitefriars, a mosque, a synagogue, the Sikh temple which had taken over the old Bamba Nightclub – explaining the nature of the project, inviting participation, and his office quickly filled with boxes of loaned material, photographs, interview tapes, lists of people still to visit. This project is about the journeys you or your parents made to come to Coventry, he told them, the ways you remember those journeys, and the ways you remember the places you or your parents came from. He wasn't surprised by the number of responses he had to these presentations. He'd learnt, working at the museum, how many people wanted someone to tell their family's story to, how often the children of people who died would bring their parents' possessions to the museum to be archived or put on display, assuming that because these objects had belonged to someone who was no longer alive they would naturally take on a historical importance, assuming that the words museum and mausoleum were somehow the same.

He wasn't surprised by the interviewees' eagerness to loan him their few treasured keepsakes – the watches, the framed photographs, the religious artefacts – trusting him to keep their last attachments to a lost home safe, pushing them gladly into his arms. But what he hadn't quite been expecting was just how readily people held these things to hand, arranged together in the alcoves of their front rooms, or across a chest of drawers in a bedroom, or filling a glass-fronted cabinet in a kitchen, like miniature museums of their own. He interviewed, and was offered material by, people from all across Europe, from India and Pakistan and Bangladesh, from Vietnam, from Africa and the Caribbean. He interviewed people from Ireland, Scotland, Wales, from Sunderland and Southport and Somerset, people who had at some point come to Coventry in search of work and ended up staying. And he found himself hoping that when people contacted him from the Irish Club one of them might start by saying so I left home when I was a young woman, heading for London, looking for domestic work. I came over on the night boat. I had to leave London just before the war ended, on account of a sort of disagreement with my employers. He wondered how that would feel, to hear the beginnings of that particular story, to be able to hear it out to the end.

They based the exhibition around a map of the world, with Coventry at the centre illustrated by an image of the three spires, and with red threads reaching out to each of the countries the interviewees had travelled from. At the end of each thread they placed a photograph of the interviewee, or of one of the objects which had been loaned for the exhibition. It took Anna and him three evenings just to put the map together, staying behind while the rest of the staff went home, passing each other scissors and paste and Letraset, talking and disagreeing about which images to use. It took them another two weeks to finish the rest of the display material, putting it together down in the conservation room, spreading the work across the wide wooden desks while they selected the best extracts from the transcribed interviews, the most relevant artefacts, the clearest images.

Sometimes, when they had finished for the evening, packing the uncompleted work away, they would stay there for a while, leaning against the table, talking about things other than work. Anna told him about her wedding anniversary, and he asked what her husband was like, what he did for a living. Chris had gone straight to a job at the car-works when they'd left school, she told him, working on the same line as his father, getting used to working long hours for good money until they closed the factory after a round of strikes. It was the worst time really, she told him, it was only a year after we'd got married and we didn't know what we were going to do. She asked him again about Eleanor, and he said well, she's better in a way, you know, with the medication, but she's still not right, and she said oh that's awful, that's so sad, how do you cope? Once she said do you ever regret it? Getting married, I mean. Saying sorry sorry as soon as she'd said it, looking away from him, picking up her bag. Saying sorry only sometimes I wonder.

She was younger than him but he only ever noticed when she said things like that, when she seemed to be asking his advice, talking to him like an older brother. There were only six or seven years between them, and even that didn't seem as much as it once had. She had dark hair, tightly curled, cut to her collarbone. She had a small flat nose, and dark eyes, and she held her hand to her mouth when she spoke, as if she was afraid of letting her teeth show. She was tall. She was slimmer than Eleanor had lately become. They talked. That was all. They worked together, and while they were working they talked.

But one evening she touched him, for the second time, and he didn't pull away or say anything to stop her. It came from nowhere, a lull in the conversation, her hand drifting to the back of his head with her eyes fixed firmly on his, her fingers trailing down through his hair to the expectant skin on the back of his neck. She said sorry, as if it had been an accident, and for some reason he said sorry too and they said no more about it, and he tried to forget the feel of her long fingers, the delicate scratch of her fingernails across his traced and tingling scalp.

They'd finished all the displays, and were going over the layout plans, disagreeing over the need for additional text and trying to work out where to put the model steam engine a Russian man had been very keen to loan. They were both leaning over the desk, the papers and designs spread across it, the glare from the desk lamp getting harsher as the evening quickly darkened outside. He was saying I'm not sure about all this Anna, maybe we should look at it again tomorrow, and then there were her fingers, trailing down to the back of his neck.

And all that happened next was he looked at his watch and stood away from the desk, turning on the main overhead light and saying I think we'll take another look in the morning. That far corner looks like it will be too cramped, visitors will be squeezing past each other. And all she did was shrug, smiling, starting to tidy away the papers from the desk. Okay, she said with her back to him. See you tomorrow, she said. He walked away, and when he got halfway down the corridor and turned back to look through the open door she wasn't looking at him. She was marking something on the floorplan, running her fingers up and down the back of her head, through the dark tangle of her hair.

It was a popular exhibition, one of the most popular of the year. Coventry's population had been growing rapidly for years, tripling even between the turn of the century and the war, so there was no shortage of people who had a story of arrival, or who had grown up hearing their parents' stories, or who could in some way relate to the themes of being a stranger in a new town, making a new life, holding on to the few fragile reminders of home. Even Anna's husband Chris turned out to have a story, muttering it so matter of factly to David in the pub one evening that David had to ask him to repeat himself to be sure he'd heard it right.

My dad came here the long way round, Chris told him, dangling his empty pint glass between his finger and thumb, watching it swing. He went east to get away from the Germans, and ended up on a boat to England, ended up in the air force loading bombs to send back at them. He watched Anna walking back from the toilets, squeezing past a group of men by the bar, resting her hand on someone's shoulder by way of an excuse me. His eyes narrowed slightly before he turned back to David.

My mum came west a few years later, he said, to get away from the Russians. She met my dad in the Ukrainian club up in Leeds, and they moved down here when he heard about jobs going on the cars. Turned out they were only born twenty miles apart, he said as Anna sat down, saying it like a well-worn punchline, sitting back on his stool and turning to look at the bar.

Your parents? Anna asked, and he nodded.

We could have interviewed them if you'd mentioned it, David said to Anna, and she shook her head.

I don't think they would have wanted to take part, she said. Chris stood up, taking their empty glasses.

They don't like immigrants, generally, he said, turning towards the bar.

He was a broad-shouldered man, and people moved naturally aside to let him pass, as if they'd felt his approach without looking. As he got to the bar Anna said, murmuring, he's working again now you know, for the parks; it'll probably only be until the end of the summer but it's something at least. David nodded.

That's good, he said. That's something.

She looked at Chris, who was laughing briefly at something the barman was saying. It's not as bad as it was, she told him now. My money's enough for us both really. David watched him heading back across the room towards them, the three drinks held awkwardly out in front of him. He noticed Anna moving the back of her thumb across her wedding ring, rubbing it clean, the same way she'd been doing a few nights earlier when she'd told him about their anniversary. Five years though, she'd said, tutting and sighing fondly, seems hard to believe sometimes, and he hadn't known whether she meant hard to believe how quickly the time had passed or hard to believe they'd got married at all.

Where's your missus tonight anyway? asked Chris as he sat down, the three glasses knocking against each other and slopping beer out on to the table.

She's staying in, David said. She's, I mean, she's a bit under the weather at the moment.

Really? said Chris. Nothing serious is it?

Well, said David, no. Nothing serious. He noticed Anna looking at him, looking like she wanted to say something, an edge of worry in her eyes.

She not made it to the exhibition yet then? Chris asked, and David shook his head no. Pity, Chris said, it's a good bit of work. He moved his hand across Anna's thigh, grasping it, leaning in towards her. It's a smart idea she had there, I reckon, he said, and David nodded in agreement, Anna smiling with surprise, turning suddenly and kissing her husband on the cheek.

David sat back a little, not wanting to intrude, a familiar resentment turning over in his stomach. He wanted to be able to sit in the pub with Eleanor beside him, having a drink with their friends and talking about the small things. He wanted not to have to explain her absence every time, and almost always to have to lie about it. He wanted at least to know how long this was going to go on for, or to know that there was something he could do about it. He wanted their life together to be the way they'd told each other it would be when they first got married, instead of the empty helpless waiting his life had become. He wanted – and he felt a rush of shame as he realised this – he wanted her to make more of an effort to get better. He couldn't be expected to wait for ever, he thought, trying to silence the words even as they formed in his head. He pushed his glass away with half the pint still undrunk.

I'm sorry, he said. I'm going to have to get going.

Anna and Chris looked round.

Say hello to her for us, won't you? Anna said, reaching her hand out across the table. Give her our best wishes and everything, she said. Chris muttered something along the same lines, and David said that he would, looking back at Anna, looking at the tilt of her head, the reach of her arm across the table, her fingers arching a little. Looking at her bottom lip, caught by the concerned bite of her teeth.

I'll do that, he said. I'll say hello for you.

37 *Framed photograph (w/broken glass), David and Eleanor, c.1975*

It was the birdsong he remembered, mostly. High up in the branches somewhere, hidden by the pale and folded first leaves of spring, a bird had started singing, the notes tumbling down into the yard. The air was wet, and clean, and still. The brick walls were streaked with rainwater, the stone paving slabs by the back door gleaming darkly. The bushes under the window were spilling fat beads of rain to the ground, nodding gently as each drop swelled and broke free. Everything felt as though it had been smoothed and shined by the rain, and the birdsong chittered against the hard surfaces like scattering pieces of polished glass. It was a slow, languid sound, barely even a song at all, more of a hesitant trickle down the notes of the scale, but there was something compelling about it, something demanding and insistent. Something about the way the sound was carried through the wet air. Something clear and bright and pure, moving in through the open kitchen window and raising tiny braille bumps on their skin, so that they could only stand and listen, and not dare to move, and not dare to breathe. Their bodies touched and pressed against each other. He could feel her warmth, the pulse of blood against her skin. The brittle words and stamped feet of a few moments before were forgotten. She closed her eyes, and the corners of her mouth lifted gently into a smile. The song stopped. There was silence for a moment, broken only by a few drops of water spattering on to the stone, and just as they were about to move, to turn away and say something, or not say anything, the song began again.

She shifted beside him, her shoulders dropping as she eased out a held sigh. She looked up into the tree, trying to spot whatever bird was up there. He leant forward and tilted his head beside hers, and as he did so the sound stopped abruptly. The light in the small yard faded, and there was a rapid smatter of raindrops which soon accelerated into the same heavy downpour of a few minutes before. Water splashed in off the window ledge, clattering lightly against the glass.

She backed away, startled, looking at him for a moment without quite meeting his eye, and edged out of the room. He watched her go. He reached out and swung the window closed, fastening the catch and wiping his wet arm on the side of his trousers, and he heard, from upstairs, the bedroom door closing gently, the slow rasp of curtains being pulled closed.

It was the first time, the only time, that he'd ever come close to hitting her.

He'd told her to pull herself together, and she'd said she'd be alright if he left her alone.

He'd come back from work and found her in bed again, sitting up against a heap of cushions and pillows with the sheets hauled up to her chest, staring blankly at the wall. The curtains were closed, and the room smelt as though it could do with the windows being flung wide open.

For heaven's sake Eleanor, he said, have you seen yourself? She looked confused, and it seemed to take her a few moments to work out where his voice was coming from. What are you doing? he said. You can't just sit here like this. He opened the curtains. He made her get out of bed and come downstairs. He put the kettle on, talked to her, tried to snap her out of it. She'd obviously been in bed all day; her hair was tangled and her breath smelt sour, and when he helped her down the stairs she felt hot and clammy and slow.

He told her that she needed to look after herself. It was the wrong thing to say.

She came through into the kitchen, looking at him curiously. What did you say? she asked, very quietly and slowly.

I'm just saying Eleanor, you need to pull yourself together, he said.

She told him it was his fault that she was in this hopeless ugly town. She said that if it wasn't for him she'd still be in Scotland, with her friends, with people who understood her. She said she wished he'd never suggested coming away here.

He told her that she didn't know what she was saying, that she wasn't making sense, that her head needed looking at. These were the worst things they could think of to say to each other, and they chose their words deliberately.

They stood there, glaring, and he felt suddenly that it wasn't even Eleanor standing in front of him, that it was somehow someone else altogether. Outside, it started to rain.

When he lifted his hand, and when he felt his hand closing into a hard angry knot, she didn't flinch or turn away. She looked at him, her eyes tracking the arc of his fist. She watched it hanging there, and her body seemed to slacken in front of him, waiting.

The sudden pounding of the rain made him catch a breath, his fist trembling weakly in the air, and he brought his arm down behind his back. Her expression didn't change. She turned away and looked out through the open window into the yard and, as suddenly as it had begun, the heavy rainfall came to a stop. A bird started singing.

38 *Wine cork, dated (handwriting) August 1975*

And then there were the good days. Sitting in the back room with the window wide open, holding on to each other after a hot and spoilt day, untightening their tensions with a bottle of wine. The air drifting in from outside, thick and heavy, hungry for rain. Children shouting, the sound carrying all the way from the park.

Eleanor leant forward to pour herself another glass of wine, reaching back to rest a hand on his knee. I was scared though, she said quietly, I really didn't know where he'd gone. He sat forward, looking over at the photograph of her father, listening to her story of being lost on the heath one summer. He stroked his hand up and down her back, finishing his glass of wine and passing it to her. He lifted the hem of her T-shirt and tucked his hand beneath it, pressing it flat against her skin.

So where was he hiding? he asked.

Out on the moor, her father on the top of the rise, his taut outline silhouetted against the raw blue sky. She watched him put a hand to his chest, catching his breath, and then she crouched down to peer into the heather, looking at a crack in the hard grey rock, wondering how deep it went, trying to squeeze her hand into the gap. She stayed there for a few moments, waiting for her eyes to adjust to the undergrowth's shade, and then she stood up. Hold up now! she called, brushing the dirt from her knees and her hands.

Her father's silhouette had disappeared. Everything

seemed suddenly very quiet. The faint huzz of the insects, the occasional pop of a gorse pod in the midday heat, the distant crashes from the shipyard in the town below. But no voices. No sign of life besides her own anxious breathing.

She ran to the top of the rise and looked but he wasn't anywhere. Maybe he'd sat down somewhere for a rest and she just couldn't see him, she thought. Maybe he'd fallen asleep and that's why he couldn't hear her shouting. Or maybe this was him vanished for ever, like Bill's dad did that time, or Annie's. Or like Grandad Hamish who got lost at sea. She wondered if she'd be okay to find her way home. She wondered if her mother would be cross with her for losing him. She walked on, swinging her arms stiffly, turning her head from left to right, scanning the hot landscape for any signs of life. All she saw were butterflies, pure white ones and red-brown ones, lifting and falling and tumbling across the heather. All she heard were the insects, her breathing, her feet kicking the dry sand along the track.

She remembered when the teacher told the class about Bill's dad. Bill sat scowling, like it didn't matter to him, like it was no bother and if anyone wanted to say otherwise they'd have him to deal with. His dad had been missing two weeks when they found him on the tideline down at Cammachmore, and they wouldn't let Bill look at him. But he said that didn't bother him, what difference did it make, and whenever she saw him he was always scowling like that, for weeks and weeks and weeks.

She hadn't got very far when she stopped and called out again. Her small voice fell flat amongst the heather and the bracken. She stood and turned and looked all around her, clenching her fists and trying hard not to be very close to tears. Maybe if she went back now and told someone, they could fetch up a whole lot of men to look for him. They could spread right out across the heather, like when the beaters sent the birds up for the guns. He might be lying somewhere with a turned ankle, and she'd never find him on her own, not even if she kept looking until it was dark. It'd be too late then, maybe.

She heard something behind her and before she could turn around there was a pair of thick strong arms wrapping around her waist and lifting her into the air, the sky sprawling dizzily away, his laughter gasping into the back of her neck. She tried to pull away but he was holding too tightly. That was a good one, eh Ellie? he said. Had you wondering there, didn't I? She didn't say anything. He let go of her and she moved away, sitting with her back to him and her arms wrapped around her knees. His hat was lying on the track a few feet away, where it must have fallen when he leapt up to grab hold of her. She felt like rushing over and stamping on it, or picking it up and running with it all the way to the sea, throwing it in and watching it fill with water and sink beneath the surface. But she didn't. She just glared at it, hotly, her eyes stinging a little. Probably she got some sand in them when he pulled her over, she thought.

You alright petal? he asked. I didn't frighten you, did I? She didn't say anything, but rubbed the corner of her eye roughly with the bony heel of her hand. She heard him shuffle and fidget behind her. She heard the snap and hiss of a match being struck, the slow sigh he always made when he lit a cigarette. Aye well, I'm here now, he said quietly.

David watched Eleanor carefully while she told him the story; how it had seemed like hours that she'd stood there in the crackling silence and wondered where he'd got to and if she should go for help, how he'd suddenly leapt out behind her, laughing, and lifted her up into the air. I told him it wasn't funny, she said, smiling.

He lifted her T-shirt higher and pressed his mouth against the warm expanse of her back. Don't stop, he said. It was so rare for her to talk like that, even to mention her family, or her childhood, or anything north of the border; and especially not in that way, the memories coming easily, her body relaxed, laughter spilling out around the words. He didn't know why she'd brought it up then, why she'd rushed upstairs to find the rarely opened packet of photographs she kept at the bottom of the wardrobe somewhere. Some distant sense memory triggered by the heat of the day perhaps, or by the voices of children playing out in the streets. Some rip in the smothering comfort blanket those pills provided. A little more wine than usual. But just hearing her talk like that, with the slow evening closing in outside, with her leg lifted up on to his lap and his fingers climbing inside the ankle of her trousers, things seemed okay for the first time in months, things seemed okay and normal. A husband and wife talking about their families, their childhoods, the things that matter and the things that don't.

She stacked the photographs back up on the mantelpiece, and opened another bottle, and they waited for the taut closeness of the air to break into rain. And as the first fat drops slapped on to the path outside she put her glass down on the table, took his out of his hand, and leant over to kiss him. She stood up, a little unsteadily, and pushed her skirt to the floor.

Hey, she said. So, do you want to, her voice trailing off as though she'd forgotten how to put it, what to do, and she lowered her head to look down at herself.

He smiled, pulling at his belt and his trouser buttons, and he said do I want to what? She clambered on to the sofa, kneeling across him, clumsy with drink and banging her knee against his hip, leaving a bruise.

I'm not sure, she said, kissing his face and his neck, twisting away to reach for another mouthful of wine. Remind me, she said. And they made tired and uncoordinated love on the sofa, rain splashing in through the window, elbows banging into the wall, her soft voice whispering delightedly into his ear even as they shifted and adjusted the awkward fit of their hips across the narrow sagging sofa, stopping and starting as one or other of them said no, ow, you're squashing my arm, you're pulling my hair, move round a bit, move back a bit; but between these uncomfortable readjustments they still found room to savour the taste and the feel of each other's bodies, to press warm skin against warm skin, to pinch and to kiss and to hold.

So it wasn't difficult, when the question arose, to know when the moment had come – to circle the day on the calendar, count off the weeks, to smile at the faint smell of stale red wine on the end of the cork he'd kept, to say, it was that night, you remember, it must have been then, of course, when else would it have been? There wasn't another time it could have been.

And something happened, something which stretched the boundaries of Eleanor's enclosed world much further than they had been stretched for a long time, some massive damburst of hormones, more effective by far than the powdery charms in those pills, roaring and singing through her body and bringing her back to life. She started to pull further and further away from the stifled stronghold of their house, setting herself targets – the park, the shops, the city centre – and when she met him one day at work, waiting outside with a cigarette in her hand and a proud smile on her face as she watched him coming down the steps, he dared to hope again that the worst might be over. She cleared out the spare room, stripping the wallpaper, repainting the walls and the ceiling, hanging up mobiles and alphabet charts, buying furniture and nappies and tiny sets of clothes. When he got back from work each evening, there was always something new in the house – a baby blanket, a set of feeding bottles, a row of toys lined up along the dinner table – and the kitchen always seemed to be full of the smells of her cooking, baking cakes and biscuits, preparing dinner, making up soups for him to take to work in a flask; and when he came in through the door she was always there to show him, taking him by the arm, saying look what I bought, isn't it lovely, isn't the baby going to love it, are you hungry now by the way, and kissing him, holding him tightly, pressing her face into the hollow between his shoulder and his neck, saying oh I'm so happy I'm so happy I'm so so happy now.

39 *Hospital admissions card, 1945 (Discovered 1976)*

The last time he went to see Julia, she didn't say anything at all. She gazed up at him from the bed, blankly, drifting in and out of a dream-drenched sleep, the covers pulled fretfully up to her chin, old before her time. Later, Dorothy told him that, four days before she died, she sat up in bed and had a suddenly lucid conversation with the doctor and her, asking who was looking after the house and whether Dorothy was still planning to take that trip to the Isle of Wight, asking how David was getting on at the museum and when he'd be down to visit her next. But nothing like that happened when he was there. She watched him coming into the room, following him with her eyes, her expression fearful and tense if it was anything. Her body gave up before she did, the muscles in her legs weakening until she could no longer stand, her bladder and bowel control faltering, her arms quivering and flailing into the air if they weren't tucked safely beneath the sheets.

I'd have been lost without her and no mistake, Dorothy told them, a few weeks after the funeral, when they were gathered at Julia's house to help Laurence sort through all the things she'd left behind. I couldn't believe it, she said, the first time she invited me here for dinner; gesturing around her as if to say, this house, I mean, just look at it. It wasn't what I was expecting, she said, laughing, not when everyone else lived in those dingy old nurse's rooms. They sat around the kitchen table, Dorothy, David and Eleanor, Susan, eating the sandwiches and cakes Laurence had laid out, and she told them all about when she'd first met Julia and how much

Julia had helped her out. Laurence hovered in the background, listening, waiting to restock any empty plates, putting the kettle back on for a fresh pot.

They'd had little in common when they first met, making hospital corners on the beds of a whole wing of new wards, but that hadn't kept them from making friends almost immediately. Something just clicked with us, Dorothy said. I never knew what it was, she was like my sister more than anything else. She showed me round London, and introduced me to people, and toughened me up. I was only eighteen when I started nursing, I needed a bit of toughening up, she said, laughing, gathering up the last few cake crumbs on her plate. Laurence started to clear their plates away, asking if there was anything else anyone wanted. They shook their heads. I hated it for months, Dorothy went on, couldn't stand it, the work, and the people, and the effort involved in just getting from place to place, but I didn't dare go back. Where I came from, people didn't do that. She laughed again. I must have seemed like a real country girl when we first met, she said, but Julia soon fixed that. She turned me into a proper Londoner. I still feel like one even now, she said, shaking her head and smiling, running her thumb along the smooth worn edge of the table.

They sat quietly for a few moments more, and then David said well, should we? And they stood up, ready to get on with the job in hand, moving back through the musty hallway with its rolled-up carpets and stacked picture frames, working their way through each room and sorting everything into categories: boxes of clothes, boxes of bric-a-brac, magazines, newspapers, printed documents, handwritten documents, photographs, jewellery, items of value, items mentioned in the will. Laurence stood around awkwardly, collecting up the mugs from the table, walking back and forth between the rooms without really doing anything, picking up the occasional ornament and putting it back down, his hands hovering uselessly above papers and boxes he seemed unable to touch. Eleanor, seven months pregnant, did what she could and sat down whenever the others insisted. And although they all tried to keep each other moving, and tried not to stop and think, they each came across something which caught them out, something which snagged a loose thread of memory and tugged them to their knees. Julia's wedding dress, still wrapped in tissue paper in the attic. A photograph of Dorothy holding a one-year-old Susan, both of them clutching their thick rubber gas masks. A cigarette holder. The two telegrams. A birthday card David had made at school, with *To Auntie Julia* smeared across it in flaking orange poster paint. Her old nurse's watch. Half a dozen pairs of mislaid spectacles, gazing blindly up at them from beneath magazines, cushions, handbags. And towards the end of the afternoon, while everyone else was back in the kitchen drinking more cups of tea, he found what he'd been unknowingly looking for all along, tucked away at the bottom of a suitcase in the attic, waiting for him.

The suitcase was full of old papers – programmes from some of the plays Julia's mother had been in, a stack of appointment diaries, thick bundles of bank statements and tax certificates. But once he'd sorted it all into piles, ready to take downstairs, there was something left over. He listened to the voices of the others floating up from the kitchen, Susan saying something about the smell of Julia's tweed coats that she remembered from when she was a little girl, Dorothy laughing, and he thought, for only a brief moment, about putting the slip of card back where it had come from. He wondered if his mother even knew about it.

A hospital admissions card, headed *Royal London Whitechapel, 29th March 1945*.

Brisk blue handwriting, the details spread neatly across the dotted lines.

Mary Friel. D.O.B. 14.11.??. Maternity.

There was an address, a King Edward Avenue in St John's

Wood, but it had been crossed out in red pen, the words *prob. false* written above it. And there was a signature, *Mary Friel,* the writing scratched and faltering, the *e* and the *l* of *Friel* falling beneath the dotted line.

He sat slowly on the chair by the small dormer window and looked at it for a long time in the failing evening light. He tried to convince himself that it was something other than what he knew it must be. He tried the name for size, and it felt heavy and alien on his tongue. *Friel.* David *Friel.*

He tried to imagine the young girl whose handwriting this was, and the much older woman she must have become. He traced the shapes of the letters with his thumb, hoping for more clues than those few words could give.

Friel.

He practised saying the name, whispering it to himself in that large bare room littered with piles of paper. He wondered why even the date of birth was uncertain. And the hunger came back once more, the hunger to know, the hunger that had never really gone away. *Friel. Mary Friel.* David *Friel.*

And someone might say, my God, I don't believe it, with the shock that comes from sudden recognition, from a memory abruptly refreshed. My God, where did you find this? Reaching out to touch it, mouthing the words written across it, saying, I never thought. I remember when. They said I couldn't, I couldn't. But however did you find it? someone might ask. I mean it could have been anywhere couldn't it? I wasn't really looking, he was going to say, smiling, shrugging, it was an accident more than anything.

An accident, like the Mildenhall ploughman tearing through thick frosty soil to haul out the treasured silver plates with his bare hands. An accident, like Julia's original slip of the tongue.

40 *Scrapbook w/postcards, tickets, maps, etc., 1979*

He stood out on the deck, watching the dockers wrestle the heavy mooring ropes into place around the bollards, watching the oily slip of water between the boat and the quay narrow to nothing, and he felt the sudden rush of tears. It was unexpected. He didn't so much burst into tears as subside into them, his face collapsing slowly in on itself, his eyes squeezing shut and his lips rolling over each other, his head bowing as though in prayer. He gripped the rail, steadying himself, grateful for the sprays of rain drifting down across the docks and flashing through the haloes around the warehouse lights. He wiped his eyes and his cheeks with the backs of his hands. The people standing around him began to move away, down to the car deck or the passenger exits, wandering off in twos and threes. A low grinding vibration shook through the boat as the bow doors opened. He looked out over Belfast, the buildings huddled together under the low grey sky, towers poking up out of the gloom, a line of hills rising faintly in the distance.

He walked from the dock to the bus station, following the directions on a map he'd brought with him. The streets were quiet and dark, as if people were waiting until the last possible moment before heading out for work, keeping their heads down and their lights low. The people who'd come off the boat with him walked quickly, holding umbrellas or newspapers up against the rain. A police Land Rover hurtled past, a skirt of steel-plating around its wheels, metal grilles across its windows, hurling up spray from the road. A man watched him from inside a dark blue news-stand, cutting open bundles of newspapers. Another man came out of a side street ahead of him, pushing a handcart blooming with cut flowers in black buckets, and he tried to nod good morning but the man ignored him. He came to a hotel with all its front windows boarded up, found his bus waiting in the bus station behind it, and took his seat.

Later, he stuck the tickets and maps and handwritten directions into a scrapbook, along with the other remnants of the journey – postcards, bus tickets, beer mats, notepaper printed with the addresses of bed and breakfast guesthouses – and he imagined someone, someone smiling, wrinkles creasing around their eyes and away from the corners of the mouth, someone saying look how close you came, saying ah but you're here now though.

He woke up with no idea of how long he'd been asleep or how far the bus had travelled. From the window he could see long sloping fields of wheat and open pasture, large white farmhouses and open-walled barns set back from the road, mournful-looking long-haired cattle standing unexpectantly in the damp corners of fields. It could have been the south-west of England, or Wales, or Northumberland, except for the hard-edged accents of the other people on the bus, or the union flags which hung limply from every other telegraph pole along the road. The hills got higher, and the fields on either side became more barren, littered with rocks and striped with marshy puddles. Sheep sprang away from the roadside, mud stained halfway up their legs, colliding with each other as they hurried away from the bus. Valleys fell away to one side, steep-sided and channelled out by narrow streams. They reached the top of the ridge, passing through a small town, and as they came down the other side, the driver changing down through the gears and leaning heavily on the brake, he saw Londonderry appear below them, hooked to the near side of the river by a long narrow bridge, ringed by a wall which no longer held the whole city within it. He changed buses in Londonderry, crossing the border soon afterwards. A soldier got on to the bus to look at the passengers. Another one walked around outside, crouching at each corner to peer at the axles, glancing up at the tops of the surrounding hills, waving them through with a swing of his heavy black gun.

Eleanor's anxieties about leaving the house went further than keeping her from walking to the shops. They made her worry about other people's journeys, and about David and Kate's in particular. When David had to drive somewhere for work she would question him repeatedly about where he was going, why he was going, how long it might take, which way he was planning to go. She took comfort in seeing him perform small rituals of safety – checking the oil and the water and the brakes before he left, putting a blanket and a first-aid kit in the boot of the car, fastening his seatbelt before she waved him goodbye. So it took a long time, when he finally decided to make this trip to Donegal, to persuade her to let him go. It'll only be for a few days, he said, maybe a week. You'll be fine with Kate, my mum will come round and help out. Please, he said. But she only asked him not to go. He said he wouldn't drive, and she said that made her feel better but she still didn't want him to go. What will you do? she said. You've got no idea where to go. What are you expecting to find? I don't know, he told her. I just want to have a look. I just want to see what it's like. But it's not safe there, she said, how will I know you're okay?

So he didn't tell her about the soldiers or the Land Rover when he spoke to her on the phone that evening. He told her about the hills, and the flags, and the sheep, and he told her about his first darkened view of Belfast in the morning.

What's the weather like? she said. Where are you now? He could hear Kate in the background, saying she couldn't hear, saying it was her turn to talk now.

It's been raining all day, he said. I'm in Donegal Town. The room's a bit small but it's clean and everything. He could hear voices in another room, and see someone moving around in the lounge, setting tables for breakfast. She asked how long he was going to stay, what he was going to do.

I don't know, he said, a couple of nights here, I think, so I can try and work out where to go next. He read the names in the visitors' book on the table beneath the phone, turning a few of the pages. How're things at home? he asked.

Fine, she said quickly. You know, fine. Weather's nice. Your mum said she might come round tomorrow.

He closed his eyes a moment. There were things he wasn't saying, and he wanted to say them. He wanted to tell her how he felt now that he was finally there, that he was at once excited and disappointed, that he'd been surprised to feel no sense of homecoming; how utterly lost he had in fact felt when he'd arrived. But he wasn't sure if she wanted to hear these things, or if she wanted him to be there at all, and so he said nothing.

And how's Kate doing? he said.

Well, she's fine, she said. You want to speak to her? He said that he did, and he listened to Eleanor holding the phone out, leaning over to Kate and asking if she wanted to speak to her daddy. He heard the soft whump of the sofa cushions, and pictured Kate burying her face in them, trying to hide herself. Eleanor spoke again. She's gone all shy on you, she said, a smile in her voice. She misses you, you know, already.

I know, he said. He hesitated, looking to see if the woman was still setting the tables in the dining room, lowering his voice. And you're okay? he asked.

Yes, she said. I'm fine. He heard the edge of her voice tighten, and knew that she'd closed her eyes.

You've been making sure you take them then? he said. You haven't missed any? There was a long silence, without even the sound of Eleanor's breath reaching down the phone line to him, and he wasn't quite sure if she was still there. Eleanor? he said.

Yes David, she said. Yes, I have. He heard Kate running into the kitchen and dragging a stool across the floor, and he heard Eleanor telling her not to do that, the phone lowered away from her face. I've got to go, she said, speaking to him again.

Right, he said, okay. He started to say look sorry, I didn't mean to, and he heard something breaking in the kitchen, a plate or a glass, and Kate screaming in surprise, and Eleanor telling her not to move. He said I love you, I'll be home soon, over the noise, but he wasn't sure if she'd heard.

On his first morning in Donegal, after breakfast, he walked through the town centre, calling into a newsagent's by the market square to buy a handful of postcards, sending one to Eleanor and Kate and keeping the rest to stick into a scrap-book. The streets were busy with people shopping, women mainly, standing at shop counters set just in from the door, loading cuts of meat and handfuls of vegetables into cloth shopping bags, chatting to the flat-hatted shopkeepers or to the women beside them in the queue. He found himself looking out for women in their late forties and early fifties, stupidly, as if he might somehow catch the eye of one and recognise something in her face, and be recognised in turn.

He walked away from the square, past a small ruined castle and across a river, looking for the town library. It was closed. There was no museum. He walked along the river to a jetty, watching some men unloading armfuls of netting from their boat. He went for a drink in a bar, barely able to see for a moment as he stepped in from outside, blinking quickly and asking for a stout. At the edge of town, just off the Ballybofey Road, in a steeply sloping field beneath an oak tree, he found a memorial stone to the famine dead, buried together there beneath his feet.

Kate said hello to him on the phone that evening, but sank into a breathy silence when he said hello back, when he asked her what she'd been doing, as if she couldn't quite believe it was him at the end of the line.

He phoned Anna, and she said oh hello, I was wondering how you were getting on. It's been quiet at work without you there, she said, half-laughing, are you heading back soon? He told her he'd be a few more days yet, there was still plenty left to see. She said well we all miss you, speaking, as she often did, as if she meant something else, something more, and he wondered again if there really was something more to be meant. The teasing sound of her voice when she spoke like that reminded him of her fingers trailing through the hair on the back of his head, or of her breath moving across his cheek when they looked over layout diagrams together, leaning over the desk, her elbow pressed against his.

He said anyway, I was just phoning to see if there'd been any post for me, any messages I need to deal with?

She said no, nothing that can't wait. We can cope without you, you know, she added, laughing.

Oh, no, yes, of course, he said. Well, okay then. I should go.

Take care then, she said as he hung up.

He left Donegal Town and took a bus to Kilrean, a smaller place which didn't look like much more than a hamlet on the map. He was the only passenger on the bus, and he sat near the front, looking through the tall windscreen. The driver didn't say anything to him. The roads seemed wider than they were in England, but less well made, unfinished, petering off on either side into broken gravelly verges. The driver would sometimes have to steer a wide swerve around a pothole or a stretch of broken tarmac, or swing on to the wrong side of the road to slowly overtake a tractor pulling a trailer piled high with muddy potatoes. Dogs, keeping sluggish watch at the entrances to farmhouse driveways, their heads wedged between their front paws, would look up while the bus was still in the distance, running to meet it, barking and jumping and chasing it furiously away down the road. What few other drivers there were would greet the bus driver with a curt wave, usually just lifting a finger from the steering wheel and nodding, and he wondered whether the driver knew them all.

They stopped outside a pair of shops and a garage. There was a man sitting on a bench outside one of the shops, a black dog curled up by his feet. There was a long burgundy car poking out of the garage workshop, the bonnet open, two men leaning over the engine together. The driver turned to him.

Are you getting off then? he asked. David looked at him, and back out of the window.

Is this Kilrean? he asked.

It is, the man said, pointing at the door to clear up any confusion.

Kilrean, Ballybofey, Raphoe, Kilross; he stayed a night in each, walking around the area, calling into a shop or a bar, ready for conversation but not sure how to begin. Once or twice, with a couple of beers inside him, he said something to a barman like, I'm looking for a woman, Mary, Mary Friel, she was in London during the war, you don't know of anyone do you? And the barman would say something like, I don't know if I can help you there, or that's a long shot isn't it, or we're all looking for a woman, son. And David would smile, and shrug, and say yes, it's a long shot, not to worry; until one evening in Kilross an older man sitting beside him said, Friel was that you said? You want to head up to Fanad if it's Friels you're after.

He phoned Eleanor each evening, a stack of small coins ready beside the phone, and told her what he'd done that day, where he was, who he'd seen or met or spoken to briefly. He turned each coin over in his hand as he spoke, looking at the dates and designs embossed on them, the harps and salmons and bulls. I know it seems strange but it feels like it's worth it, he said. I know she might not even be here but at least I'm getting a look at the place. It's something, he said uncertainly. I love you too, he said each evening. Tell Kate I'll be home soon, tell her I love her, tell her to be good. He always paused a moment before putting the phone down, listening to the click and buzz of the broken connection.

He looked out for museums, but there didn't seem to be all that many around. He found one in Letterkenny, and spent the afternoon in there, reading the mainly handwritten display boards above the few artefacts. He read about burial chambers and dolmens, the fragments of shields and beakers and belt buckles found beneath the stacked slabs of rock. He read about farming in the Middle Ages, and expressions of religious faith, and the dominance of the oral culture. He read about the coming of the English and the Scots, the battles against the landlords, the potato blight, the starvation and desperate emigrations, the villages left abandoned and burnt. He read about the uprisings, and partition, and then there were photographs to look at and his interest in the stories faded as he studied the blurred faces looking out at him from those white-washed walls. He didn't know what he was looking for; some familiarity in a glance, a nose, a jawline or a posture which might catch him by surprise, something he could recognise. Something which would make someone stop and say well now, would you look at that. He's got your eyes. He's got your smile. He's got the same tiny curl of skin at the corner of his mouth. That's the spit of you. He wanted a photo he could rip off the wall, and show to someone, and have them say something like this. It would be a start. It would be something to go on.

He remembered when Kate had been born, how people had said these things to him then. Look, she's got your eyes, don't you think? There, that smile, that's pure David Carter, look at that. It had shocked him, hearing people say this, the force of the joy which had erupted inside him, a joy which came from the knowledge, at last, of someone connected to him. Someone in the world who was truly the flesh of his flesh. The only one. There were evenings, holding Kate in his arms, or watching her sleep, when he was frightened by the strength of the feeling surging through him. It was something so much more than love. It was something which made him crumple at the sound of her breathing coming down the telephone line. It was something, he was sure, he would be capable of tearing flesh from bone to defend.

He asked the woman at the front desk of the museum where Fanad was, explaining, when she asked where he wanted to go exactly, that he was looking for someone called Friel. She smiled. Well you're heading in the right direction then, she said. You'll be researching your family tree? she asked, looking up at him through gold-rimmed glasses. He hesitated, and said that he was. She looked in her desk and found him a leaflet – *Ancestor Research, A Visitor's Guide* – and told him not to say that she'd said but the best place to start would be with Father Dwyer at the church in Kerrykeel. He'll have records, she said. But don't tell him I sent you, she said again, tapping the side of her nose. He promised he wouldn't.

There were no buses until the next day, so he spent the evening in a bar, reading a newspaper and listening to other people's conversations. He phoned Eleanor, but she was busy putting Kate to bed so they just told each other they were fine and said goodnight.

He phoned Anna, and in the middle of talking about the way small museums seemed so reluctant to keep anything in storage, crowding out their displays in a way which was muddled and off-putting but also perhaps more honest, she said I've been thinking about you a lot, have you been thinking about me?

The church in Kerrykeel was set back from the road, low and dark behind a row of trees. There was a pub opposite, single-storeyed, its windows curtained off against the outside, and a shop that looked as though it had been closed all day. He ducked under the arch in the thick boundary wall and followed a path round to the side of the building. A door was half-open, and he could see, on a doormat just inside, a man easing a pair of mud-clodded boots from his feet, his hand jammed against the door frame for support. The man looked up and saw David before he could turn away.

Can I help you there at all? he asked. David hesitated. He'd had difficulty deciding what to ask, how much he should say. The man straightened up and looked at him.

Father Dwyer? David said. The man nodded patiently. Ah, David said, well, I was wondering if it would be possible to have a look at some parish records. I'm doing some research, he said. I mean, if it's not too much trouble. Father Dwyer pulled the door open wider and stood to one side, his thick socks half hanging off the ends of his feet.

I'm sure I can spare a few moments from my busy schedule, he said. What is it you're after exactly?

As he was showing David into the sitting room, once David had tried to explain what he wanted, he said, well, we can have a look but my guess is I'm not going to be much help. He went into another room, and came back with three dark-green record books, heavily bound, the page edges thumb-darkened and worn. Can I get you a cup of tea? he asked.

David nodded. Please, he said, that'd be great. It's been a long day.

He looked at the record books while he listened to the tea being made. He wasn't sure whether to pick them up and start leafing through or if he was expected to wait. He felt nervous sitting beside them, as if Father Dwyer might take them away again, as if this was the only chance he had to thrust them into his bag and sneak off. He reached a hand out to touch the top one, and drew it back again quickly.

Father Dwyer came back into the room with a tea tray, clearing a space on his cluttered coffee table. Excuse the state of the place, he said. He sat down opposite David. Go ahead, he said, take a look. It's all there: births, christenings, weddings, funerals, the whole lot. Well, everything they tell us about, he added, laughing briefly, leaning forward to pour out the tea. David picked up the first book and rested it on his lap, heaving it open to the first page.

Mary Friel, died 1920 (born 1872), the very first entry said in a flowing hand, the glossy ink matted by the years. He glanced down the page and found *Michael Friel, John Friel* and *Dermot Friel; Bridget Friel, Margaret Friel, Nora Friel.* There was a *Mary Friel, born 1927*, two lots of *Mary Friel, born 1928*, and five lots of *Mary Friel, born 1929*. He looked up at the priest, who shrugged, raising his hands and lowering them again. It's not an unusual name around here, he said. Not an unusual name at all. You'll be tracing your family tree?

In a way, David said, turning the pages and running his finger down endless columns of *Friels*, and *Dohertys*, and *Carrs*. Another three *Mary Friels*, born in 1930, and four in 1931. Father Dwyer looked at him seriously for a moment.

I get a lot of people tracing family trees, he said. Americans mostly, more so than folk who ended up in England or Scotland. More likely to have lost touch, I suppose, he said, nudging a teacup towards David's side of the table. David kept turning the pages. *Mary Friel, died 1932 (born 1925). Mary Friel, married Sean Sweeney, 1933.*

But if it was something else, Father Dwyer said, lowering his voice very slightly. If it wasn't the family tree exactly. David looked up. If it was something else, Father Dwyer said again, then I'd say a little caution was needed. He coughed suddenly, bringing his hand to his mouth, sitting forward in his chair. Excuse me, he said. He wiped his mouth with a handkerchief from his pocket and swallowed a few times before continuing.

People can cause upsets, he said, looking down into his tea as he stirred it, when they go about the place asking questions. People can get ideas. Things can be dug up which didn't need to be. David looked up at him, his hands resting on the roughly textured pages of the record book. They heard footsteps outside, loud and brisk on the stone path, and something rattling through the letter box.

Excuse me, Father Dwyer said, putting his tea down and crossing the room to the hallway. David heard him picking something up from the mat and opening the door for a moment. The smell of cool damp air swung into the room before the door closed again.

Do you mind me asking how old you are? Father Dwyer said as he came back into the room. He was holding a thin white envelope, turning it over in his hands as if he could read the letter without going to the trouble of opening it.

Thirty-four, David said. Father Dwyer took the letter through to another room, closed a window there, and came back to his cup of tea.

Thirty-four years, he said, looking at David steadily. That's a long time now, isn't it? David closed the book, and put it back with the others. He drank his tea. He looked around the room, blinking quickly, looking at the pictures on the wall, religious paintings mostly – a crucifixion scene, a bearded man holding a baby in a temple, Rembrandt's darkly clouded image of a father resting his hands on the bowed shoulders of his son.

Sometimes people prefer to forget, Father Dwyer said.

David finished his tea, and put his empty cup back on the tray, and wondered what he could say now. He felt as though the words would fall apart if he tried to speak them, would spill wetly into the air.

You're not the only one, Father Dwyer said gently. You know that at least, don't you?

part three

He left Eleanor at home, to pack a suitcase or to decide that she didn't want to make the long journey with him after all, and drove round to see his mother, looking for a few more photographs to take with him. She was standing outside when he pulled into the small cul-de-sac of sheltered bungalows, waiting for him, watering the potted flowers they'd bought her as a moving-in present.

No Eleanor then? she said as he got out of the car, barely looking up.

No, he said, she's busy sorting a few things out.

Pity, she said, putting down the watering can and tilting her cheek towards him to be kissed, it's been a little while. Her skin was dry against his lips, and her body felt thin and fragile as he put an arm around her.

They're looking nice, he said, nodding down at the flowers. She looked at them, sceptically.

Well, she said, as good as can be expected with the light they're getting there. She turned away, leaning on the walking stick which had been propped up by the drainpipe, and eased her way back into the house. He tried to take her elbow, to support her weight, but she shrugged free of his grip and headed into the kitchen. He stood in the small entranceway for a moment, watching her stiffened movements, slower versions of the ones he'd grown up with, watching as she filled the kettle, plugged it in, opened the cupboard, took out the teabags. The bones of her hand looked as though they had shrunk, leaving the skin loose around them. There was a brown spot on the back of her wrist which he hadn't noticed before. She put a plate of biscuits on the table, and a pair of cups and saucers, and sat down. As the kettle came to the boil, David filled the pot, brought it to the table, and sat down beside her. She turned the handle towards him and waited for him to pour.

So, he said. How are things, Mum? How are you finding it? She smiled slightly, looking past him towards the window, looking over at the other bungalows with their ramped entrances and grab handles beside the door, their groups of potted flowers and thin strips of lawn.

Oh, it's all very nice, she said. I've got no complaints. It's warm, and dry, and clean. It does me okay.

It had taken them a long time to persuade Dorothy to move. They'd reminded her, more than once, that the doctor had said the stairs were doing her hips no good, and she'd told them she could get one of those stair-lift things, what did they call them? They're ever so expensive, Susan had said, and Dorothy had looked at her, narrowing her eyes, saying are they now Susan, is that right?

They'd asked her what would happen if she slipped in the bath one night and had no way of calling for help. They'd told her the house was too big for her to keep clean any longer, and she'd said well, I know that, what do you think I keep asking you lot round for? But she'd agreed in the end, grudgingly, saying she supposed it was better than going into a home like Julia had done, saying she'd go along with it if only to stop them all harping on.

The night before she finally moved out, they cooked her a dinner and kept her company until late in the evening, sitting around the same kitchen table she'd been putting food on for more than fifty years. David and Susan, with the help of Susan's son Mark, spent the day emptying most of the house, taking some things to the bungalow and the rest to charity shops and auction yards, or to their own garages and lofts.

Dorothy kept out of the way, saying she was sure they knew what they were doing, talking to Eleanor in the garden or on the way to and from the shops, and in the evening they laid the table as they would for Sunday lunch, with warmed dishes for the vegetables, white sauce in a jug, separate serving spoons, napkins in rings. Eleanor suggested candles, and they found some left in the cupboard under the stairs, and put them on the table in half-sized wine bottles with the labels scrubbed off. They poured drinks for everyone, and drank a toast to Albert, to the house, to new beginnings.

When his mother had poured out a second cup of tea for them both, he said listen, is there anything you want me to do, while I'm here?

Well you're not leaving yet are you? she asked.

Not straight away, he said, but I can't be too long. We should try and get going before lunchtime. He put his hands on the table, as if he were about to get up, and she looked at him.

We? she said. Is Eleanor coming with you now? He nodded, and Dorothy smiled.

Oh, I am pleased, she said. I never did think it was a good idea to go on your own. He shrugged, looking around the room.

Is there anything you want me to do though? he said again. She watched him for a moment and shook her head.

There's not an awful lot to be done, she said.

No hoovering or anything? he asked.

Now then, she said, watch yourself. I'm not an invalid yet. But you can wash these things when we're done, she added, glancing at the cups and saucers on the table. He nodded.

He said, almost as an afterthought, oh and Mum, I was still hoping to borrow those photos, you remember? She looked at him. Do you mind if I have a look for them? he said. I was hoping to take them with me. He said the words quickly, quietly, picking crumbs from the lace tablecloth as he spoke.

Oh, she said. Well. Of course. She nodded towards a stack of cardboard boxes behind the door. I think they're still packed in there.

Can I look? he asked again. She waved her hand towards them, nodding, in a gesture which might have meant be my guest if she hadn't also turned her face away and lifted her cup of tea unsteadily to her lips.

The albums were still packed where she'd put them when she moved out of the house, wedged in between recipe books and old gardening magazines. He stood in the corner of the room to look through them, knowing already which pictures he wanted, removing them quickly and laying them to one side on the worktop; his and Susan's first days at school, Albert and Dorothy moving into the house, a summer holiday with his grandparents, small square snapshots with rounded edges and faded colours. His mother carried on looking out of the window, fiddling with the sleeves of her cardigan, rolling the cuffs back and straightening them again. Each time he peeled back the plastic cover of an album page it made a sound like tearing paper and she glanced at him anxiously.

You will be careful with those, won't you? she said. He nodded, still flicking quickly through the heavy pages, squeezing each album back into the box when he was done.

Look, Mum, he said when he'd slipped the chosen pictures into a clear plastic binder, are you sure you don't mind?

When they'd had dinner together that evening, the night before Dorothy had moved into the bungalow, some awkward things had been said. She'd drunk too much wine, and had let her anxiety about what he was doing spill out, saying I'm not going to stand in your way but you shouldn't think I'm happy about all this, saying isn't it a bit late now, really? Saying oh this is all Julia's fault. But now, with only a cup of tea passing her lips, and with the sharp summer light filling the small and tidy room, she had nothing left to say.

Really, I don't mind, she said eventually. You go and get on with it. She stood up suddenly, looking around the room as if she wasn't sure where she'd put something, as if she wasn't sure what it was she was looking for, and sat down again. Say hello to Eleanor for me, won't you? she said, her voice sounding tired and faint. Tell her I said to look out for you.

He said that he would, and he carried the cups and saucers across to the sink, rinsing them under the tap and balancing them on the draining rack, glancing up at the clock.

41 *Cut fragments of surgical thread, in small transparent case, dated July 1983*

It wasn't until he'd been out of hospital for three or four months that Kate saw his scar for the first time. She was fascinated. She knelt beside him and peered down at it, at the two faint dotted lines either side of the ridged pinch of flesh, the scarred surface puckering away into healthy skin. He propped himself up on his elbows, watching her face, the concentration in her eyes, the pursed lips and lowered eyebrows which meant she was working hard inside her young head to process this new information. She reached out to touch it and Eleanor caught her hand with a sharp uh-uh and a shake of the head. Wash your hands first, she said, still holding on to Kate's wrist. Kate looked at her hands. They were covered in soil and grass from where she'd been digging in the far corner of the garden with the bucket and spade Dorothy had given her; looking for museum things she'd said. She stood up and went into the house, looking worriedly at David as she went.

Eleanor smiled at him and shuffled across the ground to kiss his neck and his ear. He broke off a handful of grass and threw it at her as she turned away. She broke off a handful herself, and was just about to throw it back at him, laughing at his cowering face, when they heard the gurgle and splash of water down the outside drain and saw Kate reappear at the back door, holding up her wet hands.

Good girl, Eleanor said, and Kate hurried over to kneel beside David's stomach again. She looked at the scar, and up at him, and back at the scar again. She seemed to be waiting for his permission. He watched her. Be careful, Eleanor said, moving round to sit beside her. He felt like a patient again, lying in bed watching doctors and students make comments about his body, taking it in turns to pinch and prod at his flesh.

Kate's small finger brushed against the damaged skin, pulling away suddenly, reaching back. She traced the line of the scar, and the two dotted lines where the stitches had been, and the pinched line of the scar again. She looked round at Eleanor.

It's like on my elbow, she said, sounding surprised.

Well, said Eleanor, it's similar, isn't it? Kate lifted her arm and ran her finger along the faded scar she'd got from falling on to a piece of glass in the street a year before. She ran her finger along his scar again, and along hers, and smiled up at him, the seriousness gone from her face.

It's like my elbow, she said, as if she thought he hadn't heard her speaking to her mother a moment before.

Yes, he said, it is.

Does it hurt? she asked.

No, he said, not any more. She looked at it again, thinking about something.

Have I got a pendix? she asked.

Appendix, Eleanor said, correcting her. Kate looked up at her mother, frowning.

I said a pendix, she said; have I got one too? She looked down at herself, prodding her stomach. Eleanor smiled.

No, it's an appendix, she said again, and you have got one, don't worry.

Have you got one? Kate asked, looking up.

Yes I have, said Eleanor.

But Daddy hasn't? she asked.

No, Eleanor said quietly, not any more. She looked at David, her eyes narrowing very slightly. Kate looked at his scar once more, satisfying herself that she understood, then stood up and went back to her archaeological exploration in the corner of the garden, plunging her hands into the warm soil to look for Roman pottery, Bronze Age coins, snail shells. David lay down again, the late afternoon sun on his face, and closed his eyes, his own hand reaching automatically for that stiff pinched reminder of a few months before.

He must have woken a few times before he managed to speak, struggling in and out of consciousness, because he didn't remember being surprised to see Eleanor sitting there when he finally opened his eyes.

Hello, he said, and his mouth felt swollen and stuffed with rags and he didn't think she could have heard him. Hello, he said again, the word cracking in half across his dry lips. She looked up at him suddenly, leaning forward and smiling, her eyes wet and blinking quickly. She looked very tired. You alright there love? he said, trying to lick some softness back into his mouth and his words. You been here long? She pulled her chair closer to the bed, reaching for his hand.

A wee while, she said, smiling again and tilting her head to line it up with his. He smiled back and immediately felt a swirl of nausea in his empty stomach.

What time is it? he asked, and closed his eyes.

When he woke again, there was no one there. He could feel a sharp thudding pain in his stomach somewhere. There were metal rails along the sides of the bed, and he tried to remember where he'd seen that before. There was the brown plastic chair that Eleanor had been sitting in, but there was no sign of her. The room was darker than it had been. He could hear a hushed voice somewhere and he couldn't tell if it was coming from a radio or from someone talking, or if they might be talking to him.

David? She was standing right next to the bed this time, trailing the tips of her fingers across his forehead, brushing his damp hair away from his face. He looked up at her.

Hello again, he said. She smiled, and it was a smile of such open pleasure and warmth that he didn't quite know how to respond.

How're you feeling there? she said.

Sore, he told her, and sick, and a bit dizzy. She ran her hand down the side of his face, and he turned to kiss her palm. She looked round, and leant over to kiss his forehead, his cheek, the end of his nose.

Bloody hell David, she whispered, you had me worried there for a while. She reached down for his hand, held it, pulled the brown plastic chair closer to the bed and sat down, tugging his hand into her lap. Look at the bloody state of you, she whispered.

There was a vase of flowers on the locker next to the bed, and a card. From your Mum, she said, when she saw him looking at them. She'll be back down later.

Is Kate with her? he asked.

Oh, yes, she said, I was there with them both last night. I think your Mum likes the idea of having her to stay; I think it's an adventure for them both.

Have you told her? he asked.

Kate? she said. I've told her that you had to have an operation; I said they had to fix your tummy but you're alright now and you'll be home soon and right as rain. I told her it was your appendix, she added softly. She squeezed his hand, and traced the outline of his fingers with her thumb. She seemed okay with that, she said. Oh, look at you, she said again, running her eyes across the dark swollen bruises on the side of his face, his thick and broken lips, the mottled stains across his ribs.

Someone at the other end of the ward was watching television. He couldn't see the screen, but he could see a slight flickering glow on the man's face, and hear the rustle of studio applause. He was an old man, his hair cut fuzz-close to his head, his mouth hanging slightly open. He was wearing blue-and-white striped pyjamas, and a thin grey cardigan, sitting up in bed with a pile of pillows behind him. Through the window at the end of the room, David could see the top branches of two trees, shifting together and apart in a light breeze, the dark green leaves billowing and swooping towards each other. The sky was white with sliding clouds.

I brought you some grapes she said, trying to smile, do you want some? He reached out to the bowl on the bedside locker, tugging feebly at a grape. As it broke off the stalk he dropped it deliberately to the floor, letting his hand fall weakly to the side of the bed.

I don't think I've got the strength, he said.

You're unbelievable you are, she said, biting back a smile and standing closer to the top end of the bed. You're supposed to be sick and exhausted. She plucked a handful of grapes off the stalk, her hips tilting ever so slightly towards him, and fed the grapes into his mouth, poking each one into the reluctant press of his lips, withdrawing it with a teasingly raised eyebrow, slipping it back in, running the broken edge against the licked bite of his teeth. You should be careful of your blood pressure there old man, she murmured.

I'm being as careful as I can, he replied, but you're not helping much. He reached his hand up and curled it around the lean of her waist.

She stood away from the bed suddenly, closing her eyes and covering her mouth with her hand, catching her breath, looking around to see if anyone had been watching. She shook her head at him. You'd better be home soon, she said.

I'll see what I can do, he told her. I think they're going to want my bed back before too long. She sat down, looking at him and smiling as though she were the keeper of some great secret.

A nurse came and took his temperature, asked how he was feeling, and changed the bedding. There was some blood mapped out across one of the sheets where he must have caught a stitch as he turned over in his sleep. A man came round with a trolley, selling sweets and newspapers, books of crossword puzzles. People came round with food which tasted like it had been warm for a long time, and slid it in front of him on wheeled tables. After a couple of days he was able to sit up in bed, and then to get out of bed, and then to walk the short distance to the toilet. A doctor came, dragging the curtains closed around the bed, and listened to his breathing through a stethoscope, and looked into his eyes with a bright light, and tugged painfully at the ends of the blood-encrusted stitches. Time you were off I think, Mr Carter, he said vaguely, looking around as if he'd forgotten something. I think we've done all we can, he added, and slipped away again.

A police officer came, and sat by the bed with a notebook, and asked him what had happened. He told him, more or less, and the police officer wrote it down, watching David, asking questions, asking for a better description. David said it was unclear, that things had been quick, and confused. I'm not sure I'd recognise the man if I saw him again, he said. It's difficult to be certain, he said. I didn't even get a look at his face really, it was over so quickly, he said.

He lay back in a hot bath, steam rising from the still surface of the water and filling the darkened room, clouding the mirror and the window, curling and spreading across the ceiling. The two candles at the end of the bath burnt steady and still, their light streaming up the shining tiles behind them. Eleanor knelt on the floor beside him with a handful of cotton wool.

Kate was still at his mother's. Eleanor had said she wanted her to stay there a few more days, that she didn't want her to see him like this. She'd said it would frighten her. The house felt strange without her, empty and awkward, her toys still spread across her bedroom floor, her school satchel hanging by the door. But when he'd spoken to her on the phone she hadn't seemed unsettled by what was going on at all. Are you looking after Granny? he asked her. Are you cooking her dinner and making her bed? No! she said, giggling once she realised he was joking. Are you reading her a bedtime story? he asked. No Dad, she said. You're just being silly now, she said, and asked to speak to Eleanor. He missed her being in the house incredibly. They both did.

Sit up, Eleanor said quietly. She leant over, dipping a piece of cotton wool in the water, squeezing it out between her fingers. She pressed it on to the dried blood around the stitches, the grainy crust softening and dissolving and trickling down on to his skin. The cotton wool soaked red and brown, and she reached over to drop it into the bin. She dipped a fresh piece into the water and repeated the process, looking up at him now and again to see if it was hurting, carefully dabbing and wiping away the blood until there were only the pressed pink edges of the wound, the shining black stitches knotting it together, the red dotted punctures where the thread wove in and out of his skin. Stand up, she said, and he did, and the water streamed off him with a sudden plunging rush, the candlelight flapping for a moment in the shaken air. She held a towel up against him, drying his hair, his face, his chest and arms and back, pressing it carefully against his belly. When she pulled it away, it was marked with a small kiss of fresh blood. She soaked a pad of cotton wool in iodine and held it towards him. This is going to sting, she murmured, pressing it against the wound. It was cold, and he jerked back instinctively, but she kept it pressed against him as the initial jolt became a duller throbbing pain. He sucked air through his teeth, and smiled as she looked up at him. She dropped the cotton wool into the bin. There, she said, sitting back on her heels as if admiring her handiwork, how's that now?

He looked down at the scar, pink and hot from the bath, wreathed in the steam still rising from the water. I think that'll do, he said. Thanks, he said. They looked at each other for a moment, and she held back the beginnings of a smile at the corner of her mouth. Water had run down her arms and soaked the ends of her shirt sleeves. As he stood there, looking down at her, he felt the familiar flush and pulse of an erection beginning to swell. She watched it for a moment, the shift and stretch of the skin, the darkening of the veins. She stood up, shaking her head.

You're a disgrace, she said, laughing, passing him the towel as she left the room.

Pocket address book, w/page torn out, c.1982

It was nobody's fault, he told himself later. It was just something that happened, something they'd both drifted towards without thinking it through. They spent so much time together at work, that was part of it. And they had a lot to talk about, things they could share, that was a part of it as well. They both had good reasons to stay at work late, not to go home, to find themselves yet again the only two left in the building.

We must stop meeting like this, she said to him once, laughing, as they both left the building after a long evening spent assembling new display panels. He laughed too, and said, right, well, see you tomorrow, and nodded a surprised hello to Chris, who was waiting for her at the bottom of the steps; and the next time they worked late she said, I didn't mean that you know, we shouldn't stop meeting like this at all.

She touched him, more than once, brief nudges and shoves which were never supposed to mean any more than oh stop it now, or go on then, or, occasionally, are you okay? No more than friendly, playful gestures. But he felt the soft pressure of those touches for hours afterwards, like pale bruises, and he started to want to feel them again.

It was nobody's fault. It was just something that happened.

She asked him how Eleanor was, still, and these conversations seemed to restore the innocence to the time they spent together. They made it okay; they were having the conversations good friends would have. He could say it was good for a long time after Kate was born but now she's started at school

I think Eleanor doesn't know what to do with herself, I think she's just exhausted, and Anna could say oh David I'm sure she'll be better soon, as any friend would do. It was only talking, what they were doing. He could even say well I'm sleeping on the sofa now you know, just for the moment, she says she can't sleep when I'm there, she seems to flinch whenever I go near her, she's so withdrawn, and Anna could say oh it must be hard for you David, and this could be okay as well.

It was nothing. There was nothing going on. He told himself this, many times. He asked himself what she would see in him anyway, and there was nothing he could think of, and this proved to him that there was nothing going on at all.

But she told him once, outright. She said, I like you David, you know that, don't you? She said you're so, I don't know, dependable, reliable, no, that sounds wrong, solid, I mean like strong in your own way, oh listen to me, sorry, I don't even know what I'm trying to say. Saying all this while he stood looking at her, motionless, astonished, his breath caught in a fist-like knot in his throat. And she tried again: I like it when you're around, that's all, okay? Laying her hands on his shoulders when she said this, looking straight into his eyes, and only moving away when they both heard footsteps out in the corridor.

He was putting dinner on the table one Friday night when Eleanor said someone phoned for you today, I forgot to tell you. She gazed down at her plate as she spoke, her hands flat on the table in front of her. She was still wearing her dressing gown, and her hair was hanging down around the sides of her face. Kate looked up at him, holding her knife and fork in her small fists, waiting to be told she could start. He sat down, the oven gloves still flung over his shoulder, and nodded at her.

Oh? he said, to Eleanor, only half interested, watching Kate scoop her peas into a crater of mashed potato.

Her name was Anna. She wanted to speak to you but I told her you weren't in, Eleanor said. Her voice wasn't quiet, but it sounded distant somehow, as if she was calling from another room and not sitting next to him at all.

Oh, right, he said. Something about work probably. I'll speak to her on Monday, I'm sure it can wait. He looked over at Kate, who was sticking two halves of fish finger together with a mashed potato cement, her mouth full, watching her mother curiously.

Did you have a good day at school? he asked. She thought about it for a moment.

Yes! she said. But Robin got in trouble, for breaking my pencil, because he did it when I was on the sand table, she said.

Did Mrs Ellson give you a new one? he asked. She nodded.

He glanced across at Eleanor again. She was eating very slowly, pushing small forkfuls of food around her plate as if checking to see that they were safe. But she was eating. He wanted to push her hair away from her face and be able to look her in the eye. He wanted to be able to ask how her day had been.

Kate put down her knife and fork and asked if she could go and play. He told her she could. Eleanor looked up.

Who's Anna? she said. He tried to explain.

Anna from work, he said, you know. The Assistant Curator, she does transport, young woman, dark hair. She started in '73 but she'd been doing placements before that, remember? You met her at the Christmas party the year before last, Anna Richards, you know. Speaking lightly, cutting his fish fingers into small squares as he spoke, heaping his peas up on to his fork. Speaking as though it wasn't at all important and he couldn't quite remember.

No, she said. I don't know.

Dark curly hair, he said, down to here, quite slim. She looked at him very briefly, her head held low.

No, Eleanor said, I don't know her. She got up from the table and turned the television on, sitting at the end of the sofa and resting a cushion on her lap, pulling her dressing gown across her knees. Kate stood up from the floor with a doll still in her hand and went to sit next to her, shuffling across to rest her head against her mother's arm. Eleanor edged away for a second before lifting her arm and wrapping it around her daughter's back.

Half a year later, with Christmas and New Year and winter behind them, with Kate at his mother's house and Eleanor still hiding in bed, he phoned Anna. He thought they should discuss the themes for the next foyer display, he said. As if it couldn't have waited until the next day. As if it was perfectly usual to speak about work like that on a Sunday afternoon. As if he hadn't known that Chris was going to be working away all weekend.

They talked about the foyer for a minute or two, no more, and fell silent. And he lowered his voice as he said, so, shall I come round?

She was quiet at first, and he wasn't sure if she'd heard him. He could hear a lawnmower somewhere nearby, and music. It sounded as if she had the back door open, and he imagined her sitting there with a warm breeze blowing through the house. Sorry? she said.

He looked up at the ceiling, squeezing the back of his neck.

I was just wondering, he said. If you're not doing anything. If you've not got anything to do, maybe I should come round. I'm not doing anything, he added. She hesitated for only a moment.

Okay, she said. Yes. Okay. He held the phone away from his face, looking at it, wondering what he was doing.

Okay, he said.

43 *Small fragment of metal, unidentified, 1983*

For a long time, he thought about it every day. That strange expectant atmosphere. The feeling of needing to leave but being unable to. The shock of that first touch, the dizzying force of it. Later, he found himself able to not think about it for days at a time, weeks even, caught out only by some passing reminder – birdsong, summer evening sunlight, rubble overgrown with birch trees and wildflowers. He would see these things, hear them, and he would remember.

But eventually even these things failed to bring it to mind, and he was able to go for months without remembering what had happened that day. And by the time he and Eleanor were driving to Liverpool to catch the Belfast ferry, almost twenty years later, it took something as direct as her stroking the bare warm skin of his belly and catching her finger on the old faded scar to bring it suddenly back.

She said are you sure you don't mind me coming with you? He drew his breath in sharply and laughed.

Well, it's a bit late now isn't it? he said. Her finger was still moving back and forth across the scar, looking for and finding the twin trails of tiny dotted lines where the stitches had once been, and he thought once more of the things he'd never told her, the things he wasn't going across the water to say.

The first punch was a shock. It shouldn't have been. He should have been thinking more clearly, when Chris suggested it, he should have thought about whether it really was quicker to cut across the site of the old car factory on their way back home, squeezing through a gap in the fence while Chris talked about the work he'd once done there, pointing out the brickworked outlines of the old warehouses and offices, the paint shops, the testing bays, the assembly line. He should have wondered if there was more to the conversation's drift towards marriage and trust than just the two pints of beer swimming through them, the long sloping fall of the evening's light and the birds sliding across the sky. He should have listened, and thought, and realised what might be coming. He should have known that the offer of a drink after work was out of the ordinary, that their talk had been a little too awkward, a little too forced, that Chris had seemed all along to be waiting for something. But he hadn't thought about any of these things; or if he had, he'd done nothing about them, and so when that first punch came, it came as a shock.

He turned just as Chris caught him with it in the stomach, noticing the strange grim look of concentration on his face, even as his body folded around that lump of a fist, even as his feet were scraping and scrabbling across the stony ground. He looked up, almost laughing, as if it might have been a joke or he could turn it into one, and he said what what are you doing what's this? Chris said nothing, and brought the heel of his open hand crashing into the side of David's head like a hammer.

And even as the punches were falling across his face, his ribs, his kidneys, David still found the time to be surprised, the breath to say but but what no but I didn't do anything what are you fuck I didn't do a thing. Chris laughed when he heard this, and kicked David's legs out from under him, the sun-baked concrete cracking hard against the side of his face as he fell to the floor.

What did you think you were doing, mate? Chris said, wiping his mouth with the back of his hand. How did you think you were going to get away with it?

I didn't do anything, David said, there's nothing, we only,

and Chris called him a liar, a liar and a cunt, kicking him in the side of the head as he lay on the ground.

It was a hot summer's day when he went to her house, when he telephoned and asked if he should come round and she said okay, when he walked over there and she opened the door and said hello. She'd tied her hair up, and long curls of it were falling loose across her face, and she kept blowing them out of her eyes, fanning herself with a piece of paper and saying it's hot, I'm hot, aren't you? And every time she said it she giggled, nervously or embarrassedly or excitedly, he couldn't tell. She had a laugh that made his ears flush red. She asked him in, and she poured them both a drink, and she dropped ice cubes into the glasses. She dared him to suck a whole ice cube and he dared her back, and they stood there in her kitchen with their mouths puckered around a block of ice each, grimacing at each other, her eyes watering and sparkling, and when she spat hers out, laughing, she touched him once again. Her two hands flat to his chest, gently, briefly. It had been months since Eleanor had touched him like that.

She was wearing a blue dress, a very pale blue, as though it had been washed too often, cut low and hanging from her bare round shoulders on straps as thin as parcel string. Her feet were bare. She caught him looking at her and smiled.

They sat in the front room with their drinks. They sat next to each other, and she turned towards him, folding her legs beneath her and stretching one arm out along the back of the sofa. And she talked a lot, quickly, she laughed and the way she laughed made him feel uncomfortable and good at the same time. And when she didn't talk she took a long slow sip of her drink, looking at him over the top of her glass, a long slow look which he wanted to turn away from but couldn't. He had no idea what he was doing, now that he was there, and he wanted to leave, and he didn't want to leave. She asked him how things were with Eleanor, and he said the same, that she wasn't spending so long in bed but that she still wouldn't leave the house and she still looked puffy-eyed when he came in from work. He told her the doctor had been talking about a different medication and that he wasn't sure it was really the answer. It was almost a routine conversation by then.

How long has it been now? she asked. He had to think for a moment.

He said, she's not always like it, you know, it comes and goes. She was fine when she was pregnant, and fine for a while afterwards. But it just comes on sometimes, he said. It doesn't seem like there's anything either of us can do to stop it. I'm not even sure the pills make much difference, he said; they just make it easier to deal with, they're only damping things down. She was watching him while he told her this, nodding, leaning towards him slightly.

She said, it's good, you know, what you do for her, it's impressive.

He said, well no, not really, I mean, she's my wife, what else would I do?

She was wearing a long bead necklace, she was twisting it between two fingers and when she let it go it fell against her bare skin and again he couldn't help looking.

She said, I'm glad you're here, it's good to have you here.

Well, it's good to be here, he said, trying to be mock-polite but actually meaning it. It was good to be there, on her sofa, with a cold drink on a hot afternoon, and her sitting there in that dress, blowing curls of dark hair out of her eyes, and talking, and laughing, and touching her fingers to her lips.

She said, is it? suddenly, demandingly. Is it good to be here, are you glad you're here?

Yes, he said, yes it is, yes I am, and he was confused and she was quiet.

He finished his drink. He went to the toilet. He washed his face and his hands, and when he came out of the bathroom at the top of the stairs she was there.

She was standing in the open doorway of the room next to

the bathroom, leaning against the door frame slightly, one ankle curled round behind the other. The blue dress hung down to her knees, but with one leg lifted like that it rode up higher, almost halfway up her thigh. He looked at her. That was all. He just looked at her. She lifted a hand to adjust the knot of hair at the back of her head, and she smiled. That was enough. That moment, standing there looking at her, and her smile, her smile for him, that hot day with the windows open and the sleepy sounds of summer drifting through the house, a lawnmower somewhere, children shouting, that was enough.

How do I look? she said.

She told me David, she fucking told me, Chris said. He lit a cigarette, breathing heavily, and told David to stand up, half helping and half pulling him up by the collar of his jacket. David lifted his hand to his face, checking his swollen lips, his cheeks, the bruises around his eyes, looking at the blood on his fingers as he pulled his hand away. He coughed, and spat blood on to the ground, and wondered if that was it over already.

He said, Chris, look, it wasn't like that, it wasn't, we didn't. Chris lifted his hand, already starting to turn away.

Fuck it, he said. Forget it, he said. He turned back towards David, and for a moment David thought he was reaching out to shake his hand, that this was the end of it after all; but instead he reached for the collar of David's jacket, yanking him towards the ground, leaning over to spit the words into his ear. He said, you and Eleanor, that's your problem. He said, I don't care if she's not giving you any or if she makes you sleep in the spare room or if she won't even undress in front of you ever again mate. He said, it don't bother me, it's not my problem, it's nothing to do with me, but you fucking keep your eyes off mine, alright? He said these things quietly, with a smile in his voice as though he was trying not to laugh, and he gripped David's jacket tighter, so that the collar squeezed and cut into his neck. And all David could think about, as he felt the veins on his neck starting to pulse, was that there was only one way Chris would have known about those things. There was only one person he'd ever discussed them with.

Alright? Chris said again, and David nodded, making a noise which was supposed to be yes, okay, I understand. Chris stood up straight, and as he did so he pushed David away. David felt his feet slip from under him, felt his face smack against the warm hard ground again, felt small stones and grit grinding against the skin of his cheek. There was something sharp underneath him, jutting into his stomach, and just as he was arching his back away from it, he felt the weight of Chris's feet stamping on his back, a sudden gasp of pain as the something sharp broke through his skin, gouging and twisting and tearing into his muscles and his flesh.

Chris backed off, and he rolled over to look down at the pain. For a moment, there was nothing; a rip in his shirt, a glimpse of something hard and rust-coloured. But as he looked, and as Chris began to turn and walk away, the blood suddenly poured out, seeping through the fabric of his shirt, sliding thickly across his skin. He looked at the blood, and he looked at Chris, still only a few yards off but moving further, and he looked up at the empty pale blue sky.

He washed his face and his hands, he came out of the bathroom, and there she was, standing there in that dress, looking at him. How do I look? she said, and it seemed as if she really wanted to know, as if she wasn't sure, when every inch of her was breathtaking and desirable, her elegant bare feet and the smooth straight rise of her legs, the way her dress pulled against the curve of her hips and the press of her breasts, her shoulders, her neck, her eyes. Her eyes looked strange for a moment, when he looked, anxious almost.

He said, you look good, and she said, do I? really? as if she genuinely didn't think so, as if she thought he might be humouring her somehow. As if there was no one who told her each day how very good she looked.

He said, softly, yes Anna, you do, you look very good. She smiled again, looking away for a moment, looking over her shoulder into the room. He still hadn't moved. When she turned back her eyes looked different and she wasn't smiling.

She said, quietly, looking straight at him, alright then, come on, and she turned quickly in the doorway, stepping into the room, out of sight.

He didn't even breathe.

That movement, the turn of her hips, the swing and lift of her dress around the backs of her legs.

He found it difficult to remember, later, how long she had waited, how long he had stood there looking at the open door.

He didn't move. He couldn't.

She reappeared, and when she spoke this time her eyes spilled clearly over into tears, her voice cracking. She said don't be shy. She said I thought you wanted to.

He said, I do.

She said well come on then, and she opened her mouth slightly, and there were tears down both her cheeks, shining.

He wanted her, immensely.

He couldn't move.

Later, he would have liked to have been able to say that he thought of Eleanor at that moment, that he remembered how much he loved her still and how important it was that he went straight back home and told her. Or that he thought of Kate, and how privileged he felt to be a part of her life, and that he knew with sudden clarity that he could do nothing to jeopardise that. But these things wouldn't have been true. It was only fear which kept him from moving towards her. Fear of what might happen if he did, fear of what might happen then, and next, and for the rest of his life.

He turned and walked down the stairs, slowly, his knees buckling with each step, feeling the weight of her gaze on his shoulders, watching him. He hesitated again at the bottom of the stairs, wondering whether he should turn and say something, or change his mind, or stay for another drink so that they could both pretend nothing had happened at all. He heard the swirl of her dress behind him as she turned away from the top of the stairs, and he heard her bedroom door closing, and he thought, even then, about going back. He wiped his face with the sleeve of his shirt and opened the front door, stepping out into the afternoon sun and walking quickly away.

He was surprised, as he lay there, by just how much pain there was, a ragged-edged, nameless, roaring pain. He was surprised by how much blood continued to spill out of him, pooling thickly across the cracked and broken ground. He tried to bring his hands to the place where it hurt, to see if he could take out what had broken into him, to pinch the edges of the wound and stop the endless outpouring of blood. But his hands quivered uselessly when he tried to move them, lifting weakly into the air, falling again. He turned his head, watching Chris moving further away, watching the birds cluster and sweep across the evening sky.

He thought about when Kate had been born, and the visceral sense he'd had of the need to protect her, the violence he'd felt rising in his body at the thought of anyone so much as intending her harm. He realised that he'd already failed her, and he wondered who would be there to protect her now, if they would do a better job than it seemed he was capable of.

He saw Chris turning round without breaking his stride, looking back from fifty yards away. He saw him stopping, turning again, shielding his eyes from the low sun. They looked at each other. David lifted his bloodied hands, in some feeble gesture of need, and Chris ran, stumbling, across the broken ground.

44 *Pair of child's gloves, striped, c.1983*

When Eleanor was eight years old, she told him once, she lost a pair of gloves on the way home from school. It was getting close to spring and the day had turned warm, so she'd left them in her coat pocket, not realising they had fallen out until just before she got to her front door. She spent an hour looking for them, running back to school with her head down, scanning the pavement and the gutter and the railing tops. She got to the school just as her teacher was leaving, and he let her back in to look under her desk, in the cloakroom, in the corridor, in the outside toilets, but they weren't there. She ran back to the house, her frantic search blurred by hot, frightened tears. I didn't want to get into trouble for being home late, she told him, but I didn't want to get into trouble for losing the gloves either. When she gave up, and knocked on the door, and wasn't able to meet her mother's questioning glare, she got into trouble for both. She was sent to bed without any tea, and smacked on each step of the steep stairs, and wasn't allowed another pair of gloves until she was old enough to buy them for herself. I used to wear socks on my hands, she said, when it was deathly cold, and hoick my hands up into my sleeves so that no one could see.

When Kate was seven years old, the autumn after David had been in hospital, Eleanor bought her a new pair of gloves and attached them to her winter coat with two lengths of bright red wool. She took a sewing kit out from the cupboard under the stairs one Sunday afternoon and settled down into the sofa by the window. Kate stood and watched her for a few moments, distracted from the farm she was building in front of the fireplace, a look of puzzled concentration in her eyes.

What are you doing? she asked. Eleanor looked up from trying to thread the needle, her daughter's coat laid out across her lap, the two gloves nestling together on the arm of the sofa.

I'm going to sew these gloves to your coat, she said. So you don't lose them. Kate thought about this for a moment, and turned away.

Okay, she said, as though giving permission. She went back to the farm, her grandmother watching her fondly and asking where she was going to put the sheep. In here! Kate announced, dunking the two plastic sheep into a felt duck-pond, picking up a horse and galloping it around the farm in circles, neighing loudly, knocking over dry stone walls and stumbling into a tractor, saying ow the horse has broke his leg he has to go to hospital and have stitches, her voice loud and shrill and excited. Dorothy glanced across at Eleanor, ready to shush her granddaughter, but Eleanor was still concentrating on threading the needle and didn't say anything. David came back inside from putting out the rubbish.

The aerial's come loose, he said, I'll have to go up on the roof and fix it. Or get someone round. No one replied, so he went back into the kitchen to make a start on the washing up, standing in the doorway a moment while he waited for the water to run hot, watching his wife and his daughter and his mother sitting together in his home on a quiet Sunday afternoon. He had discovered, with surprise, that this was one of the deepest pleasures in his life, to cook dinner for these three people, to eat with them, and to settle into a long afternoon of being in their presence. He liked to sit at the end of the sofa with his eyes closed, so that they would think he was asleep, so that he could be there without being there, listening to their lazy talk, Kate's babbling chatter, his mother's commentary on the afternoon's films. And he liked to listen to them before dinner, through the doorway,

Eleanor telling Dorothy about their week, Dorothy telling Eleanor about hers, Kate interrupting to ask questions and tell them both about something that had happened at school, their conversation sharpened by hunger as he kept busy in the kitchen – checking the roast in the oven, lifting it out to spoon more juices over its back, sliding a knife between the bones to see if it was cooked, draining the vegetables over the sink with a rush of steaming water – knowing that his mother would be listening, would be thinking that she'd taught him something at least.

Eleanor finally managed to thread the needle, and reached for the long hanging end of the thread, twisting it round her finger to make a knot. As she did so, the needle spilt out of her fingers and down between the cushions somewhere. She slammed her hand on to the arm of the sofa in frustration, knocking the gloves to the floor and saying a loud shit! before catching herself. David turned the tap off and stepped forward, wanting to help. Kate looked up, startled, with a hand over her mouth, saying Mummy said a naughty word, naughty word, Mummy said a naughty word, saying it almost as a song to herself, crouching back down amongst the pieces of her farm. Dorothy looked across at Eleanor, trying not to smile, and stood up.

Shall we go up and play with Sindy now? she asked Kate, reaching for her hand. Kate looked at her, and stood up as well.

Okay, she said, without seeming to think about it, and the two of them went away up the stairs.

You okay? David asked, moving towards Eleanor. She smiled, shaking her head, wiping her eyes with the tips of her fingers.

I'm fine, she said. It's just, sewing's not really my strong point, you know?

It went down the side there, he said, pointing to where he'd seen the needle fall. Stand up a minute. She stood up, and he lifted the cushion away, peering in at the fluff and the crumbs, picking out a pen, some scraps of paper, three halfpenny coins, and the needle.

It's like an archaeological dig in there, he said, smiling, handing her the needle as she sat down again; there you go.

Thanks, she said. Anyway, how about you soldier, you okay? She looked up at him, reaching out and pulling him a little closer by the hem of his shirt, lifting the thick cotton and gazing at the small dotted scar, still raised and raw. How does it feel? she asked.

It's okay, he told her. It doesn't hurt really. Just sometimes when I stand up too quickly, or bend over. She pulled him closer, and kissed the faintly bruised skin around the scar.

I'm going to have to keep a closer eye on you, aren't I? she said, trying to re-thread the needle. Do a bit more looking after you. He sat on the arm of the sofa, not sure what she meant. I'm going to have to pay more attention, she said, glancing up at him; wouldn't you say?

They could hear, upstairs, his mother talking softly as Kate's feet pounded across the floor and she acted out Sindy's catwalking at the top of her voice. He glanced upwards.

David? she said, lowering the needle and thread into her lap. David, what happened? I mean, what really happened? He kept his eyes on the ceiling.

You know what happened, he said, his voice low and steady. She noticed him gripping the edge of the sofa-arm, trying to keep his balance. I've told you what happened, he said. I don't remember all that much about it, he said.

But why would someone do that? she asked. It doesn't make sense. For no reason?

He could have told her then, he thought later, he should have told her then. Things would have been better that way, maybe.

I don't know Eleanor, he said quietly. It was just some drunk. I was just in the wrong place at the wrong time. She held his gaze, winding and unwinding the thread around her finger.

She said, I just want to understand David, I just want to know why it happened. I want to know what it is you're not telling me. She turned away, squinting at the needle, easing the thread through its narrow eye.

He said, what do you mean? He said, there's nothing I'm not telling you. It was just some drunk. It was an accident almost. Don't worry about it now, he said. He leant forward and kissed the hair on the top of her head, and she told him he was in her light. He sat back again, moving his shadow away from her face and her hands, watching as she picked up a length of wool and one of Kate's small neat gloves.

She said, it just doesn't make sense David, and he said, I know, I know.

He went outside to look at the aerial again. It was swinging in the light breeze, angling towards the roof, looking like it would take a tile off in a strong wind. He wondered who he could borrow a ladder from. He wondered if he would ever tell Eleanor what had really happened with Chris, what had almost happened with Anna. He wondered how she would react if he did. He walked to the end of the garden to put the lid back on the dustbin, and went inside to finish the washing up, watching Eleanor's sewing as he put away the last of the plates and the pans.

How's it going now? he asked her. Fine, she said, nearly done. She knotted the last stitch, snapped the loose thread across her hand, and held the coat up for him to see. The two gloves hung down from the cuffs, turning slow circles in the air, and he pictured them swinging back and forth as Kate ran towards him in the park, kicking up leaves, stumbling over divots and molehills, laughing.

There, she said, try that. David tugged at one of the gloves to test it, and it pulled away in his hand, dangling a long strand of red wool with a tail of broken stitches beneath it. He looked at her in anticipation, but she just shrugged, smiling as she pulled at the other glove and it snapped away in turn.

This is definitely not my strong point, David, she said, breaking into a laugh, and he agreed that, no, she was right, it probably wasn't.

45 *Job application form, Head Curator, c.1984*

He was going through the filing cabinet in his office when he heard someone come into the room and quietly close the door. He'd been looking through the records of old exhibitions, looking for the acquisitions list from a watchmaking display he'd put together in 1978, but when he heard Anna gently coughing and shuffling her feet he slid the drawer shut and turned around. Hello, she said quietly, not quite looking at him. He nodded.

He'd been trying to avoid her since he'd started back at work, spending as much time as possible in his office, being careful whenever he'd needed to venture into the corridors and galleries. When they had come across each other, in the staff-room, or in a meeting, they'd spoken as briefly and as distantly as possible, avoiding each other's eyes, their voices thick with self-control. Talking to her made him feel uncomfortable in a different way from before; talking to her now made him want to look over his shoulder and see if anyone was there.

Hello, he said, still holding a folder from the filing cabinet. It was clutched against his chest, as if he thought she was going to try and take it from him.

I haven't seen much of you since you came back, she said, stepping forward from the door.

No, he said. No, I suppose not. I've been catching up on some paperwork. It builds up, doesn't it? He tried to smile. He noticed that she'd cut her hair much shorter, pinning it back into a tight knot on the back of her head. He noticed that she kept opening and closing her hands, smoothing them down the sides of her skirt.

How's Eleanor? she said. And Kate? How are they both doing? She smiled, and tilted her head to one side, and he already wanted to tell her to leave.

They're fine, he said. They're both doing fine. She waited for him to say something more, and he realised he should ask how Chris was. He said nothing, and he felt his breath catch at the top of his lungs, felt his arms starting to shiver against his chest. They're fine, he said again.

Anna stepped closer to the desk. I wanted to say sorry, she said, so quietly that for a moment he wasn't quite sure what he'd heard. It wasn't supposed to happen, she said, not like that. He almost smiled, wondering how it had been supposed to happen.

He said, have you heard back from Manchester about those loan requests?

She said, you're doing the right thing you know. There was a knock at the door. He looked at her. She moved closer, until there was only the corner of the desk between them.

He said, they should have got back to us by now. It's been six weeks, hasn't it?

Not telling anyone I mean, she said, resting one hand on the desk. I mean, no one needs to know do they? There was a second knock at the door, and Christine from decorative arts came in, hesitating slightly as she saw David and Anna move a step back from each other.

Sorry, she said. Sorry, but David, there's a problem with this delivery, from the V&A, you remember? Could you come and have a look at the paperwork before the driver leaves?

I'll be right there, he said, holding up a finger to say just give us one moment. Anna looked down at the floor, and they both waited for Christine to go. He wanted to tell Anna that it wasn't for her to say whether or not he told anyone what had happened. He wanted to ask her who she thought she was to come into his office and say these things. He looked at her, his tongue fat and dry in his mouth, and he said, sorry Christine, could you excuse us, I'll be with you in just a minute. Christine looked at them both, stepped back, and closed the door. He waited for her footsteps, and heard nothing. Anna looked up and smiled.

You know Malcolm's leaving at the end of next year, don't you? she said. He shrugged, and nodded, and turned away to put the folder he was still holding back into the filing cabinet, trying and failing to hide his surprise. Malcolm Newbold was the Head Curator and had been there since the museum first opened. I thought I might go for the job, she said, but I'm not sure about it. He kept his back to her, thumbing through the files, wanting her to leave. He felt her moving closer, and wondered if that was her breath he could feel on the back of his neck.

Do you think I should? she asked. I mean, do you think there'd be any point? The uncertainty in her voice surprised him. He turned round, not understanding why she even needed to ask, why she needed to ask him. She was sucking her lip, anxiously, fiddling with the hair on the back of her head. He wanted to reassure her, despite everything, to touch a hand to her arm and say that of course she should apply, she was perfectly capable, she should know that.

He said, I don't know Anna. That's for you to say.

How about you? she asked. Will you apply?

I don't know, he said again. He moved past her, their sleeves touching as he did so, and opened the door. Christine was still waiting. Sorry about that, he said, and followed her down towards the delivery doors. At the end of the corridor he glanced over his shoulder and saw Anna standing behind his desk, sliding his papers and pencil pots into slightly different positions, adjusting the angle of the lamp and, just as he turned the corner, reaching for his chair.

46 *Hand-drawn family tree (incomplete), dated May 1984*

Kate knelt up on her chair, stretching out across the table for the big pack of felt-tip pens. And anyway, she said, Mrs Dunn said Lisa's picture was too messy to go in the class-book, I heard her saying it to Lisa, she said Lisa would have to do it again. Kate's friends both sniggered, ducking their heads as if they were still in the classroom and were trying to hide something, or as if they thought Kate's dad might hear.

Yeah and plus as well, said Becky, sitting across from Kate and chewing the end of a pencil, I heard her say she was going to send it to Tony Hart. The three girls laughed again, and Rachel stuck her tongue into her lower lip, making a sound like a der-brain.

Be funny if she did, they'd probably put Lisa Jones age five on it because they wouldn't believe she was eight, she said, and they all sank into their seats with laughter.

They worked quietly for a moment, passing the pencils and rulers and rubbers and felt-tips backwards and forwards across the table.

Have you done all the people on yours yet? Rachel asked, looking across the table at Becky's work.

Nearly, Becky said. Have you?

Nearly, Rachel said, picking her pencil up again and crossing something out. She paused. Kate, have you decided who you're inviting to your birthday yet? she said. Kate didn't look up.

Nearly, she said.

David stood in the kitchen, next to the open back door, listening. He knew he shouldn't, that Kate would see it as some kind of betrayal, would shriek indignantly if she saw him standing there, but he couldn't help it. It was the same impulse which made him close his eyes and pretend to be asleep when she came into the room, or wait just around the corner when he collected her from school, or crouch beside her bed and watch her as she slept; the need to know more about her, to gain some admittance into the ever-enlarging secret territories of her life, to be granted a glimmer of understanding of this confident child his baby girl had become.

Does your dad draw family trees all the time? he heard Becky say.

No, Kate said airily, only sometimes because most of the time he finds old stuff in the ground or at jumble sales, I think, and he collects it for the museum and he makes expeditions of it.

Exhibitions, said Rachel quickly.

That's what I said, Kate replied.

Didn't.

Did.

Didn't.

Did.

David smiled. He liked the thought of his making acquisitions at jumble sales; he wondered what misunderstanding that had grown out of, what else there was about his job that she couldn't really grasp. He'd taken her down to the museum a few days earlier, and shown her some old family trees they had in the archives, to help her understand what her teacher was asking them to do; he'd got out the long rolls of darkened paper, cracked and smudged with age, and when he'd said that the family tree she was drawing would one day look like that, faded and almost illegible, she'd only gazed at him blankly, disbelievingly, not yet old enough to share his sense of the long hurried march of time. It was only the second time she'd even been to the museum; she didn't like history, she said. She was going to be a fashion designer, she said, so why did she need to know about history?

But she'd come to him when she needed help with the

class project they'd been set, asking him what was a family tree and how do you know what to write on it and what is a maiden name, and her friends had been keen to come round and share in his expertise; had in fact squabbled, from what he could tell, for the privilege. He'd sat round the table with them, asking if they had their lists of brothers and sisters and aunts and uncles and cousins and grandparents, and the dates of when these people had been born and maybe married and maybe died, and he'd drawn an example of how a family tree might look, with the carefully ruled straight lines, the generations, the branches, the blank spaces where there was any uncertainty. He tried to explain that it didn't actually have to look like a real tree, that it was just a way people had of describing it, but they were determined to use the felt-tips so he didn't argue and instead left them to it, telling them he was going out to the garden to make the most of the first decent Sunday afternoon they'd had all year.

Who's got the green pen? asked Becky.

David opened the back door, hesitating, trying to make himself go outside.

Kate's using it, Rachel murmured, still colouring in the trunk of her tree with a brown felt-tip. She's had it for ages, she added, and Kate sighed and tutted and muttered that it was her pen anyway. Becky sat back in her chair, waiting, looking across at the other girls' work.

You haven't got all the dates on yours, she said, leaning towards Kate. How come?

My mum didn't know all of them when I asked her, Kate said, not looking up, it's all my nana's brothers and sisters and she said she couldn't remember all of them, there was too many.

Why don't you ask your nana? Becky asked.

We never see her, Kate said. Rachel looked up from her work, first at Kate, and then at Becky, and then at Kate again.

You never see your nana? Why not? she said.

She lives in Scotland, Kate said. It's too far away.

It's not, said Rachel, we went on holiday in Scotland last year so it's not too far. Kate didn't say anything for a moment.

But anyway we don't see her, she said quietly.

Why don't you phone her up and ask her then? asked Becky.

Mum won't let me, Kate said.

Oh, Becky said. The three of them were silent again, concentrating on their drawings, Becky tracing over her pencilled branches with a biro while she waited for the green felt-tip, the scrape and scribble of the other girls' pens the only sound for a moment.

They always say it's too far away but really I think my mum doesn't like her mum, Kate said abruptly. I think she was not very nice to her or something. The others looked at her. Anyway I've finished now anyway, she said, passing the green pen to Becky and sitting back in her chair.

Let me see let me see, said Rachel, pulling Kate's piece of paper across the table and looking at it for a moment before passing it back. It's nice but it doesn't look like a tree much, she said. Kate gasped.

Yeah it does, she said loudly. Yeah it does, it looks more like a tree than yours does, yours is all a funny shape, look, it looks stupid.

Looks more like a tree than yours does, Rachel insisted; your drawing's even more bad than Lisa's is so there. Kate threw a felt-tip at Rachel, and stuck her tongue out, and then smiled.

I thought you wanted to come to my birthday, she said. Becky, who'd been keeping out of things by concentrating on colouring in the leaves of her tree, looked up and smiled as well. Rachel looked at them both.

Yeah I did but I don't now, because it's going to be boring anyway, she said.

No it's not, said Kate, smiling to herself.

Yeah it is, Rachel repeated. Who are you inviting anyway then, she said, her voice wavering a little; I bet you're inviting Paul because I bet you fancy him, everyone knows.

No I don't! Kate shrieked, and then all three of them looked up at the ceiling as they heard a steady thump-thump-thump from the room above.

Who's that? Becky whispered, as all three of them ducked back down over their work.

My mum, said Kate. She's in bed. We were supposed to be quiet and not wake her up. She looked pointedly at Rachel as she said this, as if it was all her fault.

What's she doing in bed? said Rachel. Is she working nights?

No, Kate said. She's ill, she's got a cold or something like that. Have you finished yet Becky? I want to go out now.

Yeah, said Rachel, this is boring.

Nearly, said Becky, as the other two started putting the lids back on the pens. Give me a chance, you were hogging the green for ages.

David closed the back door loudly, and the girls looked up as he appeared in the kitchen doorway.

All done? he said, smiling at them; how did you get on?

There was a pause as each girl waited for the other to speak.

Alright, Kate said eventually. We're finished now, can we go out? David stood over the table, looking at each of the family trees.

These look really good, he said. Did you all manage to fit everyone in? Kate nodded; the other girls shrugged.

Yeah and we've finished now Dad, Kate said, tucking all the pens back into their plastic pouch. Can we go out?

David backed away, raising his hands. Sorry, he said. Pardon me for taking an interest. Of course you can go out – where are you going?

Park, Kate said as they all stood up.

Well, make sure you cross at the crossing, David said. Bye girls, he added, as the three of them slipped out through the door.

Bye Mr Carter, they mumbled back.

Say hello to your parents for me, he added, but the front door was already closing and they were gone.

47 *Envelopes w/Aberdeen postmarks, occasional 1984–2000*

A letter came for him at the museum. It was from Donald, Eleanor's brother, with a photograph of his eldest son's first baby, and a short note saying when he'd been born and how much he weighed and that the mother and father were doing fine. *It is strange to find myself a grandfather already*, the note said, *and young Eleanor a great aunt too. But we are none of us getting any younger.*

Where did he get the address from? Eleanor asked when he showed her, putting the photograph down and looking at the envelope instead.

Eleanor, David said, impatiently; it can't have been difficult, can it? There's only one museum in Coventry. That's not the important thing, he said. She put the envelope down, closing and rubbing her eyes for a moment.

How are you feeling? he asked. Eleanor shrugged.

Fine, she said, fine. Why?

I was just wondering, he said. Do you miss them? She sighed, and stood up, and started to clear the table.

David, she said, don't. I mean, yes. Of course I do. But there's nothing I can do about it now. She carried the dishes through to the kitchen and closed the door behind her. David gathered up the photo, the envelope, the note, tucking them into his jacket pocket.

I trust this finds you both well, the note said. *We often wonder how you are keeping.*

The letter had arrived almost a week earlier, but Eleanor had been in a strange mood when he'd got home, brittle and tearful, and on Friday morning she'd refused to get out of bed. He'd known immediately that she was having one of her increasingly unusual and short-lived depressions; that he would have to take Kate to his mother's for the weekend and let Eleanor sleep, and be there if she wanted to talk but more likely leave her alone while she waited for the increased dose of medication to grind into effect. By Monday evening she'd been well enough to come downstairs and eat with them but he'd waited another two days before taking Donald's letter from his jacket and showing it to her. He listened to her in the kitchen now, remembering when a weekend like the one they'd just had would have stretched into weeks and sometimes months; dark slow days when he would flounder helplessly and resentfully around, wanting desperately to make things better but unable to find any way of doing so.

It was hard to say what had happened, really, what had changed. They hadn't spoken about it much. When Kate was born he'd thought that she might be cured, that the energy and devotion she was putting into raising a daughter might perhaps let some light into the darkened room her life had sometimes become. But that turned out not to be quite true. And then later he'd thought, guiltily, that the time she'd spent looking after him when he came out of hospital had cured her, that being relied upon in that way had given her some strength or vitality or reason to be. But that had turned out not to be the way things were either. These things were partly true, some of the time; they helped, and she never again sank so deeply into the speechless unreachable despair she'd struggled through before Kate had been born. She still had bad days, bad weeks, but she'd learnt to live with it somehow, had lost her fear of it, had found, crucially, a sympathetic and imaginative doctor who'd worked to develop the best levels of medication and treatment for her. It had become just another part of their lives now; something they dealt with and wondered occasionally how it had come so close to breaking the both of them.

Do you want a hand in there? he called out, standing up suddenly. Eleanor appeared in the doorway, drying her hands on a tea towel.

It's okay thanks, she said, smiling. I've finished now.

48 *Photographs of Kate at eight years old, with birthday cards, 1984*

His mother spotted them first, over by the ice-cream van. Isn't that your friend from work? she said to David. What's her name – Ann? He turned, and saw Anna standing there with Chris, laughing. He felt his body tensing for a moment, and turned away.

It's Anna, he said, correcting her, reaching across for another sandwich, hoping someone else would say something. Susan turned to look.

Aren't you going to say hello? his mother asked, lifting her hand towards the two of them, trying to catch their eye. Eleanor shifted round on the blanket and glanced at David.

I see her at work every day, David said, trying to sound indifferent. She probably sees enough of me as it is, he said.

Yes, but, his mother said, waving in their direction, you could offer them some birthday cake at least. Hello! she called out suddenly, waving more vigorously; Anna! Hello! David stood, and waved as well, taking a few steps towards them. They looked over, Anna waving back, Chris nodding and moving closer towards her. Come and have some birthday cake! Dorothy called, beckoning them over and pointing at the half-eaten cake in the centre of the blanket. They hesitated, looking at each other, looking at David. Chris looked over his shoulder, and said something into Anna's ear. David watched them, and noticed Chris wiping a hand on the back of his trousers, and noticed Anna avoiding his eyes.

The birthday picnic had been his mother's idea. Susan came, with her children, and they let Kate choose three friends from her class to invite, and they all sat round a chequered blanket eating crustless sandwiches and crisps, drinking fizzy drinks, and singing happy birthday as Kate waited to blow out the eight pink candles on the chocolate ladybird cake Dorothy had magically produced from a box in her wheeled shopping bag. By the time Dorothy spotted Anna and Chris, the children had got bored of sitting down and were chasing each other around the park, playing a complicated game which Kate appeared to be making up as they went along.

Do you want to see if they're all okay? David said to Eleanor quietly, as Anna and Chris walked towards them. She looked up at him, and over towards Kate, and stood up.

Right then, she said, wandering over to where Kate and Mark were trying to pull a balloon out of each other's hands. David moved away from the blanket.

Hello there, he said, a little too loudly, holding up one hand as Anna approached, waving faintly.

Hello Anna, said Dorothy, standing up uncomfortably, brushing crumbs from her blouse and skirt. What a lovely coincidence, she said, smiling.

Hello Mrs Carter, Anna replied, stepping past David and reaching a hand out to Dorothy's arm. Someone's birthday is it? she asked. Chris stood back warily, not saying anything yet.

It's Kate's birthday, David said, turning away from Chris, gesturing over to where his daughter and her cousins and friends were still playing, noticing Eleanor watching him. She's eight, he said. Have you met Susan, my sister? he added. Susan looked up, and smiled, and they said hello to each other, Anna nodding as if she thought they might have met before, brushing her hair behind her ears.

There was a moment when nobody spoke, the children's voices careering across the grass, and then Anna said oh, yes, sorry, this is my husband Chris; Chris, this is Mrs Carter, and Susan, and you've met David before, and that's David's wife Eleanor over there. She put her hand behind Chris, drawing him in, gesturing to each of them, and Chris smiled and nodded at each one of them in turn.

No, please, David's mother said, call me Dorothy. Eleanor smiled and lifted a hand in greeting when they all looked at her. Kate stopped chasing a boy from her class for a moment to see what was happening, then ran on. Dorothy looked at David, wondering why he wasn't saying anything. Chris looked over his shoulder.

Would you like a piece of cake? Dorothy asked Anna. There's plenty to go round, she said, already kneeling to flip a slice on to a paper napkin.

Oh, no, thanks, Anna said quickly. We should be getting on, really. We've got things to do, she said, glancing at Chris, meeting David's eye by mistake and looking away.

Oh, come on, Dorothy insisted, you can take it with you if you want. It'll only go to waste, she said. Anna smiled awkwardly.

Well, okay, thanks very much, she said, stepping closer and kneeling down on the edge of the blanket. Susan shifted further round to make room for her, not saying anything.

Here you are then, Dorothy said, passing Anna a slice each for her and Chris. Thanks Dorothy, Anna said, this looks lovely. She turned, and tried to pass Chris a slice; but he was standing too far away, so David had to take it from her and pass it on himself. Their eyes met as Chris took the cake.

Cheers, he said. David looked at him. How's it going? Chris said, and David shrugged and said fine, you know, things are fine. Lovely day for a birthday party, he added, and Chris nodded.

I heard you were in hospital, he said as he bit into the cake; nothing serious was it? You alright now? David looked at him. He felt Anna glancing up at them both, and Susan turning to look across as well.

No, nothing serious, he said slowly, calmly. I'm right as rain now, he said, oddly.

Chris finished his cake, crumpling the napkin in his hand,

and with his mouth full he said something like, good, good, that's alright then, fighting fit, eh? Excuse me, he said, pointing to his mouth and turning away slightly.

Well, Dorothy said, after a moment's silence, this is lovely, isn't it? All of us together like this. She looked over at Eleanor, walking back now with Mark and Claire holding her hands, Kate skipping along behind them, the other children – Becky and Lisa and Paul – hanging back a little. We should do this more often, she said. It's such a shame your John couldn't be here though, she added to Susan, saying it almost as an afterthought, almost as though she'd forgotten he should have been there at all. He's often very busy with work, she explained to Anna. He's in management you know, she said, and Anna nodded and tried to look interested.

Chris leant closer to David, while the others were speaking, and lowered his voice to a mutter. You've never said anything, have you? he asked. David felt a pulse of adrenalin sear through his veins. He shook his head, once, almost imperceptibly, feeling his breath tighten, his eyes widen. You're not going to, are you? Chris said, as Mark and Claire threw themselves at Susan, bouncing balloons off her head and scrabbling across the blanket for crisps and chocolate buttons, and as Kate's friend Lisa said she needed to go to the toilet. David looked at Chris, and although at first he thought this was a threat, he realised, abruptly, by the way Chris was looking at him, steadily, uncertainly, waiting for an answer, that it was a plea. That somehow the balance of power had shifted between them, simply by his holding their secret to himself. He held back for a moment, and then shook his head, once.

Kate came over to David, curling her arms around his legs, pushing her face against his stomach, and as he reached down and wrapped his arms around her he held Chris's eyes for a moment longer, allowing himself the faintest of smiles. He lifted her up against his chest, feeling her thin warm arms around his neck, her legs around his hips, her hair brushing against his face as she wriggled into a comfortable position. She was too heavy to hold up like this now, but he held her tightly, briefly, and he looked at Chris as he put her back down, the smile flickering across his lips again. Chris turned away.

Thanks for the cake then Dorothy, Anna said, pushing herself up from her knees. We'll be getting on now though. Things to do, she said, smiling. She passed the paper napkin back to Dorothy, who shook the crumbs out on to the grass and smoothed it across her lap, folding it and putting it back into her bag.

Oh you're welcome, she said, it's nice to meet you again. Say hello to Daddy's friend, she said to Kate, and Kate turned in David's arms to look at this strange woman who'd been eating her cake.

It's my birthday, she said, a little too softly, overawed.

I know, Anna said. How old are you? Kate looked at her, and turned her face in to David's shoulder, embarrassed. Are you eight? Anna asked, moving closer, peering in to the gap between David and her. Kate looked out at her and nodded. I thought so, Anna said. You look very grown up for eight. Kate smiled, proudly.

I got a watch for my birthday, she announced, holding her wrist out for Anna to see.

Chris shifted uncomfortably, touching Anna on the arm, saying Anna can we, and Dorothy suddenly produced a camera from her bag.

I've just thought, she said. Could you do us a favour love, while you're here? Could you take a picture of us all? Anna glanced at Chris, and smiled awkwardly at Dorothy.

Well, I don't know, she said, I'm not much of a photographer.

Oh I'm sure you can manage this old thing, Dorothy said, holding the camera out towards her, clearing a space on the blanket for them all to sit together and pose.

Anna, Chris said again as she took the camera, nodding his head towards the park gates.

Oh it won't take a moment, Dorothy said to him, you don't mind, do you? It's so long since we've had a picture of us all together. She beckoned Susan round to kneel next to her, arranging Mark and Claire in front of them, showing Eleanor and David where they should go, telling Lisa that someone would take her to find a toilet in just a moment. Anna stood back with the camera.

Anna, Chris said. Have you told David the news yet? David glanced up from helping Kate to kneel in front of him with the cake on her lap. Anna turned suddenly to Chris, shaking her head.

What's that then love? asked Dorothy, stretching her arms around Susan and David, reaching out to pull Eleanor a little closer into the group. You've got some good news? Anna tried to laugh.

No, it's nothing, she said. Chris nudged her as she lifted the camera again.

You should tell them, he said, starting to smile. Anna looked embarrassed.

It's not you-know-what is it? said Dorothy, with a sing-song in her voice, ignoring Susan's tut and roll of the eyes.

No, said Anna, it's not that, it's nothing, really.

Oh no dear, Dorothy said. You'll have to tell us now. You can't leave us guessing like that.

She got the head curator job, Chris said abruptly, fixing David's gaze as he said it, smiling. Anna lowered the camera and looked at the ground for a moment, and looked at David, an apology briefly in her eyes.

Oh, well done! said Dorothy. Now, shall we get this picture taken?

As the two of them were walking away across the park, having given the camera back and wished Kate a happy birthday again, having said goodbye and thank you for the cake, Dorothy broke the silence by saying well really. There's no need to gloat. Really. I thought you'd been working there longer than her anyway? she said to David.

Yes Mum, he said, I have. Thanks for reminding me. He started to tidy away the crisp packets and drinks bottles, glancing over at Anna and Chris as they reached the gates of the park, Chris with one hand around Anna's shoulder, the other hand wiping the back of his leg.

He remembered things. He sat in his office at work, writing reports and assessments so that he could keep out of everyone's way – could keep out of Anna's way – and he looked out of the window, and he remembered things.

He remembered Chris swearing, asking him what the fuck he'd done, calling him a silly cunt, asking him what the fuck he thought he was supposed to do now. He remembered Chris's voice sounding very much as though he was crying. He remembered Chris sliding his arms under his body and picking him up, and the agonising pain of each of those jolting steps.

It was difficult to accept, Anna getting the job he'd always imagined would be his, the job which should have been only the first step towards all those grand ambitions he'd had as a child, as a young man, the job which now seemed feebly out of reach. It was difficult to take instructions from Anna, to have to answer to her after everything that had happened.

He remembered Anna, the way she'd stood there in that dress. Her bare shoulders. The movement of the dress when she'd turned in the doorway, the way it had swung around the backs of her long bare legs.

He remembered Chris, laying him down by the telephone box, saying bloody hell, fucking hell, you're not going to tell anyone, are you, you're not going to say it was me? Saying it was an accident, mate, fucking hell, it was an accident.

He remembered lying there on the ground, the flow of blood seeming to slow and the sound of an ambulance in the distance, watching Chris wipe his hands across the backs of his trousers as he walked away.

49 *Library tickets, green card with handwritten annotations, c.1980s*

Eleanor came to him that evening with a familiar urgency in her eyes, and they made love for the first time in months. You're safe now, she kept whispering, pulling him closer and closer against her, as if she'd understood far more about the scene in the park than he'd realised, as if by these fierce clinging acts of love she could protect him from it all.

He was reading a library book, sitting on the edge of the bed in his pyjamas and dressing gown, and when she came into the room he didn't even look up. She took the book from his hands, kissed him, and pulled at his belt and his pyjama buttons until her hands were against his bare skin, pressing and stroking and pulling and pinching. She pushed him back on to the bed, clambering after him, kneeling over his body and working her way forward until, shrugging her dressing gown from her shoulders, she could lower herself towards his mouth.

It was quick, and it was unexpected, but by then it almost always was. A stray glance, a quiet evening, a warm day, and the weeks and months of shared solitude – brief dry kisses, hugs, little more – would be swept aside in a hurried series of remembered moves and gestures. The hand on the back of the head. The unbuttoned skirt. The kneeling. The tugging at underwear. The clutching at each other's bodies. And the kissing, always the kissing. We should do this more often, they usually said, afterwards, but they didn't.

She fell back on to the bed, pulling him towards her, saying come here come here, you're safe now, come here, and as he felt the heat of her skin against his, the pull of her legs around his waist, he tried to remember when the last time they'd done this had been.

Two months, three months ago, with mud on their shoes and leaf-litter in their hair, an afternoon in the park with Kate having degenerated into a tickling match, the press and wrestle of their laughing bodies in the cold clear air reminding them again of what they'd been missing; and when they'd got home, for once she wasn't too tired, or too tearful, or too concerned about Kate playing alone in her room, and the moment hadn't passed, and they'd faced each other in their room and begun in the usual way. It was almost always the same. She would unbutton the back of her skirt, or he would do it for her. She would smile slyly, and meet his eye, and they would kiss. Her skirt would be pulled or pushed or wriggled to her ankles, and her knickers would follow, and then she would place her hand on the back of his head and push him lightly but firmly to the floor. He would kiss her, kneeling, and she would sink back on to the edge of the bed, and he would keep kissing her until she had finished. She would pause, and call him up on to the bed, and the two of them would be together again, holding, moving, murmuring.

Hey, she said, later. How're you doing? They were both sitting up in bed, dressed in their pyjamas again, reading. He looked at her and smiled.

Not bad, he said. Not bad at all. She laughed, embarrassed, and lowered her eyes.

No, but apart from that, she said. I mean, you know, what happened today and everything. He put his book down.

It's okay, he said. It was fine. Why? She looked at him and said nothing.

She said, and the job? Were you, are you very disappointed? He thought for a moment, and when he spoke he almost sounded surprised.

No, he said. No, I'm not. I thought I would be, but I'm not, I don't think. I don't know, he said. Maybe I'm just losing interest in the whole business. Maybe I'm growing out of it, he said, smiling. He picked his book up and started reading again, and she didn't ask him any more about it.

50 *DHSS Booklet,* Guide to Services for the Newly Unemployed, *1986*

This was what it took, in the end, to break him. A five-minute meeting in a basement office. A man in a suit, ten years younger than him, talking about the need for efficiencies. Talking about the importance of restructuring, the generous size of the package being offered. Economic conditions are putting the whole sector at the back of the queue, Daniel, the younger man said. It's a tragedy for heritage in the county but we have to do our best with it.

It's David, he said tautly, leaning forward, placing his forearms on the desk. It was the same desk that had been there since the museum opened, a heavy modernist piece which had seen four directors sit where the young man was sitting now, and slide important pieces of paper across its polished surface. David had even taken his place there for a week once, standing in for a director who'd gone to the British Museum for a conference. How long have I got? he asked, cutting across the young man's continued explanations. The man looked up, meeting his eye for the first time since he'd started talking. He seemed confused by the interruption, frowning slightly.

I'm sorry? he said. David rubbed his forehead, holding his hand over his eyes for a moment.

Please, he said, gesturing vaguely at the papers on the desk, don't bother with all this. Just tell me how long I've got. A month? Three months? The man looked down at the papers in front of him, as if to check, tugging at his earlobe and sweeping his hand across the top of his head.

Well, he said. If you'll let me finish.

There was a filing cabinet behind the desk that contained the records of every exhibition held since the museum opened, the loans, acquisitions, searches and sales which had been necessary to facilitate them, the planning which had gone into them, the interpretative text which had been used in the displays, the visitor responses, the press coverage, the layout diagrams, everything. And with the exception of the years 1965–1968, between the museum opening and David starting work, there wasn't a single exhibition that he hadn't been involved with in some way. He wondered if the young man knew that. He wondered if the young man knew how often he'd sat in his bedroom as a child, sketching out exhibition spaces for the air-raid finds his father brought home for him from the building sites; or how many times he'd been to London to study the exhibitions there, the correlation of displays and texts, the skill needed to draw a visitor through a collection of objects and bring them out with a lived sense of one particular moment in time. He remembered the excitement he'd felt when he first took the job, and how he'd managed to hold on to something of that excitement even as the collections were being reduced, the staffing levels cut, even as he lost faith in his ambition of one day opening a museum of his own, or saw how easily the documents and objects in the archives would rot and crumble no matter how carefully they were kept. He wondered, looking at the locked filing cabinet, if he would ever be able to do anything else.

The young man was still talking, reading through a sheaf of papers spread out in front of him, the words chattering past unheard until David caught the phrase *with immediate effect*. He looked at the man and sat further forward in his chair.

Immediate effect? he said. The man nodded.

I'm so sorry, he said, tilting his head to one side and trying to make a sympathetic expression.

Right now? David said stupidly. The man nodded again.

Bloody hell, David said. After twenty-three years? The man lifted his hands off the desk, holding his palms up towards him.

David, he said, I know. Your length of service is reflected more than adequately in the package we're offering to—

Twenty-three years, David said again, interrupting. I'm forty-one years old. This is all I've ever done. What am I going to do now? What the hell am I going to do now?

He might have signed something. He might have been handed a bundle of papers which he rammed furiously into a briefcase. Possibly the man stood and tried to shake his hand, and he either didn't notice or refused. Anna might have appeared on his way out of the building, to offer her apologies or her condolences or just to hold up her hands and say there was nothing she could have done. He couldn't remember. He wasn't sure how he got from the office to the house, whether he said goodbye to anyone on the way out, or said anything at all, shouted anything, kicked or slammed any doors. He wasn't in the mood, for once, to keep a record of the event.

51 *Video cassette*: World's Greatest Boxing Heroes, *c.1987*

He was watching one of his new videos, with his feet up on the coffee table and the curtains closed, when he heard Kate letting herself in through the front door, dropping her school bag on the stairs and walking straight past him into the kitchen. He sat up a little straighter, rubbing at the skin around his eyes and wondering what time it was. He heard her take a glass out of the cupboard and help herself to some orange squash, and he noticed for the first time that she no longer had to stand on a stool to reach it.

She came back into the room without saying anything, sitting at the far end of the sofa and slowly swinging her legs. She was eleven years old, and he realised that she was on the verge of no longer being a child. He watched her for a moment, her face lit up by the television screen, a biscuit in one hand and the glass of squash in the other, apparently unaware that he was looking at her. Her blonde hair was tied back into a neat ponytail, the arms of her small silver-framed glasses tucked into the hair around her ears. As she bit into the biscuit, she kept bringing a finger or a thumb up to her lips to poke stray crumbs back into her mouth, pinching up any that fell further down on to the front of her school uniform, her eyes staying fixed on the screen, the two men in black and white circling each other with their gloved fists raised, her face almost expressionless. He found something compulsive about watching her; something about her neat smallness, the delicate shapes of her hands, her ears, the soft roundness of her nose; something about the way each time he looked at her he saw some faint echo of Eleanor, or himself, or even of Ivy; something about the way each time he looked closely some part of her seemed to have changed, stretched and grown while he wasn't looking, the colour of her hair darkening slightly, the burnish of the skin on her face coarsening a little, the shape of her eyebrows shifting and settling, her feet stretching a little further towards the floor each time she sat at the far end of the sofa with a biscuit and a glass of orange squash. She would never again be the same as this one moment he was watching her now. Before she'd been born, he'd never understood what a privilege this would be. He watched her carefully, not quite turning towards her, trying not to let her see. She picked the last few crumbs from her sweater and gulped down the rest of her drink.

Dad, she said, turning to him suddenly, what do you do? He looked at her. She turned back to the screen.

What do you mean? he asked, taking his feet down from the table and sitting up, leaning towards her.

I mean, what do you do, she said again, emphasising the do, as if her question was obvious.

Well, he said, and then he didn't know what to say, and almost as suddenly as she'd started the conversation she seemed to lose interest.

Can I watch my programmes? she asked.

In a minute, he said. Do you mean what do I do for a job? he asked. She nodded.

Mrs Smithson went round the class and everyone had to say what their dad did, and I didn't know what to say and everyone laughed, she said, matter-of-factly.

Did everyone else have something to say? he asked her. She nodded again. Even Carl? he asked. And Robin?

Carl said his dad was an RAF pilot and Robin said his dad worked in America, she said. He smiled gently.

Oh, he said, I see. Well, you know that I used to work at the museum, don't you? You know I was a curator? Why didn't you say that? She sighed loudly, as if what he'd just said was too boring to even respond to. Kate? he said. She turned to him, resting her chin on her hand and lifting her eyebrows in an impression of her mother. Why didn't you say that? he asked again.

But you don't do that now, she said, her voice rising indignantly. I had to say what you do now not what you used to do. What do you do *now*, Dad? she said again. They looked at each other for a moment.

I don't know, he said quietly. I've been having a rest for a while, he said. Like when you have a summer holiday. She looked at him, small flickers of disbelief wrinkling across her face.

Grown-ups don't get holidays like that though, do they? she said. He stood up.

Yes Kate, he said, I'm afraid sometimes they do.

52

Hand-drawn family tree, marked 'Believed Complete', dated 1988

Eleanor went out to the garden and sat beside him, wiping the evening's dew from the plastic chair. He shifted in his seat as she sat down but said nothing. They listened to the night's sounds for a moment: the call of a bird from the tree in next door's garden, televisions chattering through open windows, traffic on the main road. She leant across and touched his leg. It's dark now, she said, are you coming inside?

It wasn't the first time she'd had to do this. He seemed to lose himself sometimes.

You'll catch a chill, she said. It's getting damp out here. Come on. He nodded but didn't move. She picked up the folded beer cans from the lawn, and rubbed her hand across his shoulders. You can't stay out here all night, she said.

A long percussive sigh broke from his lips and he shook his head as he stood up. He rubbed his face and looked around for a moment, as if he was unsure of where he was, as if he was seeing for the first time the weed-choked flower borders, the flimsy fences, the soaring leylandii three gardens away. He turned and looked at the house, seeing the light still on in Kate's bedroom, and glanced up at the roof. That aerial needs fixing, he said, again. Eleanor nodded and put her arm around his waist as they walked back into the house together.

He hadn't known what to do when he lost his job. They told him that they'd had to let him go because he was the only member of curatorial staff without formal qualifications, and they'd tried to encourage him to go in for training. We appreciate your knowledge and experience, they'd said, but the museum environment is changing. They said they were sure, once he'd retrained, that he'd have no trouble finding another job; they sent him course literature in the post, application forms, funding information, usually with a note in Anna's handwriting saying that everyone wished him well in his career development. He threw it all in the bin. I know how to do the bloody job already, he said, whenever Eleanor tried to press him on it. It's just not me, going to university, not at my age. At which Eleanor usually smiled, and stroked the hair on the side of his head, and said what do you mean your age?

It was easier when the redundancy money ran out, once he'd spent it on a wish list of trinkets and comforts and toys – a video recorder, a camera, clothes for Kate to grow out of, jewellery which Eleanor never admitted she didn't really like, a microwave, a stereo and a drinks cabinet with a spotlight that came on when he opened the door – and he had no choice but to find work again. It gave him something to do at least. They were warehouse jobs, admin jobs, serving customers at the garden centre – never jobs he was interested in – but they gave him a reason to leave the house in the morning, and they put money in the bank, and they kept him from feeling like he'd completely failed as a father and a husband. It made him feel useful again, to come home from a day at work. It gave him some of his old energy back; if not the energy to reconsider the curators' training courses he was still being offered, then at least the energy to take an interest again, to visit museums occasionally, to look over his old archives, to think about working on projects of his own. He went through boxes of old photos, arranging them into albums. He dug out the scrapbook from his trip to Ireland, reading slowly through the pages, wondering. He found the family tree Kate had drawn for her school project, looking over the faded felt-pen lines and blank spaces and deciding to finish it for her, phoning Donald to ask him for help and only realising as they started speaking how much of a shock it was to be in contact after all this time. He wrote down Donald's answers to his questions – *Ivy Munro b.1910 m.Stewart Campbell b.1900 d.1981. Hamish b.1931, Donald b.1932, William b.1933, John b.1936, Tessa b.1938, Eleanor b.1948* – and listened to Donald say that he should be sure to phone again, that it was good to be in touch, that he hoped Eleanor and Kate were both well.

He spent an afternoon filling in the missing names, redrawing the broken lines, drafting and redrafting the diagram to make all the branches fit. And it was this that he'd shown to Eleanor earlier in the evening.

Oh David, she'd said, startled for a moment and then apparently touched, looking over it, tracing the lines with her fingers. Oh David, it's lovely. But I don't think it's finished at all, do you? Really?

He'd looked at her a moment, and she'd said I'm sorry David but just, sometimes, I think, maybe you need to, I don't know. Her words stopped and hesitated under his narrowing gaze. Maybe, she said, I don't know. Maybe you should think about it again. I mean. And he'd said nothing in reply, snatching up the piece of paper, folding and refolding it as he moved towards the back door, stopping only to take a clutch of beers from the fridge.

There was no need for her to have brought that up. She didn't know. She didn't need to have mentioned it. He thought she'd just be pleased with what he'd done, pleased that he was taking an interest in something again. He didn't need to have bothered. She didn't need to have said that.

She came out to see him later, after telling Kate it was time she went to bed. Kate moaned, and said do I have to I'm not a baby any more, but she stood up all the same. Eleanor noticed her glancing out at David before she went upstairs.

She doesn't like it you know, she told him as she sat down. It unsettles her, when you're like this. You're supposed to be the steady one out of us two. He shrugged and scratched his head and said nothing.

He said there's nothing wrong with me, I'm just sitting out in the garden having a drink. There's nothing wrong with that is there?

No, she said, there's nothing wrong with that, but it's just— She stopped. She said, I'm sorry about what I said before, for bringing it up, I mean. He shrugged again.

That's okay, he said. Doesn't matter. He looked up, and saw Kate standing at her bedroom window, looking down at them both for a moment before pulling the curtains closed. He dragged his fingers through his hair and said but you don't honestly think it's something I forget about, do you?

No, she said, quietly, following his gaze up to Kate's window and turning back to him, reaching out and touching his cheek; of course I don't. But sometimes you forget to talk about it, she said. He pulled his face away from her hand, sharply.

What am I supposed to say? he said. What is there to talk about? What do you want me to say, Eleanor? His voice was tense and defensive, raised against her intrusion. She sat back in her chair, leaning away from him.

No, she said, nothing really, you're right. Nothing.

I mean, do you want me to tell you about it all over again? he asked. You want to be my counsellor or something? I'm supposed to unburden myself, am I? Like, oh Eleanor I can't stop thinking about it I feel rejected and cut adrift, oh Eleanor I need some answers oh please help me – something like that?

She said nothing, waiting for his blurred sarcasm to wear itself out.

You want me to have a weep about it or something, you think I should stop bottling it up? he said. Or maybe you think I should take up painting and learn to express my inner feelings? He reached under his chair and opened another beer. Eleanor stood up.

No David, she said. Don't be stupid. I just don't think you should give up, that's all.

He watched her walk back into the house, slam the door and tug the curtains across the back-room window. He saw the side-light going on, and the blue-white flicker of the television. He hung his head over the back of the chair and looked up at the darkening glow of the sky. He hadn't even been thinking about that when she came out. He patted the folded family tree in his pocket, checking it was still there. He noticed the faint white lights of an aeroplane overhead, the first of the evening's stars, the last of the daylight draining down to the horizon. He folded his arms across his chest. He hadn't even been thinking about that. She'd got that wrong. No. He'd been thinking about Kate asking if she could go on the school skiing trip, and having to say no, and that no matter how much Eleanor insisted that plenty of other parents would have to refuse it had still made him feel like a failure again. He'd been thinking about his father, working his hands raw each day until a few weeks before his death, and what he would have thought of a son who'd only worked half a life in cramped basement offices and dust-free store-rooms and now sat around feeling sorry for himself. He'd been thinking, again, that the loss of the job he'd been so proud of was his own fault for what he'd allowed to happen with Anna, and that he was failing his family by no longer being a working man. He'd been thinking, as he did again and again and again, that the failure to tell Eleanor about what had happened was the lowest failure of all.

He finished his beer. He tried to stand up. He sat down again. He rubbed at his face and tried to remember what Eleanor had said. He patted his pocket again. She was wrong. He hadn't been thinking about that. She thought she knew him so well, but she didn't.

He noticed that the television wasn't on any more, and then he heard the back door open again, and then he realised that Eleanor had sat down beside him. It's dark now, she said. Are you coming inside?

53 *Home videos featuring Kate Carter, 1991–1994*

The gravelled surface of a car park, the rush of traffic in the background, the flap and flutter of wind across the microphone. David's voice saying is it working? Is it on?

A blur of camera movement, a streak of blue sky and green hills, a painfully slow pan from right to left: a copse of trees by the side of the road, a low stone wall, a long stretch of meadow leading up to a hill, a noticeboard, and then Kate, turning her back as she appeared on the screen. And from behind the camera, his voice distorted and thick, David saying so here we are in deepest Warwickshire on this fine summer's day, here for a walk in one of Kate's favourite spots. Can you tell us a little bit about it Kate? The camera circling round her, trying to persuade her to show her face, while she let her long thick hair fall across her eyes, her head lowered, her hands pulled up into the loose tattered sleeves of her jumper, her legs vanishing into boots two sizes too big. Kate saying Dad, stop it will you you're so embarrassing, and David laughing, clumsily, trying to make it seem like a game, trying to make it seem as though she was still young enough to play these games. She walked away from the camera, dragging her feet, and the camera followed, David's footsteps grinding across the gravel, David saying come on love, not even a smile for us now? Her back turned, the camera no longer circling around to face her, an awkward pause. Kate's voice, drowsy with sulkiness, saying I can't believe you Dad, you're a nightmare. David, a little quieter, a little hurt-sounding, saying Kate love, just a quick smile for the camera? Kate turning, quickly, lifting her dyed-black hair away from her face, a brief grimacing smile. Is that okay? she said sarcastically, already beginning to walk away. David's voice, chuckling as if it was still a game, saying end of take one, the camera fixed on Kate's back for a moment more, waiting to see if she would turn round, and then a blur of colour and a shot of gravel as he looked for the button to turn the bloody thing off.

Kate at her cousin's birthday party, standing in Susan's elegant garden with a glass of wine and a paper plate of food, talking to some of Mark's friends and turning her back as soon as she saw the camera, the camera drifting instead across the rhododendrons and fuchsias which Susan spent so much time on.

Kate on a day out in London, standing on a bridge over the Thames, watching a barge churn upstream, smiling, saying hello Mum.

Kate on her sixteenth birthday, getting ready to go out and meet her friends, unwrapping presents from her parents, her auntie, her gran. Relaxed about being filmed now, partly because she was used to it, partly because she'd been sipping from a quarter bottle of vodka in her room – David had known about this, had been able to see it in the happy excited glaze of her eyes, and had chosen not to say anything – and partly because she was just beginning to grow out of her acute embarrassment at being seen in the world. Kate with her hair away from her face, still dyed black but knotted and piled up on to her head, frayed strands sticking out in all directions. Still wearing the ragged blacks and purples of a year before, but no longer hiding behind them, her clothes a little less shapeless and baggy, her make up less smudged. She unwrapped a large square present, saying what could it be? to the camera, and she looked genuinely pleased and surprised when she saw which band the record was by, holding it up to the lens and saying hey wow, thanks Dad, thanks Mum, leaping up in a clatter of jewellery to kiss Eleanor wetly on the cheek. Eleanor, slightly uncomfortable, embracing her in turn, saying we asked your friend

Becky and she said this was one you'd like. Kate nodding and saying I do, the camera focusing on Eleanor for a moment, her happy smile and the anxious twisting of her hands, then moving back to Kate as she ripped open her next present.

Eleanor didn't like the way Kate dressed or wore her hair, the music she listened to, the places she thought she might be going to, but she was careful never to say anything. You tell her, she whispered urgently, when they got back from a restaurant one night to find the washbasin stained an inky-blue and Kate sitting up in bed with her hair wrapped in a ruined towel. She's not going out like that, she muttered, another evening, when Kate came downstairs with stockings torn from her ankles to the hem of a very short skirt; you tell her. I don't want to get involved. Kate ignored what David said, of course, saying he was so unfair and slamming the front door as she left, and Eleanor watched her walking down the street from the upstairs window, turning to David as he came upstairs and saying my God David, what does she think she looks like? But she still said nothing; not when Kate came home with her ears bloody and studded with piercings, not when the school sent them a letter about her absences, not when she stayed out at a party until five in the morning. She faded into the background, telling David what she thought but withholding comment from Kate for fear of speaking the way her mother had once done. Sometimes, David thought, she was so busy trying not to repeat Ivy's mistakes that she was unable to see how uneventful her relationship with Kate had become. In many of the scenes on the tape, Eleanor wasn't there at all, and when she was she seemed to be pressing herself into the background, waiting for David to say something from behind the camera, waiting for the focus to move away from her.

Kate in the garden, in the summer, doing a guided tour of the borders, laughing and joking, welcoming the attention of the camera now, saying Dad planted these raspberries when I was a kid and most of them get eaten by the birds but we always get a few at least.

Kate in the garden in the winter, putting the head on a snowman with her friend Becky, throwing a snowball towards her dad, the sudden jerk and jolt of the picture as he ducks. Her hair back to something like its original colour, still tangled and long but a familiar mousey-blonde again.

This was why he'd bought the camera, using up some more of the redundancy money, so he could pin her down on tape before she'd gone. Because even when she was still thirteen, fourteen, he could imagine all too easily sitting in a quiet and empty house after she'd left, wondering what she was doing at that very moment, wishing he could picture more clearly the times they'd spent together when she'd still been at home.

Kate in her room with her hair tied neatly back, looking serious, a pile of textbooks on the desk beside her and a chewed-up pen in her hand. Saying this is my revision timetable, pointing at a sheet of paper on the wall, patchworked with highlighter squares. And how long did it take you to do that? David's voice asked, squashed against the microphone. Two days, she said, smiling and glaring at the same time. And when do your exams start? he said. Next month, she replied, standing, pushing her hand against the lens; so get out now and let me work, go on, get out! The door closing against the camera, and the sound of her happy gentle laugh.

This was his favourite scene, and the one he could hardly bear to watch; Kate on the very brink of being an adult, her purposeful seriousness reminding him of his own adolescent self when he first started work; Kate with her smile and her bursts of energy, leaping up from the desk to usher him out of the room in the same way she once threw herself at him in games of football at the park; Kate, closing the door, shutting him out, moving on, her laugh still reaching him from behind the closing door.

54 *Examination results; University prospectus, 1994*

It seemed effortless, the way Kate passed her exams and got into university. She seemed to take it for granted, just as she seemed to assume there was no reason why she wouldn't leave home and begin again in some other town she knew nothing about, with people she had to hope would become her friends. She belonged to a generation which took these things for granted, which saw staying at home as something unnatural, and education as something which could be continued on a whim, and so she barely noticed the daunted and tentative way Eleanor moved around her while she was studying for her exams.

I don't want her to think I'm worrying, Eleanor would whisper when they were lying in bed at night and wondering if she was doing okay. I don't want her to think I'll be cross if she doesn't do well. She will do well though, won't she? she said urgently.

She kept a copy of Kate's exam timetable by the bedside, hidden under some books, and slipped a packet of multivitamins into her room, and watched for some clue in her face or her voice as they ate tea together after each exam. She asked Becky's mother how she thought the exams had gone, but she didn't dare say anything to Kate herself.

And when the end of August came, after a long summer of waiting and worrying and pretending that she didn't mind, she was up and awake with the first thought of morning, much earlier than Kate was; standing at the bedroom window, looking out for the postman, waiting breathlessly for Kate to wander downstairs and find the envelope lying behind the front door. Listening to the rip of paper in the front room, leaving it a few minutes before going downstairs to see what news had finally come.

And when Kate left home the house seemed to change, doubling in size and sinking into silence. They found themselves meeting each other on the stairs like strangers, lost in their own house. It took a long time to adjust. When he got back from driving her to the university it even took David a while to find Eleanor; he called out to her as he came in through the door, and as he went into the kitchen and up the stairs, but there was no answer. She wasn't in their room, or in the bathroom, or out in the garden, and it was only when he went back upstairs that he found her in Kate's room, sitting on the end of the bed, with a pile of clothes Kate had left behind on her lap. She was folding them into neat squares, picking off long stray hairs and bobbles of lint, stacking them into a pile on the floor beside her. She barely seemed to notice him coming into the room. He kissed her on the forehead, and she smiled softly up at him.

That didn't take very long, did it? she said.

No, it was fine, he said, traffic was clear all the way back to the ring road. She smiled again, holding up a long blonde hair and twisting it round her finger.

That's not what I meant, she said.

55 Illustrated Book of Knots, *7th Edition, c.1947*

When Eleanor's oldest brother Hamish left home, before she was even born, his uncle gave him a knot-tying book as a leaving gift, saying it's not much but it'll see you well. Hamish was seventeen years old and ready to go; his bags were packed and the first ship of his apprentice life was set to leave in the morning, carrying timber to London. His parents brought the neighbours round to see him off, pushing the furniture back against the walls, hoisting open the windows to let the warm spring air in and the tobacco smoke out, baking up cakes and scones and sending young Donald round to the store for another bottle of whisky while Hamish stood awkwardly in the middle of the floor saying hello and thank you and aye I'm looking forward to it as the guests arrived and found a seat or leant against the wall or stood wherever they could find a space. Stewart made his way around the crowded room, filling glasses and saying hello, while Tessa, ten years old and forced uncomfortably into a dress, followed her father round with an overburdened plate of cakes. Will you have another piece? she said to each guest in turn, her voice quiet but confident, her gaze steady and solemn; and each of the guests, with a glass of whisky in one hand and a keen appetite in the other, said please Tessa, thank you, lifting a slab of ginger cake from the pile.

From the doorway Ivy watched her son standing stiffly in the centre of the small room, his shoulders forced back and the stubborn tuft of hair already springing up where she'd just licked her fingers and pressed it down. She knew, really, that he'd be fine when he was gone, that he'd been carrying his share of the household's weight for long enough, that he would manage on his own. But still, it was a hard thing to look at her own son, with the same snubbed features he'd had as a three-year-old, with the bumps and scars of childhood still mapped out across his skin beneath that proud new suit, and to see him as a man ready to head out into the world on his own. She watched the way he spoke to the friends and neighbours in turn, smiling and nodding at their jokes and suggestions, saying thanks for the gifts of warm socks, accepting firm handshakes and leaning forward to place brisk kisses on beaming wrinkled cheeks. Her hands twitched with the memory of holding his tiny warm body up against her face. Her hips shifted with the ghost weight of him, of bearing him or of propping his clinging body up with one arm while she busied around the house with the other. Cooking, cleaning, scrubbing, ironing. Her bones ached with the seeping tiredness of those many long years, the guilty resentment of it all, and she leant back against the door frame, still watching. She saw the way young Rosalind was looking at him, her warm eyes flicking up to his face and his chest when she thought no one was looking.

Rosalind's mother, Ellie, saw where Ivy was looking, met her eye, and smiled. Will I help you with that last lot of scones Ivy? she said, sweeping her friend into the kitchen at the back of the house, the room bursting into laughter as Stewart made some joke behind them. Aye she's a thing or two to learn about discretion that girl of mine, she muttered, as Ivy opened the oven door to a blast of hot air, sweet and damp with the smell of fresh scones.

Ivy laughed. The way she's staring, you'd think she'd never seen a good-looking boy in a suit before, she said. But I don't think you need to worry about our Hamish noticing any, he's not so quick that way just yet. Ellie fetched a cooling rack down from the shelf above the oven, put it on the kitchen table, and passed Ivy a palette knife.

Well, some are quicker than others she said, glancing

down at Ivy's almost un-noticeably swollen belly. Ivy stopped sliding the scones on to the cooling rack and looked up at her. Looks like it's not just scones you've got in the oven there, Ellie added, her eyebrows raised a little and her mouth breaking into a smile. Or Ivy said, there's something I've to tell you and Ellie said, there's no need I can see for myself. Ivy looked at her, put the baking tray down beside the sink, and rested her oven-gloved hands across her stomach.

Oh, Ellie, is it showing already? she said, whispering, her voice cracking and her eyes edged with tears. Or she turned away and said, Eleanor Davies, I really don't know what you're talking about, slamming a baking tray into the sink a little harder than she meant to. Or she looked at her friend and knew there was nothing to say.

Ellie pulled a chair across for Ivy to sit on. She sat beside her and pressed a hand to her arm, or around her shoulder, or wanted to touch her but kept her hands twisted together under her chin.

Aye love, it is, she said. Is that a problem? Ivy smiled thinly.

Of course it is, she whispered, it's a big problem, isn't it? You know I'm too old to do this all over again.

Nonsense, said Ellie, tutting, you're still young yet, and she smiled. Ivy didn't smile back but looked up at Ellie.

No, she said. You know what the doctor told me, she said. The two women looked at each other, and Ivy didn't need to remind Ellie what she meant; that each of her five pregnancies had been difficult, marked by debilitating sickness and pain, that each birth had been harder, longer, and more dangerous than the one before, that the arrival of her long-awaited daughter, the source of such happiness, had nearly killed her and Tessa both.

Aye, said Ellie, quietly. Aye, I know love. The singing faded away next door. There was a bump and a crash, and an indignant shout from young John. Ivy looked up, startled, relaxing again when she heard him laugh. Ellie smiled at her. It never stops, does it? she said, and Ivy smiled back.

No, no it doesn't, she said. Ellie took the oven gloves from her, hung them up, and popped the cooling scones on to a blue-and-white dinner plate. She passed Ivy a handkerchief from her cardigan pocket; clean this morning, she said, and Ivy took it and dabbed at her eyes and blew her nose.

I'm just wondering if it's worth it at all, you know? she said, as Ellie stood at the sink wiping down a baking tray. I just don't know why I bother, she said. You near kill yourself bringing them into the world, you break your back bringing them up, and all for what? They cut loose first chance they find, and they're gone, eh? she said, nodding her head in the direction of the other room. I'm just wondering, she said, her voice brittle with the tense shame of what she was daring to say; I'm just wondering. There's people can fix these things, aren't there? She grasped the handkerchief between her thumb and fingers, twisting it into a cord, twisting the cord into a knot. Ellie turned to look at her, and heard a noise from the far side of the room. Hamish was standing in the open doorway, looking at the two women.

Uncle James is wanting more cakes, he said, looking reluctant to come any closer. Ellie walked briskly across to him with the plate of scones.

There you go, she said, see how he goes on with these, eh? Hamish took the plate, and Ellie shut the door behind him, turning back to Ivy with her eyes wide and fearful as the scones were greeted with a cheer in the room next door.

56

Ration books, Union cards, Co-op dividend stamps, 1930s and 1940s

Well and you know our mother's not very well at all. Not at all. Donald's voice was calm and measured as it came down the phone line, and David waited for him to go on. Aye, Donald said. The doctors have told us not to expect her back out of the hospital. They've said it'll probably be months at the most, he said.

David wondered what he was supposed to say, what he was supposed to feel. I'm sorry, he said. He'd assumed it would be something like this, when the card from Donald had been forwarded on to him from the museum – *Please telephone as soon as is convenient,* it said simply – but he was still unprepared. I'm sorry, he said again.

We thought you'd want to know, Donald said, Ros and me, and the others. He coughed. We thought Eleanor would want to know, he said. He coughed again. Excuse me, he said.

He asked Eleanor if she wanted to go there, if she wanted to see her mother, and she couldn't bring herself to answer him straight away. But what did Donald say? she asked, and he told her again. Her mother was ill, she didn't have long left, they were welcome to go up and visit if they wished.

What do you think he means by welcome? she said.

It was more than five years since Kate had left home, and their lives had finally settled back into some kind of routine, some kind of direction. Eleanor was working part-time at the city council, and David had found a temporary post at the archives office. They had time to eat breakfast together, and two days a week they would catch the same bus into work, kissing each other briefly goodbye amongst the push and hurry of the nine o'clock crowds. They took it in turns to cook dinner, experimenting with new recipes they got from the friends they ate out with once or twice a week. Susan came to stay, regularly, sleeping in the room which had always been Kate's but which they'd started learning to call the spare room. And most weekends they went to his mother's, to keep her company and to do the jobs around the house she'd started struggling to do. They were almost busy, as David joked to Eleanor one worn-out evening, and they were happy, in the ordinary ways which had evaded them for so long.

A week after that first brief conversation with Donald, they met each other from work and walked home. It was cold enough for gloves and scarves, and Eleanor reached into David's pocket for extra warmth as they walked through the centre of town. They'd been talking about Ivy's illness for days, and about whether they should go up to Aberdeen. They'd argued about it, and they'd both said things they regretted, and in the end he'd said that he'd leave it to her to make up her mind; he didn't want to talk about it any more. She turned to him now, squeezing his hand, her voice low and determined. So, she said, I've decided. About my mother. I don't want to go. He looked at her. I can't, she said. It's too late now.

David had never known much about Ivy, besides the bare facts which Donald had outlined for him when he was working on the family tree, besides what little Eleanor had said. But as he spoke to Donald over those last few months, following the progress of Ivy's swift decline, he found out a little more.

He learnt that her own mother had died while she was still a very young child, and that no one had ever known Ivy mention her in company. I couldn't even promise you her name right, Donald said; it's Lizzie I think but I could be wrong – it's been known, he said wryly, before asking after Eleanor and telling David to phone again in a week for more news.

He learnt that she'd picked up most of the household's income for the first six or seven years of her marriage, taking in laundry and finding cleaning jobs in the big houses while Stewart spent his days lined up outside the shipyards waiting for rumours of work to drift in on the tide, and that she'd done all this work whilst carrying the first three of her six children. I think she was exhausted even by the time John came along, Donald said. Her sister told me that, he added, not long ago.

The phone often went unanswered when David called, and when he managed to speak to Donald he'd usually either just come back from the hospital or was getting ready to go. His voice was tired, his words strung between breathy pauses, but he never seemed reluctant to talk. He seemed keen to tell David these things, and David only had to add oh really is that right? for Donald to carry on.

She was sometimes very hard on Eleanor, he said, another time. I understand that. But she was still a good mother, you understand? No one ever went hungry in our house. And for those days, believe you me, that's saying something.

For a time, David kept these conversations a secret from Eleanor, assuming they would upset her or even that she would resent him for them. But one evening she came back from a friend's house unexpectedly early, and as she walked through to the kitchen he could see that she'd already guessed who he was speaking to. She stopped in the doorway, watching him.

Oh but she's always been able to hold a grudge, Donald was saying, I'll grant you that. She's had her fair share of those, he said, laughing in that strange rueful way he had, while Eleanor stepped closer and held David's gaze.

Is that right? he asked, awkwardly.

Oh aye, said Donald. There's a neighbour down the way here she's not spoken to for nearly twenty years, on account of an argument the two of them once had in the pub. He paused. And you know Da told me once that she didn't speak to him for a fortnight after Eleanor left with you. David looked at Eleanor, reaching out his hand and holding hers, squeezing it.

Well, he said. It must have been very difficult for them. Donald didn't say anything for a moment.

Well, aye, he said. It's a long time ago now though, he added. Eleanor was standing close enough to David to hear Donald's voice; not to hear his words perhaps, but to hear the buzz and crackle of it coming down the line.

Sorry Donald, I should be going now, David said. I've got some things to sort out for the morning.

Right you are, Donald said quickly. Sorry, I didn't mean anything just then, when I said—

Oh, no, no, David said, that's fine, not at all. I'll speak to you soon.

You don't mind do you? he asked Eleanor, after he'd hung up. She shook her head.

How're things? she asked.

She's not very well at all, he said. She nodded.

And Donald? she asked.

He learnt that Ivy had been ill before, that this was a recurrence of the same condition she'd had when Stewart had died. He learnt that Donald and Rosalind were spending most of their time at the hospital now, that Hamish and his wife were there as well, as was Hamish's daughter Cathy. He learnt that Donald had been feeling at something of a loose end since he retired. He learnt that Ivy had never really got over having to move out of the old house when it was demolished as part of the council's rebuilding programme. He learnt, more than once, that Donald thought it was funny the way things turned out.

And once Eleanor had found out, she didn't seem to mind him having these conversations at all. Sometimes she asked him, afterwards, what they'd been talking about, and asked him questions which he asked Donald the next time they spoke. Sometimes she asked how her mother was doing, although the answer was always the same; not well, getting worse. One evening, while Donald was telling him about Ivy's habit of still using a top-loader, even when all four sons had offered to buy her a modern washing machine – she's stubborn, he said, no one can deny that – Eleanor came into the room asking David if he wanted a cup of tea, not realising until it was too late that he was on the phone. Donald caught himself mid-sentence.

Eh, is that Eleanor there? he asked. Eleanor had her hand over her mouth.

It is, David said. There was a pause.

Sounds like she's lost her accent a wee bit, Donald said.

Well, I suppose she has, yes, David said. Eleanor's eyes widened at the thought of Donald saying something about her.

Mind, said Donald, it's been a while.

It has, David agreed, realising now what Donald wanted to ask. There was another long pause.

Eh, is she still there, or has she gone to put that kettle on now? Donald said.

No, no, David said, she's still here. Eleanor wiped her mouth and looked around her, and then she moved closer towards him, closer towards the voice on the phone. Would you like to speak to her? he asked. Donald said nothing for a moment, and there was only the sound of him breathing in and out.

Aye, he said. If I could. David held the phone out to Eleanor, raising his eyebrows. She looked at it a moment, wiping a hand across her mouth again, and took it from him.

Hello? she said. Hello Donald. How are you?

57 *Printed service sheet, 'Ivy Elaine Campbell, 1909–2000', 23 April 2000*

Before the service, having tea and cake at Donald and Rosalind's house, Donald showed Kate a photograph of her grandfather. That's your Granda Stewart, he said, holding it up to her. That photo was taken eighty-nine years ago, he added, as proudly as if he'd taken it himself. So don't you be getting sticky fingers on it now, he said, and everyone in the room laughed.

Oh, no, I won't, Kate smiled, perching on the arm of the sofa with a cup of tea in one hand and the photo in the other, holding it carefully by the edges.

See that wee boat there? Donald asked. They say he carried that boat around with him everywhere, after his father died. The other conversations in the room dropped away, and people turned to look.

His father made it for him, before he was lost, said Hamish.

Is that so? asked Donald, looking over at his brother, well, I never knew that. Kate looked at the photo again – Stewart holding a small model fishing boat, his brother and three sisters beside him, his mother standing behind them with a hand resting lightly on his head. She must have recognised the boat, and David was impressed that she was careful not to say anything.

I suppose you don't know too much about the family history though do you hen? said Donald, tucking the photo back into the envelope with the others.

Not really, said Kate, Mum doesn't really – you know; and

she trailed off to take a sip of tea, and Donald's weather-beaten face coloured a little. The crowded room was heavy and still for a moment, until Donald's wife got to her feet and started saying you'll be wanting another one then to each of the guests in turn, filling their cups from a huge pot on the table, cutting second slices of dense brandy-fumed fruitcake, and Kate stood and said no, not for me thanks, I think I'll just, and Donald directed her to the left of the top of the stairs.

As soon as she was out of the room, John's wife turned to David and said oh but she's the spit of her grandmother, is she not?

I suppose she is, he said, smiling.

Oh aye, said Hugh, as a murmur of agreement ran around the room, it's uncanny, isn't it? And even though of all those there Ivy's brother Gordon was the only one old enough to remember her as a young woman, they could still see something in Kate that reminded them of her. The way she lifted her head when she smiled. The shape of her eyes. Something about the way she had held herself when she first stepped into the room and said hello. Some faint echo, sounding on down the bloodline.

There was talk of arrangements, of where to park and who couldn't make it and who would be taking the cords. There were more trips to the toilet and a few more pieces of cake. And then when everyone was in the room Donald looked at his watch and said right well I think that's us away then, and they all stood and filed out of the small front room, ladies first, after you, placing empty cups and crumb-laden plates on to the kitchen table as they passed into the passageway and out through the front door to the street, all sober and dark and tight-collared. The women in rarely worn hats and M&S dresses, carrying weighty handbags and helping each other down the front step and along to the cars. The men straightening their shoulders and their ties as they stepped out into the crisp afternoon light, blinking a little, clearing their heads from the warmth of the house and readying themselves for what was to come. Everyone moving with a well-rehearsed confidence, as though it was every day they put on these clothes and drove to the cemetery to bury their mother, or sister, or aunt. Slipping into their seats in the four shining cars, scooping the hems of their dresses neatly beneath them or straightening the lines of their heavy jackets. Keeping their thoughts to themselves as they drove smoothly through the bungalowed streets and along the coast road towards the town, round past the industrial estates and through the familiar terraced streets of their childhoods.

Was that the same boat Mum's got at home? Kate murmured to him as they got out of the car at the cemetery, the one in that photo? He looked at her and nodded, holding her gaze for a moment so she could see that it wasn't something to be talked about just then.

In the evening, once people had started to go home from the wake, Donald took a large brown envelope from Rosalind's handbag and pulled out some more photographs. I thought you'd be interested in seeing some of these, he said, your line of work being what it is. He spread them out across the table. We found them in a chest of drawers in Ivy's room. David leant across and glanced at the pictures, damp-spotted black-and-white snapshots of weddings, birthdays, day-trips.

There's some other bits and pieces we found as well, Rosalind said, squeezing the edges of the envelope and tipping out a pile of ration books, union cards, Co-op stamps, pamphlets. Hamish, sitting on the other side of the table, reached forward suddenly, frowning, and picked out a grease-stained *Illustrated Book of Knots*.

That'll be mine for starters, he said. Where'd you find that?

David looked at a pale studio picture of Ivy and Stewart

holding up a young baby, the baby dressed in a long gown and white bonnet, the edges of the picture a little out of focus, none of them smiling. He held it up, questioningly.

We're not sure but we think that's Eleanor, said Donald. Doesn't look much like I remember her, but we can't think it's anyone else.

It's been a long time since I've seen this though, Hamish announced, thumbing through the book of knots, pushing his thick-lensed spectacles up his nose, launching into the story of the grand send-off the family had given him when he'd first joined the merchant navy.

David half-listened, looking through the pictures, holding up a large print of a young couple on their wedding day, two sets of parents next to them, brothers and sisters fanning out on either side. Rosalind leant towards him.

Aye, that's us, she whispered, smiling shyly, glancing over at Hamish to be sure he couldn't hear her interruption. Seems like a fine long time ago now though, eh?

There were that many folk there, Hamish continued, oblivious. David pointed to a girl in the picture who looked about fifteen, with long hair and a blank expression.

Eleanor? he mouthed. Donald and Rosalind looked at each other.

Eh, no, that's her sister, Donald said quietly. Tessa.

She's in America now of course, Rosalind added. Has been for years. She stopped herself. You didn't know that though, did you? she said, her voice dropping away.

No, David said. I wasn't sure you were still in touch.

We get Christmas cards, Donald said, no more.

Are you folks listening at that end? Hamish asked, knocking the table, and the three of them turned back to face him.

Of course we are, said Rosalind.

You carry on there, Donald agreed. David finished the whisky Donald had put in front of him and listened to the rest of Hamish's story, looking around the emptying room, wondering where Kate had gone.

58 *Email messages; printed copies dated March 2000*

He'd always known how it would be, when it happened. He would be heaving great volumes down from dusty shelves in an archive office somewhere, turning thick pages and scanning endless rows of names until he found what he was looking for. He'd be filling out small pink request slips, waiting long afternoons while under-staffed departments worked their way through to his search. He knew, or he thought he knew, that when it happened he would be sitting in a room with notices saying *Pencils only please; bags must be left at the front desk,* where no one would notice the rush of exhilaration and fear which would shoot through him as he noted down the reference numbers for the copies he required, and carried them, trembling, to the counter.

But in the end, when it happened, it was nothing like that at all. He was sitting in front of a computer screen in Kate's old room, a mug of hot chocolate going cold beside him, the modem flickering as he checked his email, listening to Eleanor brush her teeth in the bathroom, listening to the radio he'd left on by their bed.

Kate had shown him how to use the computer on her first break back from university. He'd bought it a few years earlier with what was left of the redundancy money, but had only ever used it for writing letters. She'd shown him how to get connected to the internet, how to follow the links on the different pages, how to use the search engines to look for information on any possible subject he could think of.

They'd sat side by side in front of the screen for most of an afternoon, while she showed him weather reports from Sydney Harbour, lecture notes from degrees at Leeds University, catalogues from the British Museum, the wedding photos of a couple called Jack and Mary somewhere in Florida, job adverts, property adverts, television listings, introductory guides to museums and exhibition centres, anything he suggested or which took her fancy as she clicked on the links from page to page. She kept tutting as she waited for the sites to load on to the screen, saying God I can't believe how slow this is, you should get a new computer Dad, this is well slow compared to the ones at uni, and every time she said it he looked at her in disbelief. A few minutes' wait seemed like a small price to pay for information from all over the world to come tumbling into your home.

He'd found the experience difficult to absorb at first. He'd become so used to the idea of information existing as a physical fact; books, papers, photographs, objects, the parched fragments of ancient civilisations inscribed on to stone and metal, kept secure in controlled environments. The idea that all information would eventually exist in this cacophonous airborne form astonished and alarmed him. It was overwhelming, unknowable, uncategorisable. The first few times, once Kate had finished showing him what to do and left him to it, he did nothing – sat in front of the screen with the browser logged on to a search engine, the cursor blinking impatiently in its small rectangular box. The endless choices that had suddenly reared up before him left him unable to move. He had no idea what he wanted to know.

Except, of course, that he did. He had every idea. There was only one thing he had ever wanted to know.

He started by simply entering her name into the search engines. *Mary Friel*, or *Mary Friel + 1945*, or *Mary Friel + 1928/1929/1930*, or *Mary Friel + Donegal*. The results came back either blank or with thousands of entries. So he started searching for *adoption, tracing, family history, online archives, parish records*. He looked at tourist information sites, local history sites, sites dedicated to the history of the Irish diaspora, sites concerned with the study of genealogy. And he realised, as he clicked and scrolled through the endless lists of links and databases, that the only way he would find her would be if she was waiting to be found. If she was sitting in front of a computer screen somewhere, tapped into this flood of new memories, clicking through these same sites and links with the same destination in mind. He didn't have enough information just to stumble across her on his own. She could have married, changed her name, left the country. She could have lied in the first place, and never been Mary Friel at all.

And he discovered that he wasn't alone. There were thousands of people doing just what he was doing, hundreds of thousands, listing themselves on databases and posting messages in the hope of finding the missing other. *I was born in 1953, I gave up my daughter in 1942, I saw my son for the first and last time in 1962*. He scrolled through these lists endlessly, looking for the name he wanted, looking for the date. *Mary Friel, 1945*. He chose a site to register with, paid the joining fee, and added his details to the list. *Adopted son seeks birth mother. David Carter / Mary Friel / Believed March 1945*. He put *believed* because it seemed to be the standard format, because there were so many stories of dates being mixed up, falsified, misremembered. Because people in his position were no longer sure what to believe.

When it happened, he had more or less given up. It was only habit which drew him back into Kate's old room a few evenings each week, looking for something to do before he went to bed; working his way through the lists, checking his email, searching through slowly and methodically and without any conviction that it was a worthwhile thing to do. He would sit on the folding metal chair in his pyjamas, running his bare feet back and forth across the carpet, squinting at the scrolling names or gazing blankly at his reflection in the darkened window while he waited for the modem to connect.

New Messages (1). Dear David. My mother's name is Mary Carr but her maiden name was Friel. She was in London during the war and gave up a baby boy for adoption in 1945. We'll need to talk more but I think she would be very interested to meet you.

When he called Eleanor's name, she came into the room with a toothbrush still in her mouth, her dressing gown hanging open around her nightdress. She said something inaudible, and he just pointed at the screen. She looked, and looked closer, toothpaste dribbling from the corner of her mouth as she tried to say it never is, is it? He nodded, not looking at her, not knowing what to say. They both looked at the words on the screen together, silently. She wiped at the spilt toothpaste with her sleeve, and laid her hand on his shoulder. He turned his face against her hand, and closed his eyes.

What are you going to do? she asked. He kissed her hand, and said nothing.

59 *Ferry tickets; handwritten letter; route map (from website); all June 2000*

It wasn't yet light when the ferry arrived. He stood out on the deck, his eyes stinging with sleep in the cold wet morning air. He looked out over the warehouses and lorry-parks, tracing the light-strung line of the motorway as it skirted around Belfast and headed towards the Lough. There was a map and a list of directions in the car's glove compartment, but he knew he wouldn't need them. He murmured the route to himself as the boat settled in against the jetty wall: M2 towards the airport, past Antrim, through Randalstown, through Londonderry, across the border . . .

I'm going to Donegal, he'd said to his mother, a month ago, and she'd nodded and said right then, okay, okay. I've been in touch with a woman called Mary, he'd said, as gently as it was possible to say such a thing, her maiden name was Mary Friel, and she'd nodded and smiled and said right then, okay, okay, turning her face away from him as she started to cry, and he'd noticed again how much older she was looking, the veins of her neck swollen behind the skin like knotted cords, the backs of her hands arching at the knuckle.

They'd been driving for an hour when he saw the first flag, a worn-looking union flag hanging from a telegraph pole, and he remembered how very many more there had been the last time he was there. He counted another three union flags and a half-dozen tricolours, no more. The sun began to burn more brightly through the mist hanging low over the fields, the land falling away to their left as they climbed higher. Muddy-footed sheep scrambled away from the side of the road as they passed. He asked Eleanor how she was feeling, but she was asleep, or trying to be, and before he'd even noticed how far they'd come they were driving down the long hill overlooking Londonderry, across the bridge and out along the wooded road on the other side.

They were almost twenty miles into Irish territory before he realised they'd crossed the border, that they'd long since passed the spot where once there had been concrete blocks and tall steel fences, razor wire, soldiers with loaded guns and crackling radios; now there was nothing except a gravelled change in the texture of the road. They stopped in a lay-by for sandwiches and coffee and pieces of foil-wrapped cake, looking down over the long narrow bays of the inner coastline, the still grey water glinting in the strengthening light. Eleanor stretched, arching her back and lifting her face, and leant against David's shoulder.

All this sitting down's no good for an old body, she said, rubbing the sides of her legs and bending her knees.

Well, David said, you're not that used to it. Maybe you should go for a run before we go any further, he joked, get the blood moving. She laughed sarcastically and then turned to face him.

Do you think I look old though? she asked. She lifted her hand to her hair; I mean, does this count as grey hair now?

He smiled, and looked away, and said I don't know, maybe you could call it highlights. Distinguished highlights, he said, smiling. She laughed again, swirling the last of the coffee around in the bottom of the plastic mug, stepping away from the car and flicking the dregs on to the ground. She watched the shadows of small clouds slipping across the hillside on the other side of the narrow bay. They both stood still for a moment, listening to the quietness of the morning, not saying anything.

It doesn't seem like all that long since I was here before, he said. She pressed closer against him.

It's more than twenty years, she said. Kate was only three.

I know, he said. A lorry roared and clattered past, and they turned away from the dust and grit thrown up in its wake.

Where does it all go? Eleanor said. I don't feel old enough to have a daughter in her twenties already. He slipped his arm around her waist, pushing her round to face him. And you don't look old enough either, he said, smiling, really.

I do too, she said, pulling away, embarrassed. She looked down at the water again, watching a small red fishing boat struggling out on the tide, and said, you know, when I phone her up I'm still thinking of a ten-year-old Kate answering the phone, I don't know why, I can't help it.

I know, he said, me too. And he found himself thinking about her again, about how much of an adult she'd seemed at the funeral. He wondered what she would say if he told her now why he'd made that first trip to Ireland, the one she could barely remember, and why he was making this second one now. He tried to imagine being able to say such a thing. He wondered if she would understand, or if her indignant words would be familiar: Why didn't you tell me before? How long have you known? How could you not have told me this before? He thought about the photos he had of her in the albums on the back seat, which one of them showed her as someone old enough to have been told: the young woman leaving for university, the almost-teenager starting at big school, the young girl sugar-drunk with birthday-cake excitement, the toddler sitting on her proud grandmother's knee.

They got back into the car and headed for Letterkenny.

David,

I don't think I've written you a letter since you spent that fortnight in London with Julia, when you were fourteen. Do you remember? You said you wanted to see all the rooms in the British Museum instead of just a few. I'm not sure if you managed it. I can't remember why I wrote to you then, I think I was sending you some socks, wasn't I? Or I just wanted to know how you were. Stupid really, but I think I was missing you, and people didn't use the telephone so much in those days, did they? It was strange writing to you though, it took me a long time to think what to say.

But listen to me. I'm not getting to the point at all. There are some things I've been trying to say to you, and I haven't managed, so I'm writing them down and I'll give this to Eleanor to give to you before you go. Does that make me a coward, would you say?

Now I've been sitting here for half an hour, looking at the wall, and I don't know where to start. We've been over it so many times, maybe there isn't much point trying to explain myself again. I did the wrong thing, not telling you. You know that. But I thought it was the best thing to do and maybe you'll understand that one day. Maybe you already understand but you just haven't told me yet.

The truth, David, is that I chose you. I chose to keep you. I think sometimes you forget that, or maybe you never understood it in the first place. I could have taken you back to the hospital and owned up. Or I could have let Julia be your mum instead. But as soon as I picked you up that first time, with Susan there next to me and the picture of Albert up on the mantelpiece, you were part of our family and I knew I couldn't not keep you. I was there from the very beginning, David. I might not have carried you in my womb, but I changed your nappies and I fed you, I was there when you learnt to walk, and to talk, and when you fell over and cut your knees. I don't have to try very hard to remember the weight of you on my hip, or the feeling of holding your hands above your head as you took your first steps, or the smell of your skin when I tucked you into bed at night. Your first word was Mum, David, and you said it to me.

But I can understand why you were angry when you found out. I can understand why you might still be angry now, after all this time. I think I would be, in your position. But I was never a bad mother, was I? We looked after you, and fed you, and clothed you, and tried to do our best for you, didn't we? Sometimes, and I'm sorry to say it, I don't think you've given us enough credit for that. I made one mistake, David, one wrong choice, and I don't want you to punish me for it for the rest of my life.

So that's what I wanted to say. If you're reading this you should be halfway to Mary's house by now. Be careful, will you? And say hello to Mary for me. Tell her I'd like to meet her one day, if that would be possible, if it seems like things are working out that way.

There's a programme starting that I wanted to watch, so I'll leave it there. I think I've probably said more than enough already anyway. But I hope you find what you're looking for over there, David, and I hope you'll be able to tell me something about it when you come home. Phone me if you get the chance, if you want to. And please be careful.

Love, Mum

They arrived in Letterkenny just after lunchtime, crawling the last couple of miles through traffic cones, surrounded by the heaped mud and painted stakes of new building works, bulldozers and diggers circling through the fields on either side of the road. Eleanor unfolded the emailed directions and waited for David to ask for them, but even here, as he drove through the crowded and narrow streets of the town centre, past the bus station and the shopping arcade and the school, he could recite the route by heart. They drove out of the centre along a main road, past an estate of new bungalows, and then suddenly they were there. They parked the car outside, and sat for a moment, looking. This is definitely it then? Eleanor said. He nodded, squeezing the back of his neck. You okay? she asked. He looked at her and smiled weakly.

I don't know what I'm going to say, he whispered. She put a hand on his knee.

You'll think of something, she said. Come on.

They got out of the car and stood at the front door. She looked at him. He wiped his face with the back of his hand and he knocked.

60 *Biscuit tin, rusted, used as money box or for keepsakes, c.1944*

When Mary's husband died, her eldest daughter persuaded her to move into town, into a small bungalow just around the corner from her, so that she'd be closer to other people if anything should happen. She hadn't liked it at first. She'd missed the open fire, the view across the fields, the smooth shine of the worn stone floor. She'd missed the smell of their clothes hanging together in the wardrobe. The weekly steaming ritual of the bath being filled. The photos and drawings pinned up across the walls, the tools hanging up on the back of the door, all the familiar bits and pieces of a home she had spent a lifetime making her own. The walls were thin in the new place, the doors hollow, and the electric heaters took so long to warm up and cool down that she had to watch the weather forecast just to know when to turn them on.

You're only lonely without Daddy, her children told her, when she said she wanted to go back, and she didn't think they were right but they were. You'll get used to it, they said, you'll like it there soon enough, and she found it hard to believe but she eventually did. She started to like sitting by the window, watching people walk in and out of town, waving back at anyone who smiled or waved. She started to like not having to worry so much about dust and draughts and smoke and ash. She liked being able to put her wet clothes into a machine and take them out as dry as if they'd been on the line for a week. And now that she had two rooms she didn't need, she liked having the children come to stay, bringing their own children with them, and boxes of toys, and new photographs for her to put up on the wall, filling her front room with stories of their new lives and jobs in the places they'd settled now, retelling old stories of the life they remembered growing up with.

And one day, barely stopping to think what she was doing, she told her eldest daughter what had happened all those years ago, when she worked in the big house in London, and got into trouble, and had to come home with her hands empty and her heart broken. You can understand why I didn't tell you before, can't you? she said, when her daughter had finished asking questions, and Sarah nodded, and shook her head, and said well of course, I suppose I do.

She'd thought that would be the end of it, a sad story to add to the collection, but Sarah began to ask more questions, and write things down, and to ignore her when she said that was enough she didn't want to talk about it any more it was done it was finished. And one day Sarah came round saying something about the internet, explaining things which were hard to take in for a soul who'd grown up with no telephone and no electricity and a postman who only came once a week if at all. I've found him, Sarah kept saying, and it took her some minutes to understand what her daughter meant.

I've found him. He's coming over to see you.

She wondered if it really could be as simple as that. She wondered if she was ready, having imagined it and prepared for it all those years, to finally open the door and say hello to him after all. She asked Sarah if she was sure, if there wasn't some mix up with the dates, if it wasn't odd that he was asking for her by her name and not by the name she'd given all those years ago, but Sarah said no it had to be right, it had to be him, he must have discovered the real name somehow and it was surprising what computers could do these days.

Aren't you excited? she kept asking. Aren't you pleased?

61 *Paper package of selected photographs (reprints), c.1950–2000*

Well. Now. This is something, isn't it so. She stood in the doorway, looking up at him, her hands clasped together, a short white-haired woman with taut reddened skin and soft blue eyes, smiling faintly and saying well, well, right then.

Mrs Carr? he asked.

Ah, call me Mary, she retorted, laughing briefly and shaking her head. So, she said again. You'll be David. He nodded, and when he tried to say yes, that's me, I'm David Carter, his mouth went numb and only the first cracked half of his name came out. He nodded again.

She nodded back, as if agreeing with him, and unclasped her hands. Well, now, she said. He had no idea what to say. He just looked at her. Her mouth was small, the corners pulled tightly back into her cheeks. Her nose was very slightly turned to one side. She had a dark brown mole on the side of her face, just lower than her ear, with two thick hairs springing out of it. Her eyebrows were thick, and neatly arched, blackened with a little make up.

A voice called out from behind her in the house somewhere: Mummy, will you not invite the poor man inside? He heard quick, clipped footsteps, and a woman a few years younger than him appeared, smiling nervously, touching Mary's arm, saying I'm sorry, please, come inside would you?

I've got some things in the car, he said, half turning away, gesturing over his shoulder.

Oh, leave those for now, the younger woman said, get yourself inside and sit down. You must be tired. That's an awful long way to drive. Most people fly these days. She backed away from the door, as though drawing him in. Mary didn't move, looking up at him, squinting slightly, not quite smiling.

Well, he said. We thought we'd make the most of the journey. Enjoy the scenery, you know. He caught himself, and indicated Eleanor, saying sorry, this is my wife, Eleanor. The three of them said hello to each other, Mary's daughter introducing herself as Sarah and asking them again to come inside. Mary backed away, following her daughter into the lounge without actually turning away from him, her smile beginning to broaden. They wiped their feet on the mat and followed her.

There was a table by the window, set out with a spread of sandwiches and cakes, home-made biscuits and shortbread and soda bread, cups and saucers, a jug of milk, a bowl of sugar. He heard the younger woman's voice from somewhere, and saw her silhouette through the frosted glass panels which divided the kitchen from the lounge. Is tea okay for you both? she asked.

Please, he replied, glancing at Eleanor, that'd be great, thanks.

Take a seat there, she said, appearing in the doorway, I'll be right through. He sat at the table, and when he turned to smile at Mary, to perhaps say something, he realised she'd slipped away to the kitchen. He could see her silhouette through the thick glass. Eleanor was still holding the bag of cakes she'd brought in from the car. I, well, I brought these, she said, stepping towards the kitchen, lifting one of the cakes out of the bag. I didn't realise you'd – and she gestured towards the table, so covered with home-baking that there was little room for anything else more than a pot of tea. There was a moment's silence, and he heard Sarah say oh before she caught herself and took the bag from Eleanor. Oh well that's smashing of you, she said; we'll certainly not go hungry now, will we?; laughing a little too loudly and saying thanks again. Eleanor turned to him, pulling a brief embarrassed face, and edged round the table to sit in front of the window, and when he sat down beside her she reached across and squeezed his hand.

It was a large room, made larger by the wide open screen of the window which took up the entire end wall. There was a gas fire set into the redbricked chimney breast, turned on low, a broad mantelpiece crowded with framed photographs and painted china figures. He looked at the photos and wondered how long it might be before he knew who all those faces were, knew their names and their stories, if he would meet them, if he would come to think of them as brothers and sisters and cousins. He wondered if it would come to that at all.

Right then, here we go, said Sarah, carrying a teapot and a place-mat into the room, sorry to keep you waiting there. Mary followed, staying close to her daughter.

Not at all, David said, standing up without really knowing why, this is great, thanks. She looked at him, smiling.

Oh, it's only a pot of tea now, she said, it's not all that much. He smiled, dropping his head, embarrassed. Anyway, she said. Sit yourself down. I'm going to keep quiet now. I'm sure you and Mummy have a lot to be talking about.

Mary looked up at Sarah, and at David and Eleanor, and leant forward to serve the teas. She trickled a little milk into each cup, and then took the pot in both hands to pour out the tea before sliding a cup across the table to each of them. She looked up at David, finally, and smiled. They looked at each other for what felt like a long time, taking in the details of each other's faces, the folds and creases and colours of the skin, the shape of the eyes, the way that the light coloured and shone in the eyes, the cut of the hair, the weight of the hair, the way the hair fell across the other's face or down the sides of the head, the line of the jaw, the shape of the chin, the colour and shape and tiny movements of the mouth and lips.

Well, she said. Now. Here we are then. So.

He smiled. Yes, he said. Here we are. It's been a long time, he said, smiling, and they both tried to laugh.

It has, said Mary, holding his gaze, it has.

Longer for you though, he said, saying it half as a question but knowing it was true. She considered the thought for a moment.

Aye, I suppose so, she said, a few years more at least, in a way. He hesitated and pushed on.

No, a lot longer I'd say, he said. I didn't know until I was an adult. I was twenty-two when I found out. Her eyes widened a little. She put her teacup down and peered at him. Sarah leant forward in her chair.

Is that so? Mary asked. Well, there's a thing. I'd never thought of that. She picked up her teacup again. Well, she said, shaking her head, well, there's something.

Didn't you ever wonder? asked Sarah. Did it never cross your mind? He looked at her. I mean, sorry, she said, it's not really my business, but. She sat back in her chair. I wonder why they waited so long to tell you, she said, I wonder what it was – Mary turned to her, frowning, and Sarah stopped herself. Sorry, she said. Look at me now. It's not my place, I'm sorry. She pulled the collar of her blouse away from her neck and looked towards the gas fire. Are you too warm there? she said, to David and Eleanor, and they both shook their heads.

No, he said, it's okay, I'm fine, thanks. He glanced across at Mary, her face patient and impassive. He was surprised by how calm everything had been so far, how formal. He had thought, on the many many occasions he had imagined this scene in his mind, that by now there would have been tears, garbled explanations, tentative embraces. He realised, already, that this was unlikely.

They didn't tell me, he said, answering Sarah's question but looking at Mary as he spoke. My father died before I found out, I'm not sure that he knew either. As he said the word father he noticed something flicker across Mary's face, some slight pinch of the lips, a turn of the head, and he realised that there was going to be an awkward uncertainty around their use of these words. A friend of my mother's told me, he said. It was an accident. She was getting old, and forgetful, and one day she lost sight of it being a secret at all, and told me as though I'd always known. He was surprised by how easily the words were coming. He had the sense that now he'd started he'd be able to talk until the light failed outside, and on until the sun came up again.

Well now, Mary said. That must have been some surprise. He laughed, nodding, covering his eyes for a moment, clearing his throat. She looked at him, smiling faintly, pleased with her own understatement.

Yes, he said, you could say that. It was something of a surprise. He finished his tea, and she immediately reached over to refill his cup.

And have a cake there, she said, pushing the plate across the table towards him. She refilled her own cup, and the pot trickled empty. She turned to her daughter; would you make us another pot Sarah? she asked. Sarah stood up and moved towards the kitchen, taking the pot with her, keeping her eyes on David as she left the room. Eleanor stood up as well, suddenly, and said I'll give you a hand, touching David's shoulder as she edged back round him and followed Sarah into the kitchen.

Well then, Mary said, here we are. Let me get a look at you, properly. He turned more fully towards her, feeling his face colouring under the fixed attention of her gaze. She sat back in her chair, slowly looking him over, measuring him out as an artist might measure out a life model before setting the pencil against the page. Stand up, she said softly. He stood, moving away from the table, aware of Sarah standing close to the frosted glass. Mary got up from her chair and stepped back a little, looking up at his face, moving around him. He followed her with his eyes, watching her steadily taking him in, and realised with a hard inward jolt what she was doing. The tears came then, at last, hot and stinging at the corners of his eyes, and he did his best to keep them hidden there, blinking them back, biting the inside of his cheeks. He saw that the rims of her eyes were reddening as well, and her small bony hands were curling into red-knuckled fists. I'm just wondering who it is you look like, she said, whispering.

Before Julia had let things slip, it had never occurred to him to wonder who he looked like. He had the same colour hair as his father, and the same colour eyes as his mother, and that seemed enough. He grew at about the same rate as his sister, and when they were younger and had their hair cut the same way there had been a similarity between them, and so there had never been a reason to think about it. He'd wondered, once he knew, if his mother had ever worried about these things as he was growing up, if she ever checked his growing hair for telltale signs of redness, or scanned his face for freckles, or looked into his eyes for any giveaway flecks of green. He wondered how she might have explained these things away if they had appeared, or if she might perhaps have used them as reasons to tell him the truth.

When he'd found out, he'd stood in front of the mirror with a family photograph held up beside him, looking for similarities, astonished at how few there were. It had never occurred to him before. But why would it? he asked Eleanor angrily, when he told her and she asked him this. Did you never look at yourself next to them and wonder? she said. Why would I think to do that Eleanor? he'd almost shouted, angry that she seemed to be implying some fault of his own, some blindness, some weakness in the ease with which he'd been taken in. That my parents spent my whole life lying to me? he said, shaking his hands in the air, why would that cross my bloody mind Eleanor?

I've got a few things in the car, he said later, as they were finishing the second pot of tea. I brought a few things with me. Mary and her daughter both looked at him, not sure what he meant. He stumbled over his words anxiously. I brought some things, in the car, he said, I mean, just some photos and things, I thought you might like to have a look, you know. Sarah looked at her mother. Her mother looked at David. I mean, only if you want to, he said. I thought you might like to see what I looked like growing up, where I lived, that kind of thing. Mary didn't say anything for a moment. He could feel sweat forming in the folds of the palms of his hands. He saw, from the corner of his eyes, Eleanor looking at Sarah, their eyes meeting, some understanding passing between them.

Well, Mary said, smiling. It would be one way to begin, wouldn't it? Her voice caught slightly as she spoke. Please, she said. I'd like that very much.

And at first it was just as he'd always imagined it would be. Mary and Sarah standing back while he opened the albums and the scrapbook and laid them on the table, pushing back the plates of cakes and biscuits, the basket of bread, leafing through the pages: photographs of him as a child, of the house in Coventry, of his mother and father in the garden; photographs of Julia, of her house in London, of Laurence glowering at the camera; photographs of summer holidays with his grandparents in Suffolk. A page of wedding photographs. A photo of Kate, taken when she was a baby. Another one of her eighth birthday, and of her leaving for university. And, tucked loosely into the pages of the scrapbook, his birth certificate, the hospital admissions card he'd found at Julia's, a map of all the places he'd been to the first time he'd come to Donegal.

He turned the pages backwards and forwards, looking at Mary, not knowing where to start, not knowing if he should say something. Eventually, he stepped back, gesturing vaguely at the opened albums as if to say here, help yourself, please.

She stood in front of it all, uncertainly, resting her weight on the edge of the table, her glance scattering from the album to the scrapbook and back to the album again. Sarah stood in the kitchen doorway, her back half turned, and Eleanor sat on the sofa. David watched her, this woman, as she looked over his life. She was so very different from his own mother was all he could think. Quieter. Shorter. Fuller in the face. Her voice, when she spoke, seemed lighter, calmer, more ready to listen. He wondered how the two of them would react to each other if they ever did meet. He wondered if it would ever come to that.

She turned to him, the rims of her eyes reddening again, opening and closing her mouth as if she wasn't quite sure what to say. Perhaps you should tell me about some of these, she said. He nodded, and stood a little closer. He reached across the table and started to point things out. Here, this is my mother. My father. Me. My sister. Our house. My first day at school. My first day in my job at the museum. That's Eleanor, of course, and our daughter. She leant over each photograph as he described it for her, peering at it closely, tilting the pages towards the bright light from the window, touching her finger, once or twice, against the face of the person pictured.

And this is when you moved into the new house then? she asked, pointing to a picture of the four of them by the front door, Susan clutching her father's hand, David held against his mother's chest. David looked at it a moment.

Yes, he said, that's 1947. I would have been two, two and a half more or less. Mary looked at him, oddly, as if trying to remember something, as if there was something she wanted to ask. But she turned the page over without saying a word.

This was how it was supposed to be. This was what he had planned. She would look at these things closely, ask him what that was, who this was, what they were doing in the picture and what they were doing now. And he would tell her. It was all he'd ever wanted, someone to tell these things to. My father was a builder. My mother was a nurse during the war. My father made this garden himself, when we moved to Coventry; look, he planted these, and these, and these. He died when he was fifty-one, exhaustion they said but we think now it may have been asbestos. This is my Auntie Julia. A friend of my mother's. She was a nurse as well. She wasn't my real aunt but I was very close to her. When I started working at the museum she came up especially to see me and made me give her a guided tour. This is when I met Eleanor. She was working at the tea rooms at a museum I visited for work, up in Aberdeen. She wrote her address on this napkin look. I know, it's funny, isn't it, the way these things happen? This is our wedding certificate. This is Kate again, this is her graduation photo – Eleanor was furious with her for not smiling.

Once, just once, she turned away from him, fumbling into the sleeve of her cardigan for a screwed-up tissue and holding it tightly against her face, covering her nose and the corners of her eyes, nodding her head soundlessly. He turned to the window, standing very close to the glass so that the warm light shone against his wet face, listening to Sarah saying oh Mummy, hey now, wishing it could be him folding his arms around her and holding her comfortingly against his chest. Just once, and it only took her a minute or two before she turned back to him, saying oh well will you look at me now, you mustn't take any notice, wiping the tissue around the edges of her eyes and tucking it back inside her sleeve. Where were we then? she asked, smiling.

When he talked to Eleanor about it later, he said I don't know though El, it's strange, I think she knew even then, don't you? I think she knew as soon as she opened the door. But she was still so interested, she asked me all those questions, and then she cried like that, did you see? I can't really work it out, he said, and Eleanor sighed impatiently and said David, it's a bit obvious, don't you think?

She'd looked through almost everything in the albums when he noticed her hesitating, looking as though she wanted to turn away, to sit down and bring the scene to a close. He reached past her and picked up the hospital admissions card. And there's this, he said. She nodded, looking at it, and he could see that she'd been looking at it all along. I found this when we were clearing out Julia's house after she died, he said. I don't know why she had it. She must have taken it just in case, in case my mother ever needed to know, or in case she thought I might want to know. My mother said she had no idea Julia had taken it, he said.

Is that so, Mary murmured, looking closely. Mary Friel, she said softly, as if trying to remember writing those words, as if she wasn't sure that it had ever been her name at all. He didn't say anything. Sarah moved closer to them, looking over her mother's shoulder.

She told me they panicked when you didn't come back, he said, and maybe Julia took this in case there was some trouble about it. She told me they tried to find you but there wasn't enough information here. She looked, and nodded.

Well now, she said, taking the card from David's hands and laying it down on the table without quite letting go. I suppose it's my turn now. Would you get me those albums from the bureau in my room? she said, over her shoulder, and Sarah turned towards the door, gesturing with her head for Eleanor to go with her. They listened to the two of them walking down the hall and away into another room.

Mary turned to him, and put her hand on his, and he realised immediately that he knew what she was going to tell him, and that there was nothing he could do to stop her saying it aloud.

What you should understand, she said very quietly, letting go of the card and stepping back slightly, is that most girls would have given false names to the nurses, you know? For fear of someone being told.

She didn't look at him as she spoke, and at first he wasn't quite sure what she'd said.

Absolutely, she said, they'd have given false names. That's what I did, she said.

I can't find them here, Sarah called through from her mother's bedroom, and Mary left the room to go and help her.

So when they sat down on the long plump sofa opposite the gas fire, Mary adjusting the cushions behind her and opening the first of the albums out across their laps, they knew, they both knew what was happening. But neither of them said anything about it. Sarah, standing back again, watching from the kitchen doorway, didn't know, and so perhaps it was for her that they kept quiet. Eleanor, sitting at the table in the window again, didn't know, although she immediately saw some small change in David's manner, and in his voice, and so perhaps it was also for her that they kept quiet. Or perhaps it was because they weren't quite sure and they both preferred, for the moment, not to know.

Well then, Mary began. I suppose my story's longer than yours, on account of my being around a lot longer, so it's a good job we're sitting down. He smiled, and leant a little closer towards her, a little closer to the pictures in the album.

So, she said. This is the first photo of us. This is us at my sister Cathy's wedding, all of us except Jack, who was away. I'm fifteen, that's me there, see? This would have been just before I went over to England for the first time, she said. Just before we went to the hiring fair in Derry.

He listened to the words, to the soft drifting sound of her voice, and he looked at the pictures. He found his hand moving towards each photograph the way Mary's had done at the table, as though his fingers might feel something more than he could find with his eyes, some extra detail, some texture or colour or life. But there was only the glossy press of the cellophane laid over each page, the slight ridge of each photograph's edge.

She talked on, explaining each picture, talking around it, telling the story of growing up in such a large family, of having to follow her brothers in travelling for work, of what had happened in London, of coming home to raise a family of her own. She sent Sarah back to her room to look out the biscuit tin from under her bed, with her rainy-day money in; will you look now, she said, that's the same tin I had back then. The words came easily, the story tumbling out with the pictures the way that she'd always imagined it would, sitting in a room with the fixed and silent attention of a man like this, her long-rehearsed words filling the room. She talked on, and he listened, and he asked questions, and she answered, and she was still talking by the time Sarah had turned on the side lights, and cleared the table, and twice offered them another pot of tea.

And when she had finished they both sat together for a time, not speaking, their hands touching lightly against each other, both knowing what needed to be said now but neither of them wanting to be the one to begin.

62

Bill for room and board, Conway's of Letterkenny, June 2000

As they were leaving, Mary produced a package of photographs, reprints of the ones she'd shown him in the album. It was neatly tied with string, and wrapped in a plastic bag to keep it out of the rain. I'd still like you to have these though, she said, all the same. If you'd like them. David took the package, and nodded, and tried to say yes, thank you, I would. Eleanor moved away to the car, and Sarah backed away into the house, as if they thought they should make way for one last private moment; but as the two of them stood there they could do little more than smile.

I'm sorry, said David.

Oh, not a bit, said Mary. It's you that's come all this way now. He shrugged. I should be apologising to you. I think Sarah got a bit carried away with herself there, I think maybe she found what she wanted to find, you know? I think she didn't stop to be sure. She only said you were coming a few days ago, I haven't had a chance to . . . she said, her voice fading, her hands reaching for what she was trying to say. It would have been nice though, wouldn't it? she said. Before it was too late. She stopped, and closed her eyes, and he thought about calling Sarah back outside. But it's okay, she said, finally. I don't mind. And I don't think you'll mind, will you?

No, he said. No, I won't.

It's better than nothing though, isn't it? she said, almost smiling, and he could only nod in reply.

They didn't drive straight to the hotel. It was earlier than they'd expected, and Eleanor said they should have a look at the scenery while there was still some light. They drove north out of Letterkenny, following a road he half remembered from his previous visit, heading up towards the Fanad peninsula. They didn't speak much. Neither of them seemed certain what to say.

Are you glad you came, at least? Eleanor asked eventually, and he took so long to answer that she thought he hadn't heard her. They drove into a small market town, coming to a river at the bottom of a steep hill, and as they crossed an old stone bridge he glanced at her and said yes, yes I am.

Well, she said. That's the main thing. They followed the road out of the town, through another small village, and out to the shore of a long narrow bay, pulling off the road on to a gravelled car park by a slipway. He turned the engine off, and they watched a pair of men working on a fish farm in the middle of the bay.

I was expecting more people though, he said. Not that it matters now. She shifted in her seat, turning her body towards him, waiting for him to say more. He opened the car door. I thought there'd be a whole crowd of them there, he said, waiting to meet me. I didn't think it would just be the two of them like that. I think I thought it would be more of a get-together, he said, swinging his legs out and resting his feet on the gravel.

Maybe that would have come later, she said softly. He looked at her, and she saw for the first time the disappointment he was feeling, etched across his face, darkening in his eyes.

Maybe, he said.

He got out of the car and wandered over to the water. She reached for the door handle on her side, but stopped, letting her hand fall as she watched him kicking small stones from the concrete slipway into the sea. She thought he might pick one up and skim it across the water, remembering when she'd first taught him how, a young woman showing her landlocked boyfriend the way to search out a flat stone and curl his finger around its corner, to bend his knees as he flicked it across the waves. She remembered his boyish delight when he'd finally made one bounce, and she wondered whether she'd ever really imagined, then, still being with him now, still being able to see that fizzing, sparking, skinny young man in the ageing figure he'd become, with his greying hair, his loosening skin, his tired and heavy heart. She couldn't remember being able to think that far ahead.

He didn't skim any stones. He kept his hands in his pockets, and his eyes down, and the waterproofed men on the fish-farm rafts finished up their work, and a pair of diggers on the other side of the bay fell quiet and after a few minutes he got back into the car.

It's getting dark, he said. Shall we go back to the hotel?

She waited until he'd run a bath and settled into it before asking him anything else. She put the lid down on the toilet and sat there, watching him smooth soap lather up each of his arms and across his chest, watching him slide down into the water to rinse it off.

She said, David, were you surprised though? The way it turned out? He looked at her, sitting up a little straighter. He splashed water over his face, and wiped it away with his hands. She said, tentatively, I mean, could you not have asked a few more questions before we came over? Didn't the dates seem wrong from the start?

I don't know, he said. It seemed to just about fit. I think it was Sarah who got the dates muddled. You know she was doing all this without telling her mother? he said, turning to Eleanor. Eleanor's eyes widened and she shook her head.

No, she said. Oh no, really? David nodded, and shrugged, and sat forward to wash his feet.

Maybe I knew all along, he said. Maybe Mary did too. Maybe we were both just kidding ourselves, really. She leant towards him, her face in her hands and her elbows on her knees, waiting for him to go on. He looked at her, almost apologetically. I wanted it to be her, he said. I so much wanted it to be her. And I assumed Sarah was talking to her mother about it, checking things. I just didn't know. I thought it was worth taking the chance. He sat up straighter, sluicing handfuls of water across his body. I had all this stuff, he said, waving his hands as if to conjure the photos and scrapbooks out of thin air. I just wanted to hear what she would say, he said. He slipped back down into the water, closing his eyes and laying his hands across his face, and she stood up to leave.

But there was so much more I would have told her Eleanor, he said, his voice muffled by his hands. There was so much I wanted to be able to say. She looked at him.

I know, she said. He lowered his hands, and looked at her. I know, she said again.

She closed the bathroom door and left him to it, turning on the television news, looking at the supper menu and the tourist leaflets in the folder by the bed, wondering what he thought he was going to do now. Later, she heard the water draining from the bath, and the rattle of it being refilled, and she looked up to see him coming out, avoiding her eyes, sitting on the edge of the bed with water trickling down his hunched back. She said nothing, but undressed quickly and quietly, slipping into the bathroom and closing the door behind her. She expected to find him asleep when she came back out, or watching television, or sitting blankly by the window, or even to have gone out walking and left her a note. So she was surprised, when she opened the bathroom door, to find him waiting for her, with his towel wrapped around his waist and a look in his eyes that she recognised at once.

Really? she said, arching an eyebrow and taking a towel to dry her hair, nodding over at the supper menu: aren't you hungry?

Really, he said, moving towards her, placing his shaking hands against her warm damp skin.

It was always almost the same. The unbuttoning of the back of the skirt. Half a smile at the corner of the mouth. Her hand, sooner or later, on the back of his head. Sometimes the smile would come first, sometimes the unbuttoning, and sometimes, catching him by surprise, the hand pressing lightly on the back of his head, making him kneel.

They would almost always be in the bedroom, and almost always on the bed, the curtains closed or half open, the window hauled up or bolted down, the lights on or off or lowered. Sometimes the rain would hurtle across the roof and against the window while he pulled her shirt or her sweater up over her head, pressing his mouth against her neck and her shoulder and her collarbone, kissing her throat until her familiar faint sighs brushed against the top of his head. Sometimes the evening's light seemed to last for hours, the warmth throbbing up from the hot dry streets and in through the open window while they lay naked together on the bed. Sometimes the sky would be flat and still and grey.

There would be the feel of her thighs beneath the stretched fingers of his hands, hot and red from the bath, still smelling of soap and towel, or cold from a long day outside. The skin gradually less smooth than it had once been, less soft, her waist a little fuller, her legs a little heavier, and what Kate had once called her creases becoming ever more pronounced beneath the touch of his own ageing hands.

Sometimes it would be snowing, and the room would be filled with a wavering white light, shadows and refractions falling across the walls.

She would step backwards, and sink on to the bed, and lie back with her legs trailing to the floor, both of her hands pushing against the back of his head, and he would follow her with his mouth.

Sometimes, when they were older, his knees would make a cracking sound as he lowered himself to the floor. I think I'm getting too old for this, he would say, and she would shush him as she worked her fingers into his hair. Sometimes his jaw would click, loudly, and they would both have to stop and laugh for a moment.

It would be in the morning, when neither of them were in a hurry to go out, or it would be in the afternoon when they both got home, or it would be last thing at night. It would almost always be the last thing at night.

She would shift on the edge of the bed, and make the sounds he liked to hear, and almost always reach that moment, the jerking forward of her head, the sudden lift of her legs around his ears, the look of someone bolting awake from a dream before settling gently down with a long slow sigh.

He would trail his fingers across her waist, her belly, her breasts. He would pinch her skin. He would stand up – and sometimes it would take him longer to stand than it might once have done, pushing himself up from the floor with a hand on the edge of the mattress, rubbing his knees – and he would look down at her, stretched out, lying across their bed in the bedroom they had shared for so long.

There were times when they went without these things for weeks at a time, months, a year. There were times when they undressed in the evenings with their backs to each other, or in another room, climbing into two halves of a silent bed and staring at opposite walls of the room in the near-darkness. There were times when they slept in different rooms, and woke a little colder than usual, blinking, trying to remember what was wrong.

Sometimes he would bring her a cup of tea in the morning and put it by the side of the bed and open the curtains a little. He would watch her, as fragile-looking in sleep still as she had always been, her eyelashes flickering, her clenched hands drawn comfortingly up against her face, and want nothing more than to climb into bed beside her, to curl up into her warmth. He would wake her, a hand resting on her shoulder and his voice low and steady, and tell her that he wanted her to take the pills before he went to work.

Sometimes she would bring him a cup of tea in the morning, and he would already be awake. Sitting up against the wall in the corner of Kate's old bed, reading, or watching the grey light brighten through the open curtains. Unable to sleep because he'd already slept through most of the previous day. Without his work, he told her once, the work he'd spent his whole life either doing or preparing for, he'd been lost for what to do with his time. I feel so tired all the time now, he would tell her, his voice flat and low. I feel uncomfortable, like I need a bath or like I need clean clothes. I feel like I'm letting you down and I can't do anything about it, he would say, his head lowered, his voice drained. I know, she would tell him, touching his hand. Really. I know.

The doctor told me I should find a new hobby, he said to her once, coming back from an appointment. They caught each other's eye in sudden recognition, and laughed for the first time in weeks.

She would almost always open her eyes after a few moments, propping herself up on her elbows and looking at him expectantly, or sitting forward and drawing him towards her, kissing and stroking and taking him into her mouth until he was ready to join with her on the bed. Sometimes it took him longer to be ready than it once had. It seemed to be one of the things that happened, with the cracking knees, the thinning hair, the fatter waist; a slower response of the body to the prompting of the excited mind, or the mind simply slipping for a moment to something else altogether; to whose car alarm that was going off outside, to how Kate was getting on at school, to whether tomorrow was the day for putting out the bins.

Sometimes the phone would ring, and they would ignore it, letting its shrill little grab for attention go unanswered while they moved closer together in the familiar way. Sometimes the phone would ring and one or other of them would say sorry, hold on, but it might be, I was expecting, and leave the other one waiting, impatiently or patiently or finding their place in the book they were halfway through.

They tried to use the lounge again after Kate left home, when they had the house to themselves once more. They tried – after a slow stunned month of feeling lost in their own home, of not knowing quite what shape their days should take now that they didn't have a daughter to feed or provide for or watch growing up – to undress each other on the rug in front of the new sofa, and to kiss, and to relearn what it meant to be just the two of them in their world. But they would hear voices somewhere, footsteps, and turn to the door suddenly, or check for the third time that the curtains really were closed, or be distracted by the draught coming under the kitchen door, and they would almost always move back up the stairs to their bed.

Sometimes he would shape a hand around her breast, and hold it there, still, feeling its weight as they moved.

Sometimes he would reach behind her and trace his fingers up and down her spine until she shivered.

His sister's children had left home two years before Kate did, rushing off to university in London and in Leeds, and she'd warned them what it would be like. You spend so long fitting your life around theirs, she said, you forget what you used to do before they were born. You look forward to having all that time to yourself, and then you want to phone them every night to see how they're getting on. She came to visit them a lot after she and John were divorced, staying with Dorothy or, later, in Kate's old room. He was a very good man, she said to them once after a bottle of wine, a very good father, but I was just so bored. We had nothing to say to each other, she said.

They waited a moment, settling together on the bed, and she tilted his head up with one finger so that she could kiss his throat. He shifted her arm so that it stretched out across the pillow, and held it there with his fingers curled into her hand, and they began to move. The bed was smaller than theirs, and softer, and for a moment it felt strange. But the bath had woken them up a little, and they were both full of nervous energy from the way the afternoon had unfolded, and it felt good to be doing this thing that was almost but never quite the same. It was the first time they'd been away for the night together since before Kate had been born, and there was an excitement to being in an unfamiliar bed, and a comfort to being in each other's familiar arms. She reached around to the back of his legs, tracing a line from his thighs to the back of his neck.

Their bags were on the chest of drawers by the door, the envelope of reprinted photos Mary had given them as they left spread out to one side. His trousers, shirt and jumper were folded across the back of the dressing-table chair. Her skirt was heaped halfway between the bed and the en suite bathroom. The fan in the bathroom was still whirring, shakily. They could hear the voices of the kitchen staff echoing up from the courtyard below.

He shifted his weight a little, and slid one hand beneath the small of her back. She kissed him, hard, pulling his mouth down to hers with both hands on the back of his head. He caught his breath and hesitated. She tipped back her head, pushing her shoulders into the bed and lifting her back into a shallow arch. He kissed her throat, her cheeks, her eyes, her ears, quickly, holding her face between his hands. She lifted her legs a little higher, the rough soles of her feet scratching against the backs of his knees.

He dipped his head, awkwardly, and kissed each of her breasts. They heard the fan in the bathroom stop, and were suddenly more aware of each other's sounds: their breathing, their small concentrated gasps, the soft percussion of lips against skin. She circled her fingers across his back, scratching a sharp line from his shoulder to his waist, until suddenly, as always, there it was. She watched him, holding his face in her hands, catching her breath even as he was gasping for his. And the look in his eyes, as it almost always was, was a look of wonder and surprise, as if even after all that time it was something he hadn't quite been expecting, something he didn't quite believe he deserved.

He lay back on to the bed and pulled the covers up across them both. The light was fading outside, the noise from the bar getting louder as more people arrived for the night. She spread her fingers out across his chest as his breathing slowed and tugged gently on his ear, leaning towards him to whisper, hey, don't fall asleep. He turned his head on the pillow to look at her. She smiled.

What do you want to do now? she asked. He smiled and closed his eyes for a moment more. David? she said, nudging him again. He opened his eyes and looked at her.

I want to go home, he said.

ACKNOWLEDGEMENTS

My family, Alice, Kim and Mark, Jane and Cormac, Rose Gaete, Randal and Jennifer Faulkner, John and Chris Consella, Pamela Wood, Maggie and David Jones, Derek and Becky Porter, Beatrice von Rezzori and all at the Santa Maddalena Foundation, Rosemary Davidson, and Tracy Bohan.

A NOTE ON THE AUTHOR

Jon McGregor is the author of the critically acclaimed *If Nobody Speaks of Remarkable Things*, and winner of the Betty Trask Prize and the Somerset Maugham Award. He was born in Bermuda in 1976. He grew up in Norfolk and now lives in Nottingham. This is his second novel.

A NOTE ON THE TYPE

The text of this book is set in Berling roman. A modern face designed by K. E. Forsberg between 1951–58. In spite of its youth it does carry the characteristics of an old face. The serifs are inclined and blunt, and the g has a straight ear.